The Wolf and the Fox

The Wolf and the Fox

The Partisan Campaigns of Major Jacob Clarke

Erick W. Nason

Strategic Book Publishing
www.sbpra.net

For information about special discounts for bulk purchases, please contact Strategic Book Publishing, Special Sales, at bookorder@sbpra.net.

ISBN: 978-1-68235-885-6

"We fight, get beat, rise and fight again!"
Nathaniel Greene

"We are soldiers who devote ourselves to arms
not for the invasion of other countries, but for the
defense of our own, not for the gratification of
our private interests but for public security."
Nathaniel Greene

"Promises you make to yourself are often like the
Japanese plum tree—they bear no fruit."
Francis Marion

"What a strange pattern the shuttle of life can weave."
Francis Marion

I want to thank my team-Ed Forte, Sandra Rose and Samantha Botros who help to bring the story together.

Thanks Team!

TABLE OF CONTENTS

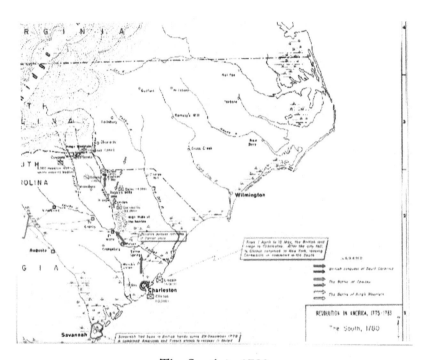

The South in 1780

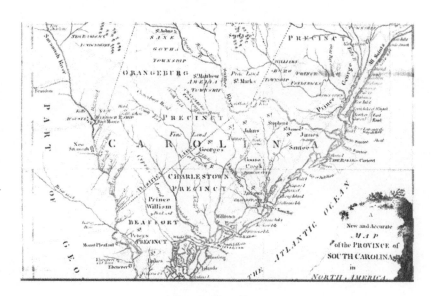

South Carolina

PROLOGUE

Jacob slowly moved through the water, carefully placing his feet before putting any weight on them. The only sound around them was the songs of birds and insects, gurgling water, and the breeze in the trees. His clothes were a faded brown and light tan hunting frock instead of his blue regimental, though he did still wear the black leather helmet of the Second South Carolina.

Behind him was his eldest son, Patrick, crouched low, mimicking what Jacob did. Near him were Samuel's twin boys, Robert and Thomas. Jacob's other son Richard was back at their camp on Snow Island with the wolves, keeping a watch for Marion.

They were out to make sure no one was taking an interest in their camp location, and Jacob wanted some more field time with the boys. As much as he didn't want to bring them along, they were the same age he was with the Rangers in New York. What was stranger that his wife had insisted.

"You know we must do our part," his wife had told him when he stopped in to get his hunting clothes, having removed his uniform except for the helmet.

"Who else can answer the call? Besides, who is the best for them to learn from, then their father and uncle?" Maria stated and to the point, hands on her hips. Samuel's wife, Otti, nodded in agreement. She worried about Samuel, not knowing his fate but knew in her heart he was still alive and surviving.

Maria looked into Jacob's eyes, softly caressing his face with her hand. "It's not over, and you must go. The boys are old enough to be in the militia, so I want them with you. No one will argue if they are serving with you. Besides, they are safer riding with you and Marion than staying here with those damn Loyalists running around."

Jacob nodded, knowing it was foolhardy to argue with his wife. Then, taking a deep breath, he let it out and smiled in agreement. Maria returned the smile, "See, that was not so hard, was it?"

Jacob looked at his wife, "What will you do? Are you safe?"

Maria snorted and stood tall and proud with a hand on her belt knife.

"Anyone foolish enough to mess with my family or me will have all of us to deal with it. Come after one of us, hurt one of us, and you will face all of us! Peter and a few other older hunters are staying behind."

Then a mischievous grin appeared on her face. "Besides, who will keep you informed of the coming and going of these damn Bandits who call themselves Loyalists. No one will suspect Otti and me to be other than good, loyal citizens running their farm and business. We'll open our eyes and ears and let you all know."

"Yes, yes, we will!" Otti stated with heat, looking intently at Jacob. "We will make them pay for what they did to my Samuel, and if it can end this war sooner, the better!"

Jacob shook his head to concentrate on their movement through the water. Jacob led them toward a concealed position. From there, they were to watch a bridge. So much has happened after the fall of Charles Town, leading him up to his knees in swampy water. Times are more dangerous now than they had seen before.

While the city had been under siege, Jacob and Jean got Marion and the governor out of the town before it was entirely encircled and cut off. Governor Rutledge left to gather the militia in the High Hills of the Santee while they moved an injured Marion to his home.

Marion had not wanted to participate in the party during the siege. As the rest of the officers were drinking, he tried to leave. However, as was the standard practice for safety, they locked the first-floor doors and windows so the drunk officers would not be a danger to themselves or the populace in the city.

Marion had gone up to the second floor, found a window open, and tried to climb down. However, he had lousy footing and did not fall correctly, landed and in the process, broke his ankle. Jacob and Jean smuggled the injured Marion out of the city and safely saw him home.

On the other hand, Samuel was not with them but with the regiment when the city surrendered. He and the remaining men of the Second Regiment laid down their arms, were rowed out onto the Cooper River, and loaded onto prison hulks anchored out in the middle of the river.

While at Marion's home, they learned how these Green Dragoons closed the noose around the city, striking at Biggings Bridge and chasing off all South Carolina cavalries. Once Charles Town fell, Lord Cornwallis was given the command, subduing South Carolina and bringing them under control.

As Jacob moved slowly forward, his legs making small ripples, he smiled as he recalled that resistance began to rise as soon as the British attempted to take control of South Carolina. The leader of these Green Dragoons, Tarleton was his name, went riding about the countryside, looking for the remnants of their army.

He found a group of Continentals near the Waxhaws, who had been heading to support Charles Town and, having learned of the city's fall, had stopped. Jacob was informed that this Green

Dragoon charged and the Continentals gave one volley for their honor before attempting to surrender. But unfortunately, the dragoons did not honor the surrender and cut down most of the men in a wholesale massacre.

Not knowing how much of the story was true, Jacob didn't care other than be wary of this Green Dragoon. Of course, sometimes reports are made or blown out of proportion to meet a need, but this does sound like it could have happened. But, of course, he hadn't been there; just another loss of their men against the British.

After a short moment, the sound of voices could be heard coming from the direction of a known bridge. Jacob raised his hand, and the boys froze and slowly crouched lower in the water but not before they had tied their shooting bags higher to keep their powder dry.

Slowly moving forward, Jacob lay concealed behind large Cyprus tree roots sticking out of the water, taking off his helmet before looking around the tree. First, four horsemen on the bridge appeared to be civilians talking to one another. They were not armed, so Jacob could not tell if they were Loyalists.

They spoke of a party to be held later in the week and what they should bring. It appeared they must have made up their minds and continued riding down the road with no indication they were looking for their camp. Satisfied, Jacob slowly backed away, turned, and motioned the boys to follow him to the base.

The movement back to the camp was uneventful, and after getting a reasonable distance from the bridge, Jacob led the boys out of the river and back onto dry ground. As he led them back, he recalled how his old friend, Thomas Sumter had returned to action to face the British. He had resigned from his commission and went home and thus wasn't in the city when it surrendered.

From what Jacob learned, Sumter had learned this Green Dragoon was heading into the High Hills of the Santee, so

Sumter put on his regimental uniform, kissed his wife goodbye, and headed up into North Carolina, where Governor Rutledge had gone to get help. After that, Sumter was commissioned to return to South Carolina and take the fight to the British.

From the Catawbas, Jacob learned that Sumter had passed through, and some two hundred joined him. The locals elected him as their leader, and he built a force to face the British. He took this brigade and engaged the British at Rocky Mount. Jacob also heard that Major Davie from North Carolina led an attack on Hanging Rock, while Sumter had focused on Rocky Mount. They would not go quietly into the night.

Then up north, in the upcountry where the New Acquisition Militia and other local militias were resisting as well, what Jacob learned was being called "The Presbyterian Rebellion" as they fought against one of the Green Dragoon's captains, Captain Christian Huck. Jacob also heard of much plain murdering, as now Loyalists sought retribution against the patriots. The bloody tide had, for the moment, turned against them.

As Jacob moved cautiously, he looked back, and his boys were doing what they had been taught to do, scanning while they moved; he nodded to himself how well they were doing. Finally, after a short but quiet movement, they came up on their base, where Marion and the few men they had were camped. The sentry spotted Jacob who waved, and nodded for him to come in.

Relaxing slightly, they entered their small camp in a small clearing surrounded by Palmetto Palms and other vegetation. Their horses were picketed nearby and had laid their bedrolls around the tree trunks. Jacob motioned the boys to head to their bedrolls while he went to Marion.

Sitting on a log with his injured leg in front of him, Marion was not dressed in his regular officer uniform. Instead, he wore a rough, coarse linen red jacket and plain trousers; though, like Jacob, his black leather helmet sat next to him.

Marion's servant Oscar hovered over him, ensuring he ate their little food. Then, when Jacob approached, Marion smiled while Oscar nodded.

"See anything we need to be worried about?" Marion asked, and Jacob shook his head.

"I guess there is a party going on," Jacob replied, "guess we didn't get the invite."

Marion chuckled. "I dressed for just such an occasion," then looked seriously at Jacob.

"Time to get back into action. I learned that our new commander, the hero of Saratoga himself, General Gates, is marching south from North Carolina with the new Southern Army. So it's time for us to ride north, meet with the general and receive our orders."

Jacob nodded and smiled. He, like Marion, was ready for some action. "When do we leave?"

"First thing in the morning, see to your gear, men and horses." Marion looked toward Jacob's camp, "I am sure the wolves are ready for action as well."

Jacob nodded to Marion and Oscar before returning to their campsite to get their gear together, what little there was.

***

General Cornwallis reviewed the map on a table left behind, his office in a suitable house in Charles Town. He learned that the house had been the headquarters for the rebel commander General Lincoln. Following his orders from General Clinton, he was to secure the interior and stabilize it before he could lead an expedition northward into North Carolina.

Looking at Major Ferguson, "How do we stand with our Loyalist forces."

"Sir," Ferguson began, "we have mustered about eighteen hundred men formed into six regiments in the Ninety-Six District. But, unfortunately, we are lacking arms at the moment to equip them fully."

Cornwallis nodded, recalling that as soon as the city fell, a careless worker and the quartermaster failed to check to ensure the muskets were unloaded. As a result, one fell over and caused a catastrophic explosion destroying a thousand muskets and hundreds of pounds of powder. Until they secured some more, the powder would be rationed. Once they secured some more, he needed morentil they secured some more.

"Yes, yes, we are aware. But, like the other regiments, you will have to do with what you have now. Until we can secure more, or through combat action, you can take more; you have what you have."

Ferguson nodded his head in understanding, though he didn't like it. "Yes, sir, then I will see to securing the interior."

Standing erect, he saluted General Cornwallis before turning and heading out of the house. Cornwallis returned to the map and looked at his deployments. Then, he began tracing lines from Charles Town to key towns in the interior.

"Ferguson will head up-country and deal with that matter while Colonel Brown and his King's Rangers will secure Augusta. Then Colonel Balfour, with his three regiments of Provincials, will hold Ninety-Six, and Lord Rawdon, with two regular regiments and the Volunteers of Ireland, will secure Camden. Colonel Turnbull was at Rocky Mount with Delancy's Brigade. Tarleton and his Legion were rooting out rebels in the low country."

As Cornwallis thought through his deployments, his fingers traced the lines from Charles Town to these critical positions.

Then he stood back and looked at the map; only the up-country near the Cherokee Lands wasn't fully secured, and some of the areas in the low country. But the rest was lining up nicely.

He placed his finger on Georgetown and chuckled. A schooner sailed in and captured the port and the city without firing a shot. Now a detachment of infantry was moving to secure the town and protect the King's Road along the coast. He then looked up at the long border between North and South Carolina.

"What about those rumors of a new Rebel Army? Our sources indicate that this rebel government appointed Horatio Gates as the new commander."

Cornwallis shook his head, recalling when Gates was serving the King. He thought he was a good administrator, but as a field commander, Cornwallis had doubts. "He did have the arrogance of a field commander," Cornwallis whispered to the map, "but lacks the skill." Cornwallis made a mental note to have his information network keep their eyes and ears open. So far, his plan was coming together.

***

Since April, Major General De Kalb had marched from Morristown, New Jersey, with his fourteen hundred men of six Maryland and the one Delaware regiment. Accompanying his column was artillery from the 1st Continental Artillery. The column marched with the men's wives and children following behind. As they had no horses or wagons, the men had to carry everything on their backs.

He had hoped to get more reinforcements along the route, but surprisingly none did. De Kalb couldn't understand this. Were they all not fighting together? The Governor of North Carolina refused to send troops and made it clear he was not happy he was in his state. All he could do was lead his army southward with the sick, the laundresses, and the other camp followers bringing up the rear.

When they arrived at Buffalo Ford on the Deep River, they received the news that Charles Town had surrendered. Morale began to dip in the army, having learned that Charles Town fell, and the people they came to support would not even help them. So they were left on their own, starving and waiting for direction.

That's when the news arrived that Major General Horatio Gates had been assigned as their new commander and was on his way. Hope was restored amongst the Continentals that now, under Gates, they would get their reinforcements, but most of all, food and supplies to keep them going were coming as well. The first indicator that Gates was on the way was when De Kalb received his orders from Gates, relieving him as the overall commander but remaining as a brigade commander.

When Gates arrived, he looked down at the poor condition of the men, similarly amazed that no supply depots had been established along their march route in North Carolina. But, as De Kalb tried to explain the situation to Gates, he would have nothing of it.

"Tell the men that supplies and rum are still on the way. Until then, the men are to hold themselves ready to march at a moment's notice."

De Kalb followed his orders and waited for the next instructions, suffering alongside his men. Finally, after three days, Gates ordered the army to march south while he sent most of the women, camp followers, and part of their baggage to Charlotte to form a depot. Most of the officers, De Kalb included, wondered why they were marching without resupplying. Some of the officers even whispered, "treasonous decision."

As the army marched southward, De Kalb and Colonel Otho Williams from Maryland approached General Gates with a proposal.

"Sir, perhaps we should look at a route that will bring the army through Salisbury, Charlotte, then to the Waxhaws. It is all rich farming land and staunchly anti-British. The army could rest and resupply there."

Gates waved his hand at the suggestion. "We may move forward and starve, or stay here and starve. Then, when the army stops for lunch, we'll hold a quick council of war to discuss it."

De Kalb and Williams accepted the answer and returned to their units. Disappointingly, the army did not stop for lunch, and no meeting was held. Later in the day, orders were passed down the line; the army would march straight away toward Camden via the most direct route.

De Kalb and Williams shook their heads, as this was not only one of the most barren, poor counties for food but also very pro-British. The army would not find any support in this area of South Carolina. However, none of the officers questioned the orders and plodded on down the road. Unfortunately, the men's morale did not improve, as no supplies were delivered, and they continued to march on empty stomachs.

When the army arrived at Mask's Ferry, they found some Indian corn ground into flour to make biscuits for the army. Gates learned that the North Carolina Militia was at Lynche's Ferry, and he needed them. His concern was that they would go home after they fought, and he needed them for the fight. So he decided to move the army toward Lynche's Ferry, as Gate told his adjutant, "To save the militia from themselves."

While the army was en route, Lieutenant Colonel Armand's Legion of cavalry and infantry arrived from Wilmington, North

Carolina. Part of his cavalry were survivors of Pulaski's Legion from Savannah Georgia. Although, de Kalb shook his head. Gates appeared not to know how to use cavalry to scout and screen the army. Instead, he saw cavalry horses pulling wagons for the army. The evident disgust on the faces of the dragoons highlighted the growing friction. He and some of the other officers had a hard time maintaining order and discipline.

The wagon masters had to be routinely ordered not to allow riders on the wagons, especially women. Baggage would be tossed aside as the wagon masters ignored the order and let the women ride. The starving men would be caught plundering supplies, what little they had.

To maintain order, Gates directed that roll calls be done four times daily. If soldiers were found absent from roll call, the punishment was death. But, de Kalb shook his head; this draconian method wouldn't keep morale up and could lead to a mutiny or increased desertions.

The army finally crossed into South Carolina, and Gates ordered the army to stop and camp. The men ate their fill along the fields of green corn growing along the Pee Dee River. Unfortunately for Benjamin Thurman, it was his plantation that the army camped on. They stripped him of his green corn, and the army also went after his unripe peaches and apple orchards. Some officers even used their hair powder to thicken soups from green corn.

The army could not march within a day because most men had severe diarrhea and weakness. While the army rested for a day, Colonel Porterfield and his light infantry joined the column. In addition, survivors who had escaped the Waxhaws and Charles Town, mainly North Carolina and Virginian troops, joined. Gates was pleased to see his army was growing, though he was disappointed at their current physical condition.

Nevertheless, he must resume marching soon and bring the British to battle.

**

Samuel leaned back against the rough wood of the bulkhead. The daily sweating had begun as the heat from the outside summer sun baked the old hulk. Little air moved through the main deck where they were held, though still dark but crammed with prisoners. His shirt clung to him like a second skin. Breaches were torn and had holes in the knees.

Since their surrender, he had been locked up with the other regiments' men, primarily the First and Second Regiments and militia, who refused to be pardoned. What surprised Samuel was that after a few weeks, the British would send Loyalist recruiters to see if anyone would join their ranks.

Some men quickly agreed, more out of necessity than they were willing to fight. Looking around the crowded interior of the hulk, Samuel could understand why some were willing to take the King's shilling. He ran his hand over his sweaty scalp, the bald area where he had been scalped, and then down his long growing hair.

They were fed twice daily, lining up with his bowel to get his scoop of gruel. It wasn't much, but at the moment, it was all he had. He slowly ate his gruel, chewing on it so it soaked into his gums before swallowing. He savored what he could while ignoring the bland or sometimes foul taste.

If there was one comforting thought, it was that the British did remove the shackles, and he could move around though there wasn't much room to move. At least once a day, the guards would allow them up on the top deck to get some fresh air, but it was almost like a tease, as it wasn't very long before they were sent down below.

The other major challenge was the smell of those unwashed bodies in tight quarters, sickness and disease, and piss-pots. The smell was overwhelming, competing with the little in the tight space. *"I'll never complain about the hot, humid air out there,"* Samuel thought as he leaned his head back against the bulkhead and closed his eyes, *"It's a lot better than this!"*

CHAPTER 1

AUGUST 1780: BACK IN ACTION

Jacob, the boys, and the rest of the twenty men packed their gear and loaded them on the back of their horses. The wolves sat on their haunches, ready to follow Jacob. Marion mounted his horse, Oscar helping to set his leg in the stirrup before mounting up on his. Jacob looked around at their small band, but all were loyal to Marion.

Along with Jacob and his three boys, Marion and Oscar, there was a mixed bag of veterans who were white and freed black men who believed in the cause for freedom. They were armed with various weapons, from rifles to muskets and fowling pieces. They had a small amount of powder and shot, so they had to be careful if pulled into combat.

Once they were all mounted, Marion ensured his helmet was straight before leading the men out of the camp. They walked through the swamp, the horse's hooves making the water swirl and bubble. After leaving the swamp, they rode along the road toward the border with North Carolina. The wolves ran alongside, ranging ahead and along the side of the trail.

They ensured they avoided known areas that supported the Crown in an attempt to move unobserved. Granted, they were all in civilian clothes, primarily hunting-style frocks, and split shirts. However, Jacob observed that Oscar was the best dressed out of all of them. The dust started to kick up from the hooves, beginning a light layer of dust on their clothes.

It was August 4th when they arrived at Thurman's Plantation and the camp of the Southern Army. As they rode up to the sentry, they were halted by the sentries on the edge of the base.

"Advance and be recognized!" the sentry shouted.

Marion halted the column and advanced up to the sentry. "Lieutenant Colonel Francis Marion, Second Regiment South Carolina Continental Line, here to report to the commanding general."

The one sentry looked at the other, who shrugged, then turned back to Marion and presented arms.

"Pass, sir! The general's headquarters is over by the large kitchen house."

Marion nodded to the sentry and motioned for the rest of the column to follow. The sentries looked at Jacob and the others as they passed, their clothes dirty and dusty from the road, and gave an odd look at the wolves who trotted by. The soldiers returned to their normal stance, leaning on their muskets and watching down the road.

Jacob looked over the camp with a practiced eye as they rode through the center. Shaking his head, he didn't like what he saw. Although the men were mainly lying, he saw many men by the field latrines. The air smelled of sickness.

"Papa, is this what it was like when you were in the army?" Patrick asked, and Jacob shook his head.

"No, we seemed to have been treated better than this."

Riding on Jacob's other side, Jean shook his head, "Even we were in better shape than this, even in the heart of the cold winter up north. Mon Deu!"

From what he observed, Jacob could figure out why the men were in such bad shape as he saw the piles of green corn and old corn being ground into meal by hand grinders in the field kitchen while men made Johnny Cakes and biscuits.

As they rode by, the men all stopped and looked at them, and Jacob even saw them pointing at them and some snickering.

"Well, that answers it," Jacob remarked to Jean, "I wouldn't even feed that to our pigs and cows back home."

"Is this normal?" Jean asked, and Jacob shook his head no. The column continued to plod through the camp, drawing the attention of Gate's men, who pointed at them.

They found Gate's headquarters next to the kitchen building, one of the few tents. Marion halted the column and had all of the men dismounted. Then, motioning Jacob to accompany him, Marion reported to General Gates.

"Stay with the men," Jacob told Jean, "Keep them together, don't let them wander off."

Jean nodded and had the men see to their horses and their gear. The wolves plopped down on the ground under the shade of a tree, watching the activity around them.

Bending into the tent, Marion and Jacob took off their helmets, held them in their left hand in proper military fashion, and reported to General Gates, sitting in a field chair behind a field desk. He looked up when Marion and Jacob entered and stopped before his desk.

"Sir, Lieutenant Colonel Francis Marion, Commander of the Second Regiment, South Carolina Continental Line, reporting to the commanding general."

Gates looked up, then slowly stood and saluted Marion, though Jacob noticed he was looking at their dress with a somewhat disdained look.

"Where is your regiment, colonel?" Gates asked.

Marion looked Gates in the eyes directly. "Sir, I have a few men with me, including Captain Clarke and a few survivors from the First and Second Regiments. The rest are prisoners in Charles Town, sir."

Gates nodded, "So, you don't have a command then if your regiment is no longer operational."

Marion pursed his lips together but nodded. Jacob was starting to dislike this General Gates but kept a stoic face. *"Must be another of these former British officers who switched to our side. His arrogance shows through."*

"Sir," Marion began, "I have my men with me, and I can gather more. We know the area well and can serve as scouts for the army, find the best routes for you, and ensure no British or Loyalist force is waiting in ambush."

Gates thought about it before responding, "I shall think about it. Then, when I make my decision, I will call you. You are dismissed."

Marion, followed by Jacob, came to attention and saluted the general before turning and leaving the tent. After placing his helmet on his head, Marion had a stern look.

"Well, that didn't go as expected," Marion grumbled, "what do you think of our commander?"

"Jack Ass," Jacob answered without pausing, and Marion chuckled.

"Now, that's not nice to say about our commanding general," Marion playfully chastised Jacob, then nodded. "But accurate." They returned to the men, mounted, and turned their horses away from Gate's tent.

Marion, with Jacob, led the men over to an open area in an orchard and set up their camp. First, they ran a rope between the trees to picket their horses, then set up their bedrolls. Next, two men began building a fire, while another two went to the quartermaster to see if they could get supplies.

The boys, who now had good practice, set out their ground cloth and blanket for a pillow, the temperatures warm enough at night that it wasn't necessary to use them. They checked their muskets and, making sure they were cleaned, leaned them against a tree they had camped next to. The wolves came over and sat near the boys, who gave them some jerked deer meat.

Looking around, Jacob could see they were still drawing the attention of some of the Continentals and the militia, and they all seemed to be pointing at them and laughing. Jacob's eyes hardened, and he shook his head. The wolves looked over and gave them all icy stares, challenging them to approach. The soldiers thought better of it and returned to their duties.

One of the black men of the unit, Jehu, had been with the regiment since the Fort Sullivan days and finished his three years before returning to farming. When he heard that the city had fallen and Marion was on the run, he searched for Marion and joined their small band. He walked over and stood beside Jacob, looking at the men pointing at them.

"What are they pointing and laughing at, Jacob?" Jehu asked.

"Us, they're laughing at us," Jacob answered.

"Humph," Jehu responded, shaking his head, "they are only slightly better dressed than us. Maybe they should spend some time in the swamp. Bet we can outfight them, though."

Jacob smiled and nodded. "Aye, Jehu, you're probably right. Let's care for the men and horses; ignore these prideful fools."

Jean and the men who came from the quartermaster shook their heads. "What we have in our haversacks is better than what these poor souls are eating, Jean commented in disgust. "We also saw a lot of the men sick, barely can move. This army can't fight, at least not in the next few days."

Jacob nodded, and they joined the group around their fire, pulling jerked meat and Johnny cakes they had made before leaving their camp in the swamp.

"So, what do we do now, Jacob," Phillip asked, one of the veterans who had done their time and had gone home. The boys edged over to see what Jacob would say.

Jacob smiled and shrugged his shoulders. "Hurry up and wait, I guess. The commanding general will let us know in the next couple of days. I recommend getting as much rest as possible; we have a whole army around us. So take advantage of it."

Gates did make them wait for a couple of days. Jacob thought it was to allow the army to regain its strength before continuing the march. Then an orderly came for Marion, who again insisted Jacob accompany him.

When they reported to General Gates, his belongings and tent were being packed and loaded into one of the wagons. When Marion and Jacob stood before him, Gates nodded to Marion.

"Ah, colonel, I have your task. I want you and your, ah men," Gates paused, and once again, Jacob noticed the slight distaste in the face of Gates, and Jacob thought Marion saw it as well. "To head down to the area around Georgetown and the Williamsburg Township. I want you to be the herald to let the good people know I am coming to stop this wanton destruction and cruel barbarity that the British are inflicting on them. Then, rest assured, we shall drive them back to Charles Town!"

Gates paused as he paced, caught up in his bluster. However, Jacob did see Marion roll his eyes as Gates wasn't looking.

"While in the Williamsburg Township, gather information, and I want you to destroy every boat you can find. I don't want Cornwallis using them to escape my wrath!"

Marion nodded his head, "Are you sure you don't want us to scout ahead of you?"

Gates waved his hand at the suggestion. "Pah, I have those Armand's Legion horsemen; they can screen the army."

Marion continued. "Yes, sir, but do they know the area as well as we do, every road and path?"

Gates looked directly at Marion, "I do not intend to hide from the British like some others."

Marion and Jacob bristled at the veiled insult but said nothing. "I will march this army directly to their new outpost at this Camden and deal with it. Then Cornwallis will have to march out of Charles Town, and I'll give him a thrashing like I did Burgoyne at Saratoga!"

Marion slightly shook his head but bowed in acceptance. "Yes, sir, we'll depart for the Williamsburg Township immediately."

Gates waved his hand in acceptance before packing his items. With Jacob following, Marion turned on his heel and returned to their camp.

"Your assessment of our commander was spot on, as usual, Jacob," Marion stated, looking straight ahead, "what a Jack Ass!"

They rolled up their blankets and gear and tied them to the back of their horses. Once all was set, they mounted, and Marion led them out of the camp and back onto the road. After traveling a mile, they picked up the trade road to take them to the Williamsburg Township.

Jacob road next to Marion, "What will you do when you get there? Can you order out the militia as a Continental Officer?"

Marion thought about it and shook his head, "No, I don't believe so, and as the governor is away, I never received a militia commission. Furthermore, I have no authority over any militia company; I hold no rank." He then looked over at Jacob.

"Don't you still have rank in the militia?"

Jacob nodded, "Yes, I am still a captain in the Goose Creek Militia."

7

"Well then, if they don't follow me, they sure will follow the great Captain Clarke, a survivor of the gauntlet and years of battle!"

Jacob looked over at Marion, who had a twinkle in his eye, and Oscar, who was riding behind Marion, who was laughing behind his hand. Jacob just shook his head.

"We will have to see once we get there."

***

John James, looking to mobilize resistance against the British, spoke with the other Scotch-Irish families around Williamsburg Township and waited patiently in the British commander's house in Georgetown. Now that Charles Town had fallen, he had met with the different clan leaders on what they should do.

He believed they should do something about it; however, not all shared the same view. Some clan leaders agreed, while the others would only decide once they knew the British intent for their area.

So now, he was standing in a rather lovely house hall, waiting to meet Captain Ardesoif. He paced back and forth, listening to the "tic-toc" of the large grandfather clock standing in the corner of the room. He had come in peace and unarmed, only here as a concerned citizen, to speak with the commanding officer.

After waiting a while, a servant motioned for James to follow. He nodded, and the servant turned and led him to a large writing room. Captain Ardesoif was writing on parchment. He then placed his quill down and looked at James standing before him.

"Yes, what can I do for you? He asked.

James straightened out his coat before answering. "Sir, I come on behalf of the large families from the Williamsburg District and would like to learn of your intent for our township. Specifically, sir, what is your intent for our people?"

Captain Ardesoif looked at James directly, "Why sir, it is simple, be good loyal servants of the crown, answer our call to defend your homes from these rebels, and do your duty."

James stared back, "What if we chose not to? We prefer to remain free to make our own decisions, including not serving in your militia against our neighbors?"

A hard look came across Ardesoif as he stood and slowly drew his sword from its scabbard.

"Then sir, I shall require unqualified submission of your people, and as for you," Ardesoif advanced and raised his sword to strike at James. "I shall see you hang!"

James quickly reached down, grabbed a chair, and blocked the sword as it approached him. Then, using all his might, he threw the chair and struck the captain in the chest, knocking him over his desk.

Spinning quickly, James sprinted for the door and mounted his horse as Captain Ardesoif called for his men. Then, taking off in a dead run, kicking up dust and gravel, James rode out of Georgetown and continued on his gallop until he reached the township's safety.

When he arrived, the word went out about the British intent and their attempt to hang James. It spread through King's Tree, Cedar Swamp, Pudding Swamp, and finally, Lynch's Lake. The news angered the Scotch-Irish, so they gathered their muskets and began forming militia companies.

The companies moved to and formed a single battalion in Williamsburg, and they all agreed that John James would be their major and command them. They would not give up their freedom and independence, and they sure as hell would not submit.

***

Tarleton was leading his troop of horses, intent on bagging this Thomas Sumter. Following the crushing and bloody defeat of the rebel army under Gates, General Cornwallis consolidated his hold on the area and moved the army up to Rugeley's Mill. As the army marched, Cornwallis learned that Sumter had taken not only their small fort on the Cary's Plantation but had captured a vital supply train of fifty wagons and three hundred head of cattle. Cornwallis presumed he had British prisoners who had been captured, and he wanted Tarleton to recover them.

"Move as quickly as you can," Cornwallis commanded, "I will send Major Ferguson and Lieutenant Colonel Turnbull to block his escape. I want you to be the hammer to their anvil. Destroy this force like you did those other rebels, recover our supplies, and if he has prisoners, recover them as well."

He had the light infantry from the 71st Highlanders and his cavalry, who were making good time. The weather was warm. The road was hard and not muddy, making movement easier. However, he was following the Wateree River, having estimated where Sumter was marching and encumbered with wagons and cattle, "I need to move faster," thinking to himself, Tarleton knew he could bag this rebel commander quickly enough. When his lead scouts came riding back, the sun had set, and he halted the column.

"Sir, we have found them!" the excited scout reported. "They are just up ahead on the other side of the river."

Nodding, he went forward with his second-in-command, Captain Ogilvie while the rest of the column waited. Finally, the scout led them to a spot where sure enough, just across the river, the campfires of a good size camp could be seen. Tarleton pulled out his telescope, trying to take what he could in the fading light.

He could see the cattle, the wagons, and many rebels sitting around their campfires.

"Well, now, it seems the game is afoot!" Tarleton lowered his scope, "Remain here and observe. I will ensure you are relieved every hour while the rest of the column gets some food and sleep."

Sumter's men broke camp and continued along their route on the opposite bank. The scouts reported their observations to Tarleton, who nodded and finished eating his hard biscuit as the column made ready to continue their pursuit.

I am going to have to find a place to cross soon, or I may lose him and those supplies," Tarleton thought as he mounted his horse. Once the column was ready, they began their quick pace, and the chase resumed. The infantry had a problem keeping up, having exhausted themselves the previous day.

It was only a short ride when they came across some boats and began to ferry his men and horses across the river. As the men crossed, Tarleton paced and thought about what his options were, which were limited. Finally, he decided, nodded, and called for his officers.

"We'll have to move faster to catch this Sumter. So we will double up on the horses, one infantryman with a dragoon. The rest of the column will move normally and join us after we crush this Sumter and assist us in herding the cattle, the wagons, and any prisoners we take."

Captain Campbell of the 71st nodded in understanding, and Captain Kinlock of the Legion nodded. Once across the river, the chosen men mounted up behind the dragoons, and when ready, Tarleton led the column out at a trot. The rest of the Legion was forming and would follow on short notice.

***

Sumter had stopped their march at Fishing Creek; his men were exhausted from marching in the heat and herding the captured cattle and prisoners. Feeling safe, having not seen anyone coming after him, Sumter ordered the men to rest and relax. The Catawba River and Fishing Creek protected them, so he felt they could relax.

Having removed his boots, Sumter was reclining under one of the wagons, wiggling his toes.

"Oh, that feels so much better," Sumter commented, "these old feet are feeling their miles."

Colonel Winn was close by, reclining back against the wagon wheel, eating a fresh peach, and nodded his head.

"Aye, that be true," he commented as he took another bite, "very true."

Sumter had posted sentries to keep an eye out for enemy forces while the rest of the men had stacked their arms and were trying to cool down from the heat. A few had stripped down and were in the stream bathing, and many were under the wagons for shade. They were camped on Reeves' Plantation, and as he was a Loyalist, Sumter had no sympathy for him.

The men stripped as many fresh peaches from his trees. Even a few went over and shot a couple of the cows they would eat. Then, they began cooking fires as the shooters cleaned the cows and cut the meat. Sumter looked around and was satisfied that everything was in order, and he leaned his head back and closed his eyes.

"What a way to fight a war," he mumbled as he fell asleep, "I hope it stays this way."

Another portion of the men had found two hogsheads of rum and was heavily drinking. The men were breaking out in song, and a good amount quickly became drunk due to the heat and dehydration. Colonel Taylor went to where Sumter had started to snore and took a seat. He, too, pulled off his boots, giving a satisfied sigh.

Close by, sitting on a log, was Elizabeth Peay, who had followed Sumter's force as her husband was with him. She was breastfeeding her baby, thinking about how her life had been turned upside down. Their home had been burned. They lost everything, so her only choice was to shadow the army before eventually falling in with them. She had no choice, as she and her children would have starved.

Her horse was tied to a branch on the stump, and her Negro servant played with her other child. His horse was tied next to hers. She shook her head, rocked gently back and forth as her baby fed, and looked up at her with happy eyes. She smiled down as her child cooed.

There was a sound of muskets firing; Taylor looked over as he was about to take his other boot off.

"What's that firing?" he asked, and Colonel Winn shrugged.

"The men are shooting the cows for fresh meat; we're going to eat well tonight."

He nodded and was pulling off his second boot when the sound of a bugle blared across the field. Colonel Taylor looked over as Sumter's eyes snapped open, and he sat up.

"Oh hell, they found us!"

***

As Tarleton led the column, two ladies came onto the road and waved at him to stop. Holding his hand up, he halted the column. Then, bowing from his waist, Tarleton addressed the two women.

"Good day, ladies; how may I assist you? Tarleton asked, and the ladies curtsied.

"Good day to you, sir," the first woman stated, "I believe we can assist you. If you are looking for that rebel army, we just passed it camped near the Catawba River and Fishing Creek junction."

Tarleton smiled, "You have my complete attention."

The two women gave precise information on the location of Sumter's force, how they were camped, and the best way to get there. Tarleton nodded and smiled at the two ladies.

"Thank you so very much!" Tarleton replied with a deep bow. "You have provided a service to the King that will be hard to repay."

The ladies smiled, "You can repay us by getting rid of these criminals and bringing order back to our homes."

Nodding once more and tipping his helmet, Tarleton smiled and gave the command to move. Using the directions provided by the ladies, he found the trail they had described. Tarleton had the light infantry dismount, and Tarleton instructed Captain Campbell to lead his men forward while they followed.

After moving down the trail, the infantry spotted the sentries watching the ravines. The infantry halted and passed the word back to Tarleton. He looked over his shoulder and drew his sword.

"Draw sabers!" Tarleton ordered, and the Legion Cavalrymen drew their sabers. As the cavalry was being prepared, the infantry began to move forward when one of the sentries spotted them and opened fire. One of the advance guard dragoons fell from his horse, angering Tarleton. Nevertheless, their complete surprise had been foiled.

"Charge!" he commanded, and the Legion bugler called for the charge. The horses leapt forward, and the men gave a yell as they began to thunder across the field toward the camp. Then, as the horses poured out of the woods, they formed a line and charged forward with their sabers raised. The infantrymen, having fixed their bayonets, charged alongside.

The horses surged across the field, thundering hooves throwing up dirt clods. The drunken men scrambled and tried to run in different directions, the horsemen chasing after them, sabers slashing downward. The green-coated men of the Legion cut down what few men who had stood and defended. Hearing the bugle and the sounds of the charge, Elizabeth Peay clutched her baby close to her. She dropped down to lie next to the log. The Legion's horsemen jumped over the log, hooves flying over the hiding woman and her crying baby. Her servant was also lying, clutching her other child in protection.

A few of Sumter's men took position behind the wagons and began to fire upon the charging cavalry and infantrymen. A lucky shot caught Captain Campbell of the 71st, knocking him to the ground. Most of Sumter's men ran as fast as possible toward the woods, hounded by the Legion cavalry.

The scene was complete chaos; riderless horses from Sumter's command were running in all directions, along with the captured cattle. The men who had been bathing were caught in the water. The attacking infantry moved to the water's edge and fired at the easy targets.

The infantry stopped firing, an officer holding up his hand. "You rebels in the water; you stand no chance. Surrender and make your way to the shore, and we will see you treated fairly."

The few men who had been bathing looked at one another and then down at the few floating bodies which had already been shot. Knowing they had no chance, they nodded and reached the shore with their hands raised. The infantry backed away from the water's edge to give them room to come on shore.

When all were standing on the shore, hands raised, the British officer turned to his men. "Present!"

The surrendered men dropped their hands in shock, "What are you doing?"

"Fire!" was commanded, and the infantry fired at point-blank range, knocking down all the men who had just surrendered. The officer moved amongst the fallen men; one still breathing stammered, "You promised to be fair!"

After drawing his pistol, the officer walked up and shot the man. "I did say you would be treated fairly. Like the rebel scum, you are. Fairly treated, fairly executed." He motioned for his men to reload and they continued their sweep of the camp; the sound of fighting still could be heard. Once his men were ready, he nodded, and they moved across the camp, clearing the line of wagons.

Sumter mounted a horse and was hatless, bootless, unable to rally his broken men. However, their cannon was manned and could get off one shot before the cavalry fell on them like hawks, slashing with their sabers. Then, seeing there was nothing he could do, Sumter yelled out. "Every man sees to themselves!" He then turned his horse and galloped into the woods with only three other men following.

A short time later, the fighting stopped, and Tarleton consolidated his command. The infantry of the 71st rounded up all of Sumter's men. Some, including the last of the Continentals that Gates had sent to Sumter before his defeat. All of the British prisoners were released. Tarleton dismounted and tied his horse to the wagon under which Sumter had been lying.

Reaching under the wagon, he retrieved Sumter's coat, breaches, hat, and boots. Holding up the coat, he tossed it into the wagon with the breaches and hat. He did admire the well-made boots and nodded to himself. "Looks like they will fit."

Tarleton watched the camp where his men led the prisoners into a line, securing muskets and the wagons. He took out his canteen and took a long drink of the warm grog he carried. He reached into his coat pocket, pulled out a silver flask, and took another sip. He took off his helmet and set it on the wagon, using a handkerchief to wipe the sweat from his forehead,

His adjutant road up and stopped before Tarleton with a giant grin on his face. Smiling, Tarleton looked up, "Report."

"Sir," he began, "We recaptured forty-four wagons, approximately a thousand stand of arms these rebels will no longer use, and about three hundred prisoners."

Tarleton nodded, then saw the lifeless body of Captain Campbell of the 71st being carried in by his men.

"Our losses?" Tarleton asked.

The adjutant looked at his notes. "Our returns so far show nine dead and six wounded."

He stared at the grey, dead face of Captain Campbell. *I wonder if it was fate or bad luck,* Tarleton thought. *Seeing Captain Campbell burned this Sumter's house, fitting justice, fate?*

Again Tarleton nodded, then looked out over the camp. "What about their losses?"

"We have found about fifty dead rebels, sir. It could be more that floated down the river or were wounded and died in the woods. We did find several blood trails."

Tarleton nodded, "Have our dead and wounded loaded on the wagons; prepare to move out."

The adjutant asked, "What of the rebel dead?"

Tarleton looked over, "Leave them where they lie, someone will see to them, or the animals will take care of it."

The column was reformed, and Tarleton placed his helmet back on and mounted his horse. He rode to the head of his column; he could see his men were happy, caught up in their victory over the rebels. Tarleton was delighted, his men performed well, and he was proving the need for mobility to stop these rebels.

Once he reached the front of the column, he looked behind them and at the expectant faces of his men. Then, raising his hand, he motioned forward, and the column began their return trip toward Camden. *"His lordship should appreciate our accomplishing his mission."*

The British column marched away, the wagons creaking and the cows mooing as they were herded along with the Continental and rebel prisoners. Tarleton looked back and reflected on fate, as now the men who had been prisoners of the rebels were guarding their once captors, their roles reversed.

Elizabeth Peay remained next to the log until she heard silence, indicating the column had departed. Then, slowly rising, she looked over the log to see the British were indeed gone. Coming to her feet, her servant came over with her other child, whom she hugged closely.

"Are you all right, mistress?" her servant asked, and she sighed in relief, nodding her head. Then, she handed her baby to the servant, "I need to go find my husband." He nodded while cradling the baby while holding the hand of her other child.

She ran across the strewn field, the ground torn up by the charging hooves and broken and dead bodies. Elizabeth searched and, with dread, found the dead body of her husband. Collapsing to her knees next to her husband, she wept. Now she had no idea what to do.

Standing up, she looked at the lifeless face of her husband, dabbed her eyes with her handkerchief, and set her goal of heading to her family in Virginia. She wandered around the field, looking for a horse. The British had taken hers, and the thought of walking to Virginia was daunting.

She heard a whinny and found a gray horse who had been wounded but standing. She led the horse over to where her servant and her children were. Then, she made a bandage for the horse using several shirts lying about. The servant found a couple of full canteens and some haversacks with rations.

Elizabeth mounted the horse, hanging the canteens and haversacks from the saddle, and she cradled her baby in her lap. Then, taking one last look at her dead husband, the servant carried her other child, kicked the horse, and began the slow journey to Virginia.

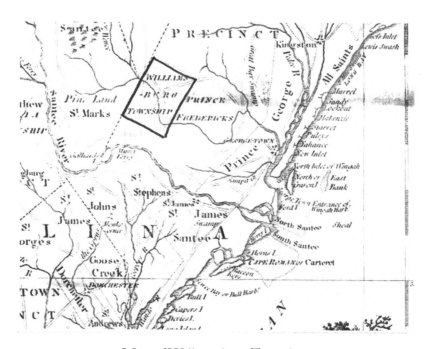

Map of Williamsburg Township

CHAPTER 2

A NEW COMMAND

With their merry little band of twenty men, Jacob and Marion trotted along the dirt road, the day's heat making them sweat and the dust sticking to them. They followed paths and roads that avoided any area known for their Loyalist support. Jacob wondered how they would be received once they arrived in Williamsburg; would they accept Marion as a leader?

"What's your plan, Marion?" Jacob asked, "What are we going to do?"

As they plodded along the dirt road, Marion thought about it before answering.

"Well, we are in a tight spot, to be sure," he answered, "We will do our best to follow General Gate's orders, secure the boats and see what mischief we can do."

Jacob nodded, "We'll just have to see what happens when we get to Williamsburg."

Marion, in turn, nodded. "It's all we can do at the moment."

It was midday when they rode into the town square of Williamsburg and were surprised to see four militia companies standing around. As they rode past, the militiamen whispered, "It's Marion, look, it's Marion!" Then a few even called out to either Marion and even Jacob.

He looked at the assembled men and began recognizing a few. They had served with the Second Regiment in the early days, at the beginning of the war, and Fort Sullivan.

"Well, that's an interesting turn," Jacob commented. They saw what had to be the officers having a meeting under a large, broad-limbed oak tree. They rode over and dismounted, and as soon as Marion and Jacob were off their horses, John James called out.

"Colonel Marion, Captain Clarke, so bloody good to see you both!" he said as he came over and shook their hands. "We feared the worse that you had been taken with the city or with Gates."

Marion looked over at Jacob, then back at James. "What do you mean about Gates? We have been traveling the last couple of days and had no news. What have you learned."

The four company commanders, William Armgarett, John Baldwin, David Gordan, and Robert Hudson, joined James, Marion, and Jacob. James shrugged his shoulders and began explaining the news they had just received.

"Well, we just learned that Shelby up at Musgrove Mill defeated a British and Loyalist force," James explained with a smile, and Marion nodded.

"That is good news," Marion responded, then James slowly shook his head. "Let me guess; the bad news involves Gates?"

James nodded, "Then you may not have heard, Gates was soundly defeated outside of Camden; Lord Cornwallis destroyed the new army."

John Baldwin snorted, "Heard old Gates broke the record of riding some one hundred and seventy miles from Camden back up into North Carolina, did it in under three days."

"What about Sumter," Jacob asked, "We heard he was given a commission and headed back down this way."

James looked at his company commanders and shook his head again. "That Green Dragoon and his Legion caught him with his pants down near Fishing Creek. He was routed, and his men scattered to the four winds. There is no one left."

Again John Baldwin snorted and shook his head. "Word is he got caught with his pants down or off. Heard he rode away as fast as he could with nothing but his shirt on his back."

Marion had a stern look, and he began to pace as he thought about their situation.

"While we have no army, there is still us. Therefore, we can fight against the British, and we will resist and keep fighting, so help me, God!"

With a determined look, Marion turned and looked at James, "Will you and your men follow me?"

James looked at the four company commanders, who nodded their heads enthusiastically.

"Sir, we followed you before. We will surely follow you to the very gates of Hell if need be. We're your men!"

James held out his hand, and Marion accepted it. "You will still command your men, James. Do you have a commission?"

James nodded, "Yes, sir, I am a major."

"Good then, Major James," Marion stated.

"We will recruit and gather as many old veterans as we can. We must be mobile and on the move. We can't let them find us and finish us. Rather we must be fast, find them, and bring the fight to them on a field of our choosing."

James and the four commanders nodded, "Form your men so that I may address them," Marion commanded, and the four turned to head over and get their companies ready. Jacob watched them go and then looked over at Marion, who looked at Jacob, then winked.

"See, that wasn't so hard."

Jacob shook his head but smiled as they headed to the companies formed for Marion to speak to them. Again, Jacob watched as Marion addressed the man. Again he spotted several familiar faces in the ranks, who were beaming, seeing that Marion was there.

"Men, as you are probably more aware than I was a short while ago, it's not looking good for our cause," Marion stated. "You have heard about Gate's defeat and Sumter being driven off. That there is no Southern Army, again."

The men murmured and nodded, knowing the situation, before turning back and watching Marion.

"I am here to tell you, there is still hope, and it rests with us. We will take up this challenge and meet the barbarity and destruction caused by the British and their Loyalist friends. Let our actions speak louder than words!"

Marion watched the men's reaction, who nodded, and even a few cheered, "Huzzah!"

Marion waited until the men quieted down.

"Now I know you are under the command of Major James here, a fine and capable officer. So what I am asking you, will you follow me as your overall commander, with Major James in charge of you, even if I don't hold a militia commission? Captain Clarke will currently serve as our mounted infantry element."

The men looked at one another, quiet discussion going on among them.

"What say you? I leave it to a vote as you are the men following myself and Major James into harm's way. Discuss and then vote."

Marion stopped to allow time for the men to discuss, but it was a swift discussion. Finally, everyone began to nod their heads in agreement.

"Sir, there is no need to vote," one of the men from the militia companies stated, "We all agree to follow you as our overall commander and under the command of Major James."

Then the man turned and faced the companies, "Three cheers to Colonel Marion, hip hip Huzzah!" The men gave their three "Huzzahs," Marion nodded and gave his instructions with a slight blush from their acceptance.

"All right then, let's get down to business. We need friends, people we can trust to be our eyes and ears, who get information to us but do not get themselves in trouble with the British or their Loyalist friends. Once we learn of a good target of opportunity, then we'll see to it."

Again the men nodded their understanding and talked amongst themselves. Marion nodded.

"Commanders, see to your men. Let us get this started!"

The company commanders saluted, and Marion returned to where Jacob and the others stood.

"Let's find a place to stay and look at our first action."

***

With his company from the 63rd Regiment of Foot, Captain Roberts watched as his men herded the next batch of one hundred and fifty rebel prisoners into line. First, they encouraged the prisoners to form a column on the dirt road using their bayonets. Then they took up positions around the column, keeping the prisoners in the line.

He looked at the downturned faces of the rebels, their morale having been crushed at their defeat and their commander abandoning them. But, thinking back to the battle, he respected the one general who stayed and went down fighting with his men, this de Kalb fellow.

Roberts shook his head. This de Kalb, a proper Bavarian, who had served in a real army, gave it all up to lead these rebels? "He showed much bravery," Roberts said with a sigh, "more than I can say about their commander, Gates."

His lieutenant looked over, having heard the comment, "Sir?"

Captain Roberts looked at his lieutenant and smiled, "Oh, nothing, just musing about these rebels and the men who lead them. Let me know when the column is ready to march."

The lieutenant nodded, then approached the sergeant responsible for the guards. A Prince of Wales American Regiment sergeant approached and saluted as he waited.

"Sir, I have the guides who know the area we will march toward. Do you mind a specific camp location along the way to Charles Town?"

Returning the salute, Roberts stated, "We'll take the main road south toward Charles Town; we should be able to make an abandoned plantation on the Great Savannah, just north of Nelson Ferry."

The sergeant nodded, "The guides need to know exactly where we are going. Do you know the name of the plantation owner?"

Roberts smiled and nodded, "I believe it used to belong to that rebel Sumter who just heard about being chased out of South Carolina by Colonel Tarleton."

The sergeant nodded, "Yes, sir, I believe I know the very plantation you are speaking of."

"Excellent, lead the way when the column is formed," Roberts commanded. The sergeant saluted and went over to stand with the guides and explain their destination.

"To the front, march!"

Roberts looked over, and the column of prisoners began to shuffle forward, the guards moving alongside with the bayonet-tipped muskets covering the column. He went over to where his horse was tied and mounted it. Then, they went over to where the guides were waiting. When the column arrived, he nodded to the lead element, who turned and led the way down the road. Roberts took up a position near the center of the column.

As the column of prisoners marched by, a worker at the old Kershaw Mercantile stopped sweeping and watched the column of dejected prisoners walk past. He had heard all the details of where they were going and decided now was the time to act.

Frederick Nasonne didn't like what he saw and wanted to do something about it. It wasn't right in his mind, and then, with a quick nod, he decided. He went inside the shop, leaned the broom against a corner, then took off his workman's apron. Standing there, looking out the window at the prisoners walking by, was the shopkeeper for Mr. Kershaw, Daniel Peak. Frederick just shook his head.

"I have to do something. I can't just sit here and do nothing," Frederick explained, "I didn't serve all those years upcountry against them damn Cherokee to see this happen. So I have to go."

Daniel nodded, "I understand," he said and shook Frederick's hand. "If anyone comes looking for you, I'll say you visited your poor old, sick mother upcountry."

Nodding his head, Frederick smiled in thanks before heading out behind the shop where his horse stood. His trusty rifle, showereng bags, and gear were inside the back door. He tied his pack onto the saddle before leaping up with his rifle.

Turning his horse, he took another trail that paralleled the road heading south, knowing he would have difficulty finding anyone still resisting the British. But, as a Mounted Ranger during the Cherokee Wars, he recalled a Jacob Clarke, whom he knew about and lived in the low country. If he could find Jacob, he could direct him to someone who would do something about the prisoners.

***

Marion, Jacob, and James were bent over, looking at a map showing their operating area. They knew the British, of course, controlled the area around Charles Town, and they controlled Georgetown and Camden. But, at the moment, they were holding the interior between those towns.

"How accurate is your information John," Marion asked as he traced his finger along the road from Camden toward Charles Town.

"The British have been moving prisoners from the battle almost daily from Camden to Charles Town," answered James. "Based on the information we received, a column was spotted departing Camden about a day ago."

Marion nodded. He sought a suitable place to ambush the column and rescue the prisoners. This victory would boost the locals' morale and perhaps e volunteers for his group. "If we knew exactly where they are going."

"Nelson Ferry," a voice said from behind them, "They are heading for the old Sumter place above Nelson Ferry."

All three turned to see a tall rifleman standing at the door and a militiaman, dust from the road on their clothes. Marion looked at the men, while Jacob thought he recognized the rifleman but wasn't sure from where or when.

"You are?" Marion asked.

"Frederick Nasonne, Sergeant Frederick Nasonne, formerly of the South Carolina Mounted Rangers under Sergeant Folk. This is Zacharia Owens, a local who knows the area very well.

His brother, Hugh Graham, served with the Second Regiment during the early days."

Jacob snapped his fingers, "That's where I know you from, the Mounted Rangers up at Fort George."

Frederick looked relieved when he saw Jacob was there. "It's good to see you again, Captain Clarke; I was hoping to find you but was directed over here instead." He then looked around with a puzzled look.

"Where is Sergeant Penny? Normally he is right alongside you."

Jacob had a troubled look. "Prisoner, I am afraid; he was taken in Charles Town."

Frederick nodded, "Sorry to hear that. He is a tough one. If anyone can make it, it is him."

Jacob nodded thanks, then turned to Marion and nodded, "I know him; we served together before our Middleton days. I recall Hugh from the early days, a good steady man." He looked at Zacharia, "If you are anything like Hugh, I will have you."

Marion appeared satisfied. "So they are heading to Sumter's place north of Nelson Ferry?"

Frederick nodded, "Aye, sir, heard it from the guides themselves speaking to the guard commander."

Marion nodded, then looked at the map. "How many men are guarding the prisoners?"

Frederick thought, "No more than a small company, about twenty men or so."

Marion looked at the map and began formulating an idea and the beginning of a plan.

"We have them outnumbered, we can pick the location of the ambush, and we can quickly hit, then fade away."

He then looked at Zacharia, "Do you know a way to get to Nelson Ferry quickly and undetected?"

Zacharia nodded, "Yes, sir, I know a couple of paths that can get you there quickly."

Marion smiled and rubbed his hands together. " Gentlemen, I believe we have our first task."

Jacob, along with James, nodded their heads in agreement. Marion looked at the map, circling Nelson Ferry with his finger. "We will have to move now, but we need to get eyes on them to confirm their presence.

"I'll go," Jacob volunteered, "I'll take my small force and see if we can detect the column and follow them to where they camp. Then, we will meet you at the old Barber's place south of the Ferry and report what we find."

Marion nodded, "Sounds good; go gather your men, and I'll get the rest of them ready to go."

"Sir, if I may," Frederick added, "May we ride with Captain Clarke? Then, between Zacharia and I, we can lead them to the spot as I have been tracking them on the way down here."

"Good idea," Marion commented, "We'll meet you at the Barber's place at nightfall."

Nodding to Marion, Jacob, Frederick, and Zacharia headed over to where the boys were, the wolves and their initial men.

"It's good to be riding with you again, Captain Clarke," Frederick stated as they walked along, "It has been some time."

"Aye, it has." Jacob replied, "We visited old Fort George some time back; it's in a sad shape now; all that is left are the memories."

"Hugh mentioned you several times Captain Clarke," Zacharia stated, "How many of his tales are true?"

Jacob laughed, "Maybe a few of them; soldier stories get slightly exaggerated over time."

After they arrived at their small camp, Jacob gathered the boys, along with the wolves, Jean, Jehu Jones, and William Lee.

Once gathered, he introduced Frederick and Zacharia, then explained their mission.

"We just learned that some of the prisoners are being marched to Charles Town," Jacob explained, "Frederick here, who used to serve with me with the mounted Rangers, is going to lead us to where we can observe the column while the colonel brings the rest of the group. Zacharia will also join our merry band; he knows the local area well."

"What will we do then?" Richard asked, and Jacob smiled.

"Simple, we're going to rescue them!"

The men nodded in approval. "See to your gear and mount up; we ride as soon as we can," Jacob commanded, and the men turned to gather their gear and weapons and get their horses. Frederick and Zacharia went over and returned with their horses. They waited with Jacob, who was checking his bags on his horse. Frederick looked down at the wolves lying on the ground, waiting.

"Nice wolves you have there," he commented, "are they useful?"

Jacob looked over at the four wolves, who looked up in anticipation. "They have proven to be excellent trackers, silent and efficient. Besides, it reminds me of the good old days with Rogers when we had our wolves then. They spotted hidden enemies more times than I can recall. So I think they will serve just as good here."

The boys and the others walked their horses up to Jacob, Zacharia, and Frederick and then mounted their horses. The wolves sprang onto their feet, waiting expectantly, their tails wagging. Jacob looked over his small Band of men, saw everything was in order, nodded, turned his horse, and began to lead them out of the town. The wolves already sprinted ahead, the horses kicking up small poofs of dust.

Marion came out to watch them leave. "See you at the rendezvous!" he called out, and Jacob waved back. Frederick took the lead as they turned off the road onto a hunting trail. The wolves stayed close but, their noses were either in the air or sniffing along the ground.

After a short ride, Jacob could see through some breaks in the trees that they were following the Congaree River, heading northward toward Camden. Jacob thought back to when he met Joseph Kershaw, who wanted to change Camden's original name of Pine Tree Hill. He was finally successful in 1768.

Jacob halted the Band so the horses could rest, the men could stretch their legs, and he could get his bearings. Then, Jacob walked up to the edge of the woods. He looked at the river and the open fields along the side. Then, nodding his hook it all in and recalled the different landmarks from memory.

Frederick, Zacharia, and Jean joined him. "We should be getting close to where the next group of prisoners should be making their way toward Nelson's Ferry that crosses the Santee River," stated Frederick, and both Jean and Jacob nodded.

"There is one other trail we can use if we need to get closer or if they get ahead of us," commented Zacharia.

Jacob then pointed slightly northwest of where they were standing. "The Old Barber's place is just up the river; we'll meet Marion and the rest of the men tonight."

Frederick and Zacharia nodded and followed Jacob back to their band, who mounted their horses as Jacob did. Once all was ready, Jacob nodded to Frederick, who continued down the path. Looking up, Jacob could see the sun was past its midpoint and heading into the afternoon hours. They rode for another hour when Frederick halted the band.

"We should be in a good position to observe and follow the prisoners from here," Frederick stated, and Jacob nodded.

He dismounted, followed by the rest of the Band. Jacob pointed to either side of the path.

"Conceal yourselves as best as you can. Frederick and I are going out to the wood line to keep an eye out for the prisoner column. Jean, you are in charge here. Once we spot them, be ready to mount and follow until we find where they camp. That's where it will be the best place to attack them."

The men nodded, moved into the trees, and tied their horses. After securing their horses, Jacob and Frederick moved through the trees until they came to the edge of the trees and bush and found a place to sit and observe the road. While they waited, in a low whispery voice, they caught up on their lives and what happened after the Anglo-Cherokee War.

The sun was beginning to get low when Jacob spotted the lead party of British redcoats marching. They stopped talking, and Jacob pulled out his telescope. The lead British soldiers had bayonets fixed and watched the road in front of them. Then right behind them, came the prisoners and their guards.

Focusing the telescope, Jacob spotted the few blue-coated Continentals and the rest of the prisoners who were only in their small clothes or split shirts. Looking closer, many of the prisoners showed they had given up. Red-coated guards were placed out along the column, then at the end of the column.

Returning to their horses, the men quickly rose and, seeing Jacob nod, mounted up. They followed the column slowly, staying far enough back to avoid being observed but not lose track of the column. The sun was setting and was only slightly above the trees when the prisoners turned off the road that led to the Great Savannah.

Jacob and Frederick dismounted and went up to the edge of the woods. Once more, they observed what the British and the prisoners were doing. Taking out his telescope, Jacob observed the British moving the prisoners into a large plantation house, and he started to chuckle to himself.

"What is so funny?" Frederick asked in a whisper.

"I think good ol' Sumter would be rather put out when he learned the British used his house to hold Patriot prisoners."

Frederick nodded, "I believe you would be right, Jacob."

As the sun set, Jacob continued to watch the plantation house. All the prisoners were inside and at least two guards were at the door. The rest had stacked their arms, started cooking fires and began to eat their meals. Some British began carrying their packs into the house but left their muskets outside. From their vantage point, they could see candle light coming from rooms on the first floor but nothing from the second floor.

"The British must hold the prisoners on the upper floor rooms while they use the lower rooms for their quarters. Perfect!"

Jacob was nodding, then closed his telescope with a soft click. "Let's get the band and head to the Old Barber's Place. I want to drop you off so that you can get a good vantage point on the house, and we can bring Marion and the others to you."

Frederick nodded; it made sense. So Jacob, Jean, and the band walked with their horses and wolves. They found a point, a huge old oak tree that was easy to see in the dark and from where Frederick could climb up to and keep an eye on the house. Jacob handed him his telescope.

Jacob left William and Jehu with Frederick while the others rode to the Barber's place. Then, using the darkness to cover them, they returned to the main road and headed to the ruins that were once the Barber's Farm. It was only a short ride from Sumter's Plantation, and Jacob led them into the barnyard area and moved into the shadows to wait.

Checking on the boys, "Check your muskets, and then get something to eat. Going to be a long night," Jacob instructed, and the boys began checking their muskets before pulling out some biscuits and dried fish. After they finished, Jacob came over and checked on them.

"Get some rest; it may be a little while before the colonel gets here," Jacob says softly, "We'll keep watch."

Having learned the importance of resting when you can, the boys didn't argue, looked for the best they could for a comfortable spot, and closed their eyes. Jacob watched them briefly, nodding as he could tell they were only snoozing and could come fully awake at a moment's notice.

Jean stood with Jacob in the shadow of the old barn, watching the road.

"Should be an easy go, no?" Jean whispered, and Jacob shrugged.

"Should be easy if we catch them by surprise and asleep. If we move fast enough, we should be able to take the guards and the redcoats, so none of the prisoners are injured."

Near midnight, Jacob heard approaching horses from down the road. He woke the boys, who sprang to their feet, coming fully Jacob smiled, "Easy lads, it's the colonel."

Marion led the rest of the men into the farmyard, looking for Jacob, who had kept his band concealed. Looking around, Marion let out a low whisper, "Captain Clarke?" Quickly, Marion saw the golden eyes of the wolves come out, and Jacob appeared from a shadow and approached Marion's knees.

Leaning down, "What have you seen?" Marion asked in a low whisper.

"There is between one hundred and twenty, maybe even one hundred and fifty prisoners, being guarded by only a company of British. They are sleeping in Sumter's old place on the Great Savannah. Frederick is still up there keeping an eye on things."

Marion nodded, and Jacob returned to his band, mounting his horse. He led his small group to Marion's, seeing Hugh Horry had joined them along with Major James. "Lead on Captain Clarke," Marion instructed, and Jacob, with the wolves and his small band, led the raid forward. Following Marion were around one hundred and fifty men in a column of two.

Jacob led them down the road in the light of a bright moon, no one speaking or saying a word. The wolves kept pace, staying close to Jacob and the front of the column. The night air was quiet but expectant. The energy was growing amongst the men, finally going to get back into action after their loss of Charles Town. Jacob could sense the growing excitement, the tension before the coming fight.

The great oak tree where Frederick, William, and Jehu watched was looming in the distance. As they arrived, Jacob could see a shadow detach from high up in the tree, make its way down to the ground and come over. It was Frederick who reported to Marion and Jacob.

"No change, other than most British have gone to sleep. There is at least one fire still burning, and there is a roving guard. No candlelight from the top of the first floor, though I did see one on the top floor. I believe it was guards checking on the prisoners." Frederick handed the telescope back to Jacob.

Marion waved over the other officers, so Hugh and James joined Marion and Jacob. Marion was formulating a quick plan in his head. He rose in his saddle, looking at the house in the distance. He settled in his saddle, nodded, and decided on his plan.

"All right, we have a great opportunity here," Marion began. "We must strike hard and fast, encircling the house, catching the British by surprise. First, we must ensure the safety of the prisoners, then we either kill or capture the enemy. After that, surprise, speed, and violence of action will allow us to prevail. Any questions?"

They nodded their heads, ready for action. Frederick went over and mounted his horse; with William and Jehu waiting, the three joined Jacob. Marion looked intently at his gathered officers.

"Hugh, lead us out and clear the right side of the house; John, you follow and go to the left. Jacob and I will secure the house. Be sure of your targets; we have friends in there. Ready?'

All the men nodded, and Marion drew his pistol. "Let's see to it then!"

Turning his horse, Hugh smiled, drew his sword, and called, "Follow Me!" Horry's men fell in behind, followed by Major James and his men. Once they had passed, Marion, Jacob, and the other raiders rode toward the plantation house. The horses went quickly from a walk to a trot, then into a gallop.

"Ka-Pow!"

A sentry, who of all times was awake for a change, heard the approaching horses of Horry's men, fired a warning shot, and fled toward the house. The alert served as a starting gun, and the horsemen urged their horses on faster as Horry led his men to the right while John James led his horsemen to the left. Finally, Jacob and Marion rode right at the center of the courtyard in front of the house and quickly began to dismount as the horses came to a sliding halt.

"Go for the muskets!" Jacob ordered, and his boys, Patrick and Richard, ran forward and knocked down the stacks of muskets into a clattering pile. Jean, Zacharia, Robert, and Thomas charged two British soldiers sitting around the fire smoking.

37

As they rose to meet the threat, they were hit by large, flying blurs of furs as the wolves charged into the two shocked men. Two wolves per man were quickly brought to the ground, their throats crushed by their jaws.

Jean stepped up and placed the muzzle of his rifle in the startled face of a British soldier trying to rise. Zacharia placed his musket against the second man's chest.

"Sit!" Jean commanded, and both men sank back down to the ground and raised their hands, watching the muzzle only inches from his face. The boys were flipping the muskets, dumping the powder from the pans and making them safe.

Knowing the boys were covered by the wolves, Zacharia, Jean, Jacob, and Marion burst into the front door just as a few British soldiers came stumbling out of a room from the right. Jacob quickly ducked, putting his shoulder into the stomach of a charging British soldier, while Marion pulled the trigger on his pistol. The soldier flew backward into the room that Marion had hit.

Stunned by the sound of the pistol going off so close to his head, Jacob lifted the soldier he had hit up and over his shoulder while he drew his tomahawk. Then, as the soldier lay stunned, Jacob finished him off with a tomahawk strike in the back. Then he kept moving, heading for the stairs in the center of the hallway, while the rest of Marion's men broke left and right to capture the shocked British soldiers quickly.

Bounding up the stairs quickly, Jacob, with about six other men, fanned out at the top. Two guards were in the hallway in front of four doors, and a lantern was on the floor. They appeared to be just coming around; perhaps they had been sleeping when they attacked and the shock affected them. They both realized they were under assault and brought their muskets up to their shoulders.

Dropping quickly to the floor, Jacob rolled forward, came up under the British soldier, and knocked his musket off with his tomahawk just as he fired. There was a thunderous explosion in the close confines of the hallway as three muskets went off, the two British guards and James Grover's from the band. The musket Jacob had struck fired, and the ball entered the door, missing Jacob.

Grover's shot hit the British soldier as he fired wide and missed, crumbling to the ground. Swinging his tomahawk, Jacob struck the other British soldier in the face and he collapsed to the floor unconscious. Jacob, Grover and, the rest of the men quickly surveyed the hall and saw no more threats.

"See to the prisoners!" Jacob commanded, and they went to the doors.

"We, friends, we're coming in!" yelled Grover as he opened his door; Jacob did the same to the door the British soldier had fired through. Slowly opening the door, with what light the lantern provided, Jacob could see dozens of faces looking back. Jacob also saw a wounded man sitting on the floor.

"Bring the lantern; we have a wounded man!" Jacob yelled, and one of the men brought the lantern over. Jacob knelt to look at the wound as one of the men held the lantern up to show at least thirty men tightly packed inside the room. He looked at the injured man; it appeared the ball came through the door and struck the prisoner in the shoulder. One of the prisoners was winding a strip torn from a shirt over the wound as a bandage.

"Who are you people?" asked the wounded man.

"Captain Jacob Clarke, formerly of the Second South Carolina, now part of Marion's men."

The wounded man nodded, "Captain Edward Duval, formerly of the Second Maryland now. We were part of the great expedition of General Gates that met its ultimate end up north."

Jacob nodded, "Let's get you and your men outside."

Following Jacob, the prisoners followed the band through the house and into the courtyard. As Jacob exited the house, the sun was beginning to rise, making it easier to see. On the far side were about twenty British soldiers and some Loyalists under guard by Major James' men.

The Marylanders joined the other rescued men and Jacob, reported to Marion. He was found speaking to an unknown person, with Hugh and John James standing with him. Jacob could tell that the prisoner was a British officer and only wore his long shirt.

"Captain Roberts, you and your men will follow our directions; you are now considered prisoners of war until we can determine your final disposition either as prisoners or offer you parole. Then, you may return to your men."

Captain Roberts gave a curt nod, then was escorted by two men over to where the British prisoners were kept. Marion turned and had a pleased look on his face.

"How did we do?" Marion asked. "I learned these guards are from the 63rd Regiment of Foot, some Loyalists from the Prince of Wales American Regiment, escorting men from Delaware and Maryland."

Jacob nodded his head in confirmation. "Yes sir, the one wounded prisoner I found said he was from the Second Maryland."

Marion nodded in turn, "Any other casualties?"

"Two wounded," reported Hugh Horry. "The British had six dead, and we have twenty-four prisoners, including their company commander."

"Let's address the freedmen, and perhaps they will join us?" Marion stated and headed over to where the former Continental prisoners were standing. They appeared to be in a discussion, pointing in their direction. Some men were nodding, and some were shaking their heads.

They all stopped talking and looked at Marion as he approached the group.

"Gentlemen, while your arrival here in South Carolina may not have been at the best of times, you are here now as freedmen. I intend to move you away from here and from the British, where you will be safe for a while."

A man stepped forward to address Marion.

"Ah, if I may ask, whom am I addressing?" he asked.

"Lieutenant Colonel Francis Marion."

The man nodded, "I am Major Patton, from the Delaware Regiment. Ah, sir. We gave our word that we would behave like good soldiers and continue our march to Charles Town as we promised."

Marion was not the only one shocked at the request; Jacob, Hugh, and John were surprised at what they had just heard.

"So, if I am following correctly, you and your men want to go on to be prisoners in Charles Town?"

Major Patton looked over his shoulder at the other men, half nodding in agreement.

"May I ask why?" Marion asked quietly, though Jacob thought he caught some tension in the sound.

"To be honest, we feel we would be better off with the British than with men who look like you." Major Patton explained, and Jacob shook his head. The same friction that came up with Gates, how they disapproved of how they looked instead of looking at what they did. Looking over at Marion, Jacob saw that he was staying composed.

"Then, Major, I wouldn't be able to trust a man in action based on their willingness to give up when given a chance to fight for freedom. While I did not personally see or hear how you did in the previous battle, if you and your men do not want to continue the fight, then march to Charles Town. We will not support you or stop you."

Major Patton only nodded, then turned, and motioned with his hand to move; about eighty men continued their march down the road, heading for Charles Town. The rest of the men stood there, looking at Marion. Then, looking back at them, Marion explained, "We'll take you to one of the camps in the area. Until then, rest, and I'll see what I can do for you from what supplies we have on hand."

Marion, Jacob, Hugh Horry, and John James, moved to the side.

"Hugh, you will lead the advance guard, James; you will escort the prisoners while the rest assist the rescued prisoners. Then, we will head over to Snow Island and camp there." Once Marion issued the instructions, they turned to gather their men and begin the trek over to Snow Island.

Once the column was formed, Marion led them out and started a slow but steady pace over to Snow Island. As they marched as individuals or small groups, the former Continentals began to desert. By the time they arrived at Snow Island, only three of the one hundred and fifty of the rescued remained.

Jacob shook his head. They had more prisoners than rescued Continentals. While he could understand that the defeat crushed their morale, he could not see how they freely gave up their freedom while there was still a chance to resist. Jacob moved over to an open area on the island, dismounted and secured his horse to a tree.

Major James took the prisoners and marched to a friendly town where they would be held until a Justice of the Peace finalized their parole. As Jacob started to set out his ground cloth, the boys, along with Frederick and the rest of their small band, came over and joined him in preparing their camp.

"Hell of a way to fight a war, eh?" Frederick said as he set up his camp. "We go through all that, spotting them and then rescuing them, only to have them turn right around and either stay prisoners or desert. No damn appreciation for what we did!"

Jacob nodded his head in agreement. "Still though, we did show the British they are not safe, that they will have to be more careful now on the march. We hurt them, and we will keep hurting them. That's what counts; granted, it would have been better if some of them had joined them, but we sent a message."

Frederick nodded his head, seeing Jacob's point. "Aye, you're right; we gave them a message. I hope they understand we're not going down without a fight!"

***

Samuel was leaning against the bulkhead as usual, used to he sweat streaming down his chest and face. He was snoozing, listening to the drone of flies that buzzed around the inside of their holding area. Then, there was a commotion as voices were heard commanding on the deck above them.

"Must be new arrivals," Samuel thought. As the sound of feet coming down the stairs had Samuel open his eyes to watch, the new prisoners move onto their deck, filling the spaces where the recently dead had been removed. They were all in their shirts and breaches, no coats or frocks and only a few still had their stockings on. None had shoes.

Paying the newcomers no mind, Samuel returned to his daydream world where he was with his family back on the compound, hunting deer and raising their children. Later in the day, he overheard a conversation between the new arrivals and the other prisoners that got his attention.

"So, we are, marching down the road from Camden, and the British take us to this fine plantation house. There, they stuffed a good chunk of us into these rooms, locked them up and put guards outside. Well, there was such a sound in the early morning, someone attacked the house and opened the doors for us. A big fellow with a scar on his face, fought like a devil with a tomahawk. A tomahawk! Would you believe that!"

Samuel's eyes popped open, and he jumped to his feet and ran to the group talking.

"This big man with the scar and the tomahawk, did he give his name?" Samuel asked urgently, excited at whom he thought it was.

The man sat for a second before snapping his finger. "Aye, he did. When we were helping the captain who had been wounded, he stated his name was Clarke, a Captain Clarke formerly of the Second Regiment South Carolina; why?"

Samuel couldn't contain himself any longer. He reached out, hugged the man who gave him the news, and kissed him on the cheek before he began dancing around, singing, "He's alive, he's still alive! Nothing can kill him; he's alive!"

While Samuel pranced around, the man pointed his thumb at Samuel, "What's his story?"

One of the older prisoners shrugged, "He is one of the original prisoners from the fall of the city; he's nuts. He survived a scalping and a long time in the field; his brain must have gotten softer."

Breathing heavily from the exertion, Samuel returned to his spot and sat down.

"Jacob is alive, and maybe Jean is too. I have to get off this floating death trap, but how?"

Samuel looked around at the crowded deck; many prisoners were malnourished and sick, lying in filth. The others walked around them, knowing they were doomed. Then there were the new arrivals. He knew he didn't have the strength to swim even if he could get into the river.

As he rubbed his chin, a plan began to formulate. A slow smile began to creep across his face as the plan solidified. Then he began to nod slowly, believing that he had found the plan that would work. Now, all he had to wait for was the opportunity to knock.

CHAPTER 3

ON THE OFFENSIVE

When the news of Marion's successful raid of the prisoners reached Cornwallis, who had secured the Kershaw House as his headquarters, having heard of the information about the prisoner rescue, he was livid. An area he thought was secure was altered as these rebels could freely move into and attack his men.

Hands behind his back and deep in thought, Cornwallis approached the large window that looked out into the house's front yard. He had moved his office to this spacious room on the second floor. Outside, the engineers and soldiers were busy erecting defenses around the house, making the house and its surroundings into a fortification. Sighing, Cornwallis returned to the table in the center of the room.

Looking at his map, the Williamsburg Township and its vicinity to Georgetown, he contemplated how this could have happened. Then, using his finger, he traced the known roads that bisected the district, running through Georgetown on the coast and out into the interior like Monk's Corner and King's Tree.

He did recall a message from Captain Ardesoif about a representative from the people of Williamsburg on their intent.

"Intent! Our bloody intent is to see our land and people secured, and these rebels and Banditti are stopped. Then, we will be in control, and they will respect our authority!"

Cornwallis made his mind up and sent for Major James Wemyss of the 63rd Regiment of Foot. After sending a runner to fetch Major Wemyss, he also sent runners for Colonel Samuel Bryan of the North Carolina Volunteers and Major Harrison's South Carolina Loyalist Rangers. As Cornwallis thought about it, he would throw in the Royal North Carolina Regiment for good measure.

"I will hammer these rebels and break them now, including those supporting them. I will see them crushed before they can organize. Then the region will be pacified, and we can march north."

"Sir, Major Wemyss and Colonel Bryan are here," stated the orderly, and Cornwallis waved them in. Shortly, the two officers arrived, stopped and saluted. Cornwallis gave them a stern look.

"Gentlemen, I have a critical task for you," Cornwallis directed, and the two officers nodded.

"Major Wemyss, you will march the 63rd along with Colonel Bryan's North Carolina Volunteers, the Royal North Carolina, and the South Carolina Loyalist Rangers. You have heard of these bandits that struck the company from the 63rd escorting prisoners from our latest victory."

Major Wemyss nodded adamantly, as it had been one of his companies. Cornwallis continued.

"Then Major Wemyss, I am giving you a chance to redeem you and your unit's honor by leading an expedition into this Williamsburg District, to King's Tree of all places, and bring these rebels to heel."

Cornwallis paused again and gave both officers a stern look to drive his point home.

"You will make them pay; punish them! Anyone supporting these rebels will be dealt with, and any rebel found will be hung as they are no better than the treacherous \bandits they are.

Furthermore, any arms concealed from us shall be confiscated, and that person subject to the King's justice!"

Major Wemyss had a slight smile on his face, "Sir, what do you mean exactly by King's Justice?"

Cornwallis gave him a leveled, intent stare. "Anyone found supporting, harboring, or concealing arms will be arrested and their property forfeited. In addition, you will burn everything they own to the ground as a message to those supporting these bandits that will not be tolerated. Do you understand your task?"

Both officers nodded, especially Wemyss, who was using their highest effort to conceal the desire for the wanton destruction he would lay upon the land. Nevertheless, he was looking forward to the expedition.

"Then see to your men, move on to King's Tree, and do your duty!"

Both officers saluted, spun on their heels, and headed out the door just as Major Ferguson entered, looking at their backs. Now he was wearing a uniform of the Royal Americans, a redcoat with green facings and cuffs. He then turned and approached General Cornwallis, who had moved back over to a large window, looking out the front yard of the Kershaw place.

"Sir, you asked for me?" he asked. Cornwallis, deep in thought, turned and almost jumped when he realized Ferguson was standing there.

"Ah, major, glad you have arrived. Are your men ready to march?" Cornwallis welcomed Major Ferguson.

"Yes, sir," Major Ferguson stated. "I have organized my freshly raised Loyalist companies; they are all armed and ready to march."

Cornwallis nodded his head and smiled.

"We are about to depart from here and move on Charlotte up in North Carolina. You will be responsible for securing the army's left flank. You will move into the Ninety-Six District and raise more militia to serve the King."

Major Ferguson nodded, understanding his instructions.

"We have received reports of rebel activity in the up-country. Once you have enough men, you will move northward into the up-country and seize these rebels as you see fit. Make sure they understand what it means to defy their King. Am I understood?"

Ferguson stood rigidly and nodded. "Yes, sir, clearly understood."

"Good then, see to your men, and when the army marches, you move along the flank. Dismissed."

Ferguson saluted, turned, and departed to see to his men. Cornwallis watched him leave, then turned and returned to the large window overlooking the yard. The army was preparing to march, packing their gear for war.

"Humph, disrespect me and my authority; I will make them pay! I will show them who is really in charge here!"

***

The sound of chains jingling, the snort of oxen, and the crunching sound of wooden wheels rolling along on the dirt road was closing in on Jacob and his band of men concealed in the brush and palmetto ferns. He had smudged his face with a bit of powder mixed with water and mud to take the shine off his skin.

His boys were to his right, concealed and looking down the length of their muskets. Frederick and some of their band's other original members were on the left. Their information network alerted them that a supply run to Georgetown was moving along the road. Now, it sounded like the carts or wagons were closing in.

Looking over, he saw his boys were relaxed, breathing steadily, with no excitement. Jacob had to admit it filled his heart with pride to see how grown up they had become and were becoming expert fighters as he had been in the early days. Then, allowing a quick smile and a nod to himself, he returned to watching the road.

Soon, two advance guards of red-coated men, though they had green facings instead of the regulars. Jacob nodded again, *"Provincials, probably local Loyalists who joined Cornwallis."*

While waiting for the advance guard to pass, Jacob sighted the wagon driver, a military man in uniform and not a local farmer or wagoner. Jacob had told his men not to shoot any contracted farmers, only to engage military targets, including Loyalists. Slowly his rifle tracked the wagon, and when it came alongside Jacob, he pulled the trigger.

As the soldier toppled off the wagon, the rest of the ambush fired, causing numerous soldiers marching alongside the wagons to collapse to the ground. Not to lose the element of surprise, Jacob and his men charged through their smoke to engage in close-quarter combat with their knives and tomahawks. It was a quick and bloody fight.

Jacob moved along the line of carts as his men held a couple of farmers with their hands raised. He noted that his men shot very well, able to distinguish the military targets from the civilians. His men were securing muskets and cartridge boxes and seeing what was in the wagons. What surprised Jacob was what was in between the wagons.

Oxen were pulling two 3-pound field cannons; the farmers, with their hands raised, had been leading the oxen pulling the cannons. Jacob inspected the guns; they had full ammunition boxes and caissons full of shot and powder. A large smile crossed Jacob's face.

"Well, now, how about that?" Jacob asked as he stood before the terrified farmers. He looked into their eyes, and he could see the fear was there. Who knows what stories and lies the British had told the farmers about them? Probably they were demons with horns who ate children.

"Are you loyal subjects?" Jacob asked, "Or were you simply contracted to pull these guns?"

"Sir … sir … sir, if I may?" One farmer stammered. "We were hired to pull these guns to Georgetown and return home. That's all."

Jacob gave them a look that said, *"You better not be lying to me,* " *which seemed to be received as the two farmers shook* in fear.

"I will have to secure these guns and oxen, so they don't reach their destination, you understand."

The other farmer looked up in shock, "But they are our oxen. We need them on our farms. So, what are we to do for planting?"

Jacob looked over his shoulder at the horses pulling the wagons and carts. He then turned back and pointed over his shoulder at the wagons and carts.

"We'll trade your oxen for those carts and horses."

The two farmer's eyes grew wide; they looked at each other, then back at Jacob.

"Truly, just a cart?" One farmer asked, and Jacob shook his head.

"All of them. Divide them between the two of you and go home. But, of course, you may want to dump the bodies out of them. We need one cart for the supplies we are taking. The rest are yours. Are we of an accord?"

The two farmers looked at one another, nodded, then turned, spit in their hands, and reached out to Jacob. Spitting in his hand, they sealed the deal. He looked at them both intently.

"You may want to tell your friends how we spared you, and we're not your enemies, Bandits, or devils. Whatever story the British are feeding you. We are good South Carolina men fighting for our homes and families. That is all. Understand?"

Both farmers nodded, and Jacob smiled in return.

"Go home to your families; take care of them for us."

Jacob returned to his men, who were mounting up, Richard holding the reins of Jacob's horse for them. Frederick was up on a cart filled with all the captured muskets, cartridge boxes, and food, his horse tied to the end of the cart. Once he mounted, Jacob pointed his horse into the woods and led his band back to camp with their two new cannons and supplies.

"This should please Marion," Jacob stated, and his son nodded. "Should please him indeed."

When Jacob and his men arrived at the camp, Marion was pleased. "Excellent job, Captain Clarke, excellent!"

Jacob looked at Marion with a concerned look. "Doesn't having these guns defeat our purpose of keeping on the move?"

Marion shook his head. "No, we'll use them. We'll build a small redoubt at Port's Ferry and see what happens."

Again, Jacob gave Marion a concerned look, "If I may ask, sir, like what?"

Marion looked directly at Jacob. "First, it shows we will resist. They don't control the interior. For our supporters, it will show we are here for them. Those who support the King are not in control. If we are lucky, we will draw the British out and meet them on a field of our choosing. A winning situation, I believe."

Jacob nodded in agreement; it did make sense. "You are correct, sir; we'll see what attention we attract.

***

Maria and Helga drove the cart to Mr. Marshal's Mercantile with a fresh load of salted venison and skins. Maria wore her typical working clothes, male-style leather pants and a linen shirt. Helga was dressed similarly. Laying at the bottom of the baseboard of the cart was a loaded blunderbuss, just in case.

As they approached a curve in the road, they could see the front of an approaching column of British soldiers. Maria pulled the cart off to the side to make room for the marching soldiers to go by. They sat in their cart, attempting to look as demure as possible, not to draw attention. Helga watched with large eyes as the soldiers marched past, their feet kicking up dust.

They were the lead elements of the 63rd, following General Cornwallis's orders to head toward Kings Tree and to stop the rebel activity there. Four men, abreast, came marching by at a leisurely pace but alert. A few even tipped their hats to Maria as they passed by. She placed a pleasant smile on her face and nodded in reply.

Her eyes, on the other hand, were taking in everything. She was counting, remembering the color of their facings, anything unique about their uniforms. Helga did the same thing; she was watching intently; though her outward appearance, she was just a curious little girl.

"Those are many soldiers marching by," she commented quietly to Maria, "are they going after Papa?"

Maria watched and observed the column, noticing the transition of the North Carolina units as they passed by the parked cart. They, like the 63rd, waved and tipped their hats to Maria and Helga. She played it up, smiled, and waved at the passing soldiers. Maria nodded, playing like good little Loyalists.

An officer on a horse rode up and stopped before the cart. He bowed from the waist and tipped his hat.

"Good lady, what news can you provide us on the road ahead? Have there been any reports of Banditti or brigands about?"

Maria placed a pleasant and warm false face on, "Oh good sir; it is so nice to have the brave soldiers of the King protecting us helpless citizens. The Bandits you speak of have not troubled us lately, but there have been in the past up in Cheraws. Oh, the horror tales we have heard; so happy you are here, colonel, to save us."

"It's only major, good lady. Major James Wemyss at your service," Wemyss replied. "We'll see to your safety and not to worry; once we are done, you will not have to worry about these rebels and their friends. You can rest easy at night!"

Bowing and tipping his hat again, Wemyss returned to riding along the column as it wound down the road. Once the road was clear, Maria flicked the reins, and their horse continued toward Goose Greek and the Mercantile.

"That was unique, wasn't it, mama?" Helga asked. "I have never seen so many soldiers at once. Is that the whole British Army?"

Maria shook her head, "No, that was just a few of the regiments, I think your father calls them, not the whole army. If they were marching by, the line would go miles down the road."

Helga's eyes grew large again; the thought of a line of soldiers several miles long seemed impossible to her.

"Tell me what you saw; what made it so special?" Maria asked, and Helga began to recite what she saw, from the colors of the uniforms and what she saw that stuck out in her mind. Maria nodded, placing it all in her memory that she would use later.

When they arrived in Goose Creek, they pulled the cart to the back of the shop, where the workers began to unload.

"You stay here," Maria told Helga, "I have to see someone real quick for Uncle Peter."

Helga nodded, sitting on a barrel, as the men moved the venison and leather into the shop. Maria smiled, entered the shop, and looked for one of the clerks. She joined the main room of the shop, looking for Andrew Hoskins. Instead, she found him sweeping up an area in the back corner.

When she entered, he saw Maria holding a red bag. Looking around quickly, making sure no one was nearby, he nodded his head quickly, then placed the broom down and went outside. Maria followed.

Andrew was waiting beside some horses tied to a trough, drinking water. First, Maria ensured that no one was nearby and would not draw attention. Then, as Andrew was checking the horses, Maria kept a horse between them and blocked her from anyone walking by.

"Andrew, you need to find Jacob; we have a word for him," she whispered, and Andrew replied with "Yes."

"Let him know we saw a large column of British and Provincial soldiers heading down the road toward King Tree. Our best guess was about three hundred in four units. We know the commander, Major James Wemyss, was with them."

Andrew grunted; he understood, and Maria headed back into the shop and, with Helga, took the cart now loaded with empty barrels for the next load from the compound. Andrew continued his job at the shop until his workday was over. Then, putting away his apron and mounting his horse, Andrew quickly exited the town.

Once he was away from eyes, he kicked the horse into a gallop and took off down the road, following the main road until he found his secondary trail that headed toward Williamsburg, but stayed away from the main road that the British were on. Through the night, Andrew rode until he arrived at a small farm on the outskirts of Williamsburg.

Andrew dismounted, went up to the door, and softly knocked. After a short while, a man came to the door. The fire and the light from the inside framed the figure.

"Ah, Andrew, what brings you this way, nephew?" the man asked.

In a low voice, Andrew stated, "Need to find Jacob or Marion; we have news."

Nodding his head, "Ah, I see, not a family visit." The man looked past Andrew to ensure the coast was clear before replying in a low voice.

"Snow Island, they just got to Snow Island."

Andrew nodded and shook his uncle's hand. "Pass my best to Aunt Betsy." The man chuckled and slapped his nephew on his shoulder.

"Be safe out there, dear nephew; keep doing God's work. Pass my best to your mother, will you?"

Andrew nodded again before turning and remounting his horse. Turning back onto the road, Andrew followed the road out of the area and then, in the moonlight, found the landmark of an old oak tree next to the trail that led out toward Snow Island. Andrew knew this was dangerous as he approached a camp with active, alert guards.

Andrew dismounted, tied his horse to a branch, and made his way along the trail. The night sound of insects and the breeze through the trees was the only sound until he heard the distinct "Click" of a hammer being cocked.

"Hold there," a voice called out, but not in a loud voice, only loud enough for Andrew to hear.

Andrew froze, "Liberty more than life," he called out, and a man appeared from around a tree, his musket at the ready. He walked up to Andrew and looked closely at him. "You have something for the colonel?"

Andrew nodded, and then the man turned and Andrew followed the sentry into the camp. After following the sentry for a short distance and passing through thick vegetation, an open space appeared, and Marion's camp came into view. A few smalls were built under broad-leafed plants, breaking the smoke that disappeared into the treetops.

The sentry brought Andrew to where Marion sat on a crate, talking with Oscar. "Sir, this man says he has news for you."

Marion nodded, and the sentry turned and returned to his post.

"Hello, Andrew," Marion began, shaking his hand, "What news do you bring."

"It came from Mrs. Clarke, sir," Andrew began, and Marion nodded. "She spoke of a large group of British regulars and provincials under the command of a Major James Wemyss. She said they are heading toward Kings Tree."

Marion nodded, "Sounds like we drew their attention as we had hoped. Thank you, Andrew." Then Marion paused and thought of something.

"How was Mrs. Clarke? I am sure Captain Clarke is going to ask."

"Determined," Andrew responded, "That is a very determined woman there. I would hate to get on her bad side."

Marion chuckled, "I will let Captain Clarke know. Be safe on your way back; keep us informed of all activity you see or from Mrs. Clarke."

Marion watched as Andrew disappeared before heading to where Jacob and Major James sat with their men, eating a meal and cleaning their muskets.

Jacob looked up when Marion arrived and stood along with Major James. "I take it you have a task for us?"

Marion shook his head, "I could be coming over to check on you and want your wit and warm company, Captain Clarke."

Jacob stared deadpan at Marion and continued, "Where are we off to?" Marion just shook his head.

"Sometimes I check on my men, but as usual, you are correct. We have a report from a very reliable source that a good size column of British regulars and Provincials are marching toward Kings Tree under Major Wemyss."

Jacob nodded, "You think they are coming after us, after our successful raids? Who is the reliable source?"

Marion gave a crooked smile, "Your wife passed it through our contact at the Mercantile."

Jacob smiled slightly, "Any word on how she is doing?"

Marion chuckled again, "Andrew said determined, and he would not want to make her angry at him."

"Smart man," Jacob replied, then, after a deep sigh, got down to business. "What are your orders?

"You and Major James will take a company, locate this British column, and determine their strength and identity. Then, report back with the information; this is a scouting trip only."

Major James nodded, "When shall we depart?"

"As soon as you are ready," Marion instructed, "This column is on the move; the sooner we can identify them and determine their size, we can decide whether to engage or withdraw."

Understanding their task, Jacob gathered his band of boys, the wolves, Frederick, and a few others; Major James went to get one of his militia companies. As they prepared their gear, Jacob explained their task of scouting out this new force of British and Provincials. Once everyone was ready, they mounted their horses and waited for Major James to arrive.

Major James led his men over, and Jacob nodded for him to lead the way; his band would follow. They took their position in the column, the wolves trotting alongside as their flankers. After sloshing through the swamp, they took to a road and began their journey toward Kings Tree.

Major James led them on a trail parallel to the known main road heading through Kings Tree and toward Williamsburg. It was around midday when Major James halted the column. Every third man held four horses while the rest cautiously advanced into a thicket that could see the road.

Jacob had the boys hold the horses while he and the rest of their band advanced and found a concealed position in the thicket. Jacob went to Major James, took a seat, and waited. Sweat began to trickle down Jacob's face as the day's heat settled on their shoulders. While the scrub concealed them, it was also very stuffy, and the men began to sweat.

As they waited, slowly baking in the heat, the only sound was that of the cicadas and crickets in the tall grass. Jacob slowly shook his head and then used a handkerchief to wipe the sweat from his face and eyes, some water dripping from his nose. Spying through the bushes, the road was about thirty feet away, which would allow them to watch the column but not risk being observed.

"They better get here soon," Jacob thought, *"Sitting out here in the heat will start to drain the men soon if we have to do anything."*

As if on cue, "Soldiers approaching" was whispered down the line, bringing the men back from the brink of becoming zombies. Jacob pulled out his telescope and focused on the lead element of the column. Jacob saw they were all green uniforms, almost like his old Ranger uniform.

"Provincial Rangers are in front; they appear to be alert," Jacob whispered to Major James, who nodded. As they passed, Jacob and the others began to count the number of men in the unit, which reached a hundred. Then the next regiment came into view. These men were British regulars by their uniforms and the way they marched.

Jacob focused on the uniform's details, "Believe it is the 63rd, same men we hit rescuing the prisoners at Sumter's old place. They had called themselves the 63rd."

Major James agreed as he pulled out his telescope and watched the men march by, counting.

When the next unit appeared, which wore a redcoat with green facings, it had to be a Provincial unit. "I counted about two hundred of the 63rd," James stated, and Jacob confirmed, "That's just about the entire unit."

They spotted an officer on a horse in the center of the column, "that must be Major Wemyss," Jacob remarked, "Marion had told us." They continued to watch and count the men of the provincial unit marched by, counting about fifty men. The last unit to pass by was another Provincial company that totaled fifty men.

"From my count, that is about four hundred men," James remarked, "which outnumber us about three or four to one." Then Jacob could see James was deep in thought, and then Jacob could tell that James had come up with an idea as a smile crossed his face.

"We could do something about it right now," James stated.

Jacob looked at him, already having a good idea of what he had in mind.

"We can get ahead of them and hit the rear of the column in a location that will constrict their movement. But, at least leave them a message that they are not safe from us."

Jacob could see Major James was set on his idea and would not be able to talk him out of it. Still, he had to remind him of their task.

"If I may, Marion only wanted us to scout this column out. We did and counted that they have way more men than we do as a whole. He did not task us to attack. I believe it would be fool hearty to do so."

Major James nodded his head. "Noted. Still, we have the advantage. Let's use it!"

Major James spun and gathered his men; Jacob shrugged and headed over to where the boys were holding the horses. The wolves were sitting on their haunches, waiting expectantly.

"Were there a lot of them, Uncle Jacob?" Thomas asked, and Jacob nodded as he took his reins.

"Aye, lad, there is a good number of them. Major James wants to whittle them down, so stay close to me."

With an excited look, the boys mounted their horses and pulled in beside Jacob. Frederick, along with Jehu, James, and William, joined them. They waited until Major James led his group out before they followed.

Using the same road, they were able to trot ahead of the column, the breeze of their movement helping to dry some of the sweat from Jacob's face. After a short ride, they approached a choke point where the main road began to cross over a swampy area. The road was on an elevated causeway that would present the British and Provincials as excellent targets. Major James dismounted and had everyone tie their horses to trees, as he would need every shooter he had.

Moving alongside Major James's company, Jacob found good shooting positions. He looked band to ensure the boys had a thick tree trunk between them and the ambush line. Everyone settled into the ground, concealing themselves as best as they could. They readied their rifles and muskets, and sweat started to bead on their faces.

Luckily, they did not have to wait very long when the lead element of the Provincial Rangers appeared, and they readied their weapons. Major James looked through the bushes and smiled.

"Wait until they march through. Then, we'll hit their rear as it will be tough for the front to respond through the swamp."

The command to hold until the end was passed across the ambush line, and the men settled themselves into good shooting positions, ensuring their muskets and rifles were deep in their shoulders. Then, as the column marched, the numerous barrels poked through the branches and followed the enemy soldiers.

Jacob watched the center of the column go by, Major Wemyss on his horse, slowly moving along with his men. Looking at the man, Jacob wondered if he should take the shot and kill their commanding officer initially; perhaps it would discourage the regulars and the Provincials.

Shaking his head, Jacob waited until the last unit appeared, and he could see Major James coiling like a spring, ready to initiate the ambush.

"Fire!"

Major James yelled out, and the scrub and bushes they were concealed in erupted into fire and smoke. The men on the causeway were caught in the center of the ambush. Many spun and fell into the swamp and onto the causeway.

"Load!" Major James yelled as British commands could be heard in response to the ambush.

"Fire by pairs!" Jacob commanded that one man fired, the other would cover as he loaded, then the second man would fire. The snap and whiz of British and Provincial balls began to fly around and over the ambush line, as they had no idea of their exact position.

The men loaded and fired, the smoke billowing before them and becoming caught in the leaves and branches of the bushes, obscuring them and the British. Jacob could hear the sound of battle shifting to their right flank; the British were fighting through the swamp to get into a position to flank their line.

"We're being flanked!" Jacob yelled over to Major James, who looked in the direction that Jacob was pointing.

"Plug that hole, please!" James yelled, and Jacob nodded his understanding, grabbing his band of fighters.

"With me, lads," Jacob yelled, "We have some business on this side!"

As they finished loading on the run, Jacob, with the boys, followed by Frederick, Zacharia, and the rest of his band, moved past Major James's men until they came to the right flank of their line. Then, as the grey smoke of their musketry began to blow away, Jacob could see Provincials in the red-faced green uniforms, sloshing through the swampy water to take up a firing position.

Dropping to their knees, the band members did the same, taking cover behind the large cypress roots and tree trunks, bringing their rifles and muskets to the shoulder. Jacob aimed at a Provincial struggling in the mud, and his right leg sank to the knee. He looked up long enough for Jacob to see his expression.

"Fire!"

Jacob pulled the trigger on his rifle and watched the stuck Provincial, whose leg was still in the mud up to his knee, flop over his back, a large spray of mud and water flying into the air. The rest of the band opened fire, catching the hapless Provincials struggling in the muck.

A battle cry went up on their left, which Jacob assumed Major James must have ordered a charge. Pulling his tomahawk, Jacob motioned forward to attack. As he turned and began to move into the swampy area, the band drew their knives and tomahawks, and a few loaded their muskets on the run.

Yelling at the top of his lungs, caught up in the moment and releasing the pent-up energy from the ambush, Jacob charged into the muck but jumped from root clump to root clump. As Jacob rushed into action, a part of his mind heard his boys behind them, also giving a battle cry as it blended in with his.

The band slammed into the Provincials, who had been in the process of reloading. They attempted to move through the mud and muck to get into a flanking position against Major James. Now they were caught with unloaded muskets and the fury of the attacking band. One soldier lowered his musket from the hip, pointing at Jacob.

Seeing he was being aimed at, Jacob struck the musket with his tomahawk, forcing it out of the way from him when the soldier pulled the trigger. He hit a provincial next to him, the ball smashing through his side and forcing him to bounce off a tree and collapse into the mud.

Following through, Jacob spun and struck the soldier at the junction of his neck and chest, the blade of his tomahawk biting deep. The soldier collapsed to his knees, staring in shock up into the face of Jacob. Then, using his foot, Jacob kicked the dead man over and spun to see how the boys were doing.

He was surprised when he saw they had four provincials standing with their arms raised, their muskets sinking into the mud where they dropped them. The three of them and Frederick pointed their loaded muskets at them. Frederick saw Jacob was looking over, nodded, and winked that all was ok with the boys.

"Right, off you go!" Frederick yelled as he and the boys led their prisoners to the rear, where their horses were. Jacob smiled despite the fighting and carnage around him, then turned and joined the rest of the band as they were pushing the Provincials back.

From his left, Jacob could hear an intense fight going on, which he assumed was between Major James and the rear unit of the British column. Jacob began to load his rifle as the band fired and supported each other by bounding up and firing from a tree, their partners covering them as they moved.

"Captain Clarke, fall back!"

Jacob turned to see a runner from Major James waving at him.

"Captain Clarke, Major James is withdrawing! Grab your men!"

Jacob nodded and turned to call his band when he saw an officer on a horse ride up to the rear to see the action and was beginning to point out and give orders for men who must be coming from behind him. Seeing an opportunity, Jacob raised his rifle and aimed at the British officer on the horse. A perfect target.

As Jacob pulled the trigger, as luck would have it, the officer bent down from his saddle to hear a report from a subordinate. Instead of striking the major, Jacob's rifle ball flew over his back to hit the officer riding next to him. That officer tumbled out of his saddle; the intended target flinched and sat up to see what had just happened.

"Band, fall back to the horses!" Jacob yelled. Then he looked again at the startled officer, a lucky man.

"Next time," Jacob growled, "you won't be so lucky next time."

Turning, Jacob jogged with the rest of the band as they headed back to their horses, helping to lead the other prisoners they had captured.

***

Major Wemyss wiped the sweat from his eyes with his handkerchief before stuffing it back in his left sleeve. The heat, the bugs as he swatted them away from his face. Wemyss just shook his head and hoped to escape the miserable swamp.

The sound of firing from their rear caught his attention, and he spun his horse around.

"Contact, contact rear!" was shouted down the line, and Major Wemyss made his way forward, his lieutenant riding with him.

"An ambush, sir?" the lieutenant asked, and Wemyss just shrugged.

"We'll see if it's these bloody rebels or banditti." Wemyss turned his horse and started at a trot toward the column's rear. As he rode through, the Provincials turned about and headed to support the column's end. The Royal North Carolina had their men turned and began their trot down the road toward the sound of battle.

The North Carolina Volunteers were in disarray from the initial ambush on them as the rear company. When Major Wemyss arrived, he began shouting orders to the Volunteers to reform.

"Form line on the right, left company begin to swing around!" Wemyss ordered, and the Volunteers split their men, so half remained with the line, the other half to begin a sweep of their left.

"Give me a report!" Wemyss yelled, and a lieutenant came running up from the volunteers. As the sound of action was nearly deafening, Wemyss had to lean down from the saddle so the lieutenant could speak in his ear.

As he leaned down, he heard a "crack" and felt the heat of a ball missing him, followed by the sound of it striking flesh. The lieutenant beside him groaned in pain and then toppled from his horse. The body hit with a wet "thud" as it landed on the churned-up muddy road.

Fear, something Wemyss cannot recall truly feeling, looked up in shock toward where he believed the shot had come from. He quickly looked but could not see anything but feet moving and body shapes running through the grey mist of battle.

"Bloody hell, that was close!" he remarked, then looked over at his lieutenant's fallen body as it lay in the mud. "Too close," Wemyss recalled. But, as he looked up, it seemed the rebels were pulling back, and the sound of battle was diminishing.

"Search the woods, see what you can find," Wemyss ordered, and the men of the North Carolina Volunteers began to deploy and advance to where the ambush had been initiated. With fixed bayonets, the men moved into the brush in line, searching for any rebels or injured Provincials.

Major Wemyss dismounted and sat on a log as the North Carolina Volunteers cleared the woods and brush. He pulled out his handkerchief, wiping the sweat from his head. Wemyss wondered if it was sweat from the heat or the narrow escape. A dark thought began to settle in his mind.

"These bloody bastards tried to kill me. Me! Of all people, they tried to kill me. I will show them what it means to take a shot at me. I will make them all pay. They will pay dearly!"

A captain approached and stood at attention, waiting for Wemyss to recognize that he was standing there. After a short moment, Wemyss's head looked up and at the captain.

"Yes?"

"Sir, we have the returns from the action," the captain answered, and Wemyss nodded his head to go on.

"Sir, we have located ten men killed, another twenty wounded, and around fifteen unaccounted for. We believe they may have been taken prisoner."

Major Wemyss nodded slowly and then looked at the reporting captain. "And?"

"And, sir, we have captured ten of the rebels."

Major Wemyss smiled and rose to his feet. "Well then, let's see them to Kings Tree, where we can judge them fairly in a court of law." He grunted as he mounted his horse and set foot in the stirrups.

"Then see that they are hung fairly."

***

Word reached Marion that Major Wemyss, now identified as the commander in the column, had received additional reinforcements from Georgetown. He had caught their attention. They were now looking at an overwhelming force of four hundred more Loyalists and British Regulars joining Wemyss, bringing his total strength to six hundred men. At the same time, Marion had only around sixty left.

The prisoners had been turned over to local authorities, who issued them paroles and let them return home. None of the prisoners came anywhere near their camp. It was now only our small group of fighters. A good number of Major James's militia was sent home to await call out.

"Six to one are not good odds," Marion stated one night as he, Jacob, Frederick, and Major James sat around a small fire. They all nodded their heads in agreement. Marion thought for a while before letting out a deep sigh and stabbing their small fire with a stick he had been poking the fire with.

"Well, we have no choice but to withdraw," he stated, making the decision.

"Where to?" Major James asked.

"Up to North Carolina, where we can resupply, perhaps a change of clothes or something for these rags of ours. We'll strike camp and head north in the early morning."

"And the cannons?" Jacob asked.

"We'll bring them along the best we can," Marion answered. Jacob nodded his head.

"See to your men. Get some rest, as we're going to be in the saddle for a while," Marion instructed, and the men returned to their smaller camps. Jacob with Frederick went over to their band of men; the boys were already asleep with the wolves curled up next to them. Jacob laid down and the exhaustion of the day and the previous activities allowed him to fall asleep quickly.

In the morning, the sky was still grey with a slight pink as the sun began to rise. Their bedrolls were packed and tied to the back of their horses. Jacob and his band rode over to the redoubt built at Port's Ferry.

They had no proper limber or harness to connect the cannon to the spare horses; they used what ropes they had with them. Jacob looked at their creation with a critical eye and shook his head. It was not pretty but, for the moment, functional.

"Captain Clarke, ready to go?" Marion asked, with Oscar riding next to him. Jacob turned to look up at Marion.

"It should hold. We'll take the rear of the column," Jacob replied as he mounted his horse. After thumping his heels on the horse, Marion nodded and led the column toward the road. Once the end of the column rode by, Jacob led his band forward, who was leading the horses pulling the cannons.

By midday, they had to stop moving to re-secure the guns as the lashings came apart. Both Jacob and Marion were becoming frustrated as their movement was being slowed. Jacob kept a small section of his band to watch on their rear in case the British caught up with them on the road.

The final decision concerning the guns was made when they arrived at the Little Pee Dee River. While running a little high, they could cross on their horses as the water approached their bellies. But, on the other hand, the guns would need to have to build rafts. Marion stared at his cannons, the water, then back to the guns.

"Sink them," he stated. "They are more of a hindrance at the moment, which could kill us. So, sink them; the British or their Loyalists can't have them either."

Jacob nodded, motioning for the boys to join him on the riverbank, and began unlashing the guns. They did keep the powder bags as they needed the gunpowder but left the shot in the ammunition boxes. Then Jacob and the boys pushed the cannon, so it rolled into the river until it sank. The river finally grabbed it and sank beneath the water with its wheels turning.

The second gun followed the first one after all the powder was removed. When that gun sank beneath the river water as it gurgled by, Jacob and his boys remounted their horses and followed Marion across to the far side. They rode for the rest of the day and into the night when they finally arrived near Amy's Mill on Drowning Creek in North Carolina.

As he had planned, the men could rest in a more secure location, away from British or Loyalist eyes and ears. Marion secured some new frocks and split shirts for the men whose clothes had nearly rotted off them. Food and additional supplies were brought in and the men began feeling healthier and ready to go back into action.

After a few days, Marion was itching to get back into action. He also knew that he needed good information before he could do anything. He called Major James and Jacob over to his fire. When Jacob arrived, Oscar stirred a rabbit stew over a small fire and nodded.

"Good to see Master Clarke," Oscar replied with a steady, deep voice. Jacob smiled and shook his head.

"I'm no Master Oscar. I am a simple man," Jacob replied. "You can call me Jacob." Oscar did not know how to react, but when Jacob reached out to shake his hand, he took it and smiled.

"Yes sir, Jacob, it is," he replied, "Master Marion will be along directly. He was over in the wood line."

Major James joined them and sniffed the pleasing aroma of the rabbit stew. He also nodded to Oscar.

"You keep Marion healthy and happy," he said, then laid his finger along his nose. "You didn't hear that from me."

Oscar smiled once again and gave a low, rich laugh. "Yes, sir, I will do my best."

Marion arrived and nodded when he saw Major James and Jacob waiting for him.

"Gentlemen, it's time to get back into action," Marion began. "Before we re-enter the fight, I need to know what is happening. Therefore, I am sending you two with a small section of men to collect information and see what our British friends are doing around Georgetown. I will follow up with the rest of the men in a few days. We will meet back up near Kingston Township.

Jacob looked over at Major James, who nodded, "Jacob, bring your band, and I'll bring Captain Mouzon's men. We will leave when everyone is packed and ready to ride."

Jacob nodded and then turned to nod to Marion, who nodded back in return. "Good luck out there," Marion called out as Jacob and Major James went to get their men ready to ride.

CHAPTER 4

A CHANGE OF COLORS

Samuel waited; he knew the recruiting party would soon be out on the hulk as usual. What news from the outside world only came from overhearing the guards talk between themselves on deck. From what he could determine, the interior was not remaining citizens were resisting the Crown's consolidation of their power.

He also enjoyed hearing stories amongst the guards of the bloody ambushes and attacks by different rebel groups. Samuel recalled names like Thomas Sumter being thrown around and a vicious group of Bandits operating between Goose Creek and Georgetown. Samuel smiled to himself. If he had to make a guess, he knew who those Bandits were.

Samuel's patience finally paid off, and the recruiting party arrived. They clumped down the stairs from the upper deck, resplendent in their fine red coats with green facings. They strode into the center of the deck while the prisoners watched them from the sides. Standing behind the recruiters were two regular British soldiers, bayonets fixed on their muskets.

"Good people, a moment of your time, please," the recruiter began in a cheerful voice, a smile on his face. "I am here to offer you a way to amend your sins against the King and country. I am here to offer you a means of redemption; who among you would not want to seek redemption!"

The prisoners just stared back, but a few, like Samuel, were nodding slightly to themselves, though his motives were completely different from theirs. A good number of them glared at the recruiters, hostilities in their eyes, while others had nothing in their eyes as they already had given up hope and were waiting to die.

"We're here to offer you land to have a farm. Pay of eight shillings, clothing, food, and the knowledge you are doing the right thing, that your King and Country will re-embrace you as one of his long-lost children. All you have to do is sign and join the Provincial regiments to protect these good people and save their homes. What is not more honorable than that?"

A few men held their hands and shuffled forward, intending to sign up for the Provincials. Samuel waited until a good number of the prisoners turned away before he made his move. Then, keeping his head down, Samuel shuffled up, joined the group herded together, and was led up onto the main deck.

Samuel squinted, the sun light so bright that he held his arm up in front of his face, shielding his eyes. The recruiters waited for the recruits to gain their vision and when they could see, they moved along to a longboat bobbing alongside the prison hulk.

Samuel moved over and sat in the middle of the boat, still keeping his head down. Luckily, his hair grew so long and wild that it hid the bald spot on top of his head from the scalping. Looking up slightly, he could see some faces peering through the few old gun ports used for windows. It did not matter to Samuel; his plan was already in motion.

"Push off!" was commanded and the longboat with its cargo of recruits for the Provincials pushed away from the hull, oars dropping into the water, and began rowing them back to Charles Town. Samuel did everything in his power to contain the building excitement within him. Instead, he put a false face on, looking like a sad man who had made a hard decision, for they had no choice.

It was a short trip, the longboat arrived at the pier, and the recruits were off loaded and made their way to the oyster shell walkway. Once they were formed, a guard of four regular soldiers, with muskets at the shoulder, escorted them to where the old powder magazine had stood before it blew up.

Inside, there were still signs of the deadly explosion, blackened walls, buildings from the fire and smoke, and some apparent new construction to replace damaged building parts. They were led to a wall tent where the recruiter transferred them to the officer of the day for the South Carolina Loyalist Militia.

"Sir, recruits for your regiment," the recruiter reported to the officer, who returned his salute. Samuel stood in line with the other men, looking around. He could see other groups of men wearing skimpy clothes who must have been recruited from the other prison hulks. Men were being separated into different groups.

"Listen up!" the officer called, having been joined by three other men in regular clothes, but all had a green sprig of pine in their hats.

"I am Lieutenant Moore; let me be the first to thank you for your service and for answering the call from the King and your country. Through service, you will find redemption. Now, who among you can ride a horse well?"

A few hands went up, and one of the Loyalists came over, took charge of those men and led them to another depot.

"Any of you experienced with artillery?" the lieutenant asked, and no one raised their hands. "How about seamanship, any sailors amongst you?"

A couple more hands went up, and they were led off. Samuel surmised they were now recruits for the Royal Navy. The lieutenant turned and looked at the remaining men who stood before him.

"This must mean you are all infantrymen, which is needed. Sign or make your mark in the book, and we'll move you to the quartermaster for uniforms and a good meal!"

The men seemed to accept their new fate, shrugged, and stood a little straighter, especially after learning they were getting new clothes and a hot meal. However, Samuel kept his false face on, waiting for the right opportunity to make his break and escape.

***

The fire was snapping and cracking as Maria scrubbed the color of a British officer's white shirt. Helga had just shuffled over to drop off an armload of firewood, turned and headed back to get another load. Maria and about ten other local women were the laundresses for the British staff in Charles Town.

Otti had taken over her duties as the eyes and ears near Goose Creek, getting the information out to Andrew at the Mercantile. Here, she listened to the gossip of the officers' wives and the men, who seemed to look past anyone doing their laundry. She may keep her eyes down and play meek, but her ears were always sharp and alert.

Helga also played an essential part, as she did the chores to keep the laundry working. Maria had Helga keep her eyes and ears open as no one bothered to conceal their conversations when a child was working nearby. Helga's quick mind and memory recalled everything she heard and saw and reported to Maria. She would pass the information through trusted friends in the city, who smuggled them out to the resistance.

Her shoulder and back ached from the scrubbing; she pulled her hands from the soapy water and looked at the water-logged and wrinkled skin on her fingers. Luckily, her hard life of living in the compound and working leather had already hardened her hands and fingers, so the water did minor damage. It did make them slightly softer, though, from the soap.

Helga came trudging back with another armload of wood and dropped it on the pile. When she turned, Maria could see she had a pout on her face.

"What's wrong, Hassie?" she asked Helga in a low voice. Helga looked over her shoulder into the camp the British garrison was using near the headquarters. She turned back to Maria but pointed with her thumb over her shoulder.

"One of those stupid boys made fun of me, called me names," she replied testily. "I didn't like it."

Maria nodded and smiled at Helga. "It's ok; it's just words."

Helga sighed and shook her head and Maria placed a concerned look on her face. "What happened?"

"Well, as I said, they were calling me names and I didn't like it. So I did what you told me to do, walk away. And I did."

Maria sighed in relief, knowing her daughter did have a short fuse from time to time.

"Until they followed me and threw a rock at me."

Maria could guess what probably happened but had to ask. "And what happened next?"

"Mama, it wasn't my fault. They started it!" Helga exclaimed. Maria looked at her daughter, waiting for her to continue.

Helga sighed, "I tried to ignore them as you say and walked away. But I also remember what Papa says about standing your ground and defending what you believe in."

Maria nodded, "And?"

"And I punched the boy in the nose. Blood went everywhere, he fell and started crying and they all ran away. So now they don't call me names anymore!"

Maria covered her mouth, trying not to laugh aloud. She held out her arms and hugged her daughter. "You did the right thing, though you shouldn't have punched the boy in the nose."

"He deserved it," Helga said in a muffled voice, speaking into Maria's shoulder. Releasing Helga, Maria smiled. *"You have your father and me in you and I shouldn't expect anything less."*

"How about you go over and help Mrs. Bishop scrub those stockings for a bit," Maria said, and Helga smiled, nodded, then turned to head over to Mrs. Bishop's tub.

Maria watched her daughter, growing tougher by the day. She had to grow up quicker then she had liked, but now, they had no choice. She returned to washing the shirt, thought of Jacob, Jean, and Samuel and wondered what they were doing or if they were still alive.

She chased the thought away as she held up the shirt, now freshly scrubbed, and the stains from the collar were gone. She could not afford to be a weepy, desperate woman like many she saw following the city's surrender. Jacob wanted her to be strong and she will. It will take more than this to break her spirit. But she also knew deep in her heart Jacob was alive.

Wringing out the remaining water, she headed to where they had stretched a clothes line to hang their laundry. Using wooden pins, she placed the sleeves on the line and it began to flap in the slight breeze.

She then sensed someone was approaching her from the rear slowly. Maria controlled her fear, slowly slid her hand down to the belt knife at her waist and slowly pulled it from her sheath. Then she felt the body touch her back and a hand came around toward her shoulder and neck.

Using her instincts, she quickly bit the edge of the hand, then, taking her left hand, clamped down on the arm, pulling the attacker off his feet and throwing him to the ground using a hip toss. Then, pulling the knife the rest of the way out of the sheath, she raised the blade to strike at her attacker.

"Maria, it's me, Samuel!"

Hearing Samuel's voice and seeing she had knocked off his hat, saw the bald spot from his scalping, stopped the downward motion of the knife inches from Samuel's throat. Samuel shut his eyes as the blade came within inches.

Maria dropped the knife and very unladylike, hugged Samuel as he was lying on the ground, and she was on top of him.

"Nice to see you too, but could you mind getting off of me?" Samuel asked, and Maria fell over laughing so hard in a release of pent-up fear and emotions. She lay there next to Samuel and was both laughing and weeping at the same time.

Samuel picked himself up, wiped the leaves and grass from his newly issued Loyalist clothes, and placed his hat back on his head. Then, while Maria was still laughing and weeping simultaneously, he shook his head but could not help but join in and began to laugh along with her.

Holding out his hands, he helped Maria back up to her feet. Then, smoothing out her apron, Maria led Samuel over to the tent she and Helga used to sleep in, what was known as the refugee camp. He sat on a small log around their cooking fire and Maria looked critically at him.

She saw the sunken eyes and cheeks, how the uniform hung off his frame. "Samuel, are you alright?" She asked, and Samuel just shrugged, knowing what she was alluding to.

"We didn't have great cooks like Otti and you out there on the hulks; we were lucky if we got fed at least once a day. Sometimes they would forget for a couple of days. Men began to die, a few at first, then more. They would add more prisoners, and our meals never improved."

Samuel stopped talking, his gaze far off and Maria knew he recalled unpleasant memories. She reached behind her and gave Samuel a hunk of freshly baked bread. He slowly pealed portions of the bread and slowly chewed on it.

As he chewed, he looked directly at Maria. "I have no news of Jacob or Jean. Did they escape? Did they get out of the city?

Maria nodded, "He did. Jean and he stopped by right after they pulled Marion and the governor out. They hid their uniforms and put on their hunters' clothes. Then they rode off to join Marion with the boys and the wolves.

Letting a sigh of relief, Samuel began to giggle lightly to himself. "Well, if anyone could have pulled that off, it would have to be those two. There were stories, but nothing solid. Not knowing was driving me mad!"

Then they talked, explaining what happened in the line and how Samuel went from being on a prison hulk to escaping. Maria caught him up on what was happening with the compound, what she had heard of Jacob and the boys.

"Uncle Samuel!" Helga squealed as she ran over and jumped on him, knocking him over from the log where he had been sitting. Then, as Helga began to fire off hundreds of questions, Samuel went, "Shhh," and held his finger up along his nose, "I am in disguise so I can get back to your Papa; you have to be quiet."

Then he looked at Maria, "You said my boys were riding with Jacob and Marion?"

Maria smiled and nodded. "If they had to join the militia and go off to fight, who best than Jacob?"

Samuel sat in wonder, hearing his boys growing up, "Who indeed."

Then he changed thoughts, "Otti? How is she doing?"

Maria explained how Otti was now collecting information on the British and passing them on to Marion. Samuel had a proud look on his face. His wife, his family, and theirs were in the fight together. Samuel talked of the rumors about a hard-hitting group between Goose Creek and Georgetown.

Maria nodded, having heard the same stories in the headquarters and other British officers.

"Then that must be those two, stirring up all the ruckus," Samuel stated, and Maria nodded.

"Well, I better get up there then; make sure those two stays safe," Samuel stated as he stood up and straightened his uniform. Then he looked earnestly at Maria.

"Let Otti know I love her, miss her and think of her daily. That I am doing my best to stay alive as she instructed."

Maria stood, smiled, and gave Samuel hugged. "I'll let her know and I have a way of getting you to Jacob without being seen.

Samuel nodded, "Well then, let's get started."

***

After being washed and clothed in a Loyalist uniform, the former prisoner stood before General Cornwallis. Cornwallis stared at the man, who was offering his services to the crown.

"Your name, sir?" Cornwallis asked.

"Gainey, sir. Micah Gainey."

Cornwallis nodded, "I was told you have an offer for me?"

Gainey stood attention straight. "Yes sir, let me hunt down these rebels, especially Marion and any survivors from the Second Regiment."

Cornwallis could see the conviction, the anger in Gainey's facial expression and tone of voice.

"I take it you have a personal reason for this?" Cornwallis asked.

"Yes, sir," Gainey answered. "I have personally been slighted and insulted in front of all of the regiment's men, suffered under Marion's strict discipline and all because of that damnable, by the regulation Captain Clarke! I come from a good family and will not tolerate being treated the way they treated me. I seek, no demand, the satisfaction of bringing them to justice!"

Cornwallis could see he was determined and nodded his head. Who else is best to chase down this Marion he began hearing about than someone who had served under him?

"Mr. Gainey, I am commissioning you a Major in our Militia. I will see that you are supplied with both men and cavalry and are tasked to find these brigands and bring them to justice. Do you accept this responsibility?"

Gainey stood at rigid attention and saluted. "Yes, sir, you can count on me!"

Below the open window, Helga had gathered twigs, placed all she had heard in her memory, and headed back to the laundry, where she would let Maria know everything she heard.

***

Big Harpe and his little brother Little Harpe, along with a few of their gang, rode their horses along the road toward Camden. Even his girlfriends, Susan with his baby son and her sister Betty. Little Harpe was deep in thought as Big Harpe rode along, chewing on a long stalk of grass.

"Are you sure this is a good idea?" Little Harpe asked his brother, who looked over at him, his heavily scarred face still giving him the shakes.

"Of course, it's a good idea. Too many are looking for us and it's hard to live. We join one of these Loyalists units, get fancy uniforms, get paid and are allowed to go after these same people we have been going after, except now we're safe. We're doing it for the King, so we're legitimate, or so they say."

Little Harpe sat and thought about it more, then shrugged his shoulders.

"Aye, you be right about that. Would be nice for a change to get paid and some of the spoils from the war,"

Big Harpe looked down at his little brother and gave an evil smile.

"Now you're thinking!"

As they rode into Camden, they saw earthen redoubts and a log palisade constructed around a large house. A troop of Tarleton's Dragoons trotted by, wearing their green uniforms and black helmets with a horsehair tops. Both Harpes watched them pass by.

"Think we could get into a unit like that one?" Little Harpe asked.

"Only one way to find out," Big Harpe rumbled, turned his horse and headed into the camp at Camden.

***

Maclane rode his horse into Cheraw and made his way over to the town's bowling green, which also happened to be next to a tavern called the "Red Rose." Dismounting, he tied his horse to a post and entered the pub where a small trial was being conducted.

"Having been found guilty of treason and supporting these rebel Bandits, Robert Miles will forfeit all property and be sold into servitude to pay for your crimes for no less than ten years."

Maclane stood in the back, joining the crowd of others murmuring over the trial verdict. The man who stood accused, hands in shackles, stood with his head bowed. Maclane saw he had no emotion, even when he was led away to face his justice.

Once the observers of men and women began to disperse, Maclane approached the man who appeared to have served as the judge. He was speaking to a local militia member when he looked up at Maclane as he approached and stopped before him.

"May I help you?" the man asked, and Maclane nodded.

"Who are you, sir?" Maclane asked.

"Lt. Colonel Joseph Robinson and this is Captain Hailey of the South Carolina Royalists. Who may I ask is you?"

Maclane smiled and pulled a sealed envelope from inside his waistcoat. "Major Maclane, currently assigned to the staff of General Earl of Cornwallis. I am here to work with you directly to end the area's rebel problem."

Robinson looked at the document.

"To whoever bears witness of this order, know that Major William Maclane, formerly of the 64th Regiment of Foot, does work directly for his lordship General Cornwallis. Therefore, all assistance will be provided to Major Maclane as he has the authority of the general, and all will support and see to his wishes.

Those who fail to support or follow the orders of Major Maclane are subject to military justice and will be punished for failing a direct order as issued by the general himself.

Given under my hand, Lord Earl Charles Cornwallis, Commander."

The royal and Cornwallis' personal seal was affixed to the document. Everything was in order.

"I see; how may we be of assistance, Major?" Robinson asked. Maclane pulled up a chair, sat down and raised his hand to get a serving girl's attention by holding up three fingers. She soon came over with three mugs of ale and Maclane handed them to Robinson and Captain Hailey.

"Gentlemen, from what I saw, you are already on a good start. My task by his lordship is to bring these rebels to heel. It seems you are already doing that, so I am here to work with you on this matter. I am an expert in getting information out of people, then I pass it to you and your men go round up these traitorous bastard and we'll bring them to justice."

Robinson glanced at his second in command, shrugged and turned back to Maclane, raising his mug.

"I believe we have an accord. Let us work together to bring the King's Justice to the district and see the protection of our good citizens and the destruction of our foes!" Robinson raised his mug, and Maclane raised his mug. Then Captain Hailey raised his mug and all three clanked their mugs.

"I'll drink to that!" Then, Maclane said as they sat down and developed a plan to secure the district.

***

Jacob and his band, plus Major James and his group of men, rode along the road in the dark of the night, though a bright, full moon was shown on them. A pleasant warm breeze caressed Jacob's face, a scent of mint in the air. The night insects buzzed and chirped and while not his style, Jacob relaxed in the saddle and enjoyed the moment.

Jacob's mind wondered like it always did when in the saddle, though a portion of it was on alert in case they ran into the enemy. His thoughts stretch out to Maria and how she is doing as he learns she is the information reporter. Marion told him he did ask on his behalf how she was doing and was told she was doing well.

Then he thought of Samuel, hoping he was still alive and not on these prison hulks he had heard of from people down in Charles Town. The stories he heard made him shake, imagining what it would be like to sit in those hulks. Then, shaking his head, Jacob returned to his vigilance of watching the woods.

They returned to Port's ferry and dismounted in the woods behind their old redoubt, now without cannons. Jacob went about setting up lookouts while arranging for the camp to be concealed. He knew Marion would be arriving in a day or so and wanted the camp already set up.

"Frederick, we need you to ride into Goose Creek to our friends and secure some supplies before Marion arrives," Jacob instructed. Then on second thought, "Take my boys with you as well."

Frederick nodded, went over and told them of their task to go to Goose Creek before the boys could finish their camp. They were heading near their home, even in their tired state from the long ride. Their excitement bubbled up. Jacob stood back and watched them get ready, knowing this was more of a morale thing for them and for as much as they had seen, something they needed.

Once Frederick and the boys were ready, they trotted out with the wolves following, except for Waya, who stayed next to Jacob. Once they were clear, Jacob returned to business, set up his camp before checking on the men and the horses and assigned work priorities.

***

Mary Frith sat in the corner of the inn, sharpening her knife, ignoring the people around her who were drinking and talking about the local activities. Much talk of the growing fight between Loyalist and resistance groups across South Carolina. After tending her unique garden, Lavinia Trout entered the inn and looked over at Mary.

She walked over to the bar, packed some tobacco in her pipe and blew a long plume of grey smoke into the air using a candle to light it.

"What's bothering you, Mary?" she asked, looking at Mary as she sat slumped in the corner with her knife. She stopped sharpening and gave Lavinia a stern look.

"I'm bloody bored; that's what's bothering me!" Mary exploded; though she tried to keep her voice down, she had pent-up feelings. Although she looked around to see if anyone noticed, she did not see anyone who appeared to have noticed. She pouted and went back to sharpening her knife.

Mary sat there smoking her pipe, looking at her young protégé. She was content in her livelihood, though she had to admit when the Harpes and the other members of the brigands were robbing the new settlers; the coin coming in was great. Even the selling of the goods and other items taken in the raids had been outstanding.

Now that the focus had shifted to the south. The Harpes and the others had headed in that direction to go to the fight. For the moment, nothing was going on upcountry, which was OK with her. Still, Mary wanted adventure; she was still young and sought it.

"Go find some action then, girl, if you are so bored," Lavinia stated, "Head to Camden or wherever these Crown forces base out of. You wear men's clothing anyways, go offer your services as a spy or a cutthroat; I am sure they will hire you."

Once again, the sharpening stone stopped moving and Mary looked up. "You think so?"

Lavinia just shrugged and puffed on her pipe.

"What can they do, say no? Then come back here, and we can find you something to do. But, of course, you can always find this Maclane fellow and still work for him."

Mary smiled, sheathed her knife as she stood up and headed to her room to pack her things. Lavinia just watched her go, smiled around her pipe and then went to work wiping down the bar to get ready for the nightly patrons.

***

Frederick and the boys slowly approached Goose Creek; he watched their excitement grow as they recognized landmarks having been gone for a good while. Finally, he led them across the street from the loading area of the mercantile, the wolves trotting along. Dismounting, they were tying up their horses when the wolves rose and took off in a dead run.

"*What in the bloody hell, where are they going?*" Frederick thought as he watched the wolves drop off in a dust cloud. He watched them head toward a group of carts that had just arrived in the loading area and they seemed to be jumping around a woman and two men.

"Mama!" one of the boys yelled and took off in a run, followed by the other three. There seemed to be a reunion and Frederick guessed it must be a family reunion. Shrugging and ensuring they were not drawing attention, headed over.

When Frederick approached, both wolves, Maus and Claus, were spinning around the legs of a woman and a man he did not recognize, and the two boys, Robert and Thomas, were hugging both. Jacob's boys, Richard and Patrick, had smiles and must have known who these people were.

"*Hmm, I wonder if this is the boy's mother,*" said Frederick, who stood with the group. The woman was well built, wearing men's clothing, with dark blonde hair and blue eyes. The man took off his hat to wipe his face and saw he had a bald spot on top and must be Samuel from the description Jacob had given.

"If I may, you must be Otti and Samuel, from how Jacob described you. I suggest we get indoors so we don't attract more attention." Frederick suggested, and they all went inside. Richard and Patrick were standing next to an older man with a pipe in his hand, who Frederick guessed were Peter.

"Peter?" Frederick asked and Peter winked and nodded back. They all went inside the mercantile's storeroom, and Andrew was already there.

"Don't worry; Mr. Marshal is away in Charles Town, so we're all alone now," Andrew stated, and they all sat down on crates in the storeroom. Samuel, Otti and the boys sat close together, Frederick with Richard and Patrick with Peter.

Peter rocked with his pipe in his mouth, a big smile and twinkle in his eyes. At the same time, Samuel and Otti were reacquainted with the boys who were stumbling over as words flowed out, as they told of their actions and narrow escapes.

Frederick looked over at Peter. "I had heard stories about Jacob and Samuel here from the Anglo-Cherokee War and even back when they were with the Rangers. But, as you were with them, how true are they? Did Samuel survive a scalping?"

Peter chuckled his pipe, puffing in time with his chuckle. He took the stem from his mouth, "The stories you heard probably don't come close to what Jacob, Samuel and I saw up north."

"So, they are just rumors and stories, then?" Frederick stated and Peter shook his head.

"No lad, they are more likely zat they are much less than what truly happened. They did much more but won't brag about it or talk of it."

"Well, this has been lovely and all," Samuel stated as he stood up, "We best see to getting supplies and getting them out to Marion and Jacob."

They all stood up and got down to business moving the boxes and barrels of smoked venison, bread, salt fish, rice, and some other root vegetables while dropping off skins for the mercantile. Once all the carts were ready, Samuel climbed up inside one that he had left some room in and settled down.

"No need to advertise that I am back," Samuel stated as he sunk lower in the cart, "besides, it would be a nice surprise for that old wolf Jacob anyways."

Once he was settled, they covered the supplies, and the drivers, including Peter and Otti, took up their reins. Finally, Frederick and the boys got their horses, mounted up, and escorted them to the camp along with the wolves.

Frederick rode next to Otti as she handled the reins with ease, and he spotted the blunderbuss leaning in the floorboards under her seat. Light snoring came from under the cover, Samuel having fallen asleep. Otti looked over her shoulder at the sound, smiled and returned to looking ahead. She could see Frederick had an inquiring look on his face.

"Long night" was all Otti said, and Frederick did not pursue it.

"When we get to the camp, we have important information for Marion; the British are planning to come after him and have spies out looking for his camp."

Frederick nodded, "We'll make sure you speak with Marion as soon as you arrive."

***

Maclane slapped the mosquito that had landed on his neck; but his attempt at being quiet and immobile was not working. His scouts from the Cheraw District were in a line, watching the road coming south from North Carolina. He felt this was their route if any reinforcements or rebels were coming down.

The flies and other insects buzzed around his head as he sat in the muck and mud of their concealed position, watching the road. Maclane missed his office over in the South Sea Mercantile; He shook his head; the odd fate that was working for the crown, his very office was destroyed by the Royal Navy. He shook his head, *"Bloody fortunes of war."*

Still, he was promoted, not marching in the line, getting shot at, or ambushed. He was still operating as an independent command and could make his own decisions; as long as he kept now Lieutenant Colonel Bedlow informed on rebel activity, he could continue with his business.

Scanning with his eyes and ears, Maclane heard and saw nothing to draw his attention. The only sound was the constant buzzing of flies and mosquitos near his ears. Frogs chirped from dark water and from time to time, the sound of something big swimming through the nearby brook made him wonder if it was one of these great lizards he had heard about.

These Loyalists did impress him; they had been very thorough and effective. Through fear and intimidation, they learned that this was the road that rebels made their way down from North Carolina. Doing sweeps through the local towns, no rabble-rousers were located; everyone appeared to be behaving themselves.

A sound of horses could be heard coming down the road, the Loyalist next to him making sure he was aware of the approach. The men sunk a little lower behind the bushes and trees as the sound of hooves came closer. Maclane waited in anticipation; hopefully, all of their work would pay off.

Soon, the horsemen came into view, led by a shorter man in the saddle, who appeared to be wearing one of these South Carolina helmets. Excitement coursed through his veins as the horsemen trotted by.

"Could this be one of the rebel gangs operating in the area causing General Cornwallis so many issues and problems?" Maclane thought as he watched the horsemen trot down the road, heading south.

They waited until the sound of hooves had disappeared when they rose from the concealed positions and headed for their horses. They had to report this to Cornwallis and dispatch cavalry and infantry to finally catch this phantom in the night.

***

Marion sat with his leg up on an empty cracker box, resting his aching leg. Oscar was sewing up a tear in one of his stockings. Jacob had just lit Marion's pipe and handed it to him when the sound of carts could be heard. A runner from the watch came over, "Sir, supplies are coming in; Sergeant Nasonne is leading them in."

Marion nodded as he puffed on his pipe, "Jacob, go see to the supplies if you please."

Jacob nodded and headed to where the carts were stopping and lining up. Frederick and the boys rode by, leading to their camp; all had strange, knowing smiles. Jacob shook his head, wondering what had gotten into them. He looked down and even the wolves appeared to have a grin on their muzzles as they trotted by.

Looking up, Jacob was surprised to see Peter and Otti with a couple of the waggoners they use from the compound. When Peter saw Jacob come out of the trees, he raised his pipe in greetings with a giant smile.

"Why are they all smiling? Have they lost their minds?" Jacob thought as he came up next to the cart. He detected a sound of snoring that seemed vaguely familiar. Then it came crashing down on why everyone was smiling and Otti and Peter were

there. Jacob tore the cover off the cart, and Samuel snored loudly in the bundles' middle.

"Sergeant Penny, stand to!"

Bolting straight up, Samuel jumped to his feet, automatically triggered by Jacob's command of standing to. However, there was not much room in the cart, Samuel began to lose his balance and fell back into the cart. After the excitement of seeing his long-lost friend, Jacob reached in, grabbed him, and pulled him from the cart.

Setting him down, Jacob looked upon his friend. Emotions overwhelmed Jacob, learning Samuel was alive and with them once more. Jacob wrapped his friend in a bear hug,

"About time you showed up," Jacob commented, "running a little late."

From his muffled voice from within Jacob's hug, "You're smothering me, you big ox!" Jacob released his friend, who stood there, catching his breath.

Samuel smiled, then answered, "Had to give those lobster-backs some hard time, keep them focused on me while you got away. Now that you're back in action, I have returned to resume my duties of watching over you and Jean."

Then he looked around in a panic, "Where's Jean?"

"I am right rear, you old pirate," Jean stated as he came rushing up; word had arrived in the camp of the supplies being delivered with Samuel. Jean had no problem embracing Samuel in a hug, which surprised Samuel. A slight tear rolled down his cheek.

"Better stop that; you're squeezing what water I have left in me." Samuel sniffled once, then smiled and returned the embrace to Jean. Jacob just smiled as Otti walked up next to him.

"I need to speak with Marion," she said, "We have news that must be passed." Jacob nodded.

"See to the unloading and in helping Sergeant Penny get to my camp. See, he gets a horse and that bag I have been saving for him." Frederick nodded and, with the boys, began to offload the supplies as Jacob walked over to where Marion was sitting.

"How is Maria doing?" Jacob asked and Otti smiled. "She and Helga are responsible for sending this news we must share. They are working in the main headquarters in Charles Town, washing clothes and listening. They are doing well."

Jacob nodded, "Who is running the compound?"

"Peter and the men are still running the compound, and I bring the supplies to Mr. Marshal. So far, no one has bothered us."

Jacob nodded and then, unexpectedly, reached over and hugged Otti's shoulder, in which she smiled and hugged his waist back.

Marion was still sitting on his box when Jacob and Otti approached. Marion looked up and lowered his pipe. "Ah, good lady, do you bare me good news?"

Otti shook her head and knelt to speak evenly with Marion.

"I am afraid not, sir; we learned that the British are sending men to find you. They are getting men off the prison hulks to use. That's how my Samuel was able to escape, but our contacts overheard they have a man from your old unit who is coming after you."

When Otti said "contacts," he looked up at Jacob, believing he knew the contact. "Would you have the name of this person hunting me?" Marion asked.

"Micah Gainey, I believe, sir."

Marion knitted his brows together, recalling the name. Jacob, on the other hand, placed Gainey.

"Disciplinary problem. Liked to drink on duty. He stated it was just like grog, but only better. So you held a court martial when he was drinking on guard duty and sharing it with the guard detail."

Marion nodded, "Yes, now I recall. I had him demoted, fined, and twenty lashes for actions unbecoming. So he is volunteering to come after me. Well, we'll see about that!"

CHAPTER 5

BLUE SAVANNAH AND THE TEARCOAT

Marion waited until they received word that Gainey was coming for him. Until then, they prepared by inventorying what weapons and supplies they had. Between Jacob's band and Major James and his militiamen, they had only around seventy men. While they now had several days' worth of dried, smoked and salted food, powder and shot became an issue.

Jacob, Major James, and Marion checked everyone to see where they stood on arms. Each had their own, from the fowling pieces some men carried for duck hunting, muskets like the Brown Bess and even some French Charlevilles, some carbines, rifles like Jacob, and even blacksmith-made swords from tree saws, for men who had no firelocks.

Samuel was beaming as the bag he had laid aside for him contained his favorite weapon, a blunderbuss. Marion even nodded, "I much rather we all had fowling pieces," he commented.

"Why is that sir?" Jacob asked.

Marion looked thoughtfully at him, "Goose shot will tear a man right out of the saddle; get more damage out of it."

Jacob had to nod in agreement, mainly as they serve more as mounted infantry than true cavalry; it's better to use fowling pieces or, in Samuel's case, a blunderbuss. They still had enough shot and powder for a small engagement but not enough for any significant campaigns.

Marion looked over the gear, most of the leather products were surviving, but the men's clothing was starting to wear a bit thin. Linen on hot days and in the swamp, saw more tears and seams coming apart faster than usual. The men were becoming very handy with needles and thread. Most evenings around the camps, the men had sewing circles, repairing their gear while socializing.

Word finally arrived that Gainey, now a Loyalist Major, was leading a legion of cavalry and infantry out of Cheraw and were heading their way. He had over two hundred under his command\ and Marion had only his seventy. Jacob and Major James sat with Marion, going over their options.

"Gentlemen," Marion began, "We know Gainey is coming. We generally know how many cavalry and infantry he has thanks to our eyes and ears and we know we're outnumbered. So, what options do we have?"

The three men thought, looking at the small fire cracking in its pit, throwing its glow on their faces. Then, finally, Oscar approached, bringing Marion a cup of tea.

"We can move, avoid contact," Major James said. "We must conserve our strength until we can get more men."

Marion nodded, then looked at Jacob, who nodded in agreement. "We must be careful; the locals rely on us for morale. We get beat, they get beat and the Crown wins. Perhaps wait to fight another day when we have an advantage."

"Attack them. They wouldn't expect it."

The three looked up at Oscar, who had made the suggestion, standing off to the side as he looked back. Oscar looked at all three officers and continued. "It has always been your way to do things the enemy does not expect you to do. For example, to be in a location where you are not supposed to be. They would not expect you to attack, so attack fast and use shock as a weapon."

Marion nodded and chuckled. "Oscar, we may make you into an officer soon enough!"

Oscar waved both hands. "No, no, sir. I am happy to serve you."

"But he makes sense," Jacob stated. "If we ride in, strike them hard and fast, we can divide the cavalry from the infantry, hit them in detail and keep them from concentrating on us. Who dares win, remember?"

Marion smiled and nodded his head. "We'll ride at first light. Then, as we are all in our normal clothes and not uniforms, have the men place white pieces of paper in their hats so we can identify them," Marion paused for a second, "before we blast them out of their saddles."

Having settled on a plan, Jacob and Major James headed to their respective groups and told their men to prepare for their attack. First, Jacob had his band check their muskets, inventory the amount of shot and powder they had and then check their horses and tack. Next, Jacob checked his gear, then went around and checked the others.

Jacob's band were the original men who had joined Marion just after the fall of Charles Town, but now as Marion was in command, they followed Jacob. These men were the last of the First and Second Regiments and veterans who had answered the call. Then there were the boys and even the wolves who were members of the band. As he checked them, he ensured they all had white paper slips in the helmets and hats.

"You boys doing alright?" Jacob asked as he checked on his sons and nephews, who nodded energetically. They still had the energy of youth, though he could see in their eyes that distant look of someone who saw more than they should have. Jacob wondered if he had the same look when he was younger with the Rangers.

"Yes, you did," Samuel replied behind Jacob as he approached.

"Yes, what?" Jacob returned.

"The looks in their eyes. You and I did have that same look, both the hunger for excitement, though what we saw was starting to fill the back of our minds. I know what you were thinking about the boys; I thought the same thing."

Jacob snorted and then smiled at his long friend. "It's good to have you back."

Samuel smiled, cradling his blunderbuss in his arm, "It's good to be back."

Jacob could see a new depth in Samuel's eyes, of new horrors he must have witnessed while a prisoner. But Jacob also knew it was not time to ask.

"I'll tell you about it later when I am ready," Samuel replied as he turned and headed over to his horse.

"What, you can bloody read minds now?" Jacob shot back.

"Yes, yours!" Samuel returned.

The band mounted up and joined Jacob, standing next to Marion. As they entered, Marion nodded to them and then Major James and his group joined. Then, looking over the assembled riders, Marion nodded to them all.

"Men, I will not lie. We're outnumbered. But then again, when are we not outnumbered?"

The group all chuckled at the comment. Then Marion gave them all a hard look.

"Also, it's one of our own. Anyone who had served in the Second may remember Micah Gainey, who was not a model soldier. He offered his services to the King and leads the force against us. We'll hit the cavalry first and then go after the infantry. The more we can eliminate, the better off we'll be."

Marion looked at all the men once more before turning his horse and leading them out. Jacob rode next to Marion as the column wound out of the camp and onto the road. Before Jacob could ask, Marion spoke.

"Our friends reported that Gainey is located near Queensboro. So, we'll look for him there."

Jacob gave Marion a surprised look, "Can you read minds as well?"

Marion chuckled and shook his head, "No, Jacob, but I do know, as a good officer, you want to know where we are going. That's all."

Marion led them through McCrea's Crossroads and headed north toward Queensboro in the Cheraw district. Their eyes and ears had spotted both men on horses and infantry marching south out of Cheraw. Reports of heavy Loyalist activity kept any support for Marion up there as they dealt with the Loyalist threats.

Samuel came trotting up and rode next to Jacob. He had a very pleased look on his face, enjoying the ride. Jacob had to chuckle at the site of his friend enjoying the moment.

"Good to be out?" Jacob asked and Samuel smiled. "You have no idea!" Even Samuel's wolves seemed to be happy jogging alongside his horse.

They were cresting a rise when below them was the town of Queensboro, and a troop of horsemen who had to be part of Gainey's command appeared to be posted on the road. Without waiting for Marion's command, Major James spurred his horse, giving a battle cry with his men following close behind him.

"Impetuous fool!" Marion yelled as he charged after him. Jacob's men, while only slightly better disciplined than the others, exploded out as Jacob waved his arm forward, and they charged.

Then, with hooves thundering, James and his men spread out into a wedge, with Marion coming close behind and followed by Jacob.

Strangely, for horsemen blocking the road approaching the town, Major James and his group, who came thundering over the hill, crashed into the Loyalists, who seemed to be caught by surprise. Jacob led his band off to the side and made another approach through an alley as Major James and his men clashed with the Loyalists.

Pouring into the town center, Jacob spotted a second set of Loyalists, a man he recognized. Gainey himself was there and was looking toward the sound of the clash. Jacob gave a war cry and charged out of the alley, followed by his men. As they cleared the alley's opening, Samuel fired his blunderbuss with telling effect as three Loyalists and two of their horses fell screaming to the ground.

Seeing he was being attacked, Gainey wheeled his horse about and took off in a dead gallop. Jacob continued to follow, his boys and wolves right behind him. A few of the band lowered their muskets and took a few of the dismounted men prisoners. Jacob tried to catch Gainey, but he was moving too fast and the distance between them was growing.

Jacob raised his hand, and they came to a stop. Shaking his head, Jacob did not want to pursue it as it could lead them into an ambush.

"Papa, look!" Richard yelled out and pointed to where another group of Loyalists was riding away and Major James, all alone, was chasing them. Spurring his horse into a gallop, Jacob and the boys, with the wolves in full sprint, charged out after Major James, with Jacob muttering, "Bloody fool!"

The Loyalists rode into thick brush and trees, and it appeared James was about to ride right behind them.

"Major James, hold!" Jacob yelled out and luckily did get Major James to hear him. James pulled on his reins and his horse came to a sliding halt. The wolves tore into the woods, and hooves could still be heard.

"Come on, Jacob, here they are!" James yelled, excited and caught up in the chase. Jacob slowed to a trot, rode up to James and shook his head.

"We don't know who is in there, what we're riding into," Jacob explained. "Remember Marion said Gainey had infantry coming. It is a good way to be killed or captured. So, let's do it on our terms."

James knew Jacob was right and nodded his head. "Aye, you're right, as always. Wasn't thinking straight." James gave Jacob a sheepish grin and Jacob grinned back.

"We know, we know." Jacob whistled, and the wolves came trotting back with somewhat satisfied looks. They turned and rode back to the town where Marion was waiting.

"We asked the prisoners where the infantry was and they said they are coming down the same road, should be about three miles or so. We need to ride now if we're going to catch them by surprise."

Jacob and Major James nodded, and Marion led them out of the town as a small section led the prisoners away and secured any supplies from the captured horses. Marion led them on a hard trot and was only on the road for about ten minutes when they ran into the lead element of the Loyalist infantry.

Jacob had to admit that the infantry reacted rather well as they pulled the reins on their horses. Instead of panicking and running, they quickly began to form into line as the column's rear began to deploy on either side of the lead element. The lead element lowered their muskets and fired a semi-ragged volley, in which Marion turned his horse and led them back.

As they turned, he yelled over to Jacob. "Hang back; make sure they follow us. I have a little surprise for them!"

As Marion rode off with the rest of the column at a gallop, Jacob believed he knew what he was up to and hoped he had a good location in mind. He turned his horse and saw that the Loyalist infantry was, in fact, in a full run after them.

"Alright, lads," Jacob instructed, "Let's give these good men some exercise!" Kneeing his horse, Jacob led them on a trot that kept them just ahead to stay out of musket range but not too far, where they couldn't be seen. The boys kept looking over their shoulders at the running Loyalists.

"Eyes front lads," Jacob commanded, "remember we're fleeing from the mighty site of those Loyalists! The boys chuckled but did as they were told. Jacob watched the ground to ensure they followed Marion's trail, then nodded. He knew where they were riding toward, the Blue Savannah.

As they just left the tree line and entered the savannah, Jacob kicked his horse into a gallop. "Now, lads, ride like the wind!" The horses' hooves thundered and threw up clods of dirt. Soon Jacob saw Marion come out of the tree line before them and he led his horsemen into it. When they came even with Marion, they pulled up on the reins.

As Jacob had suspected, the rest of the men were in an ambush line. Their muskets, fowling pieces and swords were at the ready. Jacob spun his horse around that was breathing hard, and his band joined the ambush line. Marion mounted his horse and had his fowling piece ready. Now they waited for the Loyalists to arrive.

The horses were able to catch their breaths when the lead element of the Loyalists came into view, not running as fast as before, but still in pursuit. Then, as the savannah opened, they did precisely what Marion had wanted; they opened up in more of a staggered column than an organized line. Now it came down to timing.

"Wait for it, "Marion commanded, his hand held to his side, palm facing back toward them. They all watched the approaching infantry, even the horses getting anxious and began pawing the ground. Even the wolves were waiting in anticipation, low growls coming from their throats.

"Wait for it," Marion commanded as his arm swung up.

When the Loyalists were where Marion wanted them, his arms shot up and then forward.

"Charge!"

They all kicked their horses simultaneously, the wolves taking off like a shot. Once more, the men released their pent-up energy by screaming war cries from the veterans' deep voices and the youthful voices of the boys. They burst from the trees and the Loyalists all had shocked faces.

"Boom!" Samuel's blunderbuss mixed with Marion and the other's fowling pieces loaded with goose and other shots. Instead of using his rifle, Jacob decided to use his tomahawk. Like the other men using the homemade swords, he rose in their stirrups and brought down heavy swings of their blades on the heads and shoulders of the Loyalists.

The Loyalists were caught hard in the ambush but still tried to defend themselves when a small group did get a ragged volley off that sent three of Marion's men tumbling from their saddles. Then, swinging his tomahawk to the left and right, Jacob hewed a path of destruction through the Loyalists. First, Jacob poured through the line of infantry and then spun around to attack. The wolves had double-teamed, and each brought down a Loyalist.

The Loyalists broke, all running in different directions like chickens running from a wolf. Marion had Major James sweep in one direction, and Jacob, with his band, sweep in another. Most of the Loyalists were running for the safety of the swamp. When they arrived at the edge, Marion called a halt.

Caught in the energy of the attack, Marion's men yelled and cursed at the running Loyalists as they splashed through the swamp away from them. Marion ordered them all to hold if they were trying to lure them into an ambush in the swamp where they would have the advantage. A few men fired their muskets at the running Loyalists and Marion yelled for them to save their ammunition.

They returned and stripped the dead of any shot, powder, muskets, food and equipment they could use. The few wounded and prisoners they had were secured. Marion led their column out until they returned to McCrea's Crossing, where the prisoners and wounded were deposited with the local sheriff and were given their parole not to fight again.

Then they rode back to the camp; Jacob had to admit the morale of their men was very good now. Once again, they stopped a more significant force and chased off another commander. The word will spread like wildfire of their success, which should bolster the morale of the local people.

Jacob did worry that their growing fame would also be a curse, drawing the attention of a larger force. Still, the people needed a good story to show the resistance was there and that they were fighting for themselves and the cause. They arrived at their camp and Jacob had his band take care of their horses, weapons, and personal gear. They had to be ready to ride at a moment's notice.

Later that night, a company of volunteers arrived outside of their camp. One of their trusted militiamen had been contacted and he led these sixty volunteers to the road just outside the center. Marion, with Major James and Jacob, went out to meet them. These volunteers had brought their muskets and fowling pieces like the others. They even had their gear and bedrolls, and most had experience in the militia. Marion nodded and welcomed them all to the group.

***

When the news of Gainey's rout by a smaller brigand force reached General Cornwallis, he was livid again.

"What in the bloody two Hells is going on here!" Cornwallis roared as he crumbled up the message from Georgetown and tossed it into the fire. He began to pace about the room, his hands held behind his back, shaking his head.

He stopped, looked at his wall map, traced the road network from Kings Tree through McCrea's Crossing and went to Georgetown. Cornwallis's lips became a tight line, turning white. Then, settling on a decision, he called for a messenger.

After scribbling a quick message, he handed it to the orderly, who reported.

"Have this delivered to Major Wemyss immediately! Make sure he understands that he is to execute immediately with extreme prejudice!"

The orderly nodded, turned, and went off to get one of the messengers, who quickly mounted his horse, took off at a gallop and headed for Major Wemyss's camp. As Cornwallis heard the horse's hooves thunder off into the distance, he returned to the wall map.

"Let's see how they will handle this," he remarked as he looked at the stretch between Kings Tree and Cheraw. "This should put the fear of God and the King in their hearts."

***

Smoke rose like deathly fingers into the afternoon sky as the British column marched through the countryside. Having received the urgent message from Cornwallis, Major Wemyss began his campaign. His own 63rd Regiment of Foot, the Royal North Carolina Provincials, and the South Carolina Rangers are at his disposal.

Major Wemyss did not particularly like the South Carolina Rangers; he felt they were more irregulars and plunderers than professionals like his own regiment. Still, he did have a use for them, and they were being very effective.

To ensure he had covered enough of the territory to send a message to the rebels and the Loyal Subjects, he began a sweep seven miles wide, starting at Kings Tree, and he intended to head northeast until he reached Cheraw. There, he knew he had a vital, Loyalist-controlled region. However, the rest in between was very questionable.

Major Wemyss's message was clear, "If you hide arms from the King, make war on his loyal subjects and soldiers, support the rebel brigands, then all is forfeit to the Crown as punishment." As he sat upon his horse, the flames of the burning house flickering in his eyes, and he smiled.

Watching his men deploy as they searched for the hidden arms and supplies, he knew these locals must be hiding from the Crown. He felt justified in his action, following General Cornwallis' orders to disarm these rebels most rigidly.

An aide rode up and reported to Major Wemyss. "Sir, may I have permission to speak freely?"

Wemyss looked over and seeing he was caught in the excitement of the raid, allowed it. "Yes, you may speak freely. What is on your mind?"

The lieutenant paused, getting his thoughts together before asking. "Sir, is this right? I mean, burning and destroying all of these homes? Do we know truly if they are rebel sympathizers or not?"

Wemyss turned and gave the lieutenant a stern look. "Of course, I know if they are loyal or not. We ask them if they are concealing from the King and if they are good, loyal subjects. Most we have found are not and must be taught a lesson. They will learn their place."

Major Wemyss kneed his horse and began to walk forward, the lieutenant riding alongside, watching the activity around him. At a farm they were passing, the family was outside their home, fear in their eyes as the Rangers held them in place with bayonet-tipped muskets.

The rest of the Rangers were leading the cattle off to be eaten later, smashing the family's loom and burning a mill in the distance. They were also bayonetting all of the sheep, laughing as they were enjoying the wonton destruction. The lieutenant looked at Major Wemyss's face and knew he had no way of getting him to change his mind, a contented look upon his face.

Major Wemyss looked over at the lieutenant, who seemed to have stopped speaking. "Is there anything else, lieutenant?" Wemyss asked, and the lieutenant shook his head no.

"Then you best return to your duties then," Wemyss commanded, and the lieutenant nodded and rode off, leaving the major to enjoy the view of the destruction.

***

When the news of the path of destruction reached Marion, he called an immediate meeting with Major James and Jacob. Following the rout of Gainey, Marion, with their new sixty men, rode back up to North Carolina to be refitted and supplied to the best of their ability.

Dr. Wilson from the local area had ridden north, bringing the news of the destruction. When Major James and Jacob arrived, Marion introduced Dr. Wilson to them. "Tell them what you just told me," Marion instructed.

Dr. Wilson nodded. "As I told Francis, the British are on a rampage in South Carolina. A path almost seventy miles long from Kings Tree to Cheraw, they destroyed everything. It didn't matter if they supported our cause or even were Loyalists. They destroyed everything!"

He paused, gathering his thoughts before continuing. "I saw with my own eyes the destruction, the murder! Adam Cusack had tried to defend his family and home, fired at one of those Loyalist Bastards. His wife and children tried to get between this British commander, this Major Wemyss, to save Adam, but he nearly ran them over with his horse. So he had Adam hung right there in front of his family. I tried to stop him."

Dr. Wilson stopped, looking down into the fire and then finished. "I failed. He hung Adam, and I believe that man even enjoyed it! This man is evil incarnate, the Devil himself. He must be stopped!"

Marion rested his hand on Dr. Wilson's shoulder and gave a reassuring squeeze before looking at Major James and Jacob. "Well, lads, what do you think?"

Jacob could see the hard line on Major James's face and knew his answer. "Well, sir, we know we will be outnumbered, but as you have stated before, when are we not outnumbered," Jacob began, then gave Marion a straight, level look.

"We need to make this officer and his men pay. What we do in battle is one thing, but to make war on simple farmers and their families, just killing sheep and cattle for the bloodlust or sake of killing, then it's no different than murder. To hang a man for defending his home and his family makes him worse than a criminal. They all must pay!"

Marion nodded. "Gather the men; have them cook up what rations they have. We ride in the morning."

Jacob and Major James nodded in understanding and went to their respective units. Jacob called his men together and told them what was happening in South Carolina.

"They're burning and destroying everything?" Richard asked and Jacob nodded.

"Aye, lad, I am afraid so. This is how they make war and don't seem to care about who they hurt."

"Even these people who are considered Loyalists?" Patrick asked and again Jacob nodded.

"How do you fight something like that?" Jehu Jones asked, and Jacob nodded his understanding.

"With heart and trust in your mates, we will be victorious as a team. No one can win against that type of destruction. We have to work together and trust one another. In the end, we will be victorious!"

Jacob looked at his band. From the old veterans to his boys and even the wolves who sat there with their tongues hanging out, smiling in the method of the wolves.

"We all trust you, Jacob," Samuel nodded firmly. "We'll follow you to the gates of Hell to pull the tail off the devil if need be!"

All of the band nodded and cheered in agreement. Jacob just smiled. "It works for me," he answered, "See to your gear and we'll ride in the morning."

As the sun rose the following morning, Marion was already up, Oscar on his horse next to him. Jacob and Major James brought their groups up and nodded they were ready. The new volunteers were placed under Major James' command.

"We're going to be riding hard to get down there and hopefully catch some of these vaunted British or Loyalist officers still in the Williamsburg area."

With that, Marion turned his horse and the march was on. True to his word, Marion led them on a mile-eating pace to get them across North Carolina and back into the district. Even Jacob had to admit the pace was rugged and tough on his backside as he was getting sore from the ride. No natural breaks other than walking their horses for a bit, then picking up the pace again.

In all, Marion led them on a forty-mile trip, crossing three rivers in the process and as the moon began to rise, arrived at the Williamsburg District. They moved into a campsite, and after establishing a guard force, the men started to take care of their horses and get some rest. Marion sent out a scouting party to locate the location of Major Wemyss or any other Loyalists.

It was near sunrise when the scouts returned. "Sir, we found Colonel Ball and his Loyalist militia. They are at Dollard's Tavern over next to the Black Mingo. They appear to be using it as an outpost."

Marion nodded and then called for Jacob and Major James. When they arrived, he began to lay out his plan. "Well, it's not Wemyss, but I can settle for Colonel Ball. He seems to be forted up at the Dollard Tavern and that's where we'll hit him."

Using a stick, Marion drew out his plan in the dirt. "We'll cross here on the bridge, then split into three attacking columns, catching them between us." He then looked at Jacob and Major James, "If possible, I want to take Ball alive so he can answer for his crimes, understood?"

Jacob and Major James nodded their heads in understanding. Marion smiled and let out a long sigh. "It's getting rougher, isn't it," he asked. "Before, we were just simple soldiers. Fighting a war was so much easier. Now it was not so simple; there was no clear description of being a combatant. The lines have blurred, no longer clear. It's a sad state we have entered, gentlemen."

They waited until the afternoon before mounting their horses and heading out to attack. Marion wanted to attack in the dark when the Loyalists were more and likely asleep. Marion led the way as always, with Major James and his band, then Jacob and his band. During the fight, James would be the left column and attack the tavern, while Jacob would strike the right and ride around to cut off the retreat.

The ride was uneventful, the men keeping quiet and their thoughts to themselves. Then, finally, the sun sank, the moon rose and almost full moon, which Jacob didn't like how bright it was becoming. But, it would work; to their surprise, if someone was awake, they could be seen in the moonlight. Soon, the bridge appeared and Marion led them across.

The "clunking" sound of horses' hooves on the wood planks grew louder as the numerous horses crossed over, even at an walk. Jacob was surprised at how loud it was in the still night air. Then, as Jacob and his band began to cross, there was the sound of a sentry's musket going off.

"Well, so much hoping we catching them asleep," Jacob thought as the column leaped into a gallop as the attack was initiated. Major James and his column broke off to the left as planned; Jacob led his band to the right. What surprised Jacob was that he watched Major James dismount early and begin a charge toward the tavern on foot.

Jacob led his band along the Black Mingo Creek to get behind the tavern. Jacob held up his hand when they arrived, and they all dismounted. The select few held the horses' reins as Jacob led the rest of the band in a sweep toward the back of the tavern. The

Band quickly spread out; their muskets, rifles and even Samuel's blunderbuss were at the ready. The wolves advance alongside Jacob, slinking low to the ground as on the hunt.

"Crack, boom!" A volley could be heard coming from the front of the Tavern and Jacob could not determine if it was the Loyalists or James.

"Pick your targets!" Jacob yelled as they advanced, "When in doubt, charge them and knock them down. Then we'll see who they are."

It sounded like a battle was starting from the front as both sides exchanged musket fire. No one appeared to be leaving from the back of the tavern. Jacob angled his band to come from behind the Loyalists. He had to be careful not to be caught in a crossfire between the Loyalists and James.

Keeping a slight angle on the tavern, Jacob could see around the corner where a line of troops, Jacob assuming to be Loyalists, gave a ragged volley toward James' direction before turning and heading straight at him.

"Fire!"

Jacob gave the command just as the fleeing Loyalists came around the corner of the tavern, trying to flee toward the creek. With the thunderous roar of Samuel's blunderbuss and the other muskets and rifles going off, many of the Loyalists crumbled to the ground. What survivors there were, dropped their unloaded muskets and raised their hands. Having heard the blunderbuss, the other Loyalists turned sharply and ran in a different direction.

After everyone reloaded, Jacob escorted his prisoners to the front of the tavern, where Marion and Major James were waiting. Marion was rubbing the nose of a fine horse with a somewhat satisfied grin on his face. Jacob pointed to where the other prisoners were being gathered, then reported to Marion.

"Well, that bastard Ball got away, but I have his horse. What a fine animal. I'll borrow him for a while and name him Ball."

Jacob just nodded his head, not sure how to respond. "How did we fare, sir?"

Marion looked to where Major James and his men were going through the supplies they had captured. Marion let out a long sigh.

"We did well. We captured the horses, arms and powder and shot. But I also lost some good men in the process. I would never have guessed that Ball would have come out of the tavern to fight, thought he would force us to lay siege. But, instead, that one volley of his killed three of our men and wounded a good number more. Men, we can't afford to lose."

Jacob had to agree, but from what he saw, it had been worth it. They needed to capture their baggage, horses, arms and supplies. It also conveyed that what they did when they burned and destroyed the farms would not be tolerated; they would be brought to justice. But, unfortunately, it just may take some time.

Once they secured the prisoners and the supplies, Marion led them back to their camp. The prisoners were dropped off at the local authorities so they wouldn't know where the base was. Once in camp, the new supplies were distributed, especially the powder and shot. Anyone who was still carrying the homemade swords was given a musket.

Jacob, with his boys Patrick and Richard, were sitting around a small fire, the wolves lounging nearby. Patrick sewed a hole in his shirt and Richard cleaned his musket. Jacob had a small pot on the fire, melting some captured musket balls to pour the lead into a mold for his rifle.

He watched as the lead spread out and liquefied before pouring it into his mold, then let it sit as the lead hardened.

"Papa, do you think this war will ever end?" Patrick asked, and Jacob nodded.

"Aye, lad, I do. It's just going to take some time, that's all."

"Then another war will start, won't it?" Richard asked as he finished placing his ramrod back in its keeper. "You have been fighting wars since you were our age, "Mama and Uncle Peter said. Will that happen to us too?"

Jacob thought about it and shrugged. "Good question, and I have no answer. I would think by now man would tire of fighting, all of the blood and loves lost, that they would find a better way of settling differences."

Jacob reached down and opened his mold and a shiny new silver rifle ball fell onto a rag to cool and harden. Then, dropping another captured musket ball into the spoon, Jacob laid it on the fire to start the process again.

He then looked at his boys, who were no longer boys. Both were lean, hardened, muscled men now, having to grow up in the crucible of war. They still had youthful eyes but with a deepness of seeing too much death and destruction so early in their lives. He had mixed feelings when he looked at them, sorry he had taken them into battle but proud to have watched them grow into such fine men and soldiers.

Jacob just smiled and looked at his sons. "That will be up to men like you, whether another war will come or peace. It will be all up to you."

***

The ball came whizzing past as Big Harpe ducked around a tree and Little Harpe fired down the hill at the approaching riflemen. After signing up at Camden and with their knowledge of the up-country, they were assigned to Major Ferguson and followed him into the Ninety-Six District.

While in the district, Ferguson sent a newly paroled rebel to take a message to the rebels living in the upcountry. He had demanded that they give up this rebellion and return to be faithful and loyal subjects to the King, or he would lay waste to their homes with fire and sword. He even threatened to release the Cherokee on them once again.

Even Big Harpe knew that threatening the up-country men was a mistake and he knew the threat of using the Cherokee was empty. Granted, he had been all for the destruction, but he was missing the old days of robbing and pillaging on behalf of the King. Even Harpe also knew not to pick a fight with a force larger than yours.

This was the situation he now found himself in, as he was fighting for his life, and it was an odd feeling. Ferguson had taken them to the top of a large hill named King's Mountain, thinking he could hold off the rebels. But instead, the rebels were using their rifles efficiently, knocking down these 71st Highlanders.

Taking a deep breath, Big Harpe came around his tree, did a quick aim and fired, not knowing if he hit anything. As he loaded, his brother yelled, "So, this is the great opportunity you spoke of, right? Of looting and pillaging once more for the King, right?"

Big Harpe just looked at his brother and gave him a hard, dirty look. "Just shoot."

As they were loading, the Highlanders were charging across the field. Their bayonets lowered to force these riflemen off the top of the hill. Big Harpe looked over and saw their illustrious commander on horseback, wearing a very distinct colored coat and not his normal officer redcoat. Big Harpe could see the situation was getting desperate.

"Go get the boys!" Big Harpe yelled at Little Harpe, "I think it's time we find a better place to be than here!"

Little Harpe nodded and gathered the men who had been with their gang when they joined. Big Harpe was watching the ebb and flow of the battle. The British were getting handled by these riflemen. He saw a few white handkerchiefs go up from some of the Loyalists, where Ferguson could be seen riding over and knocking them down with his sword.

Little Harpe returned with the three men. "Where are Benjamin and Charles?" Big Harpe asked, and Little Harpe shook his head.

"Bloody Hell, they both owed me money!" Big Harpe grumbled. He then looked over the battle and saw the signs that it would not be much longer.

"All right, lads, be ready to move when the time is right," Big Harpe grumbled, then went back to watching the fight. Ferguson was riding around, trying to rally his men. Finally, they were at the breaking point. Then there was a sound of numerous rifles firing at once and Ferguson tumbled from his saddle and crashed to the ground.

"That's it, boys, let's go!" Big Harpe yelled and led his men away from the fight. Quickly moving from tree to tree, Big Harpe led them to the mouth of a ravine that ran down the side of the hill. Moving while maintaining their balance, the men followed Big Harpe, who surprisingly could move so fast for a man of his size.

He weaved through the rocks and over the down trees. Then, he sank to the ground in a flash and his men followed. A group of rebel riflemen was climbing up the hill on the lip of the ravine. Their attention was focused on getting to the top, where the sound of celebration could be heard.

Big Harpe kept moving, and they somehow evaded all of the rebel riflemen and got away. Then, as they were moving along the bottom of the hill, Big Harpe quickly halted them and brought his finger up to his lip. Just before them were picketed horses, and two young boys with muskets were watching them. Big Harpe gave a crooked, evil smile.

Turning, he pointed to one of the lads, then to himself, then to his brother before pointing back at the second. His brother understood and handed his musket to one of the men before drawing his knife. Big Harpe handed his musket, then flexed his large fingers. Then, crouching, he slowly made his way toward the boys looking up toward the top of the hill and not in their direction.

Moving quickly, Little Harpe grabbed his target just as Big Harpe grabbed his just as the young boy turned to face him. Little Harpe made quick work of his, sinking his knife in the boy's throat. Big Harpe wrapped his hands around the throat and squeezed so hard you could hear the sound of cartilage and bone breaking.

Enjoying his sadistic pleasure of choking the boy to death, Big Harpe dropped him like a rag doll onto the ground and motioned for the other three to come up. Little Harpe did not show emotion other than wiping his knife blade on the boy's shirt. Finally, little Harpe received his musket and followed Big Harpe to grab a horse.

"So nice for these fine people to leave horses for us, wouldn't you say?" Big Harpe quipped before giving an evil chuckle as he mounted up on a horse. All of them had a horse and took four extra with them. As they rode away from the battle site, Big Harpe looked forward to seeing what they found in the bags, hoping for some rum and food.

"Turned out alright," he said to his brother, "we'll head back and rejoin the forces and see where we can go next."

Big Harpe's laughter bounced from the trees as the leaves fell onto the dead, staring eyes of the two boys whose bodies were left behind.

***

Major Wemyss re-read the letter, crumbled it and threw it in the fire. He had a furious look on his face.

"Sir?" his orderly asked.

Letting out a deep breath with a "humph!" He looked at his orderly.

"Pack your things," he told him, "We have just received our new orders. I am to take command of the garrison at Camden. Colonel Balfour has assigned the task of clearing the countryside and bringing these rebels to justice to a Colonel Tynes of the South Carolina Loyalists."

Wemyss shook his head and grumbled, "A Loyalist! So, they will entrust this task to a Loyalist of all people?"

Still, he knew he had to follow orders, whether he liked it or not and accepted his new assignment.

"Put out the word; we march at dawn."

***

Marion fumed as more and more details of the destruction reached him, of the refugees making their way to different towns and families with only what they had on their backs. The more he heard, the more he wanted to bring justice to these British and Loyalist leaders.

As it had been some time, Marion had released the Williamsburg Militia and Major James to their homes. But, as it was fall, he knew they had to get their harvest. Moreover, they had received the news that the up-country riflemen had dealt

Major Ferguson a heavy defeat at King's Mountain, which did bolster his morale.

Jacob and his band stayed with Marion and Oscar to watch over his old commander. Samuel would take the boys out and scout the area around their camp, ensuring no one was looking for them. Jacob sat with Marion and Oscar; the chill of the air required Jacob to put on his old, well-worn blanket coat.

Oscar made sure Marion wrapped himself in a blanket before their small fire, just big enough for warmth but not to give their position away. Marion looked at Jacob, appreciating that he had strayed with him.

"You know, you should be a major with everything you have done," Marion stated, "Actually, you should be a colonel with your command. I know you have much more experience at this than I do, and you are one of the best I know."

Jacob snorted but smiled at the praise he had received from Marion. "I am happy serving under you with my merry band of misfits."

Marion chuckled and nodded. "Aye, they are a merry band of misfits, to be sure." Even Oscar smiled and agreed that Jacob's band was a bunch of unique characters, especially now that Samuel was back with them. But then, there were the wolves, Waya lying next to Jacob, his golden eyes watching all.

Later that day, Samuel and the boys returned and reported to Marion and Jacob.

"Nothing seen or heard," Samuel reported, "Seems Major Harrison is good at hiding or is out of the area. No one has seen his group of South Carolina Rangers." Samuel spat on the ground after saying "Rangers," detesting their use of the term as he feels they had not earned it as he and Jacob had.

"I do have some good news, though," Samuel continued with a grin and then pointed over his shoulder as a man approached from behind wearing hunting clothes and carrying a rifle, being escorted by all things, Samuel's two wolves.

Marion stood up, allowing the blanket to fall to the ground, but Oscar grabbed up. Jacob rose as well as the man came up and introduced himself.

"Captain William McCottry at your service, sir," he said as he reached out to shake Marion's hand. "My company is at your service. We want to do something about the destruction of our friends' and neighbors' homes."

Marion smiled and nodded, "Then I welcome you and your men. While we don't have much to offer, let us know if you require anything."

A few days later, a train of pack horses arrived, led by Otti and accompanied by three Catawba Indians and Peter. After dismounting, Otti went to see Samuel and the boys while Marion, McCottry and Jacob met Peter and the Catawbas.

With his ever-present pipe in hand, Peter smiled when he saw Jacob and the others, though Jacob had to admit his old friend looked older than he had.

"Ah, mine good friends, so gut to see you again!" Peter said warmly and shook everyone's hands. "May I introduce Nopkehee, Issae and Totiri of the Catawbas, who decided to winter with us and help where they can."

Jacob shook their hands and the three looked at one another and then asked, "Okwaho?" Jacob smiled and nodded.

"General Green River sends his best and wishes you a good hunt."

Jacob again nodded, "How is the General?"

"He has taken a group of warriors, fought with Major Davie up at Hanging Rock, and is taking the fight to these friends of the British. We have no Cherokee to fight, so we go after these friends of the Crown."

The three nodded their heads, appreciative of the news they brought.

"We also have a word of a new commander in the area, Major Tynes and his Loyalists are camped nearby, over by the Tearcoat if you're interested," Peter informed, and Marion brightened.

"Well, I'll take him if he is available," Marion stated, then turned and headed back to his camp to begin planning. McCottry went with him, while Jacob stayed with Peter and the Catawbas. Jehu and the others were helping to unload the bags of supplies from the horses.

"Not much, I am afraid," Peter said as he puffed on his pipe. "At least some more dried venison and some powder vie vere able to get."

"How is Maria doing and Helga?" Jacob asked, and Peter winked.

"How did you think we got the information about dis Tynes fella?" Jacob smiled and patted his friend on the shoulder. "Take care, my old friend."

Peter nodded, "You too."

Jacob turned to the Catawbas and grasped their forearms, "May your hunts be true." Meanwhile, Samuel said farewell to Otti and joined Jacob as they headed to Marion's camp.

"Let's call in the militia, get the word out to Major James to meet at McCrea's Crossing tomorrow and we'll pay Tynes a visit."

Jacob sent a few of his band to contact Major James and his captains, call out their men, and assemble at the Crossing. The rest prepared their weapons and gear, then mounted their horses. Marion would lead the way, with Jacob followed by McCottry's men.

When all was ready, Marion led them and headed to the Crossing at the trot. They arrived first, as expected and Marion moved them into the woods while keeping a man posted to watch the road. After only a short while, the first of Jacob's band returned, leading some of the Williamsburg men. Then Major James arrived with his company of men. Around a hundred men joined Marion, giving him a force of one hundred and fifty fighters.

Leading the column again, Marion took them along more minor roads and trails that took them in the vicinity of the Tearcoat but not on the main roads where they could be spotted. Finally, as the sun descended toward the horizon, Marion halted the column close to the Tearcoat Swamp.

"Jacob to the front, please," Marion passed, and the word was sent back, and Jacob rode up to the front.

"Jacob, we need to scout out their camp. We know they are along the Tearcoat, but we do not want to tip our hand. I want your boys to scout them out, have them carry fishing poles or something, so they don't draw attention."

Jacob understood what he needed and returned to his band. "Patrick and Richard, I have a task for you. Leave your muskets, but go cut some fishing poles."

The two boys looked at one another, shrugged and did what they were asked to do. After finding some bamboo, they cut two cane poles and rigged some string to make it look like fishing poles before returning to Jacob.

Jacob nodded in approval. "Ok, lads, you have your mission to do. Marion wants you to scout out and find the Loyalist camp. Locate it, remember what it looks like, where they have guards, and return."

The two boys smiled and nodded as Jacob continued. "No heroics; go and see what you can find. If they call out to you, tell them you are fishing. If they challenge you, run. Understand?"

Again, both boys did, and Jacob nodded. "Take the wolves with you; that should be enough for them to leave you be."

Jacob nodded and smiled, and then the boys shouldered their poles and headed along the Tearcoat. The wolves trotted alongside the boys, making it look like the two local boys going fishing with their dogs. Jacob watched them go; Samuel joined him and watched them disappear into the woods.

"They're no longer boys," Samuel stated with pride, "Mine are not boys either. They have all grown."

Then he looked at Jacob with a grin, "Like little you and me back in the day when this mess all started."

Shaking his head, Jacob chuckled and checked on his to ensure they were ready. While time seemed to drag on Jacob as this was the boys' first independent action, they were only gone for a couple of hours. band

The spotters sent word the boys were approaching, and they were sent to Marion, where Jacob, McCottry and Major James waited.

"Yes sir, they are there," Patrick reported. "They have a camp in the bend between the Tearcoat and the other river. It's an open field, they have three large fires burning and most of them were lying about, sleeping."

Marion nodded; Jacob asked, "Did you see any sentries?"

Richard nodded, "I saw maybe two, but they were mostly talking with the others, not watching the woods. They were all singing and laughing. I don't think they know we are here or even care."

Patrick shook his head, "Deplorable camp, no discipline, papa and you, Uncle Jacob, wouldn't have had it that way."

Both Samuel and Jacob chuckled, Jacob responding with, "They are not well-disciplined Rangers like the two of you. Good job!"

Marion smiled, "Good job, lads, good job! Exactly what I needed to hear."

"Go see to your gear, boys," Jacob instructed, and the two boys smiled and headed back to their horses. Marion turned to Jacob, "You have some good lads there, Jacob. You should be proud."

Jacob smiled and nodded, "Yes, sir, I am. They really would be excellent Rangers back in the day."

Marion made his decision on how they will attack.

"We'll follow the boys back to the camp as they know the way. We will go in three columns, Major James; you take McCottry's riflemen and head to the left. Block any escape in that direction. Jacob, you take the right and do the same; I will lead the center. We will wait until about midnight. They should be mostly asleep. Then, I will fire my pistol, which will signal the attack. See to your men; we step off soon."

Jacob and the others nodded and then turned to go to their units and companies to get ready. When Jacob arrived at their horses, "Secure the horses, we're marching in from here. Patrick and Richard, you are leading us back to the camp. We move soon, so ensure your horses are tied and grab your muskets."

He then turned and patted both boys on the shoulders. "Marion was very pleased with you two, and so am I. I am very proud of you two. Good job!"

The boys had big smiles and returned to being all business as they secured their muskets and got ready to lead the men. Jacob and his band went over to where Marion was waiting. He had left a few men behind to watch the horses. He nodded to the boys.

"Lads, lead us out. Take us to the camp."

The boys nodded, having a serious looks on their faces, knowing they were once more given an important task. They turned and led the column into the woods and along the route to the camp.

Jacob thought it was effortless to find the camp, as they could hear the singing and laughing shortly after leaving their horses and he could smell the smoke from the fires. Still, it was good to have the lads leading the column; it made them better leaders. The two stopped and held their hands up; Marion moved to the front. Patrick led Marion forward and pointed through the bushes at the camp.

Marion nodded, patted Patrick on the shoulder, and returned to the group. Jacob contained his smile, seeing how Patrick was taller than Marion. When Marion returned, he pointed in the two directions; Major James nodded and led his company while Jacob turned and motioned for his band to follow him.

Though it seemed the Loyalists were not paying any attention to the woods, Jacob moved slowly but carefully to avoid making noise. As the sun set, the long shadows concealed them like wraiths as they stalked around the camp. The wolves kept looking in the direction of the camp, sniffing the air and the multitudes of scents coming from that direction.

Jacob halted his column at the edge of the Tearcoat Swamp and where the Black River joined the swamp. He motioned for everyone to slowly settle down into sitting positions, their eyes toward the camp. The sun had set and darkness covered the land, the cold beginning to settle on their shoulders.

Quietly, Jacob moved along the line and had his men put on their blanket coats; he had them all made to keep warm. Even he pulled out his trusty fur-lined hat instead of his old helmet. Leather did not help in the cold in keeping warm. Then, knowing they had a few hours to wait, Jacob went to his band, had them group into four men while two sleep while the other two watched.

Jacob remained awake, watching over his men while they waited to attack. Through the trees, he could see the glow of the fires that must have grown bigger into bonfires to warm the Loyalists. He could hear the laughter and the singing coming from the camp. Shaking his head, Jacob was amazed these Loyalists were not following any common sense to being safe unless they felt secure and controlled the territory. Jacob knew they were about to get a hard lesson.

As it was approaching midnight, Jacob had all his men wake up and stand up to get the blood flowing in their limbs, fighting the cold. Through the trees, it sounded like a card game was being played.

"Hurrah! At him again, ah damn!" A voice could be heard bouncing from the trees. "Now, Aye, that's a dandy! My trick by God!"

Jacob shook his head and brought his men online. Then, sensing it was about time to attack, he slowly advanced until they could see the bonfires through the leaves. Jacob and his men remained in the darkness.

"Don't look into the fires," Jacob whispered, "You'll be blinded."

"Ka-Pow!" The sound of the pistol echoed amongst the trees in the darkness.

At that moment, the adrenalin rushed as Jacob led his band forward in a charge. Their pent-up energy, being quiet for so long, was allowed to explode out and they gave a blood-curling war cry as they burst from the trees just as a few Loyalists were up and were looking in the direction of Marion's shot.

"Fire!" Jacob commanded. The band halted, brought their muskets and rifles up, and fired into the rising mass of awakened Loyalists. Then, using the light provided by the bonfire, Jacob aimed at a group of officers sitting in the middle of the camp, who had to be the card players.

Spotting his target, Jacob pulled the trigger and the rifle barked. One of the officers toppled over with his playing cards flying from his hand. Major James and McCottry's riflemen opened fire from their side as Marion and his group came crashing through their side of the woods.

The Loyalists just sprung up from where they were sleeping and, seeing the force attacking them and caught in the shock of the attack, took off and sprinted into the swamp. None stood to fight, while James, with McCottry's men, chased them to the swamp's edge, firing at the running Loyalists while yelling and cussing them.

After loading his rifle, Jacob motioned for his band to follow him as they swept through the camp, looking for any prisoners. The wounded Loyalists were secured, ensuring they had nothing on them to be used as a weapon. Jacob went over to where the officers had been playing cards.

He found the man he shot, the ball tearing through his head, exploding out the back. A second officer laid on his back, sightless eyes looking to the heavens. Jacob noticed he had the ace, deuce, and jack of clubs in his hand. The rest of the playing cards were scattered around the two dead men. Jacob continued their sweep until they met up with Marion. Once the camp was secure, they took stock of their victory.

"Sir, we found six dead Loyalists and captured fourteen wounded," Captain Witherspoon reported.

Marion nodded, "Our losses?"

Witherspoon smiled, "Not a one, not even a scratch!"

Marion smiled and Witherspoon returned to Major James. Then Captain Mitchel reported.

"Sir, we count eighty horses, their baggage, eighty stands of new British muskets with shot and powder and all of their rations."

Marion could not help but smile, and the others were smiling. Everyone moved with a bounce in their step. Though it was now early in the morning after a long day, the men showed pride in their efforts. This total victory would not only be a morale booster to his men but to the locals as well.

Once everything was secure, Marion led them back to their horses and they mounted their horses. "What am I to do with all of these prisoners?" Marion asked, looking at the numbers they had.

Looking up, he saw Jacob and Zacharia riding up. "Sir, Zacharia here suggests what we can do with the prisoners."

Marion laughed and shook his head before looking at Jacob. "I keep wondering if you can read minds, Jacob, but you are correct. I was thinking of what we were going to do."

Jacob smiled and nodded toward Zacharia. "Zacharia here says Hugh Graham could hold them until they can be transferred or paroled. We could even get supplies from Hugh."

Marion nodded, "Sounds like a good idea. Zacharia, you and Jacob will please lead us out and take us to the farm."

Zacharia smiled and nodded, "Glad to be of service, sir."

The column snaked through the countryside, ensuring the prisoners were guarded and could keep pace with the column. Jacob made sure they had advance guards, led by Frederick, as Zacharia led the column to Hugh's farm northwest of Kingstree.

It was toward early evening when Zacharia led the column into the farm of Hugh Graham, Hugh himself coming out of his house to see who had arrived, musket in hand.

Zacharia, Jacob and Marion approached Hugh on his porch. His eyes grew wide and a smile broke out across his face.

"Well, bless my soul, what a site to see! Colonel Marion, Captain Clarke and Zacharia, what brings you to my humble home?"

Zacharia smiled, "Good to see you, Hugh; the colonel here needs to drop off these prisoners and perhaps get some supplies from you if possible."

"Of course, of course," Hugh replied, "Stay as long as you need. I'll send one of my boys to fetch Colonel Giles with his militia to take charge of the prisoners. Then join me for dinner; my wife would be pleased to meet you all."

Jacob looked at Marion, who shrugged, then answered, "We would be pleased to join you for dinner after seeing to the men first."

"But of course, I understand, sir. We will have dinner ready and you can join us when you are ready." Hugh replied before heading into his house. Shortly, a boy of about twelve came out of the house. He was throwing a shooting bag over his shoulder and had a musket in his hand. Then, after mounting his horse, he took off to get the local militia commander.

Jacob saw to his men, then sent a small detail to help pack up some supplies from Hugh. Zacharia then joined him and they headed to Hugh's house, Marion joining them right after. They knocked0 and Hugh opened the door with a smile. "Please come in, sir, please come in!"

They sat at a simple meal laid out before them, Hugh's wife pleased to be providing for Marion with what they had. The meal was a simple stew, fresh crusty bread\ and a decent port to sip. Mrs. Graham had a lovely tea for Marion. But, of course, Hugh wanted to be caught up after he left the regiment to come back and take care of the farm.

Soon stories were being passed and laughter and cheer went around the table. Jacob admitted that it was good to see Marion enjoying himself, having been on the run from the British and leading this expedition against them. Once the meal was over, Marion thanked the host, and they returned to the men.

The following morning, Colonel Giles and his Lower Craven County Militia arrived to take charge of the prisoners. The wounded were paroled; Colonel Giles would lead them to a nearby town to be released, while the prisoners would be moved to a more secure area until their disposition could be determined.

Marion spoke with Giles for a short while before having the men mount up and return to their camp.

Once in the camp, the sun was creeping up and the cold morning breeze announcing its arrival blew through the camp. The men were still caught up in the victory, talking excitedly. Marion ensured all their new supplies and horses were distributed to those needing replacements.

"With more victories like this, we'll need a quartermaster!" With the other officers, Marion quipped, and Jacob chuckled in turn. It felt good; they were becoming a force to be reckoned with by the Loyalists or the British. Jacob began to believe that they were on the right path, the path to victory.

Word of their total victory spread through the Williamsburg Township, then out to the other towns of what happened at the Tearcoat. The only downside was Colonel Tynes did escape into the swamp and evaded capture.

A few days later, more volunteers joined Marion and the Williamsburg men. When questioned, some admitted that they had been with Tynes as a Loyalist as they thought it was the right thing to do. Now, they examined the Loyalist cause and even they admitted they didn't like how Major Wemyss had destroyed all of the homes. They confirmed he burned everyone's homes. No one was spared from any side.

While Jacob was not too sure about accepting these former Loyalists into their ranks, Marion allowed it though he did tell the captains to keep their trusted men watching these so-called new recruits until they proved themselves.

The word kept spreading about Marion and his men and soon people turned "Tearcoat" to "Turncoat" with the number of Loyalists that had switched sides. Jacob nodded; perhaps he was right and the tide was turning in their favor. Only time will tell.

CHAPTER 6

HALFWAY AND PROMOTIONS

Marion and his men were still riding the wave of victory, buoyed and motivated more than ever. Some of the new men who were former Loyalists began giving them information on where they thought their former commander might be running. Finally, the news was brought to Marion, who called for Jacob and Captain Snipes from Williamsburg.

When both arrived, Marion gave them specific instructions.

"Our newly joined recruits said they believe in good confidence that our illustrious Colonel Tynes is heading north toward the High Hills of the Santee. Therefore, as you have experience in that area, I want you to track him down there."

Nodding, Jacob selected a few men, including Samuel, the boys and the wolves, to be part of the expedition. "Lads, we're going hunting for Colonel Tynes. We have a good idea that he can be found in the High Hills, and that's where we're heading."

Excited to be on the go again, Samuel and the boys secured their gear and mounted their horses. Jacob led them over to where Captain Snipes and his section were waiting. The wolves trotted along, looking up at Jacob and the band.

"After you, Jacob, you know the area better than I do, so we'll follow," Snipes stated as he leaned forward, setting himself in his saddle. Jacob nodded, turned his horse, and led them from the camp and onto the road. Jacob led them to McCrea's Crossing and took a different northwest route.

The air was cool and brisk, the sky gray like lead. Jacob thought it almost looked like it would snow, though he doubted it would snow down there. "*Sure is cold enough to snow, I think,*" Jacob thought but focused on their task.

All wore warm clothes, their cloaks or blanket coats flapping in the breeze as the horses trotted along the road. Jacob took a hunting trail he and the Catawbas would use that headed north along the Santee but away from prying eyes and ears.

"You think they are heading toward Camden," Samuel asked and Jacob shrugged his shoulders.

"Would make sense," Jacob replied, "They have a garrison there and it would be a safe place to hide from us."

Jean nodded in agreement, "Seems to be more Loyalists coming out now that there is a garrison there. Would make sense he would seek shelter there."

"Should we stop at Old Tom's place?" Samuel asked, and Jacob nodded with a smile.

"Was thinking the same thing," Jacob answered. Old Tom was an associate of theirs, having served during the Anglo-Cherokee War, but time had finally caught up with him, though he still hunted. Moreover, he knew the area and would know if anyone came through.

After riding for a couple of hours, they came out of the trail and rode down a small road next to Old Tom's cabin. When they pulled up in front of the house, Old Tom came out and saw it was Jacob and Samuel.

"Ho there, boys! Out on a hunt, I see?" Old Tom asked, waving at Jacob.

"Aye, that's true, Old Tom. We're looking for some Loyalists that may have run through here."

Old Tom nodded. "I take it you boys gave them a whupping of a time? Word already reached us about that fight over at Turncoat. I take it you're chasing down some of those fellas that got away?"

Both Jacob and Samuel chuckled and nodded. "Aye, Tom, you have the gist of it. We're on the hunt for those who ran," answered Jacob.

Old Tom smiled and nodded. "Go look at the Robinson Meeting Place; I believe I heard they were there." He turned and Old Tom went back inside his cabin.

Jacob nodded, turned their horses, and led them down the road. "Can you trust him?" Captain Snipe asked, and both Jacob and Samuel nodded. That satisfied Captain Snipes, who followed along with Jacob and his men.

After a short ride, Jacob held up his hand as just around a bend was the Robinson Meeting Place, a long building where town meetings were held. Smoke rose from the chimneys and horses were tied to posts in front.

"We'll encircle the place, make sure no one escapes out a back door or window," Jacob commanded and then led them forward. Using his hands, he pointed to the left and right, and the men rode around both sides of the meeting house until it was surrounded. Jacob, Samuel, and Captain Snipes dismounted, and Patrick held their horses. Samuel carried his blunderbuss.

"In case they have second thoughts and want to make this difficult," was Samuel's justification, and Jacob just shrugged as he walked forward. Then, not even stopping to knock, Jacob pushed open the door, and the three of them entered the meeting room. Nine men were sitting and standing next to one of the fireplaces, who turned to see who had disturbed them.

"So sorry to intrude," Jacob stated as he advanced on the startled people, "You look like people we are searching for."

One man sprung up and ran to a back door, but as he was opening it, Jehu was standing there with a grin on his face. Samuel positioned himself in the center of the room and the click of his blunderbuss caught everyone's attention.

The men had crestfallen looks, accepting that they were now captured—all but one man who began to bluster.

"How dare you, sir! Under what authority do you disturb us good and loyal subjects?"

Jacob walked up and stared down the blustering man, his cold blue eyes staring intensely into the eyes of the other.

"Under my authority and that of the governor," Jacob growled, and the man backed down. "Who are you?"

"I'm the local Justice of the Peace!" he shot back and Jacob did not seem to be affected or cared.

Jacob's wolf Waya padded in, nose to the ground and approached one of the men huddled in front of the fire, wrapped in a blanket. Captain Snipes walked up and looked down at the man as Waya gave a low growl. The man's eyes were throwing daggers at both Waya and Captain Snipes.

"I think Captain Clarke, you are correct. One of those we are looking for is sitting right here," Captain Snipes indicated to the man sitting next to the fire. His blanket fell off; he only had a shirt and bare feet. Numerous scratches crisscrossed his legs from running through the swamp.

Jacob turned and approached the man indicated. He stared back defiantly, which was all Jacob needed.

"Tynes, I presume?" Jacob asked.

"That's Colonel Tynes to you!" he shot back, and Jacob shook his head.

"No, it does not. You are all coming with us to answer for your crimes against the good people of South Carolina."

Jehu waved and the rest came through the back door and helped to move the prisoners outside, including the wolves. First, the band tied the prisoners' hands together and then sat them on horses where they could control them. Once all were ready, Jacob and Captain Snipes led the men back and brought the prisoners before Marion.

They had hit the jackpot, along with a very Loyalist-leaning Justice of the Peace. But, in addition, they had Colonel Tynes and seven more Loyalists, making it difficult for them to operate in the High Hills. Nevertheless, Marion was very pleased; everything was coming together.

***

Colonel Turnbull was not pleased; everything was falling apart. First, he had received the report about Ferguson's death up at King's Mountain but now he had just learned of Colonel Tynes's camp being overrun and that he, along with some good Loyalists, had been captured by these damn rebel Banditi.

"How dare these rebels do this! Of all places, within my command!" Turnbull exclaimed as he looked at his report and began to pace the room again. "What is that bloody rebel's name?" he asked his lieutenant, who answered, "Marion, sir, we believe we have information that it's a rebel named Marion, along with some others."

Turnbull stopped and looked at his lieutenant, "Others? What do you mean by others?"

The lieutenant looked at a few documents in his hand before answering. "We believe one is a Major James who made an issue with the Georgetown Commander who tried to hang him."

He then paused and read some more documents while Colonel Turnbull waited impatiently. "Well? Out with it, man!"

"We believe one of the other rebels who may be riding with this Marion is the Wolf."

Colonel Turnbull looked at his lieutenant as if he had lost his mind. "Wolf? Is that a name or what?"

The lieutenant shrugged. "We questioned some of the Catawbas who said it was the Wolf, known for fighting the Cherokee for the British. A man who cannot die, who can walk a Cherokee gauntlet and survive, spitting blood in defiance. They say that is why the Cherokee will not support us. The Wolf will hunt them down."

Colonel Turnbull scoffed and waved his hands at the information. "Nonsense, superstitions and pure nonsense. These rebel supporters are just telling stories to scare us." He stopped, placed his hands behind his back, and thought.

"Send for Colonel Tarleton then. If we have this Marion and the Wolf to contend with, we'll meet them with our dragoons and legion."

As Colonel Turnbull waited for Tarleton to arrive, he continued to read reports of how more districts that were supposed to be under their control were slipping away and becoming supportive of the rebels. As a result, he became concerned and challenged the allegiance of these Loyalists serving under his command.

A cold, driving rain was beating against the windows of Colonel Turnbull's headquarters when the door opened, allowing a cold blast of wind to enter the room, flickering the candles. Colonel Tarleton closed the door, took off his dragoon helmet, placed it under his left arm and approached Colonel Turnbull.

Stomping his feet together and giving a half bow as required by ceremony, "Sir, Colonel Tarleton reporting as ordered!"

Colonel Turnbull returned the salute and motioned for Tarleton to join him at a side table where a map was laid out. Tarleton bent forward to look, trying to keep the dripping rainwater from splashing on the map.

"Colonel, I have a specific task for you. I need your unique skills and aptitude." Turnbull began, and Tarleton nodded.

"I am at your service, sir."

Nodding, Turnbull pointed to the map region between King's Tree and Georgetown. "I am sure you know we have a growing problem here. These damn rebels dare to attack and capture good Loyalists and turn the locals against their King. So my task is simple, ride this Marion and so-called Wolf down and stop this foolishness in this region."

Tarleton cocked an eyebrow, "Wolf, sir?"

Turnbull waved his hand. "Never mind, go after this, Marion and stop this threat. His lordship is very concerned; if we can't control the interior, he won't be able to launch our offensive into North Carolina."

"I understand, sir," Tarleton answered, "I have to refit some of my men but will ride as soon as we're ready."

"When will that be?" Turnbull asked, and Tarleton replied, "In a day or so, sir."

"Good, good. See to it then, colonel; best of luck!"

Tarleton bowed in salute, turned, opened the door after placing his helmet on, and returned to the rainy night. He walked across the town square, his boots splashing in the small puddles, and entered the Tavern where he was staying.

After entering, he shook the rainwater from his cloak, went over to a chair set before the fire, where he hung his cloak to dry, and joined his officers sitting before the fire. One of them passed him a mug of mulled wine.

"What is the word?" Lieutenant Hovenden asked after handing the mug to Tarleton.

"His lordship General Cornwallis is concerned about the rebel activity in the area, and Colonel Turnbull wants us to chase down one of these rebel leaders. One is named Marion, and for some odd reason, he mentioned one as the Wolf."

The men chuckled, "The Wolf, we heard of this Sumter called the Gamecock; how odd nicknames!"

The lieutenant nodded, as well as the gathered officers. "How long will it take to reconstitute our men and horses before we can ride?"

The lieutenant stated, "From what the quartermaster told me, two days as he is waiting on a shipment from Charles Town for tack. We can ride then after the tack is fixed."

"Well then, I suggest we rest up, as we'll be busy chasing this Marion and his Wolf for the next couple of days."

Tarleton took a drink from his mulled wine, making a joyful sound and allowing the warm wine to warm his stomach.

"How shall we search for this rebel?" Captain Kelley asked. Tarleton shrugged and smiled.

"Easily. We will not go to this Marion; we will make him come to us. When he does, we bag him and the lot of them. Easy as pie. We will just set up a trap and wait for our game to arrive. "

Close by, a serving girl was gathering up empty tankards and cleaning tables, but she kept her ears open and remembered everything she had heard. Later that night, when she was done with work, she headed to Goose Creek and passed the message to Andrew Hoskins to take to Marion.

***

When he arrived, Marion surprisingly took the news well from Andrew and told them of the trap set by Tarleton.

"I should be honored that I warrant special attention by this Tarleton to come after me. I did hear he went after Sumter and gave him a good thrashing."

When Andrew repeated what the serving girl said, including the name "Wolf," it concerned him. Marion looked at Jacob, "What's on your mind?"

"Sounds like I am making a name for myself, but likely they don't know my true name yet. My concern is for my family if they know who I am." Jacob explained, and Marion nodded as he understood the risk, as it seemed the British always retaliated with fire and swords.

"So, how do we deal with this, Tarleton?" Jacob asked and Marion replied, "When you know you're going into a trap, well, build a trap of your own."

Jacob nodded, "Ah yes, ambush the ambushers, as Rogers used to tell us."

When the day arrived, that Tarleton was supposed to ride, Marion gathered his militia and rode out to face Tarleton. Jacob's band, Major James, his group and some of McCottry's riflemen were with Marion. Using trails and less traveled roads, they avoided the main roads to remain undetected and headed in the general direction of the route Tarleton would take.

***

Big Harpe, Little Harpe and the three surviving men from his group of Bandits rode in one of the Legion's troops under Tarleton. After returning from King's Mountain, it had worked out well for them that they were not the only survivors to have arrived and no questions were asked about how they escaped.

They had been assigned to this Tarleton's Legion, for they were supposed to know the area. So, they rode to get this Marion fellow and there was also talk about another called the Wolf. Big Harpe and his brother had been allowed to loot and pillage in the area, justified as punishing these rebel supporters and it sat well with him. So, this Wolf fellow also piqued his interest.

Tarleton had decided to set a trap by attacking a local farmer and see if that would draw out this Marion. He sent the troop that Big and Little Harpe rode with, with orders to make as much noise and cause as much destruction to draw this rebel out. He would set an ambush further down the road.

Captain Kelley, who led the troop, gave the command and they rode into the farm they would use for the bait. They dismounted and began chasing the family out of the house, smashing the equipment and lighting fires around the farm.

Big Harpe carried a torch, the light from the burning stack of hay giving his heavily scarred face a more demonic look. But that glow was in his eyes, that desire to kill was rising, and his brother knew it was best to stay out of the way. The farm was large, prosperous and had many outbuildings. The landowner protested and stated they were loyal subjects to the King but Captain Kelley had his orders.

Big Harpe moved toward the slave quarters, the legion men gathering the slaves and leading them out.

"You there," a sergeant yelled at Big Harpe, "Go check those buildings down on the end, make sure all these slaves are rounded up!"

Waving he understood his instructions, Big Harpe moved off and began to search the buildings. The first two were empty and the next one had three male slaves were found hiding. Big Harpe directed his brother to take them to the front of the farm. Finally, Big Harpe hit pay dirt in the last building, a lone female slave.

"Well, now, what's this here?" Harpe said aloud, the fear in the girl's eyes fueling his sadistic need to kill. He fed off her fear; he placed the torch on the ground and advanced on the girl. His hands quivered in anticipation as the girl backed up in fear into a corner of the shack.

She began to stammer in a mix of English and her tribal tongue, Harpe hearing words like "monster" and "demon." This suited him fine, adding fuel to his fire. Slowly placing his hands around her neck, Big Harpe began to squeeze as the girl clawed at his fingers and tried to scream.

"Ah, don't do that," he said in a near whisper. "No one is going to hear you scream."

***

The burning of the farms reached Marion and his anger rose. Then, thanking the messenger, he turned and headed to where the men were camped.

"To arms, lads, to arms! Tarleton has struck, he is burning farms and we're going to stop it right now!"

The men scrambled for their gear and mounted up on their horses. Once all were on their horses, Marion waved them on and they trotted out of camp. They followed their practice of staying off the main roads and used the game and hunting trails to get over to the area where the reported burnings were happening.

Jacob began to feel his instincts kick in; something was not right. This was confirmed by all things when a young man came running out of the woods. He nearly collided with Marion on his horse. Marion pulled up on the reins and his horse came to a skidding halt. The young man bent over, breathing heavily, then looked up at Marion.

"Don't…go…it's a…trap," the boy said between deep breaths. "Saw…men…hiding…in the woods…just off the road. Men in green."

Jacob rode up and heard what the young man was saying. "Thought so. My gut was telling me something wasn't right. He is burning homes as Wemyss did, so you would get angry and ride out."

Marion, familiar with Jacob's gut for telling him something was afoot, respected it. But, with a frustrated look, Marion had to agree it had been a rash idea to charge off without knowing all the details. He looked over at Jacob.

"Could you please confirm?" Marion asked, and Jacob nodded. Then, turning his horse, Jacob rode back, gathered his band and led them through the woods.

"Keep your eyes open," Jacob yelled to his men, "Maybe an ambush up ahead."

All his men set severe looks on their faces and began scanning the woods around them as they trotted. Jacob led them on a circular route away from their trail and the area's road to see what they could spot. Finally, they crossed the main road and caught nothing; Jacob kept moving them in a circular route.

Soon, the smell of smoke was very distinct and through the trees, they could see fires burning in the field and some of the outbuildings were on fire. Turning his horse, Jacob led them toward the farm to investigate. They stopped and dismounted,

Richard and Patrick holding the horses while Jacob and the others spread out and swept through.

It appeared they were too late that this Tarleton and his men had already been there. The fields full of fall harvest were on fire, hay and corn burning and many of the outbuildings burning. As Jacob passed a small slave quarter, his senses screamed and went into overload and for some reason, he ducked.

"Kapow!" thundered as a pistol went off just to his side, followed by a thunderous roar of "You!" Jacob felt the impact of someone large hitting him, knocking him down and causing him to lose his rifle. Rolling, so the large man rolled over and off him, Jacob drew his tomahawk and rolled to his feet.

Standing before Jacob was a visage of the past, the scared demonic face of Big Harpe. Having fired his pistol, he dropped it and drew his long, wicked knife from its sheath.

"I've been waiting for you!" Harpe yelled, "I still owe you for Quebec, you bastard! You ruined all of my fun!"

Jacob stood in shock for a second, recognizing the face that was heavily scarred, scarred from the very tomahawk he carried. The one that nearly choked him to death all of those years ago. As Harpe charged forward with his knife held low, Jacob quickly dropped into a fighting stance, raising his tomahawk and pulling his fighting knife.

"Let's finish this, you cowardly murderer! Let's see how you fare this time against a real fighter and not a defenseless girl!" He clanged his knife and tomahawk together, before settling into a fighting stance.

With a roar, Harpe took a stab and swung at Jacob, who knocked the knife away with his tomahawk. Jacob followed through with a swipe and jab with his fighting knife and Harpe ducked and shifted away. The two circled one another, oblivious to the fighting around them.

When Harpe fired on Jacob, Samuel, on the other side of the huts, saw the Legion men come around the corner and fired his blunderbuss. At that point, a running fight began between Jacob's band and the Legion.

As the firing occurred, all around them was the clang of a knife on a tomahawk. Harpe and Jacob struck and parried one another. Finally, Harpe took a heavy swing at Jacob, who ducked under it and scored with his tomahawk, catching Harpe across the brow and knocking his helmet off. Enraged, Harpe came back swinging as the blood began to cover his eyes.

"Where are you?" Harpe roared as Jacob continued to bob and weave around Harpe, parrying another strike and slicing his arm with his knife. Jacob had learned his lesson, to stay out of reach of Harpe's hands. He was going to whittle him down to a size that would be manageable. Jacob could also see that the wound over his eyes was making it hard for Harpe to see. He would have to be patient for the right moment to finish it.

Unfortunately, as fate would have it, more Legion men were coming around the farm and outer buildings and Jacob's men were becoming outnumbered.

"Jacob, Jacob!" Samuel was yelling. "Damn it all; we have to go!"

Jean ran up and quickly fired at an approaching Loyalist before he could get a shot off at Jacob.

Quickly assessing the situation, Jacob could see his men were falling back, and the situation was collapsing around him. He had to withdraw.

The Legion was coming closer. Timing his strike just so, he caught Harpe in the gut with the back of his tomahawk, momentarily knocking the wind out of him.

That was all Jacob needed; turning, he took off in a run, Jean, and Samuel covering while the others ran with him back through the woods and to their waiting horses.

"I'll get you yet, you bastard!" Harpe yelled after Jacob, "I'll get you yet! I'll tear your heart out and eat it!"

Big Harpe stood there, seething, blood dripping down his face following the texture of his facial scars. He stared at the retreating forms of Jacob and the others, glaring as the flames from the burning buildings wrapped his visage in a hellish color.

"I'll get you yet!"

***

Tarleton was livid that all his best-laid plans had fallen apart, unable to bag Marion and his group of fighters. He paced back in forth, hands clasped behind his back as he thought of appropriate action. His officers waited, watching him walk back and forth.

With a quick nod, Tarleton made up his mind. "We'll follow in Major Wemyss's footsteps, as these locals appear to support these rebels and allow them to evade our capture. Therefore, they are all guilty of sedition and will be punished!"

Tarleton stopped and faced his assembled officers, who quickly stood rigidly at attention.

"We shall break up the command. Each of our troops, supported by the Legion infantry, will sweep the parish up to the High Hills of the Santee. You will secure all, and I mean all, livestock and any items that can be used to support the rebels. Then burn their houses, as they are now forfeit. Perhaps this will draw out this Marion and his men."

The troop leaders nodded their understanding and returned to their commands to prepare their campaign. Tarleton's Legion broke out and spread out like the claws on a hand and began punishing the locals starting at Jack's Creek. Every farm to every plantation was looted and burned, and their occupants were sent out with what they had to make their way southward toward Charles Town.

Tarleton led a section of his troop and road into the front yard of the home of Widow Richardson, wife of the former General Richard Richardson, who had served South Carolina during the Anglo-Cherokee War. The horsemen arrived and spread out around the farmyard while Tarleton made his way up the steps to the front door.

Turning, Tarleton watched his men move about the farm, searching the barns and outer houses. Then, smiling, he turned and knocked on the door. After a short wait, the door opened and a servant stood there.

"Yes sir?" she asked, but Tarleton only smiled and pushed his way in, followed by a few of his men.

"Is the Widow Richardson about?" he asked, and the servant nodded her head.

"Yes sir, Mrs. Richardson is out in the cook house."

Continuing to smile, Tarleton continued, "Ah, that's good, as my men and I are hungry. So, make us dinner right away!"

The servant just stood there, mouth a gapped. "Sir?"

"Didn't you understand?" Tarleton asked, "Make us dinner." He pointed to the back door, then made his way to the dining table and took a seat at the head of the table, where he kicked his boots up and crossed his ankles. The servant was still standing there with an open mouth, still shocked at what he had asked for.

"Move, you bloody fool! Make us a meal fit for a King!"

The servant darted out while some of the men sat with him, while the rest began to go through the house, looting items. A distinguished-looking woman entered the house only a short time later, followed by the servant girl.

"What is the meaning of this?" Mrs. Richardson demanded, and Tarleton shook his head.

"I never thought the colonials here would be so uneducated. The meaning of this, dear woman, is we want a meal, and we want it now. So, get your servants going and make us a meal, or we'll burn this house down."

Then Tarleton looked directly at her and commanded, "Sit."

Maintaining her dignity, Mrs. Richardson gave orders to the servant, who nodded, then headed out the back of the house while taking an empty chair at the table. Tarleton and his men watched as she tried to maintain her calm and collective outer appearance.

"Our servants are seeing to your meal, sir."

Tarleton smiled and nodded. "See, it wasn't so difficult after all. However, we are rather parched from the ride. Could you call for something for us to drink, perhaps?"

"Betsy!" Mrs. Richardson called out, and a different serving girl arrived.

"These gentlemen are thirsty; please go fetch a couple of bottles of the port from the cellar if you please."

The servant nodded and did a short curtsy while staring at Tarleton and his men before heading off to get the bottles. Mrs. Richardson folded her hands in her lap as she stared at Tarleton. "I expect this is more than a social call, as you don't appear to be refined enough to be social."

Tarleton chuckled, shrugging off the barb. "You are correct, madam; I am here because we know you are helping these rebel scum and Bandits attack good King's men and citizens."

He leveled his gaze at Mrs. Richardson, "While I may not be refined as you state, madam, I do not associate with rebels and Banditti. By the King's Law, you are no better than a criminal. Your land and property forfeit and whether you live, or die shall be weighed."

Her gaze never faltered as she stared back at Tarleton, "Who will judge me?" she asked. "You? Are you a good King's man who drives good people from their homes, burns their property, and takes their livelihood? Would it not be simpler to either shoot them or hack them down with your swords, put them out of their misery quickly?"

Tarleton just shrugged, "That remains to be seen."

Betsy arrived with a tray with four bottles of wine and glasses and passed them out to Tarleton and his men. The wine was poured, toasts made to King George, and everything else they could think of. After the bottles were drunk, Betsy was sent for more.

Then the food began arriving, Tarleton and his men began to eat while Mrs. Richardson was forced to sit there and watch, with nothing before her. As they had been in the saddle for a few days, the men ate everything that was placed before them, and nothing was left.

Tarleton was sitting back in his chair, rubbing his full belly, when one of his troopers entered the house and whispered in his ear. Tarleton smiled, chuckled and nodded his head. He then looked at his men around the table and nodded.

They pushed back their chairs and began to stand up, content with the food and drink they had just received. Placing his helmet back on, Tarleton motioned for Mrs. Richardson to stand and join him. He escorted her out the front door.

"We thank you for the wonderful meal and drink you provided to my men and me."

Mrs. Richardson nodded as she followed Tarleton out the door, with his men following her. On her front porch, Tarleton stopped and observed what was happening in the yard while she was inside.

Tarleton's men finished herding all the farm animals and livestock into the barn, then shutting the door. She looked in horror as troopers with torches came before Tarleton.

"All of the livestock is secured inside, sir," the trooper stated, and Tarleton nodded.

"See to your duties then."

The trooper nodded, then motioned with the torch. The soldier and the other torchbearers moved around the barn and set it ablaze. The flames began to race up along the sides of the barn, starting at the corners and moving to join with the other fires. The bleats and cries of the animals from the barn began to rise.

Mrs. Richardson stared in disbelief as the barn with all of their livestock burned with a thick, black column of smoke pointing like a black finger of death into the air. Then she looked around the rest of her yard and nearly fainted when she saw her husband's grave had been dug up and they were sitting next to his grave marker, the rotting remains of General Richardson were sitting, his arm resting on top of the stone.

She collapsed to her knees, seeing the disgraceful act Tarleton's troopers had done. She looked up at Tarleton, who seemed to have only a smirk on his face.

"You are a monster!" she whispered in anger.

Tarleton looked down at her in contempt. "Be happy I am not putting your home to the torch. Let this be a lesson to what happens to those who aid these rebels."

Tarleton and his men stepped off the porch and headed to their horses, "Order the men to mount!" Tarleton commanded. The Legion troopers made for their horses and quickly formed into their column.

Tarleton smiled and gave a short bow upon his horse. The barn was now fully engulfed in flames and black smoke, the odd smell of death, burned flesh and cooking meat on the wind. Then, raising his hand, Tarleton led his horsemen at a trot out of the yard and back onto the road.

Mrs. Richardson sat there on her porch in shock as her barn snapped and the flames rose higher. Betsy and the other servants stood around her, trying to comfort her as they watched the destruction.

Her eyes hard as flint, Mrs. Richardson stared at the collapsing barn, now turning into a flaming pile of timbers. She was breathing deeply, anger coursing through her veins. Looking over at her husband's grave, some of her other servants reburied General Richardson.

"Betsy, go get my horse!" She commanded to Betsy as she stood up, a very determined look on her face. "I'll make you pay for this abuse and dishonor your bloody bastard!" She turned and headed into her house to change into her riding clothes.

***

Word did reach Marion about the Tarleton raid, the burning of homes and especially what happened to Mrs. Richardson. What angered Marion was the word about how they desecrated the grave of General Richardson, who Marion had known personally. Many of the men wanted to ride out and find Tarleton and make him pay but Marion though angry himself, knew better.

If they rode off in anger and were blind to what was around them, they would get most of his men killed and would serve no good. So, therefore, they played it smart and waited until the emotions settled before they did ride out and tried to bag Tarleton.

It was a massive game of cat and mouse, where both Marion and Tarleton were hunting one another, attempting to lure each other into ambushes. Loyalists would give information to Tarleton, Jacob's eyes and ears and other locals who did support Marion would warn them of Tarleton's traps. It became a stalemate.

Through their network of informants, Maria passed that Tarleton had been reassigned. He had been sent to the High Hills of the Santee to go after Sumter, who had returned. Marion also learned of his growing fame as the Swamp Fox and his trusty Wolf.

When Marion learned of the news, he smiled and nodded to Jacob. "The Swamp Fox and The Wolf, what a combination. You have a courageous woman there for your wife," he commented. "She is cut from the same cloth as you." Then he shook his head and looked at Jacob.

Jacob chuckled, "I would say cut from leather than cloth; she is tougher than you know."

Marion chuckled and nodded, "Aye, I believe you are correct."

With the pressure off from Tarleton, Marion began to focus on his campaign to take Georgetown, the most prominent British post in the area.

Marion sat in the middle of their camp on an old cracker box, Jacob, along with Jean, Major Peter Horry, and Captain Melton, sitting on an old log, a small fire before them with a small teakettle over it. Hovering behind Marion was Oscar, preparing a tin cup of tea.

"Lads, we need to take Georgetown and we need to take it soon," Marion commented. "We're getting low on vital supplies of salt, clothing, shot and powder for the men. Though we have been doing well with the supplies Jacob and his friends have provided, it won't sustain us for a long campaign."

Jacob and the other officers nodded in agreement, Peter Horry nodding to Jacob in thanks for what supplies that Otti and Peter had been provided. Jean gave Jacob a playful punch in the arm.

"The other key point of Georgetown," Marion continued, "Would be a massive morale crusher for the British and a massive morale boost for us. In addition, it could significantly impact our operations locally."

Again, Jacob and the other officers nodded in agreement. "Well, with officers like this, Wemyss and Tarleton supporting the Crown, they have been our best recruiters so far." Commented Major James and the others chuckled in agreement.

"Oui, that they are," Jean then looked at Jacob and Marion. "I mean no offense, my friends, but during the last war, when the British burned all of the towns in Canada, it swelled our ranks with volunteers. They wanted justice for their loss. It may work for us here, in this war."

Marion nodded, "Yes, Jean, you are right about that. However, we must do our best to keep the locals on our side and don't encourage them to support the British." Then Marion paused as Oscar handed him his tea.

"We'll move our camp toward White Bay. From there, we can make forays around Georgetown to assess the situation and take the fight to these Loyalists." Marion took a sip of his tea and nodded his thanks to Oscar.

"We'll depart in the morning; see to your men."

In the morning, with Jean and Samuel with the band, Jacob packed their gear and readied their horses, the wolves sitting and waiting expectantly. Having been told they were heading toward White Bay and their investment of Georgetown, the band was ready to get back into action.

As usual, Marion was ready, Oscar on his horse next to him as Jacob led his band up to form the column. Once everyone was ready, Marion waved his hand forward, and they began their trot out of the camp and onto a trail. They began to snake through the woods toward Georgetown. The wolves loped alongside, noses smelling the air, their eyes scanning the woods.

It was an uneventful trip to their new camp at White Bay, a junction between Black and Sampit Rivers. The camp was set up in a triangle, each band taking a leg of the triangle. The horses were picketed, the men set up their sleeping areas and the guards posted.

Marion allowed the men to settle in for the night and waited until the next morning until he issued orders for the day. Then, finally, the officers gathered at the center of the camp, where Marion had sketched in the ground of the general area. Once everyone was assembled, Marion began.

"We need to assess the local situation before focusing on investing Georgetown. Major Horry, you will scout the area along the Black River and determine enemy activity. Major James, you will scout toward White Plantation. Captain Melton, you will scout toward Sampit Road. Captain Clarke scout the area of Robert's ferry along the Black River. Determine the level of Loyalist activity."

He then looked at the assembled officers. "As we are just starting, I suggest avoiding contact with the enemy as much as possible. This is a scouting mission only. I need to gather information more than fight. That will come in due time."

The officers nodded their heads and then turned to head off to their respective commands. Jacob went to where the band was camped and Samuel had everyone ready as he usually would. Jean was standing with the wolves, waiting.

"Where are we off to?" Samuel asked.

"Lads, we're scouting Robert's Ferry up along the Black River. Marion wants us to gather information only, so no direct fighting unless we have to."

The men nodded and went over to mount up on their horses. No questions were asked and they understood their task. Samuel and the boys had already prepared Jacob's horse, so all he had to do was mount up. Jean had one-half of the band ready, with expectant looks on their faces. The wolves, along with the men, looked at Jacob in earnest. Jacob smiled, nodded and led the band out of the camp.

Jacob watched the area to their front\ and Samuel and the others watched the trees and fields as they trotted along the trail. Everyone had their rifles and muskets resting on their pommels, ready to snap into action. The leaves were changing into oranges and reds, reminding him of his days up in New York. Unfortunately, the seasons changed slower in South Carolina.

It was a brisk mid-November day but not as cool, requiring a blanket coat, at least not yet. The leaves fluttered down as the breeze blew through the trees, which helped to muffle the sound of the horses' hooves on the trail.

Riding with Jacob's band was Charles Dempsey, a local leading them to the ferry, riding next to Jacob. "Not much longer to the ferry," Charles commented, "there is a rise up ahead that is just above the ferry. A good place to dismount and move in for a closer look."

Jacob nodded, "Makes good sense to me."

"Do they use the ferry much?" Jean asked, and Charles nodded.

"Aye, that they do. Everyone from the British, the Loyalists and any trade from North Carolina and Georgetown use the ferry."

When they arrived at the rise, it was a balding hill next to the trail they were using. Charles led them off to the side and dismounted. The band followed suit, Jacob pointing out a couple of men to stay behind to secure the horses. Samuel, along with Jean, the boys and the wolves, crept with their muskets and rifles, following Jacob. Charles and Jacob led the way forward, moving at a crouch, even though puffy clouds kept the sunlight dull. Jacob wanted to conceal as much of their movement as they could.

Moving through the trees and brush, the band moved slowly and quietly as Charles led them to the edge of the high ground and the edge of the trees. Charles halted and went slowly to a knee. Jacob motioned for everyone to come up online slowly and sink to the ground. Samuel and Jean moved up and lay next to Jacob.

Before they were at the ferry itself, as Charles indicated, each side of the ferry had a small shack, then the supports and the thick rope that guided the flatboat ferry across the black river. Jacob pulled out his telescope and focused on the ferry.

On the far side of the river, Jacob only saw the shack but nothing more. On the nearshore, the ferry was docked and he could see a civilian sitting in a chair before a fire. It was close enough to the river that Jacob spotted a couple of fishing poles set up, their lines in the water. No other activity was observed.

"Form groups of fours, two up, two rest. Samuel, you and the boys watch our rear," Jacob whispered his command and the band crept to comply. The wolves lay down and watched, waiting to see what would happen. Jean protected their flank.

Jacob and his band spent the day watching the ferry and only really saw two crossings of what appeared to be trader wagons. Then a small troop of horsemen arrived, drawing Jacob's attention. They wore a green uniform top, similar to the Legion, but he observed a different helmet.

Jacob focused his telescope and saw it was a leather helmet, a tall front shield similar to the old 2nd South Carolina helmet, only taller. What drew his attention was they were wearing crescents on their helmets. Jacob tried to focus more, but from their distance, he could not make out any details on the crescents. However, they did have white plumes on the side of their helmets.

"Well, now," Jacob whispered, "We seem to have more new players in the game."

The horsemen crossed over on the ferry and trotted off toward Georgetown. The ferryman went back to check his fishing lines and not having any fish, threw them back into the river before taking his seat before the fire.

The sun started sinking when a large wagon came along the road. It stopped before the ferryman on their side. Jacob pulled out his telescope and saw it was a sizeable four-wheeled cargo wagon with a wagoner and a single redcoat soldier. They appear to have cargo in the back of the wagon. An idea began to take shape in his head quickly.

It seemed the wagon was going to sit for a short while. The wagoner and the ferryman started a conversation next to the fire. The soldier was heading for the tree line, more likely to relieve himself.

Jacob quickly called in his band. "We have an opportunity here," he began, "we can secure some supplies for our camp. Charles, get our men with the horses and have them come to the ferry. We'll quickly strike, secure the supplies and get out of here."

"What about the rule that Marion said, no engagement?" Samuel asked.

"I saw only one redcoat in the tree line at the moment. The waggoner and the ferryman appear to be sitting around a fire with a bottle. Just detain them, we'll secure the cargo, and then we ride. No fighting."

Samuel nodded in understanding, and Jacob smiled with an evil grin. "Samuel, go secure the wagon and the two civilians; I'll take care of our redcoat. Jean, watch our flanks with the rest of the band."

Samuel and Jean nodded, and Jacob motioned for the band to follow him. Then, looking over his shoulders at the wolves watching him, he motioned them to follow. Jacob moved silently through the brush and trees inside the tree line and headed down the hill. The wolves moved like ghosts next to him.

They saw a flash of red through the trees and heard a man whistling to himself, along with the sound of water hitting the ground. Jacob smiled wickedly and motioned for the wolves to move toward the soldier.

The soldier was finishing buttoning up the drop fly of his breaches, his musket leaning up against a tree a few feet away, when he heard the low growls of four wolves. He froze and slowly looked up at the four wolves who were growling, their hair bristling, staring at him with their golden eyes. He began to tremble, not knowing what to do.

"I wouldn't move if I were you," Jacob stated as he came around the backside of the tree nonchalantly and approached the British soldier. He walked around and secured the leaning musket and motioned for the soldier to accompany him as the wolves closed in around the soldier, still growling. He placed his finger on his lips, "No sound."

When Jacob arrived at the ferry, Samuel had the ferryman and the wagoner under control and being guarded. The rest of the band was securing the cargo from inside the wagon. Jacob motioned for the British soldier to drop his cartridge box, bayonet, haversack, and canteen. Richard secured the items with a mischievous smile while the wolves stared and growled at the three men.

Charles and the rest of the band arrived with the horses. The men quickly began loading the foodstuff, uniforms and powder supplies onto their horses. The wolves sat but still kept the three men in their gaze. Finally, Jacob walked up to the wagoner.

"What's your story," he asked, "Are you contracted, or are you a Loyalist?"

The man shook his head, "Ah, no sir, just trying to make my way through this with my hide attached, just doing a job."

"So, you're doing this for the coin and not out of love for King and country?" Jacob asked.

"That's the bloody truth of it there; I need the coin for my family," the wagoner responded, and Jacob nodded. Then he looked at the ferryman.

"And you?"

He just looked dejected at Jacob and shrugged, "Just business. I care nothing for who is on what side or whatever you all call it. I need business like anyone else and the coin."

Jacob nodded and then looked at the British soldier, who just looked back at Jacob with a mournful look.

"Guess you are going to kill me. That's what I have been told when you bloody rebels catch any of us, so get it over with and be done with it." Jacob motioned for Jean to stay with the men and keep an eye on them.

Jacob looked at the soldier once more, then turned to head over to where Samuel was supervising the loading of the horses.

"That's it," Samuel commented with a smile, "Do we take the wagon or destroy it?"

Jacob shook his head, "No, we'll take the supplies and leave them be. We need to get the message out were not murderers like they are trying to make us out to be."

Samuel nodded and then headed to his horse, "Mount up!"

Jacob mounted his horse and walked him to where the wolves were still watching the three men. "You're free to go." Jean smiled and trotted off to mount his horse that Richard was holding the reins for him.

The three men just looked at one another as Jacob whistled, and the wolves trotted off but looked over their shoulders at the three with disappointed looks on their faces.

"You're not going to kill us," the soldier stammered, and Jacob shook his head.

"Maybe later if you keep fighting us, but not today."

Jacob turned his horse and trotted off to join the band as the three men just stood there and watched them ride off with confused faces. Jacob and the others trotted back to their camp, avoiding locals to the best of their ability.

When they arrived back at the camp, Jacob could sense a change in the mood; a tense heaviness seemed to lay across everyone. After dismounting and getting the supplies to their acting quartermaster, Jacob made his way over to see Marion.

Oscar stopped him before he could see Marion.

"May not be a good time to see Master Marion now, Jacob," he stated quietly while looking over at a pacing Marion. Jacob could see he was fuming and deep in thought.

"What happened?" Jacob asked in a whisper.

"It's Gabriel," Oscar answered, he went out with Captain Melton, and they ran into some Loyalists near Colonel Alston's Plantation. Gabriel fell; we believed he may have been captured initially, but we now learned that Gabriel was brutally murdered."

Jacob's face became hard, "Murdered? How?"

Oscar thought for a moment before continuing. "We learned a mulatto named Sweat did it, not a normal Loyalist. Just walked up to him, placed the muzzle of his musket against his chest, and pulled the trigger."

Oscar had a horrified look as he explained what had happened. "Jacob, his clothes caught on fire; that's how close he was when he pulled the trigger. That's what a witness told us."

Jacob shook his head at the needless murder that would cause a rippling effect on the rest of Marion's men and those who knew his nephew Gabriel. They would want revenge, which could lead to more murders on both sides.

"Are there patrols out?" Jacob asked and Oscar nodded.

"Yes, sir, they are out looking for this group."

Jacob nodded, looked at Marion, and decided to leave him be. While he could understand what he was going through, Jacob was not sure he could help now other than support his mourning. So, he headed to his camp to take care of his horse and see to his gear.

The following morning, there was a camp disturbance and Jacob and his band went over to see what it was. In the center of the camp was a man's body tied over a horse. Marion yelled at the officer Jacob recognized as Captain Beene from the militia.

Major Horry was standing there and Jacob stood next to him. "What's the matter?" Jacob asked quietly, and Horry leaned over and explained the situation to Jacob.

"They found the man who murdered Gabriel; Sweat was his name. While they were bringing him back to camp here, Captain Beene decided to be judge, jury and executioner and shot Sweat in the head. I guess he wanted to spare Marion the trouble."

Jacob looked over at a furious Marion and shook his head. "Trouble? It seems Marion is rather livid at the moment."

Watching the situation unfold, a very upset Marion turned and pulling a pistol from his gear, placed it against the forehead of Captain Beene.

"Should I give you the same treatment for your violation? Based on the military code of conduct, you, sir, are guilty of murder, and in the military, that punishment is death! Should I administer that punishment here and now?" Marion spat, holding the pistol in a tight grip. He then lowered the pistol and looked at the assembled men who heard the commotion.

"Let me make this perfectly clear. We will abide by the rules of war! I will not tolerate or condone anyone under my command who violates the rules and the discipline required to be an officer in this Army. If not, then we are no better than those we are fighting. Do not forget that!"

Giving Captain Beene one last look, Marion spun on his heels and headed to his campsite. "I will see to your punishment later." The rest of the men broke up and headed back to their respective camps.

The opportunity to get revenge did arrive when Andrew Hoskins arrived in the camp with news. Once he finished speaking to Marion, Jacob and the other officers were called to the center of the base. Marion was still hurting from the loss of his nephew but was returning to normal.

"Gentlemen, the time for our taking the fight back to the British has just arrived," he began as he winked at Jacob, who realized who the actual source of information was.

"We just received word that a column of the 7th Regiment of Foot and the 64th with recruits are marching from Charles Town and heading toward Camden. We will catch them on the road and strike hard. Make them pay for how they are waging war on us!"

Jacob could see the underlining of Marion's plan was to get revenge for his nephew, but on his terms and to a more significant effect than just going after the Loyalists. Nevertheless, Marion continued with the plan.

"I am calling for all of the militia to turn out. Gather McCottry's Riflemen, plus all of our groups, to pursue and engage Major McLeroth, who is leading the column. Get the messengers out; I want the militia formed by noon!"

Jacob nodded, along with the other officers present, plus the messengers who took off for their horses to gather the militia. McCottry nodded to Jacob before heading for his men and Jacob ran to the band.

Samuel was waiting, along with Jean and Jehu, at their camp, expectant looks upon their faces. The boys looked over from around their lean-tos, the wolves poking their heads out.

"So, we're going out to make them pay. For the murder of Gabriel?" Samuel asked.

"Yes, we're heading out," Jacob replied, "and I think you're right. We're going to make them pay for what they did to Gabriel. See to your gear, get ready to ride; Marion is calling out everyone."

Samuel whistled, "Everyone? Like all of Williamsburg District, everyone?"

Jacob nodded, and Samuel smiled. "That's a good number of folks there!" Then an odd, almost savage look came across Samuel's face, something Jacob had not seen before as he rubbed his hands together. "We are bringing the hate on this one; we'll make those bastards pay!"

Even Jean smiled at the thought of getting even with the British for the murder of Gabriel.

Still, Jacob gave Samuel a look of concern, though he could understand how he felt from his experience on the prison hulks and how they all liked Gabriel and the loss hurt them all in one form or another. They also felt for Marion, raising their anger against the British.

Jacob checked his shooting bag; he was getting low on balls for his rifle along with powder. He would have to make every shot count. Looking over at his band, "How is everyone set for shot?" he called.

The men checked their bags and replied with either "six balls or ten balls," whatever amount they had. Jacob thought, "Samuel, redistribute if possible; see that everyone has at least five rounds per man."

Jacob rolled up his blanket coat and placed it behind his saddle as a cold December wind blew through the trees. Winter was coming soon, and Jacob knew you could never tell what kind of winter it would be. Every year it has been different. Some of the winters were mild from what he experienced up north but some gave the north a run for their money for cold temperatures.

Settling his shooting bag on his shoulder, he moved his haversack into a more comfortable position, then mounted on his horse. Jacob reached down and patted the horse's neck, who replied with a low grunt and shook his head. Then, looking up, he saw the rest of the band had mounted up, and the wolves were sitting, all watching him.

Smiling, Jacob just turned his horse, and the band followed him to the assembly area where Marion was sitting on his horse with Major Horry, James and Captain McCottry. Jacob rode up, his band stopping and waiting as he went to report to Marion.

Marion nodded to Jacob when he stopped next to him. "Sir, we're getting low on powder and shot. I recommend that after this fight, we try to recover what we can from the battlefield and any prisoners we take."

"Sound plan Captain Clarke, a very sound plan," Marion stated and then looked at the other officers. "How are you all set for powder and shot?"

"We have about thirty rounds per man," McCottry answered and Marion nodded.

"We are in about the same boat as Jacob here," Major James said, "About eight rounds per man and just enough powder as long as they don't overfill their pans or spill them."

Sighing, Marion nodded. They always ran low on shot, powder, food, and other supplies.

More of the militia arrived and Marion asked their commanders the same question on shot and powder. Jacob watched in amazement as the entire district's militia turned out as ordered. Roughly seven hundred men were gathered and

Jacob almost felt sorry for the British; many of these militiamen were looking to get back at the British because of the death of Gabriel.

Almost felt sorry.

When Marion was satisfied that all was present, he turned his horse and he led the column of militiamen on the main road, believing he could intercept the British somewhere above Nelson's Ferry. Jacob and his band stayed with McCottry's Riflemen as they rode through the large plume of dust that all of their horses were kicking up from the road.

Jacob knew there would be a lot of luck in catching the British. While they knew the area they were marching in, numerous other factors could slow or speed up the column enough that they could miss them on the road. Marion must have thought the same thing, halted the column, and followed a trail to a farm just off the road.

Jacob and McCottry rode in and joined Marion, who was speaking to the woman of the house. "Who lives here?" McCottry asked.

Mrs. Rose had been a faithful friend and supporter, seeing she lives on the main road here. She perhaps saw the column march by." When they arrived, Marion was already speaking to Mrs. Rose.

"Have you seen a column of British soldiers pass this way, heading north, perchance?" Marion asked.

Mrs. Rose shook her head slowly, "As much I would like to assist you sir, I cannot."

Marion gave her a stern look, "Why is that good lady?"

"Because, sir, it wouldn't be right. Major McLeroth was honorable and a gentleman. I would hate to see him harmed."

Marion pursed his lips, sighed and nodded his head. "I understand good lady, good day to you."

Marion turned, the officers, along with Jacob, following. Then, finally, he turned and waved his arm, leading the column north.

"We must be ready, for I feel they are just ahead of us," Marion stated, setting a determined look on his face.

"How is that sir," Major James asked, "She wouldn't say anything."

That's the point," Marion stated, "Major McLeroth and his men passed through here; it's the only way she could deem him honorable and gentlemanly. They are just ahead of us!"

Marion had the column pick up speed while sending Jacob and his band ahead to look for signs of the British column. Jacob and his band, kicking their horses into a gallop, and the wolves keeping pace, rode on. After a few minutes of riding hard, Jacob halted and quickly dismounted.

Throwing his reins to Jean, Jacob looked closely at the road's dirt. There were clear signs of footprints of many men who had marched through. Kneeling, Jacob felt the ground for the texture of the tracks and he could feel they were fresh and not weathered. They were just behind them.

Quickly mounting back on his horse, Jacob waved his band forward and continued down the main road connecting Charles Town with Camden. They were above Nelson's Ferry, heading toward Singleton's Mill near Halfway Swamp when Jacob spotted the British column. He quickly raised his fist, and the band came to a skidding halt.

Jacob had them back up into the tree line as the area was opening up into open fields. Then, pulling out his telescope, he focused on the British soldiers who appeared to be resting. He could pick out the men of the 64th and the 7th by their uniforms and a good number of recruits in civilian clothes.

Closing his telescope, Jacob looked at Jean, Jehu, William Lee and Primus Hall, "Stay with them, keep them in sight but stay back enough not to get detected." The four nodded their understanding; Jacob turned and led the band back to Marion at a gallop. It was not a long ride when they met with Marion, who led the column at a fast trot.

"They're just over the ridge," Jacob stated, standing in his stirrups and pointing behind him. "They are near the Singleton Mill on the Halfway Swamp. I left three men to watch them."

Marion smiled hard, "Good, let's get down to business then!"

With Jacob at his side, waving them forward, Marion continued to ride down the road at a good pace, eating up the distance. Finally, they were climbing the ridge where Jean and the other three were waiting. Looking down into the open field, Marion could see the rear of the British column snaking away.

"Yes, by God, we have them!" Marion exclaimed, "Officers to me!"

The command was passed back and the officers rode to the front. "We will strike them at the next field, where we should have the swamps and trees, and they will be in the open. Lieutenant Colonel Horry, you will move to the left, Major Horry and Major James to the right. Captain Clarke and Captain Mc-Cottry will stay in the center; you are to target their officers, gorgets, and epaulets."

Marion gave them all a look and they were ready. They nodded their heads, and Marion smiled. "Alright, let's see to it then. Follow me!"

Marion kicked his horse, taking off in a fast trot, the rest of the column following with the officers falling back to their men. It was only a short ride through the trees and swamps before the following open field appeared and there was the rear of the column. Pulling his pistol, Marion yelled out, "Charge!"

Lieutenant Colonel Hugh Horry led his column to the left and his men began to fire on the rear guard of the column.

Major Peter Horry led his column with Major James to the right and began to fire on the column's flank. Marion stopped with McCottry and Jacob, whose riflemen quickly dismounted and began picking off British soldiers of the rear guard and the column's tail end.

Under fire, Major McLeroth halted the column to defend itself against Marion's horsemen. The 7th Regiment, more to the rear, was turning to give fire against Lieutenant Colonel Horry's men. The 64th tried to organize themselves while half of the regiment attempted to control the panicking recruits. Finally, McLeroth had the column tighten its ranks and move toward a fenced-off field.

Bringing his rifle to his shoulder, Jacob took a good, slow, deliberate aim at an officer controlling the rear guard. Then, taking a slow, controlled breath, he pulled the trigger, and his rifle barked, the British officer being knocked back and crashing to the ground. McCottry and his riflemen were tearing up the rear guard, who finally broke and ran to where the British were forming a defensive square.

The riflemen and Jacob's band stayed within the tree line, taking slow and deliberate fire on the British. Mainly to conserve their shot and powder; the other reason was they had them boxed up, and they were not going anywhere.

"Pick your shots, lads," Jacob yelled, "Make them count!" Jacob reloaded his rifle, took a few slow breaths, then brought it up to his shoulder and braced it against a tree to stabilize it. Then, pulling back the hammer and looking down his sights, Jacob took a nice slow breath, sighted in on a British Sergeant in the distance, then let out his breath slowly and pulled the trigger.

The rifle barked and the sergeant in the distance fell to the ground. Then, slowly and deliberately, Jacob began to load his rifle. All along the tree line, Marion and the men were keeping up a withering yet sustained rate of fire against the boxed-up British and their recruits. While the British were firing back, it appeared to be hitting nothing but trees or air.

A short time later, the call of "cease fire" was sent down the line, followed by "Captain Clarke report to Marion."

Jacob made his way down the line, shrugging when both Jean and Samuel gave him a look of asking what was going on. Then, finally, Jacob arrived where Marion, Major James, and Lieutenant Colonel Horry were standing. In the distance, a British officer with a white flag was standing, and Jacob suspected why he was sent for.

"Captain Clarke, you will accompany Major James and me to see what they want. If this is a trap, Hugh, you will take command and do everything you can to wipe them out."

Marion made sure his gear was settled and his helmet was sitting properly before stepping off toward the British. Jacob and Major James flanked Marion, walking slightly behind, making a small wedge. They walked up to the officer holding the white flag, a Captain Kennedy. He took off his hat and bowed as required; Marion nodded.

"Sir, my commander Major McLeroth demands to know why you violate the laws of civilized warfare."

Marion looked at the officer, maintaining a stony expression on his face. "I see no violations of the law of war; what does the major mean?"

Captain Kennedy gave Marion a surprised look. "Sir, you fire on pickets instead of the main line of battle. This conflicts with the conduct of warfare. You fight from the shadows no better than a criminal instead of fighting in the open as brave and honorable men do."

Marion snorted and shook his head. "Brave and honorable, you say? That is a good laugh, sir. What happens when your officers, these Wemyss and Tarleton, burn good people out of their homes like brigands? Is this an honorable way of waging war? For every home you burn, I will shoot pickets!"

The British officer ground his teeth together before responding. "Then, sir, it is my duty to issue a challenge from the major to you."

Marion gave him a surprised look, "Challenge?"

"Yes sir," the captain continued, "He will take the field with twenty of his best marksmen, you sir are to take the field with our twenty best marksmen, and we'll settle this once and for all."

Marion gave a grin, "Accepted. We will meet your twenty at noon in that open field." He pointed to an open field at an angle from both the British and his position in the woods.

Captain Kennedy nodded, turned and returned to the British line. Marion, with Jacob and Major James, returned to their lines.

"Jacob, you and Captain McCottry will pick the twenty. Major Vanderhorst will lead you in this small action."

When they returned to their line, Jacob headed down to where his band and McCottry's men were waiting and told them what would happen.

"A duel? He wants a duel?" Jean asked and Jacob nodded. Jacob was to choose his ten best and McCottry would pick his ten best riflemen, and they would meet this challenge. So first, Jacob selected Samuel and Jean, then the seven other good riflemen he had in his band. McCottry had selected his ten and they formed their company of marksmen.

Major Vanderhorst made his way down to the waiting riflemen, coming up to Jacob and McCottry, "Are these the chosen men?" he asked with a smile, seeing the selected men were excellent and experienced riflemen.

"Yes sir, we are ready to face this challenge," Jacob responded and Major Vanderhorst nodded his head. Each man checked his rifle, its flint and the powder in the pan, ensuring everything was in order. When the time arrived, they formed into a single rank of twenty men, dressing their line once they formed outside of the trees.

Drawing his sword, Vanderhorst looked at the assembled riflemen, all with set and determined looks on their faces. Jacob was the first in the rank and Vanderhorst took his position next to him. Then, raising his sword, Vanderhorst commanded, "To the front, march!"

Jacob had to admit; it felt good being in the ranks again, a simple soldier following his orders and going out to meet his foe on the field. But, surprisingly, they stayed dressed and almost looked like parade-ground soldiers as they marched out into the open field.

With the rest of the men, Marion watched from the tree line as Vanderhorst led the chosen men out onto the field. On the far side, they could see the red uniformed soldiers of the selected British soldiers. While usually discouraged, some heavy betting was going on while waiting for the engagement to start.

The British came out with more fanfare with fife and drum playing as they advanced into the middle of the field. Their commander gave them ordered arms and they waited for the riflemen to arrive. The sun reflected off their buttons and the officer's gorget.

Jacob looked down the line of men, seeing Jean and Samuel, "Watch your dress," as he kept the rank shoulder to shoulder as they did their best to stay in step. Then Jacob shifted his gaze at the waiting British, their line standing firm in the open field. Vanderhorst judged the distance and decided to advance within a hundred yards from the British, the easy killing range of the rifles they carried.

As the riflemen closed within a hundred yards, they heard the British command of "Shoulder firelocks!" Then, in perfect sequence, the men took their muskets from order to up onto their shoulders. This was the first step in the firing sequence and Jacob began to brace from the coming volley automatically.

Instead, the British give the command of "Right about face. To the front, march!" The British line turned their backs to the riflemen and marched back toward the British line. Shocked and not knowing really what to do, Vanderhorst gave the order to halt.

Shrugging his shoulder, Vanderhorst commanded, "Three cheers for Marion!"

Jacob looked and Jean and Samuel, who shrugged, then the men took off their hats and held them high as they cheered, "Hip, Hip, Huzzah!" three times. Then Vanderhorst turned them around and marched them back to their lines and into the woods.

"Well, lads, you're released to your commands. Let's see what happens next." Vanderhorst stated, smiling before turning and reporting to Marion. McCottry, along with Jean and Samuel, joined Jacob and was soon followed by the boys.

"Well now, that was rather odd," McCottry commented, and they all agreed. "Have you ever seen that before?"

Jacob looked at Samuel and Jean and they shook their heads no. Then, shrugging, McCottry joined his company and Jacob pulled his band together. He set up a rotation plan where Jacob, Jean, and Samuel would keep a third of the band on the line watching the British while the rest ate some rations and got some sleep.

The day turned to night, and in the distance, they could see fires for the British being made, along with talking, joking, and singing. Jacob looked across the field as the darkness of night swept across. Marion instructed fires to be built, as they would spend the night here and see what the British would do in the morning.

"Have your men rest; redistribute what shot and powder you need to make sure we can resume the fight in the morning," Marion instructed as he stopped by their position, then continued back to the center of their line. Jacob still looked out across the inky blackness of the night; only the flickering glows of fires from the other side could be seen and the British singing was heard.

"What do you think?" Jean asked, with Samuel standing next to them, also looking out across the field.

"Doesn't seem right," Jacob stated, "This is not like them to sit there. They almost want us to sit here and watch them."

"Deception, they are a decoy?" Samuel asked and Jacob nodded slowly.

"Do you think they got a messenger out, and a large force is heading this way?" Jean followed up\ and again Jacob nodded slowly.

"We should be ready for some company," Jacob replied.

"When do you think they will attack?" Jean asked and Jacob smirked. Jean groaned as he knew what Jacob would reply with.

"Why in the morning, of course, just like you did back in the day."

Shaking his head, Jean shook his head. "No, mon ami, that was the French. I am Canadian, remember."

Jean stamped off, Samuel chuckling. Jacob went around the, checked on his men, and told them to be ready in the morning, just in case. He also told them band to watch the British fires and see what happens during the night.

As Jacob got some needed rest, the band continued to watch the British fires across the way. Finally, around midnight, the voices began to quiet, and the fires were dying down. They did hear some voices biding their comrades a "good night's sleep and watch out for the bugs." Jean, on watch, just observed as it sounded about right, with the camp going quiet at midnight and the fires dying down. For all purposes, it appeared they had settled in for the night.

The night passed and Jacob had his band up at stand-to just before the sun rose. Everyone watched the road, the field and over toward the British camp. It was quiet, and to Jacob's ear, it was too quiet. Then, finally, the sun rose fully, cleared the trees, and shined on the field, chasing the cold night air away.

Jacob had his men relax but stay ready while they chewed on biscuits and dried venison. As he expected, Marion arrived with Oscar right behind him.

"I think we have been played, Jacob," Marion stated, looking across the field at the British camp. "Would you and your band be so kind as scout out our British friends to see if these so-called honorable men are still there?"

Jacob nodded and called his band to him. "We're going across the field to scout out the British camp, see if they are still there. Jean will take the left. Samuel, you'll take the right."

Everyone nodded and then Jacob led them out onto the field. The band fanned out into open order with Jacob in the center. Once formed, Jacob waved them forward and they began a steady advance at a crouch toward the British camp.

Moving at a crouch, Jacob scanned with his ears and strained with his ears to hear anything. The wolves had moved ahead, sniffing the ground and following trails in the grass. They crossed the fence line and could see where the British defensive line was. Paper cartridges identified the three sides of the square firing from where they fell.

Jacob halted the line and bent down to look at the grass closely. Leaning on his rifle, he could see tracks in the grass from where the men moved and, with the accompanying blood trails, where the dead had fallen. Standing up, he motioned his band forward.

The smell of burnt wood reached Jacob, alerting him that he was closing in on the campsite. Scanning, he, along with the men in the band, saw no one. No sentries, no movement, and no voices. Jacob's suspicion of a decoy was proving to be true. Confirmation occurred when they arrived at the camp area where the remains of the fires could be found still smoldering.

Fanning out the band, they swept through the camp; and they only found the baggage and equipment left behind. The British had slipped away in the night. Sighing, Jacob halted the band and had them consolidate on him.

"Patrick, Richard, tell the colonel the British are on the run, probably heading north toward Camden."

The boys nodded and took off in a sprint toward where Marion was. Jacob turned to the band, "Secure the camping area, gather all the baggage and supplies, look for shot and powder and bring them here."

A short time later was a thunder of hooves as Hugh Horry and about a hundred of his horsemen galloped past in pursuit of the British. Marion rode up and dismounted in the camp as Jacob gathered the abandoned baggage. Marion came over and nodded at the pile of supplies being collected.

"They humbugged us again, didn't they?" Marion asked, and Jacob nodded. Marion snorted and chuckled, "They wanted to lecture me on being honorable, and then when they offer a duel. Then they run away again in the night."

Jacob shrugged his shoulders. "Sir, I hate to admit it, but if you were in his shoes, wouldn't you have done the same thing?"

Marion gave Jacob a dirty look and then sighed in acceptance. "Yes, you're bloody right Jacob, as usual. I would have done the same thing."

From the baggage, they found numerous helpful items. Clothing like shirts and waistcoats, some breaches and the much-needed shot and powder were found. However, for the Brown Bess muskets the British carried, Jacob knew he could break down their cartridges, save the powder, melt the lead balls and recast them with their molds.

Because he had a reasonable size force assembled, Marion decided to take the fight to the local area. He gave orders to Major James and Major Horry to block the Santee Road and close off water traffic on the Santee River. Marion was sending a message to the British and the Loyalists that they did not have freedom of movement.

Jacob and his band were sent back to Nelson Ferry to block traffic and see what trouble they could stir up. After arriving at the ferry, Jacob concealed the men and the horses and took up a watch to see if any British supply wagons or Loyalist horsemen crossed over. Jacob had split his men, Jean leading half of the band on the opposite side of the ferry.

"Boat approaching from the north," Zacharia called out and Jacob moved up to the edge of their concealment and, after pulling out his telescope, saw a schooner coming down the river.

"Must be coming from Camden," Jacob stated as he lowered his telescope, "We're going to have to convince the captain to pull into shore to be inspected."

"Well, I can use this," Samuel volunteered, tapping his trusty blunderbuss. Jacob smiled and nodded, "Well, that would get his attention." Samuel smiled in return, and they positioned themselves at the edge of the woods.

Jacob moved into the center of the road and waved to get Jean's attention. When Jean stepped out, Jacob pointed upriver at the approaching boat. Jean stepped out just enough to see the boat, stepped back and looked back at Jacob.

Jacob made the grabbing motion with his hands, then pointed at the boat; Jean nodded he understood Jacob's intent to take the vessel. He moved back and concealed himself with his group and they waited for the boat to get even with them at the ferry.

As luck would have it, the boat pulled into the ferry, and they called out for the ferryman. Jacob, Samuel and the others were waiting to see what would happen. Jean stepped out of the woods and waved at the river schooner. One of the crew members threw a rope and Jean tied it off to a post, securing the boat.

"Well now, isn't that rather polite of them for securing themselves, just for us," Samuel commented, then cocked his blunderbuss. They all looked at Jacob, who nodded and led them out of the woods. Then, running from the opposite side when they saw Jacob break from the woods, Jean and his men swarmed over the boat's bow and pointed their muskets and rifles at the crews.

Jacob and his men did the same, the boat captain seeing he had no choice, raised his hands, and the crew did the same. Jacob used the ferry to pull themselves across while Jean and his crew secured the boat and the crew. The captain and his men were taken off the ship. They were placed under guard next to the ferryman's hut.

"Secure everything that can be used, all supplies and cargo," Jacob ordered, even equipment we could sell or trade for supplies. Then, as the men went to work stripping the boat, Jacob went to where the captain sat with his crew with a sad look.

"Who were you carrying supplies for?" Jacob asked, and the captain looked up at Jacob and answered, "Colonel Balfour, the supplies were for his garrison at Georgetown. Guess he doesn't realize you rebels are in control here."

Jacob nodded, "Where did you depart from?"

"Camden, we had taken on the cargo at the depot in Camden, mostly foodstuff and supplies gathered from up there," the captain explained, then gave Jacob a questioning look.

"Are you going to kill us?"

Jacob shook his head. "Is that all they say about us, that we're killers and murderers? Do you know how many civilians have paid for the loss of their homes the British burned and looted? Yet, you all keep up this message we kill all of our captives. If that were the case, you would be dead."

The captain nodded, "I ply my trade; I try not to get caught up in politics and this fighting. Just trying to do business, and they were paying in gold."

Jacob nodded, "Winds of war are fickle, seems you chose the wrong side." Then, shrugging his shoulders, Jacob turned and returned to the band who were stripping the ship.

The band stripped everything of value from the boat, even the sales that could be cut up for lean-tos or sold. All of their horses were carrying supplies. Then, two scouts who had been watching the road came galloping up.

"British column approaching!"

Jacob nodded, "Everyone across the river, set the fires!" The rest of the band ran over to the ferry and Jacob went over and released the crew. The few men left on the schooner set it on fire from the tar and other resources they found. The crew stood there in shock, watching the schooner burn. Jacob and the rest of the band pulled the ferry to the other side of the shore.

As the men off-loaded, securing some of the boxes to their horses, Jacob turned to see the lead element of the British redcoats come into view. They were jogging toward the landing and now the fully engulfed schooner.

The burning mast cracked, fell into the river with a great splash and blocked some of the dock. The black smoke billowed across, obscuring the band from the British.

The redcoats began to fire on the band; Jacob turned and commanded, "Send them a parting shot!"

Samuel came up and let loose with his blunderbuss, knowing it would not reach the far shore, but the thunderous roar made the British cringe. A few more men, Patrick and Richard included, came up and fired at the British. Once all the cargo was secured, they mounted and rode off, leaving the ferry on their side but cutting the rope so it could not be moved.

They rode into camp and began to offload the cargo and supplies they had taken from the schooner. Jean called for Jacob, who motioned him to come to look at one of the boxes they had just opened. When he arrived, he saw what appeared to be a large flintlock musket, twice the size of a blunderbuss.

Jacob smiled, "It must be one of those Hessian Jaeger Amusettes I heard of!" He closed the lid, then turned and called for Samuel, who came over to see why Jacob had called him

"An early Christmas gift," Jacob stated and then opened the box to show him the amusette. Samuel's mouth opened and he reached down and lifted the gun out of the box. His eyes were all a-glow.

"Did it come with shot?" Samuel asked in a calm voice, though his face showed excitement. Jean nodded and led to the other box with the solid ball and powder. He then hugged the amusette to his chest, and Jacob smiled.

"Yes, Samuel, you're now my heavy gunner, seeing we don't have artillery. Patrick will assist you." Jacob agreed, "Besides, it suits you!"

Samuel couldn't help but have a giant grin on his face, and after leaning the amusette against a tree, he began to gather the shooting supplies and shot for the gun.

"Captain Clarke, the colonel, needs to see you," Oscar stated, having come over to get Jacob. Nodding, Jacob followed Oscar to the center of the camp, where not only was Marion there, but surprisingly, so was Governor Rutledge. The governor turned, smiled, and shook Jacob's hand.

"So good to see you, Jacob, alive and in one piece!" Rutledge said as he shook Jacob's hand.

"Glad to see you as well, sir," Jacob replied, "It has been some time since Charles Town."

The governor nodded, "Aye that it has. Between meeting with the new army commander in North Carolina, leveraging assistance from North Carolina, and getting our militia back into action, I have you all to thank for it!"

Jacob had a confused look on his face and the governor continued. "News of your exploits have been the only good news we have had up north since that damn Tarleton drove Sumter back up into North Carolina. You and the men with Marion are heroes, giving hope to those who need it!"

Jacob did not know how to receive that news of being heroes and all, though he was glad they were having an impact. "Who is the new army commander?"

"General Nathaniel Greene is the new commander, and he is organizing the new Southern Army up in North Carolina and will soon be back down here to deal with the British. With that said, he wants to coordinate his actions with Marion, Sumter and the other groups fighting down here."

Rutledge pulled documents from his coat, handing one to Marion. "Colonel Francis Marion, you are now hereby promoted to the rank of Brigadier General of the South Carolina Militia, to be obeyed and followed in accordance with your rank."

Marion accepted his promotion with a nod and smiled as Rutledge turned to Jacob.

"Captain Clarke, for your unwavering support and demonstration of leadership, you are hereby promoted to the rank of Major in the South Carolina Militia and commissioned as an independent command to serve under Marion and follow his instructions."

Rutledge handed Jacob his commission letter and then shook his hand. "Having been in discussion with Marion, this is way overdue for a man of your talent and leadership. Congratulations!"

Then Marion reached out and shook Jacob's hand, agreeing with the governor. Jacob finally smiled, then shrugged his shoulder in acceptance. "I will do my best, sir."

Marion nodded, "I wouldn't expect anything less."

***

Tarleton looked at his orders from General Cornwallis. "*You are ordered to depart immediately with your Legion and the light infantry from the 71st for the upcountry. You are to find, fix and, in detail, destroy these rebels reported to be operating west of the Catawba River. Once these rebels are dealt with, you must rejoin the main army.*"

Tarleton folded his orders and placed it in his coat pocket, then looked once more into the swampy areas where they had been patrolling, looking for the rebels and this Marion.

"As for this damned old fox, the Devil himself could not catch him," Tarleton grumbled, and his men near him nodded in agreement. For all of their attempts to track him down and well-prepared ambushes, this Marion outfoxed them every time.

"Well, lads, his lordship needs us to find another rebel leader, though I feel he will be easier to find than this damnable fox."

With that, Tarleton turned his horse and led his cavalry back to where the rest of the Legion was waiting at Camden, where they could resupply before making the trek upcountry. The light company of the 71st should be there as well.

"*Outsmarted by a damn old fox,*" Tarleton thought, then shook his head, "*And this Wolf character.*"

CHAPTER 7

1781: A NEW CAMPAIGN

It was all confusion and Big Harpe was caught in the middle. Cornwallis had ordered Tarleton to chase after these rebels and they had learned that General Morgan was gathering rebels near Hannah's Cowpens. Tarleton had been marching their column through the night and early morning hours, attempting to catch these rebels off guard.

They arrived at the open field where the Cowpens was located, and Tarleton deployed his infantry into open order onto the field after they dropped all of their excess packs and gear. He even had cannon, deploying his two 3-pound guns in the center. With the rest of the Legion cavalry, Harpe was on the left side of the line, the 17th Dragoons on the right end.

The air was bitter cold; Harpe's breath was a long stream of steam and his brother Little Harpe was on his left. "Think it's going to be a big one?" Little Harpe stated as he blew on his hands to warm them, then placed them on his horse's neck to keep warm. Big Harpe only nodded, his eyes fixed on the far side.

Big Harpe watched as the infantry advanced, a mix of the Legion infantry, recruits from the Seventh Regiment, and the light infantry from the 71st Highlanders. In the distance, Harpe could see a line of rebel pickets waiting. Harpe watched as the two cannons began firing at the rebels in the distance, though he could not see whether they were hitting anything.

Soon there was the sound of musketry, though only light at first; the volume of fire began to pick up. The excitement started to race through Harpe's veins; he caressed the handle of his sword with his right hand in anticipation. The musket fire began to intensify and the cavalry was getting ready to join the fight.

Soon, the sporadic shooting changed into organized volleys, as the rebels began to fire as groups, in a well-disciplined matter, which Harpe had to admit, impressed him. He was watching the men of the Legion. The Seventh was starting to fall, including officers who seemed to be targeted by the rebels.

Harpe was watching in fascination; he had never seen a major fight before, only his hit-and-run raids. But, though fascinated, he was glad he was not out there as he watched more and more of their men fall to the ground. The rebel sharpshooters showed their skills, which were better than theirs.

"Hand to sabers!" was ordered, and Big Harpe drew his heavy cavalryman's sword he had received before the campaign. It felt good in his hand, the weight of the blade comfortable against his shoulder. The Legion cavalry began to walk their horses forward, the 17th Dragoons doing the same on the other side.

Before them, the battle was joined. The men of the 71st Highlanders had fired a vicious volley at what appeared to be the backs of retreating rebels. Now they were charging forward at the backs of the rebels. The rebels were firing by companies, turning and heading to the rear.

As Harpe and his fellow horsemen trotted forward, he yelled, "Now we bloody got them!" Then, when the command to charge was given, he let loose a loud, blood-curdling yell with the rest of the Legion cavalry. Harpe raised his heavy sword in anticipation of hacking down these hapless rebels.

Then the world exploded and the battle changed as Harpe and the cavalry had closed in to within ten yards of the running rebels. Harpe just had enough time to see a line of blue-coated infantry that had lowered their muskets and leveled at them. Then they fired a volley and balls screamed all around him.

Harpe felt a burning sensation as a ball skimmed the top of his shoulder, and a second one entered his coat and creased his side. His horse spun in place, caught in the smoke and flames of the volley, causing it to rear up. Harpe pulled hard on his reins to control the horse.

Little Harpe's horse screamed, was caught in the chest by three musket balls, and crashed to the ground. Little Harpe could barely jump from the falling horse to avoid getting caught under the animal. Big Harpe spun his horse around to face the rebels and saw they had lowered their bayonets and were charging.

Then from his right side, he saw the white uniforms of rebel dragoons as they were charging into the flank of their cavalry. "Damn the luck!" Harpe yelled, then saw his brother was down on the ground, struggling to get back up. He stayed to protect his brother as he got his footing, his saber at the ready.

Some rebel infantry closed on him and Harpe swung down with his heavy saber. The heavy blade caught a running soldier in his right arm and cleanly sliced through the elbow, hacking it off. The soldier fell screaming to the ground, a fountain of blood coming from the stump of what was his arm.

Once more, a burning sensation caught Big Harpe as one of the charging soldiers thrust his bayonet at him and caught him along his left side, just above where the ball had creased him. Bellowing in anger and pain, Big Harpe turned and hacked down with all of his might, sinking the blade into the head of the attacking rebel.

The blade was wrenched from his hand and stuck in the falling soldier's skull. "Damn!" Big Harpe yelled and, quickly reaching down, drew one of his pistols from his saddle holster. Then, taking quick aim, he fired at a rebel charging his brother with a bayonet.

As that soldier fell to the ground, Big Harpe kneed his horse, which trampled the rebel attacking his brother. Then, with his hand, Harpe yelled, "Grab it and let's go!" His brother grabbed his hand, Harpe pulled him onto the back of his horse, then kicked it into a gallop. They rode through the vortex of the fight, the rebels appearing to snatch victory from defeat.

As they galloped away, he could see off to their left that Tarleton and many white-coated dragoons were pursuing his group. So big Harpe decided to ride in a different direction and headed southwest. As they rode, they came across a riderless horse waiting, and Little Harpe jumped off and mounted it. Then the two rode on and found a trail heading through the swamp.

The two rode in silence for a few minutes, letting the emotions of the battle subsided. "Well, what now?" Little Harpe asked, looking at his brother.

Big Harpe smiled, "I think it's time for us to find a new line of business elsewhere. So we will ride back, get the girls, and head west into the Indian lands. I don't know about you, but I have had enough of this war, and it's time to move on."

"That's been the best idea I have heard from you in a long time," Little Harpe stated, and Big Harpe glared at him but shrugged.

"We're still alive, aren't we? Let's go to a new place and have some fun!" Big Harpe gave an evil smile, Little Harpe just shook his head and chuckled and the two rode off into the west.

***

Having learned that General Greene was preparing to march south, Marion sent out different groups to engage the British around Georgetown. The goal was to keep the British lines of communication stressed to keep the British constantly moving around and off balance.

Lieutenant Colonel Peter Horry was sent back to the Waccamaw Neck to collect boats and drive off cattle. Jacob's band, now Major Clarke's Independent Company of Partisans, rode along. Jacob rode next to Horry, discussing how they would conduct the raid.

"Well, we want to draw their attention," Horry stated with a smile, "so let's make some noise!"

Jacob nodded, went over to his camp and gathered his band. Once everyone had checked their gear, they mounted and followed Jacob, where they joined with Horry's troops. Looking over, Jacob noticed all of Horry's men were armed with fowling pieces. Horry noticed Jacob looking, "They are all loaded with swan shot," he commented, "going to let those Loyalists have it."

Once everyone was ready, Horry led them out, with Jacob and his band following Horry. They rode hard once they left camp and made their way over to Waccamaw Neck. Jacob and a few others thought of Gabriel and how he had been murdered in the same area. Horry led them down the main road, not trying to hide but instead wanting to draw the Loyalist's attention.

Horry split his command, setting out half of his horsemen down one of the side roads and he sent Jacob and his band further down the Waccamaw Neck area, looking for the newly identified Queen's Rangers who had mounted troops in the area. Jacob followed a road that passed several good-sized farms and plantations. As they were riding, Jacob spotted a group of men who appeared to be gathering cattle.

Raising his hand to halt, Jacob stopped his band and took out his telescope for a quick look. There were four of them, wearing the uniform of the Queen's Rangers. Two were holding the farmers at gunpoint; the other two were herding the cows. After focusing on the men, he lowered and closed it. "They are who I thought they were, Loyalists taking cows. Let's go visit them!"

Jacob kicked his horse and led his band out of the woods and into the field. The men were fanning out into a few lines across. They yelled at the top of their lungs, a warbling war cry as they charged toward the Loyalists. Jacob felt the excitement, caught up in the moment of the charge and joined in the war cry.

The Loyalists turned quickly at the sound of Jacob's men charging them; the two men herding the cows raised their muskets and fired. Then they turned and ran for their horses as the two who had been holding the farmers at gunpoint jumped up on their horses. After they were mounted, they turned to ride off.

Jacob pulled the reins of his horse and raised his rifle to get a quick shot off as the animal came to a skidding halt. A few of the others were firing from the saddle as well. Jacob saw his ball strike one of the Loyalist's horses and it fell, kicking and screaming. The rider was pinned underneath.

As the other three Loyalists took off in a gallop, Jacob motioned for Jean and Samuel to pursue, "Try to take another captive for questioning!" Jean, Samuel and about half of the band galloped past Jacob in pursuit of the other Loyalists; Jacob halted and dismounted to check on the farmers.

A man with a woman and two kids hiding behind her skirts, looked at Jacob, along with Frederick and Jehu, who approached them. First, Jacob pointed to the Loyalist, who was still pinned under his dead horse. Then, waving toward the fallen horse,

"See to that man, secure him," Jacob ordered. He then went up to the farmer and his family.

"Are you folks fine?" Jacob asked and the man nodded his head.

"Thanks to you," he answered, reaching out to shake Jacob's hand. "Those bastards were trying to take all our livestock, leaving us nothing."

Jacob looked down at the two kids, a young boy, and a girl, peeking around their mother's skirt. Then, looking down, Jacob waved and smiled, "You're fine now, don't be afraid." Then he looked at the farmer. "We'll make sure these Loyalists leave you be."

The man and woman nodded, both saying thanks as Jacob turned to check on the fallen Loyalist. When he arrived, the Loyalist was standing there; Frederick and a few of the band were standing around him. His uniform was a deep green coat and white trousers, and his black helmet had fallen off.

Bending down, Jacob picked up the helmet and looked at it. Generally, the same design as the old Second Regiment's helmet, though the front shield was taller and had a white feather in the helmet. The silver crescent had "Queen's Rangers" inscribed, and Jacob handed it to the Loyalists. He placed it back on his head and looked at Jacob.

"What is to happen to me?" he asked, looking at Jacob and the other men standing around him.

"That all depends on you," Jacob responded. "If you behave and answer our questions, we will treat you decently. On the other hand, we will give you the same if you give us a hard time. Do we understand one another?"

The captured Loyalist shrugged, looked down at the ground at his feet, and nodded.

"Where are you stationed at?" Then, Jacob asked, "Who is your commander?"

"Georgetown" was what he responded with. "Captain Saunders is my commander; our colonel was Rogers before Simcoe replaced him in the fall."

Jacob had a shocked look on his face, "Then you are not from here, are you?"

Shaking his head, "No sir, I am originally from New York. Signed up in the summer of 1776, we were to serve up there until they sent us down here." He looked down at the ground, then back up at Jacob. "All the same would rather be there than here."

Looking up, Jacob saw that Jean and Samuel had returned from their chase and were dismounting. He waved them over to the prisoner. When they arrived, Jacob continued.

"You said you were under the command of Colonel Rogers, as in Robert Rogers? Knew Ranger tactics?" Jacob asked, with Samuel first looking at Jean, then Jacob, before at the prisoner.

"Yes, sir, the man from the war with the French organized and trained us in New York. Led us on a campaign around southern New York and then Philadelphia. I have to admit; he was a good officer and knew his business."

Jacob slowly nodded, "We know; we served with him during the war with the French. The last I heard, he went out to the Ohio."

The prisoner shrugged, "I don't know all about that. I know the rebel government arrested him, he had offered his services and this General Washington had him arrested. From what I heard, that did not sit well with the colonel, so he supported the crown and raised the unit. Heard he was the one responsible for capturing a rebel spy, Hale, I think his name was."

Jacob was in shock, learning about Rogers and they were now on opposite sides of the war. But, at least he did not have to face him down here.

"Sounds like Rogers," Samuel commented, and Jacob had to agree.

The prisoner also had a look of shock on his face, "You served with Rogers, fought with him during the war with the French? So why are you fighting for the rebels?"

Jacob shrugged, "I am fighting for my home and what we believe in. Yes, I served with Rogers, but I was fighting for my friends and fellow Rangers back then."

Samuel nodded; even Jean was nodding though his view was different.

"I saw more than I wanted to, how bad we were treated by the Crown and expected to die for them. Too many friends and fellow Rangers died and paid that price. Then to be looked down upon by King and country. So now my fight is for my home and friends."

"Fortunes of war, I guess," the prisoner stated and Jacob nodded.

"Aye, I guess so." Jacob turned and went back to get his horse. The prisoner was loaded up on a horse, Jean, and Samuel following Jacob.

"Was that strange to you?" Samuel asked and Jacob nodded.

"Aye, but as you said, sounds like Rogers. He was out in the Ohio and could have been there when this war started. I'm sure it was a shock when he returned to see we were fighting the Crown."

Samuel nodded, "But our General Washington had him arrested?"

Jacob shook his head, "Don't know, sounds like politics again, so who knows what happened up there. I am glad we're not fighting him down here."

"Speak for yourself, my friend," Jean spoke, with a gleam in his eye, "I wouldn't mind a second shot at capturing him. Besides, I still have his coat; I should try to return it to him."

They were chuckling when they got to their horses and mounted up. The prisoner was on a horse, and once everyone was ready, Jacob led them back along the road; the intent was to meet up with Horry and his horsemen. They followed the Waccamaw toward Georgetown and finally located Horry, who had occupied a redoubt.

Jacob led the prisoner over to Horry, who nodded and directed him to be placed with the other prisoners.

"Looks like you saw some action?" Horry asked and Jacob nodded. He explained their contact with the Queen Rangers foraging party and what they had learned about their old mentor Rogers. Again, Horry nodded with a serious look on his face.

"Sad news, that is, about Rogers throwing in with the Crown," Horry commented, "They are based in Georgetown, you say?" Jacob nodded.

"We chased some off as well," Horry explained, "The King's American Regiment had been here, but we chased them away; they must have run to Georgetown as well. So, we'll spend the night here; go see to your men."

Jacob nodded and returned to where his band was setting up camp. Samuel and Richard had a fire going, Patrick and some others were gathering firewood, and the rest were looking at the horses on the picket. Jacob sat down on the ground before the fire, pulling out his pipe and lighting it with a burning stick from the fire. The men joined him, eating rations and speaking of the day's event.

During the evening, the sentries called out that a rider was approaching, who turned out to be a messenger from Marion. They were instructed to return to the camp in the morning. Horry passed the word in the morning that they were returning to base. Jacob gave the word to his band before settling it for the night, wrapping it up in his wool blanket.

Jacob had his band stand to, just before the sun rose in the cold, frosty morning. The men's breath steamed the air before them, but there was no sound or sight of the enemy, so Jacob stood them down and they packed up their camp for the ride. Once settled, they mounted up and waited for Horry to lead out again.

The ride back to the camp was mostly uneventful until they crossed Lynch's Creek. As the horses were making their way across the creek, water-swollen from rain to the north, a low-hanging branch caught Horry's shoulder strap and he was pulled into the stream with a loud splash. As soon as Horry hit the water, he began to flail, as he never learned to swim. Finally, a few of his men jumped in and rescued their commander, who had an embarrassed look on his face.

Jacob suppressed a laugh, though he could hear Samuel chuckling behind him as they approached, with a dripping Horry settling back on his horse. Jacob liked Peter Horry; he was a good man, though he was actually a poor rider and did not know how to swim. To make things even worse, when Horry got excited, he stuttered really badly. Still, his men followed him and Marion trusted him; all that was good with Jacob.

***

Daniel McGirtt looked at the small town of Brier Creek in the early morning light of dawn. He led his Loyalist cavalry across the Savannah and followed the river road until he came upon the sleeping town. Unbeknownst to the people of the settlement, McGirtt had vowed to kill everyone who would not follow the King. He was going to keep his vow and waved his men forward as they rode toward the unsuspecting town.

As the Loyalists rode out, they spread out into a line, McGirtt waving to the left and right as his sections broke off to encircle the town while McGirtt rode into the center of the town. His men fanned out, began to round up the civilians and herd them into the center of the town. McGirtt sat on his horse, arms crossed on his pommel, watching his men gather the citizens.

The Loyalists kicked in the doors of the homes, the sounds of crying and screaming coming from the houses, men yelling and arguing with the Loyalist troopers. Then, using their sabers and muskets, they pushed the people toward the center of the town where McGirtt was waiting. He sat up straight in his saddle, looking down at the huddled mass of citizens.

"What is the meaning of this!" a man yelled from the crowd. "What gives you the right to treat us in this fashion?"

McGirtt nodded to one of his men who approached the speaker and struck him in the stomach; the man folded and fell to the ground.

"Now that I have your attention," McGirtt yelled out. "We are here looking for rebels, Bandits, and those who would support the rebels. If you are good citizens of the Crown, then all you have to do is swear allegiance to the King and we will go on our way. If not, then you shall receive the King's justice."

"Bandits, you say," another man yelled out, "Then what makes you? Any decent person would not rouse good people from their homes on a cold day. This is why we do not want or need people like you if you represent the Crown. If this is what it means to be citizens of the King, then I much rather side with the rebels!"

Numerous angry voices and a few fists shook at McGirtt and his men. "So that is your answer, you wish to be independent from King and country?"

A good number of people yelled "Yes!" and began to shout at the Loyalists, shaking their fists at them. McGirtt gave an evil smile and drew his saber slowly, the sound of it clearing its sheath and silencing the crowd.

"I am so glad you feel this way," McGirtt stated. Then, he looked to his men, raised his sword, and gave the order, "Attack!"

The Loyalists with muskets quickly brought them to their shoulders and fired into the huddled group of citizens. Then, those with sabers charged into the crowd and began to hack at the people, who were now screaming and running in all directions.

"Burn their homes as punishment for insurrection!" McGirtt yelled out as he rode forward, swinging his sword down on the back of a running man, slicing him along his back as he fell into the ground.

A few men were wrestling with the Loyalists who had fired their muskets. Then the cavalry was charging in and slashing at these resisting men. Women were screaming, dragging their crying children through the houses and running for the woods. The Loyalists attacked the men, between muskets firing and slashing sabers.

McGirtt ran down a few of the running men, slashing down with his saber, even severing an arm from one of the fleeing townspeople. Then, he wheeled his horse and gleefully chased women and children into the woods, hollering from the top of his lungs.

"Run, run, my little pretties!" he roared as the women, children and some men ran through trees into the forest. Then, smiling, McGirtt turned and rode back into town, where the fires were starting to burn in the homes. The thick black columns of smoke twisted and hung in the morning air as the sun rose above the trees.

The Loyalists were securing items of value from the homes before burning, laughing, and hooting as they stepped over the bodies of the dead men. The loot, including bottles of rum and wine, silver and other precious items, were loaded and tied onto the back of the horses. From what McGirtt counted, fourteen men sprawled out on the ground, their blood mingling and melting the frozen earth.

Sitting on his horse, McGirtt smiled. The roar of the flames grew as the buildings all burned within the town. A rider walked up and stopped next to McGirtt, who kept watching the destruction.

"This may drive more of them to the rebel side," the voice said to McGirtt, who turned to look at the voice. Maclane was sitting there, wearing his civilian clothes. McGirtt scoffed and shook his head.

"You fight your way," McGirtt growled, "I will fight it my way. So far, my way seems to be working. How are yours doing?"

Maclane stared back at McGirtt and shook his head, "This method is brutal and pointless, contrary to the King's desires."

Again, McGirtt shook his head and snorted in response. "Are you so sure?"

McGirtt kneed his horse and walked forward as his men mounted up and reformed their column behind McGirtt. The horses clattered with the loot bags and a few bottles were already being passed around. McGirtt took a bottle and took a long pull on the bottle before handing it back and wiping his face with his coat sleeve. Then, McGirtt led his column forward and rode around the burning village.

Maclane sat on his horse, watching the town burn, every building aflame and smoke blocking out the morning sun. Then, letting out a deep sigh, Maclane shook his head in disgust. *"We're going to lose this war,"* Maclane thought. *"If this is how we fight these rebels. Perhaps I should look for a better job somewhere else."*

Kicking his horse, Maclane rode his horse around the burning town, going in the opposite direction than McGirtt's Loyalists. Looking at the dead, the men shot or slashed, staining the ground with their blood. He could also see the faces of the women and children watching from the woods. The smell of smoke and fresh char filled his nostrils as he pushed his horse into a trot and headed for Charles Town.

*****

Maria warmed her wet, cold hands over the fire as the next batch of officers' shirts were ready to scrub. They were stained red. Wine instead of blood and stain from the make-up some of the women wore in the city. Shaking her head, she rubbed her hands together as she stood next to the wall of the headquarters building for the garrison; the window was opened a crack.

While it did appear she was warming her hands, she was listening to the conversation inside by the staff. She smiled as she heard the arguing over what to do about the partisan activity near Georgetown. In her mind, she suspected it was Jacob, Samuel, and Jean; the British officers argued that it had to be Jacob.

Helga approached Maria with a questioning look as she dropped off an armload of wood.

"What are you laughing about, mama?" she asked, seeing Maria giggling.

"Oh, it was something I heard," she said as she knelt, "I think I heard the British talking about your father."

Helga smiled, "Papa must be giving them a hard time."

Maria nodded, "That he is."

Then she looked around and asked Helga, "What did you see, describe the uniforms."

Helga recited the uniforms she saw as she gathered wood around the camps. She explained the different facings on the redcoats, the additional green coats and the cavalry riding through.

"Great job," Maria commented, and Helga smiled.

"I like this game, mama. So, let's keep playing."

Maria smiled and stood up, "Yes, we'll keep playing. You can fetch another load of wood and tell me what you see."

Helga walked off, squared her shoulders and was very serious about watching the world around her. Maria watched her go and then returned to the washing. Afterward, she would meet with Andrew to pass the information on to him.

***

Jacob was called over to Marion's camp early in the morning and was surprised to see a British officer, who was blindfolded, being led into the base. Jacob stood next to Major James, "What's going on?" Jacob asked.

"Negotiations, the British want to discuss a prisoner exchange," James answered. Jacob nodded and watched as the British officer was introduced to Marion.

"I am about to have breakfast; care to share it with me?" Marion asked and the British officer accepted. Then, as he sat on a log, Marion motioned to a box; a second box was used for an improvised table. Oscar set two teacups, one before Marion and the other before the British officer.

"I am surprised to see you are drinking tea, sir," the officer stated as he sipped his tea, "I thought you rebels drank coffee in protest."

Marion chuckled. "I enjoy my tea, sir and it's rather hard to get coffee out here in the swamps."

"Ah, quite right, I see," replied the officer.

Oscar pulled a couple of sweet potatoes from the fire coals that had been cooking and, using two wooden platters, presented one to Marion and the other to the officer. He looked surprised down at his sweet potato, then back up at Marion, who was cutting into his potato.

Chewing blissfully on his potato, though Jacob suspected it was for show, Marion closed his eyes and smiled. He then looked at the British officer who still hadn't touched his potato.

"Oh, my apologies if it is not to your liking," Marion stated, "we only just got these potatoes as we have had no foodstuff in the past couple of days. I can try to see if we have some jerky or biscuits you may like?"

The British officer shook his head and began to eat his potato. They then discussed the need for prisoner exchanges as they desired the return of British soldiers and officers and they had too many of the rebels to feed and care for properly.

This continued for a while, and Marion agreed to a prisoner exchange that would be conducted later. The British officer bowed in acceptance, allowed himself to be blindfolded and was led out of the camp. Once he was gone, Marion motioned for Jacob to join him.

"You seemed to enjoy that, sir," Jacob stated as he sat across from Marion, where the British officer had just vacated. Marion gave a mischievous smile and nodded as Oscar brought the actual meal for Marion.

"It's a game. We must keep the British and their friends off balance and for them to not know what we truly have for supplies. It's what foxes do, no?"

Jacob nodded his head, the word Swamp Fox is now used extensively amongst the locals. They even speak of the Wolf who rides with the Fox that cannot die." Then, as Marion sipped his tea, he pulled out orders from his coat pocket.

"We have received a message from General Greene that in preparation for his upcoming campaign to invest Camden and the fort at Ninety-Six, we are to disrupt the supply lines that could support these garrisons. Jacob, head toward Monck's Corner and see what trouble you can stir up."

Nodding, Jacob smiled and stood up. "It would be our pleasure to cause our British friends as much trouble as possible."

"Quite right," Marion mimicked the British officer before chuckling as he returned to his breakfast and Jacob headed over to his camp. When he arrived, he explained their task to the band and all of them smiled, liking that they were taking the fight to the British and having an offensive-minded commander of the Southern forces.

"Check your weapons; ensure you have at least eight rounds of shot and powder. Bring three days of rations just in case." Jacob instructed; Samuel and Jean checked the men as the Band readied themselves for action. Once all was in order and Samuel and Jean nodded that the men were ready, Jacob mounted his horse. The band mounted theirs; the wolves waited patiently off to the side.

Jacob led his band toward Keithfield, near Monck's Corner, a known location for transporting supplies for the British and Loyalists. The day was cold and windy, grey boiling clouds filling the sky. Flecks of ice and sleet were dancing, a threat of freezing rain on the wind. The wolves' thick winter coats waved in the wind, the wolves appearing unaffected by the cold.

Bundled up in his old faithful green blanket coat, Jacob was hoping the poor weather would make any British or Loyalist sentry more concerned about their warmth than watching the area. Looking over, Samuel had his blunderbuss cradled in his arms and a happy look on his face. Jacob had to admit he liked being on the offensive instead of hiding from the British or the Loyalists.

As they rode, the weather worsened, yet it made Jacob happy, for it reminded him of his old days as a Ranger in New York and was probably preventing any sentries from doing their duties. When they arrived a few miles from Keithfield, Jacob sent Jean and a small group to see if any British were there. They remained on their horses, moving them into the trees to stay out of the cold wind and flying sleet. The wolves sat under trees, watching with their golden eyes.

The light of day was mainly grey from the boiling clouds, the wind whipping the trees about them. The air was cold and stinging, odd for South Carolina. In comparison, there had been some frigid days from what Jacob could recall, but not like the winters up north. Jacob pulled his blanket coat tighter, eyes watching the woods.

Waya walked up and sat next to Jacob's horse, nose to the wind, taking in the scents. Jacob looked down at his wolf, "Smell anything?" The wolf looked up, wagged its tail, then returned to look into the woods and sniff the wind.

Jean and his small group returned quickly and Jacob rode to meet them. Waya remained where he was sitting but watching.

"They are there," Jean said, his voice muffled by a scarf wrapped around his face. "There are several wagons and a large bonfire they are standing around to stay warm, and I didn't see any sentries, though they could be hiding from the weather."

Jacob nodded and smiled. The weather was working in their favor. He called in his band, and they circled him, their horses making a thin fog cloud from their breaths.

"Men, we're going to ride until we get close and then dismount. Then, using the weather and the trees, we can make out way over to where our British friends are; Jean will lead us.

Let us take them by surprise, try to take them all prisoner. That will send a message to our friends and foes alike. Then we'll see what's in the wagons, take what we need and destroy the rest."

The band looked at Jacob, smiled and nodded their heads in understanding. Even Jacob put on a smile. "Again, if it comes down to living or dying, kill the enemy if you have no choice. Try to take them prisoner, if possible, but your lives are paramount."

Once everyone understood, Jacob and Jean led the and onto the road and the cold, windy weather and headed toward the British camp. The wolves trotted alongside, keeping pace with the horses. It was about a quarter mile away when Jean stopped them and they dismounted their horses. Leaving a few men behind to watch the horses, Jacob led the rest of the band, following Jean.

Jacob could see Jean's footprints from scouting the area before. The men moved with their muskets at the ready, slightly crouched as they weaved through the trees. As they approached the camp, Jacob could smell the wood smoke on the wind, blowing toward them. When they reached the edge of the tree line, Jean knelt, and Jacob motioned for the rest of the band to halt. Even the wolves sank to the ground, ears perked.

Samuel made his way forward, along with Frederick and joined Jacob and Jean. Just below them was the British camp. Several wagons were lined up and the oxen and horses picketed off to the side. There was a large bonfire where a few men stood around, their cloaks blowing in the wind. A few soldiers appeared to be carrying wood to the fire.

Jacob scanned the clearing and tried to see if they had any sentries. Near the road, he saw a flash of red, which appeared to be a redcoat of a soldier standing guard but not facing the road. Looking around, he could not see any other sentries or guards. Jacob smiled to himself.

Nodding, Jacob developed a plan of action. "I will take a third of the band, circle to the left and approach from the road. Then, Samuel, you take another third and circle to the right, come in from the other side of the road. Jean, you remain here and when we give the signal, charge down from here."

Samuel smiled and nodded, and then Jean looked at Jacob. "What will be the signal?"

Jacob smiled, "When we start yelling like demons, that will be the signal."

Jean shrugged but smiled as Samuel went to get his group of men. Jacob would bring his group, and Frederick would remain with Jean. Jacob took the boys, Jehu and a few others that would be part of his group. Samuel was leading his men to the right side of the field, his two wolves following alongside. Jacob directed the rest of the men to move forward and join Jean and Frederick, his wolves following.

Jehu, Zacharia and the boys were waiting, and Jacob motioned for them to follow him as he led them to the left side of the field. They moved cautiously; the wind and weather were still covering their approach. Then, recalling where he saw the British sentry, Jacob made his way toward him. The sound of the wind was louder than their movement. Jacob held up his hand; they stopped and slowly knelt.

Looking through the trees, Jacob could quickly glimpse the sentry. The sentry was using the trees to block the wind. His hands were in his pocket while his musket rested in the crook of his arm and body. A scarf was wrapped around his head and hat, covering his ears to protect them from the cold. He looked up the road from time to time, but his back was always facing toward Jacob.

Handing his rifle to Patrick, he looked at Zacharia and Jehu. "Cover me. I am going to move up and take him, prisoner," Jacob instructed. Then, he motioned for the wolves to stay put. The two nodded and then took up firing positions as Jacob moved forward at a crouch, knife held low. He focused on the center of the sentry's back instead of his head. Jacob had learned early that sometimes if you look at their head, people could sense someone was sneaking up on them.

Moving slowly, watching his foot placement, Jacob used the wind to mask his movement and approached the sentry. The fact that a scarf covered the sentry's ears would muffle any noise Jacob would make. Moving forward slowly, Jacob could see the soldier was not looking in his direction. Instead, he spent more time stamping his feet and looking at the ground, shivering.

Jacob, slightly shaking his head, moved about a big tree between him and the sentry, his route clear toward the sentry's back. Then, staying low, Jacob quickly rushed up and wrapped his free hand around the sentry's mouth while his knife came up to the sentry's throat.

The guard stopped moving as he felt the sharp blade press against his throat. "Don't move or make a sound," Jacob hissed in the sentry's ear, "or I'll stab you here and now, leaving your body to rot."

The sentry carefully nodded his head in understanding, his movement prevented by the knife's blade. Jacob pulled him back enough so his men could see him. Jehu, with Zacharia, motioning with his head, led the others to Jacob's position. Stripping the prisoner of his musket, cartridge box and gear that Primus threw over his shoulder, he took the prisoner from Jacob. Patrick handed his rifle back to him.

They were on the reverse slope of a slight rise, still hiding from the group around the bonfire. Looking to his left and right, Jacob brought them up online and slowly moved up to the edge to see the far side of the field. Then, hoping Samuel was in place, Jacob let out a Mohawk war-whoop.

A similar war-whoop came from the other side, showing Samuel was in position. Waving his hand forward, Jacob led his band down the slope toward the bonfire. As they began to jog toward the camp and could see the bonfire below them, Jacob began to let out a loud war cry. All of his band let loose a loud, blood-curdling yell.

The British were all facing the fire when Jacob began to lead his men forward, yelling. Samuel was leading his band down the opposite side of the road. Jean was leading his group down from the side. All three were screaming like banshees, muskets at the ready as they charged toward the British. The wolves raced alongside, charging forward with a growl.

None of the British had any weapons on them and quickly raised their hands as the men poured down around them. The three columns rapidly fanned out and surrounded the outnumbered British. Jacob motioned for Samuel to head toward the wagons, Jean toward some more British soldiers standing as Jacob approached to secure the men around the fire. "Search them!" Jacob ordered.

Jehu and the others quickly moved up. One man searched while another covered them with their musket or rifle lowered. The prisoners held their hands high, cautiously watching the muskets and rifles pointed at them, unsure of what to expect. They eyed the growling wolves, teeth exposed and hair bristling. They pulled their haversacks and anything they found in their pockets. Jacob watched as Jean and Samuel did the same with their prisoners.

All the prisoners were consolidated near the bonfire. Jacob had them sit down in a group, covered by some of the band. Jacob took a count of what they had captured at the site. There were ten wagons and Jean searched for what was inside. Samuel was approaching with a group of soldiers who were taken prisoner, including a sergeant, a corporal and eight privates. They also secured a quartermaster, a wagon master and several waggoners.

"Jacob, we have some supplies we can use," Jean called over and Jacob went over to see what they had found. Some of the wagons had foodstuffs, clothing, new redcoats for the 64th Regiment, powder, muskets and even rum. Jacob smiled, "Let's get the wagons hitched and load everything, including the prisoners and we'll take them to the camp."

Some of the band went over and hitched the oxen and horses to the wagons. The prisoners had their hands tied and placed in the wagons. A couple of the band returned for the horses, and everyone mounted up. Each wagon had a few band members guarding the prisoners in the wagons. Once the column was ready and the prisoners had blindfolds on, Jacob led them to the camp. The wagons rattled and shook going over the roads and Jacob made sure they did not take a direct route in case the prisoners tried to remember the way.

When they arrived, Jacob transferred the prisoners to a collection point within the camp while Jacob ensured all of the newly acquired supplies, including the redcoats, were offloaded. "Why did we keep the redcoats?" Samuel asked.

Jacob shrugged, "Who knows, we may have to dress up as British soldiers and do some sneaking around."

Samuel gave Jacob a stern look, "Wouldn't that be considered spying? They hang people for that."

Jacob chuckled, "They want to hang us now. So, what's the difference?"

Once the wagons were unloaded, they were taken away and given to local farmers and store owners. Marion did not need them. However, the supply of food, extra muskets and powder did come in handy as they ran low.

Jacob could see the troops' morale was higher, with the new supplies and the reports coming back where Jacob and the other partisan leaders were having their way with the British. They took a few assembly areas and cargo wagons with no losses. The word was getting out on their victories and the losses by the British, showing they did not control the interior as much as they thought they did.

***

Lieutenant Colonel Bedlow met with Captain Saunders of the Queen's Rangers in Georgetown. Bedlow, like most of the senior staff, was concerned about the successes of the rebels in the area. However, the recent attacks against their supply lines, where they lost everything and the rebels lost nothing, negatively affected morale.

Using local sources, Bedlow was able to locate a rebel officer named Captain Kane, who lived in the area and had been involved in the recent raids against British supply points. Bedlow needed this Kane to make a point that the rebels would be found and punished. First, however, he needed the manpower to accomplish it.

The Queen's Rangers were the best choice for the operation; however, Captain Saunders had already asked permission to return his unit to New York. Therefore, Bedlow had to make a deal with Saunders. If he accomplishes this mission, he can authorize the Rangers to return to New York.

Sitting at a table in his headquarters, a simple house in Georgetown, Saunders looked at Bedlow, "So if we do this mission for you, how do we know we will be released to return to New York?"

"Are you suggesting that we can't be trusted?" Bedlow asked, and Saunders shook his head.

"Not at all, sir. However, there have been times when orders mysteriously disappeared or became lost."

Pulling a document from his coat pocket, Bedlow showed it to Saunders. It had the royal seal upon it. "Here are your orders," Bedlow explained, "I'll hand them to you once this mission is complete."

Sighing, Saunders nodded. "I'll get a detachment for you; when should they be ready to march?"

"As soon as possible," Bedlow explained, "We must catch this rebel by surprise. The longer we wait, the better chance this rebel will slip away."

Saunders nodded, "I go get the detachment and have them ready to go as soon as they can get their gear gathered." He rose from the table, placed his hat on, and exited the house to get the men.

Bedlow shook his head; negotiating with a commander to accomplish an operation went against his very nature as an officer. This whole war, this new way of fighting, dealing, and using brigands and rascals, had shown how low they had sunk as an empire.

When Saunders gathered the Rangers, Bedlow was waiting outside, looking at the sky. The clouds were getting thicker and darker, and the wind was picking up. Saunders brought and introduced Lieutenant Wilson to Bedlow.

"Colonel, I have thirty-five Rangers at my disposal," commented Wilson, "we are at your service." Saunders nodded, "Good hunting," before turning and heading back to his headquarters. Bedlow watched him walk away before turning to Wilson.

"We are going to use boats instead of horses for this mission," Bedlow explained, "We are going to avoid being spotted by locals who could warn the rebel. Once we get into the area, we will move quickly and capture this rebel officer at all costs so he can face the King's justice he deserves."

Lieutenant Wilson nodded his understanding, "We stand ready, sir."

Nodding to Wilson, Bedlow led the Rangers to the Waccamaw River, where five long boats were waiting. "Have your men load the boats," Bedlow commanded, then climbed aboard the first boat and took a position in the bow. The Rangers filed into the longboats, stowing their gear in the center and taking up positions on the oars.

Once the boats were loaded, Bedlow waved his hand forward and the Rangers began rowing their boats upriver. Bedlow's boat led the way, Wilson was in the second boat and the third boat brought up the rear. The oars rose and then cut into the water, the river curling along the bows of the boats.

The weather began to change for the worse, as Bedlow guessed from watching the clouds and wind picking up. The clouds opened up and a hard, cold rain fell. The wind blew hard enough to cause ripples across the river, making the rowing more difficult. The waves kicked up by the wind went against the boats, causing them to rise and fall against the current. The Rangers were pulling for all their worth against the wind, but Mother Nature seemed to have the upper hand.

The weather only worsened, and the boats were slowing down and not making good time. Bedlow finally gave the order to head for shore. In the horrible weather, the Rangers landed their boats and held them while they offloaded their gear. Bedlow turned to Lieutenant Wilson, "Have the boats return to Georgetown; we'll march from here."

Wilson nodded and told the few Rangers still in the boat to return to Georgetown. Once the boats were empty, the Rangers rowed the boats out into the river and headed south. Bedlow looked at the ugly, wet sky before returning to the waiting Rangers.

"We'll move on foot, using the road until we can find a place to wait out the weather. The rain should conceal us from any eyes," Bedlow instructed and Wilson nodded. "Have the Rangers ready to move."

Once all the Rangers had shouldered their packs and gear, Bedlow led them through the woods. It was a short distance to the road, which followed the river. Then, moving on the road, Bedlow led them northward toward the rebel's house. Luckily for them, they came to a farm, and after telling the owner they would use his barn, they moved the Rangers in.

Bedlow and the Rangers spent the night in the barn, trying to dry their clothes while getting some rest. While the Rangers rested, they rotated a guard who watched the door and the farmyard. Bedlow sat against the wall, eyes closed but listening to the activity. Wilson was checking on his men, checking their feet and getting them to change their stockings.

Closing his eyes, Bedlow napped for a bit and by morning, the rain had stopped. Rising to his feet with a groan, stretching before heading to Wilson.

"Let's get them up and get going," Bedlow stated, "Should be early enough that we should avoid any contact with locals."

Wilson nodded and with his sergeants, got the men to their feet and gear shouldered. The corporals checked the muskets to ensure they were dry and had a good prime in the pan. The men filled the center of the barn and then Wilson returned to Bedlow, indicating they were ready.

Leading them out into a cold morning, the Rangers crossed the ground covered in puddles and some frost as they made their way onto the road. Wilson directed the Rangers into two columns, one on each side of the road. As the Rangers walked along the road, they stepped into numerous puddles as they watched the woods.

They were closing in on the rebel's house and Bedlow felt the growing anticipation. To ensure they would not lose the element of surprise, as they came to a local farmhouse, Bedlow had the Rangers secure the farmer and his family and made them walk in the rear of the column.

After securing some five farms, they arrived at the home of the rebel officer, Captain Kane. Bedlow halted the column, taking out a small telescope to look around the house. He could see lights from the windows, but no one was outside. Bedlow smiled; so far, it seemed their secrecy was accomplished.

Pulling a pistol inside his coat, Bedlow led the Rangers toward the house. Pointing to the left and right, the Rangers split into three sections. One went to the left, the other to the right to surround the home and a small element followed Bedlow and Wilson. Bedlow continued to rush forward, quickly stepping onto the porch before opening the door and charging in.

Bedlow and the Rangers flooded the room, catching a man, a woman and two children sitting at a table having breakfast. Lowering his pistol, Bedlow commanded, "Captain Kane, I hereby arrest you for insurrection and traitorous acts against the King!" The man slowly raised his hands while the children began to cry while comforted by the woman.

"I surrender, sir," Captain Kane softly replied, "Please don't harm my family. I will come without resistance." Bedlow nodded and lowered his pistol. Kane came around the table, bent down to kiss and hug his wife and the children, then stood before Bedlow. "Sir, I am ready to depart."

Bedlow nodded and motioned for the Rangers to escort him outside. He looked down at the woman and the two children crying and calling for their father. The vicious look she gave Bedlow nearly made him shiver, the hatred she felt for him. Bedlow shook his head, turned, and went outside.

Kane had his hands bound, and four Rangers were ready to escort him. Bedlow looked where the small element was guarding the local farmers they had secured. "Release them!" Bedlow called out, pointing at the locals and the Rangers nodded and reformed with the detachment. The locals watched as they led Kane off and marched toward Georgetown.

It was a cold, uneventful march back to Georgetown; the rebels did not try to rescue their captured officer. He did not say much, just marched with tight lips, staring straight ahead. That did not bother Bedlow; he'll have a conversation with the prisoner later when it is more private.

It was late afternoon when they arrived in Georgetown. Bedlow released Wilson to take the prisoner to the stockade and to see to his men. As they marched off, Bedlow headed over to Saunder's headquarters. Bedlow went inside and stood next to the fire in the hearth. The orderly went to get the captain.

A short time later, Saunders came into the room, "I take it your mission was successful?" Bedlow looked at him, wondering if he was asking out of duty or if the mission was successful, they could return to New York.

Bedlow nodded, reached inside his coat, pulled out the message with the royal seal on it, and ordered the Queen's Rangers to return to New York. "Yes, captain, we got our man. As I am a man of my word, here are your orders releasing you back to New York. See to your men and the arrangements to sail for New York. I wish you safe journeys."

Saunders accepted the orders with a relieved look and nodded his thanks. Bedlow turned and headed back out into the cold winter air. As he went to his room in a local tavern, he wondered if he should look to the future, perhaps a new assignment in the Bahamas.

"*Definitely much warmer there*," Bedlow thought and then he started to go over how to work out a plan to get assigned to the Bahamas.

***

Maria was sitting in a sewing room next to where the British officers had their meetings, discussing and planning their actions. She had a pile of shirts and breaches she was sewing, and with such bad weather, the British allowed her to sew in the house. So she could hear the conversations, just like when she washed under the windows in the summer.

She only spoke broken English to the British, relying on her German to make the British think she could not understand what they were saying. She also played it up that she was simple-minded and only suitable for washing and sewing. While all an act, the British did not know better. Helga played along, enjoying the game as she sat and did the easier sewing.

From the discussion she was overhearing, the British had difficulty getting supplies to General Cornwallis and their outposts. Moreover, different rebel groups kept attacking and making transportation extremely difficult. She thought fondly of Jacob, who was, more likely, one of these groups.

"What are we bloody going to do about these damn rebels and Bandits?" One of the voices argued. "My God, that Bandit Sumter captured the wagons heading to Rawdon in Camden. Not only did he get the pay chests, but he also got the supplies and, in the process, we lost a good number of the 64th. So, what are we going to do about it?"

"What can we do? Bloody Hell, we sent Tarleton upcountry and all he seems to be doing is chasing ghosts! Now he is chasing this new commander, Greene, I believe. First, they nearly took Fort Watson, then that gang of plunderers knocked out the South Carolina Royalists. How does his lordship expect us to keep the lines of communication open when these Bandits and brigands close them up?"

A third voice joined in. "It's not easier in the low country either. Our pack of ghosts slips through the swamps and attacks our wagons and boats, taking them all. This damnable Swamp Fox and Wolf, and who knows what, are making fools of us! We appear to supply the rebels more efficiently than our men!"

"Then, gentlemen, we better get down to business and find a way to stop this mess from growing. We will be held responsible for this failure; I do not want that to happen. To be bested by a bunch of plunderers and Banditti. So let's see how we can stop them."

Maria placed the sewing down, a slow smile creeping across her face. She recalled how Jacob told her of his meeting, friendship with Sumter and sometimes fiery personality. When they mentioned the low country, Swamp Fox and the Wolf and the taking of the boats, she knew that it was Jacob and his band, along with Marion.

"At least they don't have their names yet," She thought. *"They are safe for now, but for how long?"*

Footsteps were approaching, brought Maria back to reality, and she returned to her sewing.

"Miss Faschingbauer, Miss Faschingbauer?"

Playing her role as absent-minded, Maria waited a few moments before looking up with a big grin on her face. It was one of the assistant quartermasters for the headquarters.

"Miss Faschingbauer, as we seem to have enough seamstresses here, you can go home to visit your family if you like. Would you like to go see your mother and father?"

Maria kept a big smile on her face, "Why yes, I would love to see my family, but I have all of this sewing to do."

The young man sighed and shrugged, "Miss Faschingbauer, finish what you are doing; the other girls will continue what you have started."

Maria nodded, "When should I return?"

"Late Spring, then it should be warm enough for the laundry to be more effective."

Maria nodded, and the man walked off as her heart fluttered. While he knew what she did, as dangerous as it could be, it was helping their efforts. It would also be nice to see her family and, if fate would smile a little, perhaps see Jacob.

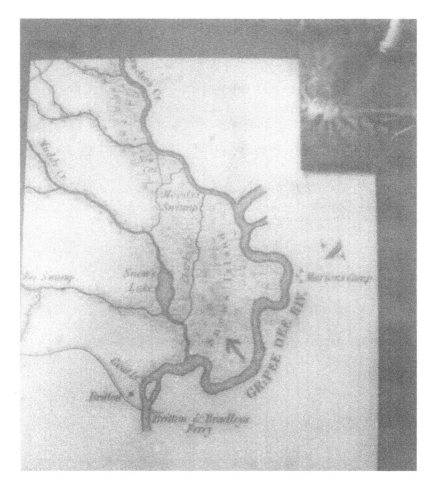

Map of Snow Island

CHAPTER 8

HOME FOR LEAVE

Marion and Oscar came to Jacob's camp; they sat around their small fire, sewing and repairing their gear. The day was clear but cold, the sun filtering through the trees into the camp. As Marion approached, he quickly motioned for everyone to sit as they were starting to stand up in his presence.

"Sit, lads, sit." Marion commented, "Good to see you boys keep your gear together to the best of your ability. Probably would be easier if you weren't camped out in the swamp and the cold."

The men chuckled as Marion watched and looked around. He could see that Jacob may have thought about where he was going with the conversation.

"I want to thank you, men, of the groups who ride with us; you have always been here. Now, I want you to go home, go see your families."

Surprisingly, it sounded more like the men wanted to stay than go home after learning that Captain Kane had recently been captured at his home by the Queen's Rangers. Marion understood it was a risk to go home, but he also knew it was a risk to his men if they did not go home and see what they were fighting for.

"Men, I am asking you to rest and see your family for a short while. Besides, we are militia and can go home when not needed. So it will be good for you, and when I need you, I will call you out and provide the location of where to meet. Now go home!"

Marion tried to look severe but cracked a smile as the men accepted and their tone changed, now excited to see family. Marion walked over to Jacob, Samuel and Jean.

"You three need a break, but I want you to pass to your family from me. I can't thank them enough for their help during this struggle. I believe the supplies and the information brought to us are why we are so effective at what I do. So, thank them for me. Now, mount up and go home."

Marion shook their hands, followed by Oscar, then Jacob nodded and they all ran back to their camping area and packed their bags. The wolves seemed to sense something was happening and waited with tails wagging. Once all was packed, they mounted their horses and gathered. Jacob addressed the men of the band.

"Be careful while you're out there, we don't know who is and who will report you to the British or Loyalists. Take care of your families, see that you keep them safe, and when Marion calls, be ready to ride at a moment's notice. I'm proud to be leading you; you're the best I have seen in a long time. Now go get some rest!"

The band broke up while Jacob, Samuel, and Jean led the boys and, escorted by the wolves, headed out of the camp. They used trails only they knew, avoiding any towns or villages so as not to be spotted by Loyalists or British sympathizers. Jacob waited until nightfall before even taking the back trail that brought them from the rear of their compound to avoid being seen.

The wolves ran into the compound first to announce their arrival. Then Jacob and the others trotted in as Peter, Gottfried, Maria, and Otti came out to greet them. Hugs were given all around, and then they made sure their gear was taken to their homes and their horses stabled; before heading into Jacob's house, Maria and the girls started making a meal for the men.

"You all need a good meal; they are not feeding you right. You are all nothing but skin and bones!" Maria commented, shaking her head, winked then headed to the kitchen area.

They all took a chair before the fireplace, the wolves curling up in their spots on the floor. Peter came over with ale tankards and even handed them to the boys. Maria gave him a disapproving eye, but Peter shrugged, "If day are old enough to fight, den day can have a drink!" Peter stared back at Maria, who shook her head, but Peter could see a small smile on her face. The boys were not boys anymore.

Jacob took a long pull from the mug, and it hit him hard, as it had been a good while since they had a strong beer.

"What news have you heard?" Jacob asked Peter and they all looked toward him as they knew little about what was happening outside their band.

Peter sat back, having lit his pipe, and collected his thoughts.

"Our old friends, the Cherokees are back," Peter started. "They attacked along the frontier but up in North Carolina und Virginia. Did not fare well, got beaten hard, then da riflemen went after the Middle Towns, burned them down."

Peter shook his head and continued with "again."

Jacob nodded. It seemed they kept using the same tactics, and he felt it was not that the Cherokee chose this on their own but had been influenced by the British and their Indian Agents. Jacob knew that all too well.

"We hear that da new commander, this General Greene, is moving around so much, dat old Cornwallis can't keep up. So it seems a race is going on and eventually, the two will come to a fight." Peter explained and Jacob nodded.

"Sumter not doing good," Peter continued. "He got stopped a few times by the British; Tarleton gave him a good pasting. They rode all over the place; some of his men called it the Sumter Rounds, as they seemed to be going in circles. Morale grew bad; many men left and went home. Then he did catch a supply train but was beaten again at Fort Granby. I heard he released his men to prepare for the spring plow, while I also heard he was taking his family to Charlotte."

Jacob shook his head while he thought of Sumter as a friend; he had heard some similar news from others about his ability to command his men. Moreover, some discussions arose concerning property taken from Loyalists that Sumter justified as they belonged to the enemy. Jacob hoped it was only a rumor, but it did not sit well with him.

Peter looked directly at Jacob. "There is a word of a Swamp Fox and da Wolf running around the swamps, giving dem Britishers a hard time. They know Marion's name, but they only know of the Wolf."

Jacob nodded and then shrugged his shoulders. "Marion knows, he learned of being called the Swamp Fox and he mentioned the Wolf is being spoken of."

"Aye, dat came from dee Catawbas, I'm afraid. They like speaking of the Wolf who the Cherokee fear and cannot die. They think it will scare the British and they will go away."

The meal was ready and they were called to the table. As they sat down, Jacob looked at his extended family, from Maria's parents, Samuel and his family and their "adopted" Jean. He was happy to see they were all still alive.

Their eyes, though, had seen different war moments and they were no longer innocent. Instead, these were eyes that had seen and experienced much, but for now, it was just family. For now, though, they were home and the war could wait for them for a change.

Jacob took Marion's advice, doing his best to rest and allow his body to heal from the hard campaigning. He spent as much time as he could with Maria and Helga, being caught up on their exploits in Charles Town. Helga spent a good hour telling her tale of helping her mother collect information and playing the game.

"Your mother told me you punched a boy hard enough he fell?" Jacob asked his daughter, who straightened up proudly, smiling.

"Yes, papa, he deserved it."

Jacob nodded, "Did he or any of his friends bother you again?"

Again giving a mischievous smile, Helga shook her head. "No sir, they left me be."

Jacob also spent some quality time with Maria, just sitting together and being caught up. "I am concerned about what you and Helga do," Jacob stated, "But Marion wanted me to thank you for the risk you two are taking."

Maria looked back at Jacob, "Is it any riskier than what you are doing? We both serve a greater good."

"And if you're caught, you could be hung as a spy," Jacob replied and Maria returned, "No different than you. Freedom does not mean it is free. Sometimes sacrifices may have to be made for the greater good. The need of the many is a heavier responsibility than the one."

Jacob shook his head, knowing not to argue or debate with his wife. "How did you get so smart?" he asked softly and she smiled, moving closer to him, "I've been around you too much." Then she hugged him tight and kissed him soundly.

Time caught up with them and while it had been a few weeks, a messenger did arrive from Marion. It seemed they had just started their rest period. Although he had to admit, he needed the rest as his body, from all the wear and tear of his life, was catching up with him.

Dismounting from his horse, Jacob noticed that Frederick had been sent to get them. He smiled and walked up and shook Jacob's hand. "It's good to see that you're rested," he began with a large grin, "Marion would like you and the others to join him at the Lower Bridge of the Black River."

Looking over, he saw his son Richard who had brought up an armload of firewood. "Richard, go fetch everyone and gear up. Marion has requested our presence."

Richard nodded and turned to get his brother, Samuel, his sons and Jean. Then, turning back to Frederick, "What is Marion up to? Have you got the message out to the rest of the band?"

Frederick nodded, "Aye, I have already met with the section leaders; they are gathering their men, and the band will all meet at the bridge. As for Marion, he cannot sit still, can he? We have been chasing the Loyalists and what seems to be only a few British regulars along the Black River. We first engaged them at Mount Hope Swamp and then we chased them down to the Black River. That's where Marion is now, fighting a Colonel Watson of his Majesty's forces."

Jacob nodded and motioned for Frederick to follow him inside his house to relax as he gathered his gear. Then, having learned that Jacob had been called for, Maria and Helga started collecting food and supplies for the journey. Frederick sat next to the fire; the wolves came over, tails waging to say hello to a familiar scent.

Frederick looked around, admiring the house and the activity. It appeared this was well-rehearsed; Frederick assumed they must have done this several times with Jacob during his life. Peter joined Frederick at the fire, staying out of the way. Frederick nodded to Peter, who nodded back.

"Da colonel ask fer Jacob and da boys?" Peter asked and Frederick nodded. Peter again nodded in response, "We'll have some supplies soon for you and da boys, fatten you up for da spring." Frederick chuckled and nodded in thanks, "I can tell you; the band and the other groups of Marion's men greatly appreciate what you do. Thank You."

Peter waved his hand in dismissal, having lit his pipe from the fire. "Ah, not a problem at all. I recall what poor rations can do to the men's morale; we vant you all to be happy."

Peter paused for a moment, his pipe in hand and eyes looking into the past. "I have soldiered a long time, with my leg though; dis is the best I can do to help and do my part."

After a short while, the boys came out, all geared up with their rifles. Jacob looked at his sons, seeing the young men they had become. While fattened by their mother's cooking, they were still stringy, lean-muscled men. Nevertheless, they all carried their gear professionally, like a second skin, and have become used to the activity.

They gathered their horses and Helga came out and handed them bundles of food and supplies. Jacob watched as she pointed her finger at the noses of the boys, probably giving them a stern talking-to about being safe. Then she hugged them and walked to Maria with a smirk on her face, from the shocked looks of her brothers.

Jacob chuckled to himself, "She is becoming more and more like you," he said as Maria came up and handed him his bundle of food and supplies. Then, looking down at her face, deep into her eyes, "We do this too much," he stated, "I am looking forward to when this all ends and we can just grow old together."

Maria reached him, placed her arms around his neck and kissed him. "I look forward to that as well."

She then gave Jacob a stern look, "Be safe!" Jacob nodded and responded with, "Be safe!"

He mounted his horse as the rest of their small group came together. Otti and Samantha walked along with Samuel and the boys, Jean coming up last. Richard and Patrick mounted their horses, and the four wolves sat on their haunches, ready to go. Peter stood on the porch and waved to them, along with Maria's parents.

As it had become a ritual, they said their farewells, be safe and the general threats of what would happen to them if either of them got hurt. This time, the men gave their jests and threats to the girls who would return to gather information from the British. Once it was all over, Jacob, with Frederick, led them out and, using the back trails to avoid any of the locals seeing them, began their journey back to rejoin the band and Marion.

***

Maria and Helga made their way into the wash area. Their bags slung over their shoulders and other belongings in a woven reed backpack. They reported to the quartermaster and were directed to the tent they had used before. After setting up their camp, they headed to the other washwomen sitting around the great tubs and tending the fires.

Helga headed over to talk and be reacquainted with the other children who hauled the wood and helped their mothers. Maria took her place with the other washerwomen and started chatting about their trip home and farm life. The woman talked and giggled as they scrubbed and worked on the dirty laundry.

From the other side of a building's corner, Maclane watched the washerwomen. Although he didn't like the fact they were so close to the headquarters, when he brought this up to the quartermaster, his response was, "The officers didn't like to walk far for their laundry, so that's why they are where they are at."

Maclane had suspicions; the rebels appeared to know much more about their activities when it was the right time to strike. When to evade their ambushers and when the supplies were moving through the countryside. Too many coincidences and Maclane knew there was no such thing in his line of work.

He watched the women chatting, like old friends in a sewing circle, their children doing chores and carrying the firewood for the laundry fires. Maclane could not put his finger on it, but something about this group of local women, recruited from the towns folk and the adjoining region, all supposedly loyal citizens.

"*But are they?*" Maclane thought, "*If I had to gather information, and how these stupid officers loved to impress women and hear themselves talk, that would be the place to get it.*" Nodding to himself, Maclane noted he would keep an eye on these helpers.

***

Robert Merritt was miserable; as he sat in the tight confines of a hut, what he over-heard was called the "bullpen." Holding the rank of cornet with the newly arrived company of Queen's Rangers. Captain Saunders' company had returned to New York. Merritt had been sent out under a flag of truce to locate the rebel leader, who they learned was named Marion. Granted, it was a ruse, but how these rebels treated him was unwarranted.

The one partisan told him this was how Captain Saunders had treated one of their captains. The captain had come to parlay in Georgetown, but Captain Saunders had him imprisoned and was still there, from what he recalled.

"Now, as your officers have seen fit to hang our men," the rebel officer commented as he was being placed in the bullpen, "If they hang another one of our officers, well, I am sorry to say, we'll hang you. Enjoy your stay!" Then he was placed inside the cell with roughly twenty other soldiers from different regiments. Merritt recognized the uniforms of the 63rd and 64th Regiments and some other Loyalists from the area.

There was a small window to let some air and light into the locked hut. Merritt stayed close to it, listening to the activity in the camp. Then, when he was able, he would look out the window, though, on a few occasions, the guard would yell for him to get back inside and try to hit him with the butt of his musket.

While he had been blindfolded before arriving, thoughts of escaping and returning to Georgetown occupied his time. Merritt sat there, looking at the window and began formulating a plan. Looking at his fellow prisoners, there was a large soldier from the 64th that would be a key element in his strategy.

The opportunity arrived when he could hear all of the activity outside the hut, Merritt assuming the rebels had departed for a raid. He would look out the window when the guards were busy and look around. He could see they were on an island of some type in a swampy area. When he looked around, he could see the camp was empty, except for a few rebels he saw moving around.

Timing would be everything; even with a small number of rebels in the area, they were still unarmed. Then Merrit reached into his pocket where his small pocketknife was, the rebels having missed it when they captured and searched him. He would have to be patient and wait for the perfect time to arrive.

It would arrive two days later when an alarm was sounded that a British patrol was nearby, and the rebels started to move around that Merritt considered the time was right. Motioning for the large soldier to come to the window, "When the guard is outside, grab him and pull him in. I'll take care of the rest."

The soldier nodded his understanding and smiled. Then, sure enough, the guard made his rounds and lined up with the window. The soldier quickly reached out, grabbed the guard with one hand, placed the other over the guard's mouth and pulled him through the window. The guard dropped his musket in the struggle as he was pulled into the hut.

As the guard was dropped on the floor, Merritt was on him, holding the knife to the guard's throat. "Easy now, lad," he whispered, pressing the blade against the skin, "no noise now." Merritt motioned with his head and the prisoners began to crawl out of the window and then helped the others out. One soldier picked up the fallen guard's musket and held it at the ready. The others started to pick up anything that could be used as a club.

Merritt was the last one out, leaving the guard inside. As soon as he wiggled out and placed his feet on the ground, he heard, "You there, hold!" Of all people, the officer of the guard was marching the guard relief around the camp. He had six other men with him, who brought the muskets up.

Not wanting to lose his freedom, Merritt devised a scheme against the guards.

"Form skirmish order! Merritt commanded and the twenty men reacted automatically, forming into two ranks at open order, twenty men strong. Though they only had one musket, the rest were armed with every conceivable club or other means to serve as a weapon. Merritt turned and faced the guard.

"Fire on us and so help me, God I'll have my men strike every one of you down!" Merritt yelled back. Merritt stared intently at the officer of the guard, hoping he would fall for his bluff. Luckily, the men figured it out and appeared more menacing, especially in their dirty and disheveled look.

The ruse worked and the six men turned and moved away from the prisoners. Merritt quickly motioned for the men to follow him and led them trotting out of the camp and to their freedom. *"It worked. It bloody well worked!"* Merritt thought as he found a road and, by looking at the sun, figured the general direction they needed to go to get back to Georgetown.

After a few days of walking through swamps and some of the roads, not wanting to be recaptured by the rebels, Merritt and his small group of twenty escapees walked into Georgetown and reported to Colonel Balfour. He explained how they had been captured, escaped, and returned to Georgetown.

Colonel Balfour was impressed. "Cornett Merritt, that was some of the best tactical decision-making I have seen in a long time. Would you accept a commission as a lieutenant?"

Merritt smiled and was slightly embarrassed, "Would it require me to leave the Queen's Rangers?"

Balfour nodded it would, so Merritt shook his head.

"All the same, sir, I would rather continue my service with the Rangers than receive the commission. Thanks all the same."

Balfour nodded his understanding. "If I were in your place, I would do the same. Go get some rest and again job well done!"

***

Marion was sitting in camp; Jacob and the other officers were going over their next plan when a messenger came riding in and reported to Marion.

"Sir, we have lost our camp on Snow Island!" the messenger stated and Marion jumped to his feet.

"Lost, you say; how?"

"From what I was told, sir," the messenger explained, "some British prisoners escaped and overpowered the guard. Colonel Ervin stated that the British returned in force and took the island under fire. The colonel resisted long enough to destroy equipment, threw our powder, shot in the swamp and then evacuated. But, unfortunately, he couldn't get everyone off the island; we guess we lost about fifteen of the sick and over twenty may have been captured."

The messenger had a depressed look on his face, being the bearer of bad news for Marion. Frustrated, with hand on chin, Marion began to pace back and forth, thinking of what to do next. Then after making a decision, he nodded once.

"Right, not much we can do about Snow Island, but we can pay a visit to our British friends and return the favor." He turned and faced Jacob and the other commanders. "See to your men. We move out as soon as everyone is ready."

The commanders nodded; Jacob headed to his band and gave them the order to pack their things. They quickly knocked down their lean-tos and rolled up their blanket rolls, securing them to the back of their saddles. As they packed, Jacob told them they had lost Snow Island.

"Oh bloody hell," Samuel exclaimed, "How did that bloody happen? Thought it was so far off the beaten trail no one would find it."

Jacob explained how the messenger had told them of the British prisoners escaping and must have told the British how to get to the island. Samuel nodded, "Well, that makes sense then. But, still, that is bad for us."

The band took it in stride, though Jacob could tell their morale had been affected by the loss of their base. He knew it would take time, as they did move around to keep the British guessing;

they had always been the chance they would find them. But, at least, their loss was minimal. It could have been much worse.

Once the band was ready, Jacob led it to where Marion, with his ever-faithful Oscar, was waiting behind them. Horry rode up, followed by McCottry and Richardson. Marion faced the groups, "Men, we're going to find Colonel Doyle and his Irish Volunteers. I learned he was the one who destroyed Snow Island. We'll return his gesture in kind!"

The men cheered as Marion turned his horse and led them out of their old camp and toward Williamsburg Township. But, as they rode, Jacob was concerned that most of the men came from that district, how many would keep their discipline and remain or slip away to see their homes.

Recalling his time on leave, Jacob could relate. However, war is never fair and sacrifices sometimes must be made. As they neared Williamsburg, Jacob's suspicion proved true. When they arrived at where Marion wanted to encamp at Indiantown, it was mostly his band and McCottry's rifles. The rest had faded away to visit their families.

When Marion dismounted and found out he had only around seventy men, he shook his head in fury. Jacob came over to report to Marion when he saw his face was a thundercloud. Oscar was there, trying to appease Marion.

"But sir, they are not regular soldiers like you," Oscar explained, "they are volunteers and miss their families, just like you do. They are only human, sir. They are only human."

Marion turned and looked at Oscar, then nodded and sighed. "Yes, Oscar, they are only human and volunteers. I sometimes forget that. I appreciate your honesty."

Oscar only shrugged and went off to make a fire to boil some water for Marion's tea. When Jacob arrived, he turned to him and nodded.

"Well, at least I can depend on you, Jacob. First, I need information about where Colonel Doyle and his men operate. I want you to take a scouting party and see if you can locate him while we wait for some of the men too," Marion paused and coughed, "ah, catch up with our column."

Jacob smiled, knowing the situation must grate with Marion, a stickler for discipline and dedication. "Yes, sir, we'll move out immediately and scout the area." Marion nodded, and Jacob headed back to his band. He called Jean, Samuel, Zacharia and Frederick over and issued his instructions.

"Marion wants information to locate the British in the area. Jean, take a group south and head over toward the Black Mingo. Samuel, take a group and head over to check along the swamp area to the east. I will take a group north; Frederick will immediately scout the area; make sure there is nothing that can attack this camp. Zacharia, take an element over to your old stomping grounds and see if you can find anything. We don't want another Snow Island."

"When should we be back?" Jean asked.

"Return by nightfall," Jacob answered, "should give you a few hours to look around. However, we don't want to make our presence known until everyone returns here."

Jean, Samuel, Zacharia and Frederick, knowing just like Jacob, that most of the men had gone home to visit since they were this close. Jacob went over and his group consisted of the boys, his wolves, Jehu Jones and Primus Hall. Jacob pulled in his group and explained their task.

"Marion wants information on the area and to see if we can find the British. We will scout out the area to the north near Lynches River. We are to observe and report only, no engagement as we are a little shorthanded right now." Everyone nodded their understanding of what Jacob wanted.

"Light marching order, we don't need to bring all our gear for this one. We will return by sundown to report to Marion. Does everyone understand?" Jacob looked at his group and with serious looks, they all nodded.

"Right then, see to your gear and mount up!" Then the band headed to their horses and Jacob went over and got his horse ready. He checked his gear and rifle, watched as Jean and Samuel with his wolves followed close behind, and then Zacharia and Frederick rode out with their groups. Jacob mounted up and his group departed with the two wolves following the boys.

"Keep your eyes and ears open," Jacob warned, "As it has been a good while since we have been through here, we don't know who is friendly or not." Jehu and Primus checked their muskets and rifles, made sure all was ready and laid them across the pommels of their saddles. Jacob nodded, turned his horse, led them out and headed north.

The day was a pleasant spring morning, but the group watched for any sign of the enemy and then took in the enjoyable day. The wolves seemed to enjoy the weather but constantly moved back and forth with the horses, their noses to the air and their ears perked. The soft thudding of their hooves on the dry dirt trail they were on helped silence their movement.

Jacob scanned, constantly searching with eyes, ears, and nose for anything that would alert him to the presence of hostile men in the area. Finally, they found a fording site across the Lynches, and Jacob led them north, keeping the river to their left side. They began to pass numerous farms, only observing farmers in their fields plowing or planting. Finally, the farms began to grow into decent-sized plantations.

It was when they were passing near one of these plantations that Jacob quickly held his fist up to halt. In the distance, he could see redcoats. Jacob moved his group into the trees and then pulled out his telescope.

In the distance, it appeared to be redcoats with thin green button lacing, collars, and cuffs. They were wearing small black helmets like the old Second South Carolina ones. Jacob lowered his telescope, *"Well, well, well. These must be the Irish Volunteers were looking for,"* Jacob thought. *"Why does everyone copy our helmets?"*

As they observed, it appeared they were a foraging party gathering supplies from the locals. However, as Jacob returned to watching them with his telescope, it did not appear the people they were foraging from were happy about it. Once the group seemed to be finished, they marched off with a small cart being pulled by an ox with the cart half-full of supplies.

"Nice and easy now," Jacob commanded, let's see where they go." So they kept the foraging party in view as they moved along the trees and bushes while keeping pace with the British soldiers. Finally, about twenty minutes later, they arrived at another plantation and another foraging party wearing the same uniforms.

As Jacob lowered his telescope, he nodded. "Well, lads, we found more of those Irish Volunteers. They must be camped in the area and sent out foraging parties, as they don't have access to their supplies. Let's get back to Marion and report this to him."

Jacob turned the group around and led them back to the camp near Indiantown. The sun was starting to set, which suited Jacob fine as it was the time for them to return anyways. Sending the group to their spot, he had them see to their horses and gear while he went over to report to Marion.

Marion looked up in expectation, "Tell me you found them?" he asked and Jacob smiled.

"Yes, sir, we found one group of foragers who led us to a second group north of the Lynches. As they were on foot, they must have a camp in that area. The locals did not look happy about them taking their food supplies."

Marion nodded, "Well, we should see to these foragers and take care of our people in the area." So they waited until Samuel, Jean, and Frederick returned from their scouts.

"The area appears to be clear of any direct British soldiers," Frederick stated, "We didn't see any sign of them." Marion nodded.

"Sir, we did receive word of sightings of these Irish Volunteers and a little Loyalist support to the south, but nothing solid," Jean reported.

"Same with us, sir," Samuel reported. "Just word about some quick sightings of these British redcoats passing through, but none of them stayed."

"The area around our camp here appears safe," Frederick reported. "We didn't see any signs of British or Loyalist activity."

Marion nodded and then looked over to Zacharia. "What news do you have?"

Zacharia shook his head. "None, sir. We didn't see any sign of the Loyalists, though a few friends confirmed they had seen them riding around, the mounted Queen's Rangers."

Marion nodded, "Then, lads, it appears Doyle and his men are to the north, on the opposite side of the Lynches. Thank you for your reports. See to your men and get some rest; we will be departing at first light."

Motioning Jacob to follow, Marion went over to his camp area, Oscar nodding to Jacob when they arrived. Oscar handed a cup of tea to Marion as he sat down on a fallen tree and sipped his tea. "Oscar, please get Major Horry and Captain McCottry if you please and have them report to me."

Oscar turned and headed to get Horry and McCottry; Jacob took a seat on another fallen tree. Jacob pulled out his pipe and, taking a flaming stick from Marion's fire for his tea, lit his pipe.

"Seems we have been doing this for ages, Jacob?" Marion asked, looking over the rim of his teacup. "We sure go back a good way, you and I." Marion shook his head, recalling in his mind their adventures together. "At least we shouldn't have more forlorn hopes, eh?"

Jacob shook his head, "No sir, I sure hope not."

Horry, then McCottry with Oscar joined them on the logs and Marion got down to business in planning their raid on Colonel Doyle and his Irish Volunteers.

"From what we have been able to scout out," Marion explained, using a stick to draw a map in the dirt, "It appears our good friend Colonel Doyle and his Irish Volunteers must have a base of operations to the north. Captain Clarke here spotted their foraging party. I intend to lead our men out and engage him at his camp. See how he likes losing his camp, just like we lost ours."

Marion looked at each of the officers present, who nodded in response. "We will cross the Lynches and head into the same area where they were foraging. We are moving to contact, not trying to avoid them this time. We will find him, fix him in place and batter them!"

Marion again leveled his intense gaze at his officers, who nodded in understanding.

Nodding himself, Marion ordered, "See to your men and mount up. Leave a small detail here to watch our camp. Everyone else in the saddle."

Jacob and the other offices stood up, headed to their camps and prepared their men. As Jacob and the band readied their gear, he explained what they would do and what they would do when they find Doyle and his men.

Samuel smiled and grabbed his blunderbuss, "I'll have my warm reception ready when we find them!"

Jacob snorted and shook his head before mounting up, the wolves rising expectantly to their feet, tails wagging, as they knew they were going on the hunt. Jacob looked down at the wolves' expectant gaze and noticed they were getting grey around their muzzles.

"I guess time catches up to everyone, even you four," Jacob commented. The wolves looked at him silently, but their tails were still wagging.

The rest of the band mounted up, automatically checking their weapons, ensuring they were loaded and had a good amount of powder in the pan. Then, holding their lock in their hands, resting their rifle and muskets across their pommels, the band stood ready.

After seeing everyone, including the wolves, were ready, Jacob led them out and joined Marion, Horry, and McCottry. Once their force was formed, Marion, with his ever-faithful Oscar by his side, led them out to the north. But, again, Marion had Jacob lead the column, following the same trail they had before.

Fording at the same site, the column splashed across the Lynches River and followed the road toward the plantations. Jacob led them past the plantations and farms they had observed before and followed the road they had observed the Irish Volunteers foraging group used earlier. It was only a short while later they came upon another Irish Volunteer foraging party at a plantation who appeared to be ransacking it.

"Got get them!" Marion ordered and Horry, Jacob and McCottry led their men forward in a charge. Yelling at the top of their lungs, Horry's men rode toward the main foraging party and opened fire as their horses slid to a halt. The shocked troops froze as Horry's men fired and began to encircle them. Nine Irish Volunteers fell to the ground and another sixteen dropped the property they had just stolen and threw their hands up.

As Horry was securing the Irish Volunteers, Jacob spotted another group trying to run away, dropping sacks and boxes they had been carrying.

"With me, lads!" Jacob yelled and the band turned to follow Jacob at a gallop. The wolves sped off toward the running Loyalists and McCottry's men followed Jacob as the Loyalists ran into some trees of an adjoining plantation.

The Loyalists were in a mad dash, heading for the river as fast as their feet would carry them. They began to spread out, the fastest of the foot getting ahead, the slower ones starting to lag. The last two men running heard an odd, heavy breathing coming from behind them. As they turned to look, the wolves pounced, two taking a man each. Both men were knocked to the ground, the wolves clamping their jaws down on their arms and legs.

As Jacob rode by, he pointed to the two pinned Loyalists. "Secure them!" A group of the band with Frederick stopped to take the two Loyalists' prisoners, the wolves wagging their tails, and at the run, took off to catch up with Jacob. They had to slow their pace riding through the trees, but then they broke into an open area of the neighboring plantation.

In the distance, the Irish Volunteers who were still running stopped at the river's edge, where a second group appeared to be destroying a ferryboat. The running Loyalists collapsed to the ground and the men destroying the boat began to form a line quickly.

"Band, to the right! McCottry, take your men to the left. Engage at will!" Jacob commanded, and as he led his men to the right, McCottry broke off and went to the left. They quickly dismounted, a few men holding the reins of the horses while the rest began to take up firing positions. Jacob had stopped beyond the range of the Loyalists' muskets, but it did not stop them from firing.

The line of Loyalists fired, their balls flying around the ground before Jacob and his men as they formed in pairs and open order. Then, at the crouch, they began to advance toward the Loyalists loading their muskets.

"Riflemen, engage at will!" Jacob commanded. He knew their muskets were out of range, but the rifles were not. The men armed with muskets took a knee to cover the riflemen, who were taking a good firing position, some standing and some kneeling. The Loyalists once more lowered their muskets and fired a ragged volley, the balls causing no damage.

Looking down his sights, Jacob slowly let out his breath and pulled the trigger and his rifle fired with a reassuring thump. Jacob's target and a couple more Loyalists spun and fell to the ground. Jacob smiled and began to load as he looked over to see McCottry and his men advancing by files. First, one fired their rifles; the other would leapfrog forward and cover.

"Advance!" Jacob commanded and the band advanced another twenty yards before Jacob halted and had his riflemen fire once again.

"Fire!" Jacob commanded and his riflemen fired at the Loyalists once they had a good target. While not a volley, still effective as a couple more Loyalists fell to the ground. Soon, the Loyalists broke and began to throw their muskets to the ground and swim across the river. Waving his hand forward, Jacob led them toward the river's edge.

McCottry brought his riflemen up alongside Jacob's men. Eight dead Loyalists and five wounded were lying on the ground, a testament to the accuracy of their rifles. Across the River, Jacob noticed another group of Irish Volunteers forming a firing line as the retreating group began to rise out of the water.

The command of "Make Ready!" was heard from the far side and the Loyalists' muskets were brought up to the ready position.

"Present!" The muskets barrels came down, leveled at Jacob and the band. Jacob did not kneel, instead stood defiantly facing the Loyalists.

"Fire!"

Jacob did not have a death wish. Instead, he knew they were out of the effective range of the Loyalist's muskets. As he expected, the balls mostly fell harmlessly into the river or the trees and brush. No one was hit. As soon as the escaping Loyalists pulled themselves dripping from the river and began running past the other Loyalists. They gave one more volley before turning and marching away.

"Reform!" Jacob commanded and a sullen Samuel came up holding his blunderbuss.

"They never gave me a chance to say hello!"

"Don't worry, Samuel," Jacob answered, "Maybe next time!"

They searched the dead for anything that could be used for intelligence and stripped them of their muskets, cartridge boxes and some personal items. The wounded were secured and led off by McCottry's riflemen. Jacob led his band back and picked up his men and the two Loyalists the wolves had tackled. They escorted them back to Marion, the wolves helping to escort the prisoners, who gave the wolves fearful looks.

Marion nodded when they joined him with their prisoners. Marion saw some blood on the muzzles of the wolves, and he looked at Jacob. "A good hunt, I take it?" he asked.

Jacob looked at his wolves, who were lounging nearby, turned and nodded in agreement. "Yes, sir, it was a good hunt!"

Marion chuckled and led the group back to their camp after dropping off the prisoners with a local magistrate for paroling them with a small detachment from Horry's men. The rest returned to their base and cleaned their gear. Then they sat around their small fires, smoking pipes, chewing on their biscuits and jerking meat.

Over the next few days, scouts were sent to keep an eye out for Colonel Doyle, his men, and the group members returning from their non-sanctioned leave to visit family. Marion learned that General Greene would be marching into South Carolina and, as he had done before, contemplate if they should ride north, meet him and report to their new commanding officer.

Peter arrived with some supplies and brought a message from Maria for Marion. Before he delivered it, Jacob pulled Peter off to the side and asked how Maria was doing. He winked and nodded.

"She is doing goot, my friend; she is tough."

Peter, with Jacob, went to find Marion so he could deliver the message. They found Marion, who nodded to them both, "I take it you have some news, Peter?"

"Ya, sir, we do."

Marion nodded and offered Peter an empty box while Jacob sat on a log.

"We learned dat Colonel Watson has been ordered to go north against Greene. Our friends in da area saw him burn his wagons and sink his guns in the Catfish. Den he was seen marching toward Camden."

Marion nodded, "Thank you, Peter, for the news. Please pass my best to our friends who help us, and please be safe."

Peter nodded, stood up, and returned to where his carts were being unloaded. Marion called for Oscar, who went to gather the commanders. Jacob remained sitting on his log as Marion began to think through the situation.

"We have a tough decision here, Jacob; what would you do?"

Jacob looked at Marion, who was looking directly at him. "Sir?" Jacob asked.

"Do we go after Watson to prevent his engagement of Greene, or do we withdraw and wait to see how it works out in case it turns into another Camden?"

Jacob looked at the small fire where Marion's teapot sat, the tiny flames dancing along the wood and embers. He then looked up at Marion, "I would go after Watson, prevent him from joining Lord Rawdon at Camden, taking that advantage away."

Marion nodded, then pulled a letter from his coat pocket and opened it. "Just received this," Marion stated as he opened the message. "General Greene has dispatched Colonel Lee and his Legion to join us with his men and supplies. That would give us an advantage, even as our wayward members return from their leaves."

Jacob nodded; that was some good news. The other commanders joined them and Marion started a council of war, laying out the same options as he had asked Jacob earlier. Besides that, he added joining their forces with Lee's Legion. The officers decided quickly to keep fighting and, with Lee's Legion, take the fight to the British in support of General Greene.

CHAPTER 9

A SPRING OFFENSIVE

Spring was arriving in full force in the city; the trees were budding, and the bushes and the flowering trees were also in bloom. The air was warmer, though some nights were cool. From within the Army Headquarters, the staff continued to plan their campaign to bring South Carolina under control. General Cornwallis was now in North Carolina with orders to head to Virginia.

Lord Rawdon had assumed command of the southern area of operation as General Cornwallis was heading north. He had moved forward to the garrison at Camden but still required Charles Town to serve as the main base of operations for the army, providing logistics and recruits to the regiments.

The staff was busy looking over maps, receiving information from their information network on the movement of the different rebel groups near Georgetown and the lower Sandhills. The staff knew they didn't have enough men to escort every wagon train of supplies, so they had to plan the best route where they had more of a loyal populace.

As they worked through the early evening, so was Maria. With her sleeves rolled up, hair falling from her bonnet, scrubbed on a dirty pair of breaches. *"Did this man wallow in the mud?"* she asked herself, seeing how caked the mud was on the knees. As she scrubbed, she kept her ears open and listened to the conversation from the staff, who had their windows open.

It had been hard to gather information inside as the cold temperatures brought many of the washerwomen inside the buildings and not necessarily close enough to overhear conversations. But, now that she was back outside, she could continue to listen and gather information. In her heart, she knew every piece of information she could glean would help Jacob.

It's been tough; they were losing washerwomen. Some had moved on to Camden with their Loyalist husbands. Others had slipped out of the city to live with their families away from the fighting. What disturbed Maria and some other women were that some other women had disappeared.

Granted, it had been some time since the old legend of "The Beast of Charles Town" hunted people before and when the war started. But then, it all stopped, and people began to feel safe at night once again. Then recently, they started to disappear and that frightened them once more.

***

As Maria worked, she was observed from the shadows. Maclane had been following and watching the entire distaff working in and around the headquarters. He was trying to determine if there was a leak and who. While a few of the distaff had moved to Camden and other garrisons, the attacks continued, so he decided none were leaks.

Then he began to follow the distaff around the headquarters, those who lived in the city and the outer towns. One by one, he followed and questioned their activities and motives. When he did not get the answers he wanted, he then had to cover his tracks. Therefore, he followed Big Harpe's evil mind and dead men, or women, tell no tales.

Maclane did not want to do it; he had to protect his identity and job, but he was starting to feel the frustration of what he thought was a losing war on their part, and he wanted to get some revenge. So he justified his killing, knowing that he was. But, he admitted in a warped way he was hurting the rebels and his enemies this way.

Now he watched this washerwoman, having eliminated all the ones working when the rebels were ambushing them. Maclane had to be patient, follow her to a secluded place to grab her, and then take her over to the old South Sea officer where he could question and, if required, sink her in the river with the other women he had killed.

Maclane leaned back against the wall, watching and waiting as the woman bent over, scrubbing, then stood up to look at the wash to determine if the dirt had come off. The light was fading, and she had to look closer at the clothes. She shrugged and went over to hand the shirt on a clothesline.

"Ms. Faschingbauer, you are one hard-working woman," a man stated as he came from around the headquarters building. "I think it's getting too dark to see. Go get some sleep, and you can start in the morning when you can see."

It was one of the quartermasters responsible for the laundry, Maclane guessed as he watched and waited. Finally, the woman nodded, moved the washing pail off the fire and using a poker, spread out the fire to die down. She then gathered her things and began to head toward the distaff camp down the road from the headquarters.

Nodding, Maclane knew this was now the opportunity. He began to follow the woman, stalking and quietly following. His mind swarmed with ideas, from how to sneak up and get her, knock her out, then drag her to the officer. Then, another thought popped into his mind, a dark and more primal idea. He had not been with a woman for a long time and other urges were rising.

"*Why not mix work with pleasure,*" Maclane thought, "*Maybe Big Harpe did have a good idea in his very warped ways.*" He focused on his quarry and moved in pursuit of his prey.

***

Maria moved along the sidewalk, her shoes crunching on the crushed oyster-shelled walkway, going over what she heard and what she should report to Marion. There are many details to go through, sifting what is essential and what is not. As she walked along sorting out the information, her senses became very alert.

Maria looked up, her eyes scanning the houses around her. Something did not feel right; a tickle at the base of her head warned of danger. She turned down the alley, which was a shortcut toward the open space that the distaff used for a camp. As she turned, she thought she spotted a shadow moving along the street.

Her heart began to race and she moved quickly down the alley, realizing that it may have been a mistake to come this way. While she held her bundle in her left hand, she reached down and gripped the handle of her belt knife. Her breath was coming heavy when she heard the crunching sound of footsteps behind her.

An arm reached her neck, but before the assailant could secure his hold around her throat, Maria spun and quickly pulled her knife, turned and sank the blade to the hilt in one swift motion. Maria looked up into the shocked face of Maclane, the warm flow of blood covering her hand. His arm slackened around her neck and he fell to the ground.

Maria looked down as Maclane lay there, blood pooling from the knife and his mouth. The shocked look remained on his face. "Wasn't supposed to be this way?" he whispered as his head finally fell back and rolled to the side, dead.

She left the knife in Maclane and dropped the clothes she was carrying on top of him. Maria spun and sprinted toward the distaff camp. Running between the tents, she quickly opened hers and woke up Helga.

Helga rubbed her eyes and asked, "What is going on, mama?" Maria replied with her finger over her lips. "Shh, pack your things. We are going home!"

Helga quickly gathered her few items as Maria did the same with what few things they had. Finally, she stuffed all their spare clothes, stockings and food into a basket backpack. Helga worked quickly and quietly, knowing her mother was serious and time was of the essence. Once everything was packed, Maria looked at Helga and nodded and Helga nodded back.

Maria smiled, "We are going to have to be quiet, so we don't wake up the others, understand?"

Helga nodded, "Can I say goodbye to my friends?"

Maria shook her head, "No, I am afraid not. You don't want to wake them now, do we?"

Helga thought about it and then shook her head. "No, mama, you are right. Let's go see Uncle Peter."

Maria nodded, "Yes, let's go see Uncle Peter."

Holding Helga's hand, Maria led her out of the camp and along a different route away from the camp. Seeing a woman and child with a backpack was more common now, allowing them to blend in with the other refugees and families. Maria led them through the north gate and followed the road north until she found a familiar route to the northeast.

Near midnight, Maria and a tired Helga arrived at a tavern owned by Jacob's friend from the Mounted Rangers, Peter Youngblood. She knocked on the door and after a short wait, the door opened, and Peter stood there with a lantern.

"Maria, what in the bloody hell are the two of you out at this time of night?" He asked as he showed them into the empty tavern. Peter looked down and saw Helga wobbling and having a hard time standing. Then quickly looking over, he could see the dried blood on Maria's hand. He looked up and saw that she had that distant look in her eyes of someone who killed their first human.

"Let's see to Helga first, and then we'll talk. So go sit for a spell and we'll talk after I get her settled in."

Maria nodded as Youngblood led a tired Helga, who didn't argue, to an open room and, after taking off her shoes and depositing her bags, helped her climb into bed, promptly falling asleep. Then Youngblood returned to where Maria was sitting at a table with a far-off look in her eyes.

He went around the bar, poured them two cups of wine, and placed one cup in front of Maria. Then, he returned to the kitchen with a bucket of warm water and soap. Then, he pulled a chair next to her and began to wash the blood from her hand.

"Drink the wine, lass. It will take the edge off," Youngblood stated as he scrubbed. He could tell she was in shock and followed his instructions. Lifting the cup, she took a drink as he continued to scour the blood away. As he washed the blood, he saw she had no injury, and the blood was from someone else. He dried her hand, returned the chair across from Maria, and picked up his cup.

"I killed a man, Peter. I killed him." Maria spoke slowly and quietly about the event. Youngblood knew she had to get it out into the open and sat there listening.

"Did he attack you, lass?" he asked and Maria nodded.

"I felt something was wrong, a sensation that made my hair stand up. Is that normal?" Maria asked, staring at Youngblood. He nodded his head slowly.

"Sometimes, for old soldiers like us, it comes with time, but yes. You can sense when someone means you harm."

Youngblood snorted, "Like Jacob and his famous gut feeling, always warned us of trouble."

Maria nodded and continued. "I felt his arm around my throat, but I was ready. I had my hand on my knife, so when he grabbed me, I turned, and my blade went all the way in. His blood covered my hand, and he fell. That's all."

Youngblood nodded, "Then you saved your life. Helga has a mother to take care of her, and Jacob has a wife to return home to. What you did was just."

Maria nodded and finished her cup. She looked up at Peter. "Is this what you or Jacob felt when you killed your first person?"

Youngblood chuckled and shrugged his shoulders. "That lass is a hard question. I don't know how long ago Jacob killed his first man, but I think I heard him talk about his time with the Mohawks and he was only fifteen or so. As for myself, yes."

Youngblood finished his mug and looked at Maria. "It haunted me for a little while, but I learned to accept it as he tried to kill me. After that, I could live with it and the others I killed over time."

Maria sat there, and the exhaustion was finally settling on her shoulders. Youngblood stood up, went over and took Maria's hand. "Come lass, time to get some sleep. In the morning, we'll see you safely home."

***

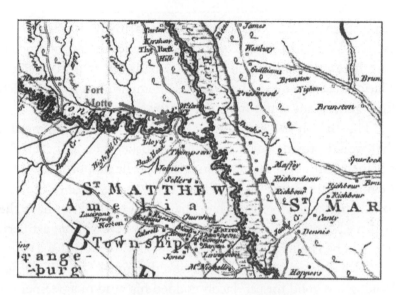

Fort Watson and Fort Motte

Jacob, Samuel and Jean looked at the British outpost known as Fort Watson. Located on top of an old Indian mound, it had three rows of wooden stakes as abatis set on a steep slope. Marion had deployed McCottry's Riflemen to keep the British from getting any water from the nearby Scott Lake.

The British had cut down all the trees around the mound that would provide cover for regular musket men and even the riflemen were at the range when firing. While supported by Lee's Legion, Marion and his men have been laying siege to the fort for the past week. Nothing had changed. They did not have the artillery Marion had requested and Jacob knew without artillery, it would be challenging to assault.

"What do you think, Jacob?" asked Samuel, "So far, it's not looking too good for us." Jacob nodded his head in agreement.

"Oui, my friends," Jean added. "Smallpox has broken out in the militia camp, and we lost about half of our force."

Jacob, still looking at the fort, nodded his head. "Aye, it is bad news, and from what I have seen with the other officers, it is starting to affect them. They are short on patience and about to start fighting one another, let alone the British. Marion is holding a council of war later to see what we can do about this situation."

When Jacob arrived at the council of war, he could feel the tension among the officers present, both militia and Continentals. He had witnessed this bickering back and forth, affecting the morale of the men and Marion's force. Finding a log to sit on, Jacob sat down to wait for the council to begin.

Major Eaton of the First North Carolina was speaking with Colonel Richardson. Major Maham was having a very animated conversation with Colonel Horry, his hands moving up and down, then circling with his fingers. Captain McCottry, like Jacob, just sat against a tree with a pipe in his mouth.

"Good idea," Jacob thought as he pulled out his pipe, filled it with tobacco and lit it using a burning stick from the small fire. Everyone was waiting for Marion and Lee to arrive. Colonels Giles, McDonald and Benton had their heads together in a tight conversation. Leaning back against a tree, Jacob allowed the smoke to curl around his face as he watched all around them.

Soon, Marion and Colonel Lee arrived and sat with the other officers in the circle. Marion looked very intently at the gathered officers. Finally, they all quieted down and looked toward Marion.

"What is the hospital report? How many have come down with smallpox?" Marion asked.

Colonel Giles spoke up. "Sir, at least twenty men have come down with the pox and are isolated from the main camp."

Marion nodded, "What is the truth behind why we are losing men to desertion?"

The colonels looked at one another before Benton spoke up. "Sir, at our last roll call, we identified at least six men unaccounted for and the day prior, four men unaccounted for. We believe it is because of the pox and the inactivity that the men are deserting."

Benton looked at Marion to gauge how he would react and Marion only nodded. "That is what I believe it is as well. We sit here, waiting to see if the artillery I asked for arrives, the men are getting restless or sick from the pox and I worry that Watson will come back with reinforcements from Georgetown and catch us between him and the fort."

There was a low murmur through the officers and nodding in agreement. Marion watched before continuing. "We need a plan, as I suspect we will not have the luxury of artillery support, nor do I wish to hazard our men in a futile assault. So, what options do we have? How can we take the fort?"

249

Again, the men began to speak amongst themselves in a low murmur. Jacob just observed from where he sat, his pipe in his hand. Maham raised his hand and Marion acknowledged him.

"Sir, I have an idea that could take the fort." He stated and Marion nodded. Marion looked at the officers before continuing. "My men and I will build a tower tall enough to shoot down into the fort where the British won't be protected by their walls. Then, if I could borrow Captain McCottry, his riflemen and some other riflemen, we could make it very hot for the British and force their surrender."

The group murmured amongst themselves; Marion looked to Lee, who only shrugged his shoulders but nodded. Marion thought about it and it appeared to make sense to him. With a nod, he approved the plan.

"As we don't have much of an option, Major Maham, let us know what support you need for your tower."

Maham nodded and smiled, "axe men, I could use some help building the tower." Marion nodded, "Then it's agreed; we support Major Maham's construction. Captain McCottry and Major Clarke, be ready to provide riflemen."

The commanders returned to their units and after explaining what they would do, many volunteered to cut wood for the simple reason of doing something instead of sitting around. When the sun rose, the axe men went to work, cutting down the trees, and then the men with tomahawks cleared the branches off, making clean logs.

The ends were notched and the base of the tower was set. As the longs arrived, they were laid in place and secured as the tower rose skyward. Jacob stood to the side, wiping the sweat from his face after helping with the construction. He looked at the fort in the distance and they did not appear to care about what they were doing. *"Of course, they may not know what we are doing,"* Jacob thought.

Over the next few days, the tower grew one log at a time. Finally, a ladder and supports were placed inside the tower to reinforce stability. Jacob, Samuel, and Jean contributed to the building, happy to be doing something for a change. The wolves sat in the shade and watched, their eyes taking everything.

The tower grew to about forty feet high and Major Maham, with Marion and Colonel Lee, looked up at the top. "Can you see into the fort?" Marion called and the worker at the top answered, "Yes, sir, I can see them plain as day."

Marion nodded, then smiled, "Well, it's no time like the present. Let's get some riflemen up there and see what they can do." Marion turned and went off to find McCottry, while Jacob and the others wiped the sweat off them and waited.

Soon, four of McCottry's riflemen, with their long rifles and shooting bags, climbed up to the platform at the top that would serve as a firing point. The riflemen took up shooting positions, bracing their rifles on the log support and aiming through firing ports at the British in the fort. As they aimed, the British soldiers were walking around, had no idea they were being targeted.

They quickly learned when the four riflemen fired and four British soldiers in the fort fell to the ground hit. The British soldiers scattered and sought cover looking at the tower in the distance. The riflemen went through their loading procedures and soon the betting began on who could make the better shots.

The British began to scurry around, having been safe behind their sloped walls, but now were under fire. The riflemen waited until they had a good target before firing, not wanting to waste their shot or powder. McCottry established a rotation plan, rotating riflemen into the tower to give the other riflemen a break to rest and clean their rifles.

On the second day, Jacob took his turn at the top of the tower with three of McCottry's men. They gave themselves room to get into comfortable shooting positions, then brought their rifles up and braced them on the log. It was a nice, sunny clear blue-sky day and they had an excellent view of the fort's interior.

Jacob could see they had dug a trench to the lake to fill a well they had dug inside the fort. Nodding his head, Jacob would target anyone getting water. Jacob checked his powder in his pan and waited for his target to appear. The riflemen sat, waited, and made small talk, reminding Jacob of when he used to go on long hunts before the war. He could see movement in the fort; the British had put up barriers and boxes to hide behind.

After a short wait, Jacob's patience was rewarded when a British soldier moving low between the boxes, had a bucket in his hand, heading for the well. Bringing his rifle to his shoulder, Jacob looked along the sights and, after judging his intended target's distance and movement speed. Jacob pulled his trigger, the rifle barked, and the man fell forward, collapsing on the ground. The bucket rolled around on its side.

"Want to have some fun?" one of the riflemen asked and another answered while Jacob began loading his rifle. "Let's see who can hit the bucket. That should wear on the nerves of our British friends. Jacob even smiled; he liked the idea as he finished loading his rifle.

Each rifleman took his turn to fire at the bucket lying on the ground. The first one fired and the bucket spun around. The men cheered and the next rifleman took his shot that missed. The third fired and he spun the bucket, then Jacob took his shot and hit the bucket. The wounded bucket spun around on the ground, then came to a rest.

The body of the British soldier began to move. Soldiers low-crawled up to where the dead man's feet were and began to pull the body behind cover.

"Do we shoot?" one rifleman asked, looking over his sights. Jacob shook his head. "Don't waste your powder," Jacob stated, "won't hit anything anyway. Let them sweat for a bit." So they remained in the roost, watching the fort interior, but none of the soldiers inside exposed themselves before their shift was over and they climbed down.

Jacob headed to their camp, leaned his rifle against a tree and took off his shooting bags before joining Samuel, Jean and the others over by their fire. They had several large trout on sticks being cooked. The wolves greeted Jacob before returning to their post of watching the cooking fish.

"I see you all had a good day," Jacob remarked as he sat down. The boys proudly smiled and held up another string of six large trout.

"Yes sir," Patrick answered, "found us a good fishing spot, so we secured fresh rations from the lake. How was your catch?"

Jacob recounted their shift in the tower, how he had the only kill and how they messed with the British by shooting the bucket.

"Sounds like you had a good day, too," remarked Richard and Jacob smiled.

"Aye, lad, I guess we both had a good day today."

Other members of the band had gone fishing as well, so their entire camp area smelled of freshly cooked fish as the men talked around the fires as the fish cooked. As Jacob leaned back, chewing on a biscuit, he recalled the times when he and Samuel had been with the Rangers, and they had done the same thing and gone fishing.

Marion gathered the men in the morning while McCottry's riflemen kept the British pinned down inside the fort. Then, standing at the edge of the woods, Marion pointed across the open area toward the fort, the slope and the wooden abatis.

"Gentlemen, I believe the time is right for our assault. Colonel Lee's cavalry has informed me there is no movement of the British heading to relieve the fort here. McCottry's men have the British seeking cover and not watching the slope. We will launch an assault, cut down the abatis and clear a path to attack the fort."

The officers looked across the field and along with Jacob, were ready to assault. They gathered as many axes as possible, their tomahawks and a few musket men to cover them in case the British resisted. Jacob brought his men up; all had tomahawks and a few axes. Lee's Legion infantry were there, as well as other militia columns. Looking left, then right, Jacob ensured the assault columns were ready before raising his tomahawk and dropping it toward the fort.

The assault columns began jogging toward the slope and the first barrier of abatis. While expecting to be fired on, Jacob had to admit it felt strange running toward an enemy fort and not being fired upon. Then, as the assault column was halfway across, a man yelled, "A white flag!" Jacob raised his hand and as they came to a halt, a white flag was being waved from the fort. A cheer went up from the top of the tower.

The assault columns returned to the camp, and Jacob was called to accompany Marion and Colonel Lee to discuss the fort's surrender. With rifle in hand and shooting bags over his shoulder, Jacob followed along with Marion and Lee as they walked up to the fort's door. The door was open and a single soldier in his regimental coat of the 64th.

Entering the interior, Marion, Lee and Jacob surveyed the damage they had wrought on the British. Off to the side was the water bucket they had shot at the day before. Jacob was pleased to see the solid hits that had put holes in the bucket.

Around the wall's interior were wounded soldiers; there was a sign of freshly dug graves, and those not injured had wild eyes in them. Jacob could see the well they had dug and the small trench that brought water from the lake. A wounded lieutenant approached the three officers.

Doing a curt bow to the three of them, "Lieutenant McKay, of his Majesty's 64th Regiment of Foot, surrenders my position and my men to you." He drew his sword and presented it first to Colonel Lee, who directed it to Marion. Marion would not accept the sword.

"Keep your sword, lieutenant and all of your officers. With your baggage, you will all be paroled and depart this place and return to Charles Town to await further guidance concerning a proper exchange of our people for you and your men. Let us know how we may assist you in evacuating the fort."

Lieutenant McKay nodded, "You're very kind, sir and we should be able to march on our own as we have already cared for our dead." He saluted Marion and Lee, Marion returning it before turning and leading them back to their position. "What is your plan for the fort?" Jacob asked.

"Burn it once they leave," was Marion's answer.

They waited until the British marched out of the fort and headed down the road toward Charles Town. Once the fort was vacated, Jacob and Marion, with a few of their men, entered the fort. After looking for anything of value, fires were set and soon the buildings and the wooden walls caught on fire.

As the flames rose and roared and the black smoke curled skyward, the men cheered their victory over the British, able to win the siege without artillery or a significant assault. Once the fort was destroyed, Marion led his men and Lee brought his Legion and they headed to the High Hills to rest and reconstitute the force.

***

The field smelled of death, bodies still strewn about where they fell on Hobkirk's Hill. Daniel McGirtt walked about the field, looking at the dead. British, rebels, and provincials. Having pushed the rebel army the day before, Lord Rawdon left the cavalry holding the hill to say he had won the battle. The men were dismounted, their horses tied to a fence leading to log town, the lumberyard outside Camden.

McGirtt walked down the hill, where more of the dead were still laid out, burial details arriving to begin digging the graves. His men searched the bodies for any trinkets or loot they could claim. Lord Rawdon had taken the rest of the army back to Camden to see to the numerous wounded.

Kneeling, McGirtt looked closely at the dead rebel, strangely naked instead of in uniform. A musket lay on the ground and he did have a cartridge box over his shoulder. *"Must have caught them washing their clothes,"* McGirtt thought, then chuckled, *"Hell of a way to go, I guess. Came into the world naked, go out the same way."*

Standing up, McGirtt kept his inspection of the battlefield when he heard the sound of horses in the distance. Looking up, he recognized the uniforms of rebel cavalry crest a hill and stopped. Turning quickly, McGirtt sprinted up the hill toward his waiting horse.

"To horse, to horse!" command was being shouted by Major Coffin as all cavalrymen began mounting their horses. As McGirtt and his men were out looting, Coffin and his cavalry already took off as McGirtt's men were mounting their saddles. Once they were all mounted, they kicked their horses into a gallop.

They rode down the hill and quickly closed the distance to the hill where the rebel cavalry had been seen. When they crested the hill, they could see the rebel cavalry enter the woods with Coffin's men in hot pursuit. McGirtt followed the dust trail of the horses, following a dirt road through the trees.

"Crack-boom!"

The woods before McGirtt erupted into a grey cloud of smoke as Coffin and his men rode right into it. McGirtt pulled back hard on his reins, yelling, "Ambush!" The sound of screaming wounded horses could be heard and some of Coffin's men quickly came riding out of the grey smoke.

McGirtt turned his horse around, leading his men out of the woods and back up the hill. But, instead of stopping, he led them onward toward Camden. "No sense in sticking around here," McGirtt grumbled, and his men agreed. After a short ride, they entered the palisaded walls of Camden and dismounted over in one of the corners.

Major Coffin and the men who had survived the ambush rode into the compound and dismounted. McGirtt walked over just in time to hear Coffin speak with Lord Rawdon.

"It was an ambush, sir," Coffin explained. "They baited us with a small element of their men, who led us into the ambush."

Rawdon nodded his head; Coffin did have a look of shame on his face, having been lured into a simple ambush. McGirtt smiled inwardly, watching this Loyalist officer fall for a basic trap that he should have known better.

"It's irrelevant at this moment, major," Rawdon explained, "Prepare your men to march. We are pulling out and withdrawing to Charles Town. I have dispatched a rider to Ninety-Six and

Colonel Cruger to abandon his position and consolidate with us in Charles Town." Then he turned and spoke to McGirtt.

"Same to you, major, have your men pack and head to Charles Town. We will consolidate there and then see to our rebel friends."

McGirtt nodded, turned and headed to where his men were waiting. "Pack your things, lads; the British have lost their stomach to fight and are running away. So, we're heading out."

"Where are we heading to?" one of the men asked.

McGirtt chuckled. "Anywhere but here. They may be giving up; I think we head north and find Bloody Bill. I heard he is not running. Let's fight with him and see what we can stir up!"

The men cheered and began to roll up their gear and get their horses packed, McGirtt thinking about how much booty they could take riding with Bloody Bill. They could profit from this loss after all.

***

Jacob and his men lay concealed in the trees, watching the British column march along the road toward Camden. Looking through his telescope, Jacob could see a few hundred British infantry and four pieces of artillery. He lowered his telescope and nodded.

"That must be Watson we were warned about," Jacob commented, "We better go tell General Greene that Watson is on his way."

Jacob mounted his horse, Patrick handing the reins up to him before he turned and mounted his horse. Once everyone was mounted, Jacob led them out with the wolves running alongside. The weather was getting warmer for early May and most men were now just wearing their split shirts or frocks. The trees and bushes were thicker with new green leaves, helping conceal their presence.

Jacob led them along dirt paths and hunting trails toward the west side of the Wateree and crossed at the ferry south of Camden. It was only a short ride when they came upon Greene's camp. Jacob halted them just before the sentries, who, after briefly asking them for the password, Jacob led them into the base. As the men were marching, there were only ground cloths or lean-tos, no tents. When they arrived at Greene's camp, Jacob halted them and dismounted.

The sentry approached Jacob, to which Jacob responded with, "Major Clarke to see the general." Before the sentry could say anything, General Greene spoke up. "Private Anderson, allow Major Clarke to enter."

The sentry came to attention, presented arms and Jacob saluted him. Greene rose, smiled, and shook Jacob's hand. "It has been some time, has it not, Major Clarke?" Jacob smiled and nodded his head.

"Yes, sir, it sure has been."

Greene nodded and then turned serious. "I take it you found Watson?"

"Yes, sir, he had several hundred men and four pieces of artillery heading this way," Jacob answered.

Greene nodded, nodding his head slowly. "Major Blair!" Greene called out, and quickly the major arrived.

"Have the army packed and ready to move; we must find a better place for our men as it seems we have irritated the local British forces."

Major Blair nodded, then turned and headed off to get the army packing. Greene turned and looked at Jacob. "If I may ask a favor, would you and your men be interested in staying here with Washington's cavalry to slow down the British?"

Jacob smiled and nodded. "We would be honored to remain here to provide a warm reception of our British friends."

"That's what I thought," Greene answered with a wink before getting his command moving. Jacob returned to his men and gave them the quick details.

"We are going to give the pursuing British a warm reception," Jacob explained, and his men all beamed and smiled.

"Ambush?" Samuel asked, and Jacob nodded. Washington's cavalry is staying back as well. I'll speak with him about how we will do it; Samuel, you, and Jean will secure what supplies you can from the quartermaster."

As Jacob's band prepared for the ambush, Jacob made his way over to where Washington's cavalry was located. Spread across the ground, Jacob could see numerous wounded from the battle near Camden. Finally, Jacob found William Washington and his cavalry and he looked up and smiled.

"You must be Major Clarke," Washington commented, "I was just told we are working together to buy some time for the army."

Jacob nodded, "Yes, that is correct. I could take my men and we will ambush them at the ferry, then ride right toward your position. Then you can take a crack at them. How does that sound?"

Washington nodded, "Sounds like a plan to me."

Jacob returned to his band. "Mount up; we're heading to the ferry to give the British a warm kiss."

As the men mounted, they laughed but were all serious about riding. As the army was being formed to march, Jacob, with the wolves, trotted alongside. The Continentals and militia were a different army they passed, compared back when Gate's commanded it. No sidelong looks or snickers, but respect was shown on the faces of the men as they rode by. The men nodded to Jacob and the band as they headed toward the ferry.

When they arrived, they found wooded spots that would give them concealment to fire upon the advancing British. Jacob spread them out, giving them all sectors of fires and that he would be the one who would initiate the ambush.

"Wait until I fire, then let them have it!" Jacob stated, and everyone nodded. Samuel had his blunderbuss out and was getting into a good firing position. As usual, he had one man holding onto five horses so they could quickly mount and ride away. Jacob checked the others, Jean, Zacharia and Frederick's sections. All were in good positions. Jacob nodded and was pleased, then turned to head back.

Jacob moved to where his group was waiting, consisting of the boys and Jehu. The wolves were waiting next to their horses, held by William Lee. Jacob was able to find a good, supported firing position leaning up against a tree, a crook in a branch making a good shooting rest.

Looking left and to his right, Jacob could see his men concealing themselves the best that they could, waiting for the British to arrive. Motioning with his hands, Jacob had the wolves lay low, but their eyes and ears were peaked, and Jacob was relying on them to hear movement before they did.

The area was quiet, insects buzzing, the water at the ferry gurgling and the light, warm breeze blowing through the leaves. The branches swayed slowly, moved by the breeze, the men staying in the shadows. Jacob's eyes kept moving, scanning, searching for the approaching enemy.

Waya's ears quickly perked up and he stared across the ferry at the road approach. Jacob followed Waya's gaze and ears, "You see something, hear them coming?" Jacob asked in a whisper.

Waya continued to stare and soon a flash of red appeared. Jacob looked intently, and sure enough, the lead elements of the British column were approaching the ferry. No drums were being played, so they did not hear them coming.

In a whisper, Jacob told the boys and Jehu to get ready. Looking over, he could see Jean and Samuel's groups were also prepared, everyone slowly sinking and concealing themselves in the brush. The men holding the horses ensured there were trees and bushes between them and British eyes.

The British began loading the ferryboats to bring them across, filling them with about twenty men each. Jacob quickly looked to his left and right, mentally projecting, *"Don't fire until I do! It will ruin the trap!"*

The first boat was using both oars and poles to push it across the river and was slowly making its way. Jacob could hear small talk and laughing coming from the soldiers on the boat traveling across the water. Standing in the center was an officer speaking to someone sitting next to him. Nodding, that man would be Jacob's target.

Bringing the Jaeger rifle up to his shoulder and aiming, Jacob took an excellent firing position aiming at the officer. While braced against the tree, he aimed along the barrel and pulled his hammer to full cock. The river was flat, so his target had no bobbing, just straight at him. Taking one last deep breath, Jacob held it and pulled the trigger.

The rifle boomed, and the ball struck the officer in the throat, tearing it out and spraying the men behind him in blood. Then, with a rumbling roar, his men opened fire to include the loud report of Samuel's blunderbuss. A good number of the sitting British soldiers fell into the boat, falling on their men or into the river. The officer that Jacob hit toppled over and fell into the river.

As Jacob and his men began to load, commands were being shouted as the survivors on the boat appeared to be shocked and just floating in the river. Then, in confusion, the boat spun around mid-river as some men fell wounded or dead, the others taking cover inside. The column started to deploy their companies on the shore to cover the boats.

Jacob and his men had enough time to reload, "Independent fire, muskets at the boats, rifles at the far side. Fire at will!" he ordered and their side of the river began to fire at targets on the opposite bank and the boats. The rifle and musket balls whistled and whizzed by the British, and many impacts were heard as soldiers spun and fell to the ground.

When the British presented their muskets to fire a volley, all of Jacob's men made sure they were behind cover so that when the volley fired, no one was hit except for the trees and the shore. Then, as the British began to reload, Jacob and his men, having reloaded, leaned out from their cover and fired once more.

The British were becoming frustrated, so the commander ordered up artillery pieces, from what Jacob could see, 3-pounders. Nodding, Jacob decided it was time to go. As the gunners dropped the tails of their guns and began the loading process, Jacob gave the order to mount up and ride. The men turned and sprinted to their horses and quickly mounted.

Boom-boom-boom!

The sound of cannons being fired was enough for Jacob and his band to spur their horses and take off. The enemy cannon balls fell into empty trees as Jacob and the band rode off toward where Washington's cavalry was waiting. Jacob looked over his shoulder and the band was following, and he could see grins on the faces of his men. Jacob had to smile himself; that was rather fun for a little fight.

Jacob waved as they rode past Washington and his men, who were concealed but ready to charge, pistols being readied. Washington waved back and smiled as Jacob's band continued toward Greene's position. Jacob slowed down the band to a walk, allowing the horses to rest. In the distance, Jacob could see a hill rising in the distance and he nodded. That would be an excellent defensive position.

Jacob led his band across the ford at Sawney's Creek and deployed before him; in plain sight was Greene's army. He had the militia occupy the empty farmhouses, their muskets pointing out the windows covering the ford. The rest of the army was deployed across the hilltop and ridges, with artillery aimed at the ford. Jacob nodded in approval.

Riding through the line, Jacob led his band to where Greene was waiting and reported.

"Sir, we engaged the advance guard of the British column. We held until they brought up their artillery to fire on us." Jacob reported, and Greene nodded.

"How many guns did they have?" Greene asked, "We heard at least three fired on us when we left." Jacob answered, and Greene nodded.

"We'll take it from here," Greene commented; the sound of pistols going off could be heard in the distance. "Seems Washington is having his turn with the British. Jacob, return to Marion with my thanks. I'll send instructions later when I may need you."

Jacob nodded, then led the band away from the line and onto the road that would take them back to Marion's camp. Samuel and Jean rode up next to Jacob, "That was fun; can we do it again?" Samuel asked while Jean chuckled.

Jacob chuckled in return, "If I know Marion, we will be doing just that soon enough." The three still chuckled and spoke of the ambush as they clopped down the road to their camp.

CHAPTER 10

FORT MOTTE AND GEORGETOWN

Alexander Cameron coughed heavily and then laid back on his bed. He was exhausted and knew his time was short. Much of his illness can be attributed to his constant interaction with the Cherokees, negotiating and constant traveling in excellent and foul weather. He lay there, looking out the window of his house in the City of Savannah.

Much had changed to get him where he is now, which weighed heavily on his heart and soul and could be another contributor to his poor health. Hence, his frustration with his government, failing to see reason and supporting his plans with the Cherokee. They had expected them to once more fight the colonials but give nothing in return.

He had tried to direct the attacks in such a way as to limit bloodshed, but he couldn't do so. In response to the Cherokee invasion came a series of punitive raids by the Carolinas and Virginians that leveled many towns and destroyed the supplies cached for the winter.

Cameron was forced to flee into the Creek country to avoid capture by the Americans. For a time, he lived with David Taitt, the British deputy for the Creek. The rebels learned he was there and sent a warband of pro-rebel Creeks to kill them all. Having learned of this plot, they fled to the safety of Pensacola in the fall of 1777.

Once more shaking his head, he recalled how he tried to perform his duties with the Cherokee but from Pensacola. John Balfour was his go-between, as Claus returned to England after they arrived at Pensacola. He was already starting to feel his age, along with John Stuart, who also showed the ravages of time.

Time did catch up with Stuart; he died in 1779, leaving his position as Indian Superintendent open. Instead of assigning him, London decided that Charles Stuart, John's assistant, would hold joint control until a successor was appointed.

"It should have been me!" Cameron thought angrily as another bought of coughing shook his body. *"I earned it and bloody well deserved it!"*

To his great dismay, the decision made in London was to appoint not a successor but successors. That decision alone would have been disappointing, but the instruction that Cameron would superintend the western division of the department would give him jurisdiction over the Choctaws and Chickasaws, two tribes with whom he had had only incidental contact.

"What were those bloody fools thinking? No wonder the rebels are winning over here!" Cameron fumed and then coughed again. Finally, he lay with his eyes closed, wheezing and sweating.

He tried to carry out his duties by sending messages from Pensacola to the tribes, but it proved ineffective. Finally, however, the question became academic for the Spanish captured Mobile in 1780 and Pensacola in 1781, forcing the British away from the Gulf Coast. Cameron traveled through the Indian country to reach Savannah's relative safety. So now he was bedridden and fighting for air, remembering his accomplishments. He closed his eyes, his breathing becoming more raged, then slowed and finally stopped altogether. Alexander Cameron, old Scotchee, drifted off into death.

***

Captain Richard Pearis looked at his new surroundings, what was being called Fort Motte. It was a long way from gathering information in Charles Town, but at least now he could be an active participant and no longer just a collector of secrets.

Built around the Mount Pleasant Plantation of Mrs. Rebecca Motte, it was a fortified position. As it seemed the Crown was having trouble controlling the interior from bandits or rebels like this Swamp Fox and Wolf, it made sense to Pearis to build these small garrisons.

The plantation was situated on top of Buckhead Hill. A deep moat and a raised parapet surrounded it. Pearis thought it was a strange twist of fate that they fortified this house. Mrs. Motte, the wife of the former Colonel Motte of the Second Regiment who had been at Fort Sullivan. He had died of sickness the year before. So she and her family were moved to the overseer's house while they occupied the main house.

Along with his company of Loyalist infantry, Lieutenant Donald McPherson was in overall command with his two companies from the 84th Royal Highland Emigrants. Supporting and scouting were Corporal Ludvick and his troop of light dragoons. They even had a small carronade cannon to strengthen the garrison.

"Yes, I believe this is a rather strong position to be in," Pearis thought as he moved down to check on his men, who were getting situated in their new home.

***

Not long after Jacob rejoined Marion, a messenger arrived from Greene, detailing them to capture or destroy the British outpost recently built on the Mount Joseph Plantation. Lee's Legion was still with Marion and had been reinforced with a 6-pound cannon sent from Greene. During the initial council of war, Lee was given the honor of reducing the position.

This made sense to Jacob, as Lee had more men and a 6-pound cannon that could reduce the fortifications and walls. So, they prepared what supplies they had, Jacob making sure his men had shot, powder and food before they rolled up their blanket rolls and prepared to mount up. Then, finally, Marion gave the order to break camp; Jacob and his band mounted their horses and joined the column for the march.

It was a warm early May day as they clopped down the dirt road, dry from the little rain and dust rising from the hooves. The jingle of the cannon's chains mixed with the clanking of tin cups and canteens on the riders. Jacob was called to the head of their column, where Marion wanted to speak with him.

"Jacob, take your band and scout ahead. Get eyes on the plantation until we arrive," Marion instructed. Jacob nodded, turned and moved quickly back to his men.

"Band, with me!" Jacob ordered as he turned and led them out at trot past the column. Soon they were ahead of Lee's Legion and were on their own. Jacob kept a quick pace but kept an eye on their horses, so they did not exhaust them in case they bumped into a British or Loyalist patrol. Finally, following a game trail, Jacob arrived on the other side of a hill from the plantation.

Having the band dismount, he had them conceal themselves in the trees while he took Samuel, Jean, Zacharia and Frederick with him on top of the hill. There, an abandoned farmhouse stood, but they cautiously entered it to ensure no one was inside. Then they made their way over to a corner of the house with bushes to conceal them, where they had a good view of the plantation.

Pulling out his telescope, Jacob scanned the position. It was on the hill across from them, making it easier for them to observe. Jacob explained what he saw as Samuel wrote it down in his notebook.

"A moat surrounds it and a wall," Jacob reported, "appears they are using the house as a garrison. I think the palisades are about nine feet tall and with ramparts roughly ten or eleven feet wide. It is faced with a six-foot-deep ditch in front. Then about twenty to thirty feet in front of that, a row of abatis. I see horses tied up, so they have cavalry, Redcoats and Loyalists in the garrison and they even have a carronade mounted."

Samuel nodded as he wrote down the information as Jacob reported it. They watched the coming and the going of the garrison. There were two guards at the entrance; they watched four horsemen depart and follow the road away from the house. Then a supply column of four wagons arrived and entered the compound.

About an hour later, Patrick came up and flopped down next to Jacob. "Lee's advance guard has arrived," he whispered to Jacob, who nodded. They slowly backed away before heading down to meet with the advance guard.

"How far back is the main column?" Jacob asked. "They are only twenty minutes behind," the corporal responded and Jacob nodded. Soon the column did arrive, and Jacob led Lee and Marion to the farmhouse and pointed out the defenses. Marion shook his head, "This is Rebecca Motte's place," he stated, "She moved here after the colonel died and to get away from the city."

Lee decided to use the farmhouse as his headquarters, able to observe the siege from there. He called up the officers, Jacob included. Lee stood out in the open, wanting the British to see they were there, and it was evident as they closed the door, they could see men lining the walls.

"Captain Finley, place your 6-pounder to rake that northern end of the position," Lee directed, and Captain Finley nodded.

Major Eaton, General Marion, we will start our approach trenches from just below, the cannon providing fire support. Riflemen will move to support positions up here on the hill and provide firing support. See to your men, get situated, then let's see to evicting these men."

Jacob nodded. While never a fan of the traditional siege tactics of the time, having been through a few sieges, but he agreed that it might work this time. *"At least it's not Montreal,"* Jacob thought as he descended the hill as Lee's men began to occupy the farmhouse. As he entered his campsite, Marion was waiting for him.

"Jacob, take a scout around the area, I would like to know the lay of the land and anyway, we could be surprised here," Marion instructed, and Jacob nodded as it made sense. Marion walked up the hill toward the headquarters while Oscar remained behind to get Marion's camp area and tea on the fire.

Jacob gathered Samuel, Frederick, Zacharia, and the boys to go out on the scout. "We are to scout the area to learn of all approaches, or the British or Loyalists could sneak up on us and give us trouble. Light marching order; we ride in ten minutes."

They quickly ran over, prepared their gear and mounted their horses. Jean came over to Jacob as he was preparing to leave.

"Your instructions?" he asked.

"Have the men rest; if they ask for riflemen to support, go ahead and send them. Try to avoid any digging details. Recall the fun we had in Charles Town?"

"Oui, mon ami," he answered, shaking his head. Jean recalled the hot days of digging and the seeping muddy days.

After Jacob mounted, his scouts arrived and Jacob led them out at a trot. Taking a circular route, Jacob led them along trails and roads, noting approaches and any bridges over the Congaree and access from the old Cherokee Road. They did not see any signs of British or Loyalists, but they kept their guard up.

When they arrived on the far side of the plantation area, they found the overseer's house, and Rebecca Motte was standing outside when Jacob rode up. She came out to greet the riders.

"Captain Clarke is it not," she asked, "You served with my husband at the fort. I recall seeing you there when we presented the set of colors."

Jacob smiled and bowed from the waste. "Yes, ma'am, it has been some time since those happier days."

Mrs. Motte sighed and nodded her head, "So true, so true." Then she looked up at Jacob. "As it has been some time, I take this is not a social call, correct?"

Jacob nodded. "Yes, ma'am, we plan on driving the British from your home. If you would like, we can escort you to where Colonel Lee and General Marion are."

Rebecca smiled but shook her head. "Thank you, but no, we are well established here and, to be honest, want to keep the children safe from any harm or bloodshed."

Jacob nodded, "Understood. We will send scouts out to keep you safe anyway."

She nodded in thanks, then Jacob turned his horse and led them back out to complete their scout of the area. When they reported to the headquarters, they described what they saw to Marion and Lee, including their encounter with Rebecca Motte.

"Don't blame her," Lee commented, "Sieges can get rather bloody."

To highlight that, the 6-pounder began to fire on the fort, planning to reduce the walls and make the coming assault easier. The men dug approaching trenches, covered by the riflemen and the cannon, for the next two days. The British carronade was in a bad position and could not be moved to fire on the 6-pounder.

Jacob continued to scout the area to provide early warning for the army in case the British had learned of the siege and sent a relief column. Jacob had led his scouts across the Congaree and, as fate would have it, spotted an approaching column of British soldiers. Leading his scouts to a concealed location, Jacob looked at the British forces.

Using his telescope, he observed the British; they were lying on their arms instead of camping. Small fires dotted the area; the men gathered around to cook their rations. No tents on site, which meant they were moving fast.

"What do you think, Jacob?" Samuel asked, "They are moving fast if not setting up a normal camp. You think they are trying to catch the army between the fort and them?"

Jacob nodded as he closed his telescope. "It looks like it to me. They can be at the siege within the next forty-eight hours if they keep pace. We better report this to Lee and Marion; we may have to set up some ambushes to slow them down."

They rode back to the camp and reported to Lee and Marion that they spotted the British column approaching.

"How long do we have?" Lee asked.

"No more than two days if they keep pace and rest on their arms," Jacob answered. Lee nodded, deep in thought.

"Colonel Lee, we have only one real option," Marion stated. Lee turned and nodded to Marion. "Which is?"

"We know we will lose valuable men if we do a frontal assault, and with a single 6-pound cannon, it will take more than two days to reduce the walls. Therefore, we need to force their surrender."

Lee nodded in agreement, "How can we achieve that?"

"Burn it down."

Lee looked at Marion, "Burn it down?"

"Yes," Marion returned. "At least burn the main house down that the British are using as a garrison. That will force them out."

Lee nodded, "But wouldn't that make us no different than what the British had done?"

Marion shook his head, "Not if we ask permission. Ask Mrs. Motte and see what she says, as it is her house."

Lee nodded and then looked at Jacob. "If you please, Major Clarke, can you lead me to Mrs. Motte so I may ask this difficult question?"

Jacob agreed and after Lee mounted his horse, Jacob and his scouts led Lee over to the overseer's house where Mrs. Motte was staying. She came out as Jacob and Lee rode up.

"Captain Clarke, so nice to see you again," she commented as they dismounted.

"You know Mrs. Motte?" Lee asked, and Jacob nodded. "Her husband was our regimental commander at Sullivan and she and the good ladies of Charles Town presented us our regimental colors."

"Ah, I see," Lee replied before he turned and after taking off his helmet, bowed adequately to Mrs. Motte.

"Mrs. Motte, I have a complicated question for you."

She looked at Lee and nodded her head. Lee sighed as he tried to devise how to ask to burn her home down.

"To save lives and prevent the unnecessary deaths of both sides, we would like permission to burn your house down."

She thought, "Do you believe it will resolve this siege with a minimal loss of life?"

Lee nodded; it was. Mrs. Motte turned and entered the house. Lee looked over at Jacob with a confused look on his face.

"Did I make her angry?" he asked in a whisper and Jacob shook his head.

"I believe she would have told you she was angry."

Mrs. Motte returned outside, carrying a bow and a quiver of arrows. "Captain Clarke, I believe you are more familiar with these if what my husband told me of your younger days, but I believe these will be the best way to set my house on fire."

She then looked directly at Lee. "Sir, you have my permission to burn my house down and see the removal of the British and their Loyalists friends from its grounds."

Lee bowed and accepted the bow and arrows. "You may have just saved numerous lives, ma'am. Thank you!"

"Until victory then?" she added.

"Until victory!" Lee answered.

They mounted their horses and returned to the camp, where they showed Marion the bow and arrows and how Mrs. Motte gave her permission to burn the house down.

"I will give them one more chance to surrender," Lee stated. Marion nodded, then led Lee over to the side of the hill facing the Congaree River. The sun was setting, and it was easier to see the twinkling fires of the British camp in the distance.

"Our guess is they will be here in a day, so whatever we plan to do, we need to do it tomorrow."

Lee nodded, then looked at Jacob. "Was she correct, Major Clarke? Do you know how to use this bow and arrows?"

Jacob nodded, "Yes, sir, in my youth, I lived with the Mohawks and the Mohicans. So, I am very familiar with the use of the bow."

Lee nodded, then handed him the bow and arrows. "Then you will take the shot tomorrow if they don't surrender."

Jacob nodded, accepted the bow and arrows and headed to the camp. He located a quartermaster and was able to secure some pitch. He then went to his camp, where as they sat around their fire, he wrapped the pitch around the arrows so they would burn like a torch.

The wolves watched quietly, along with the boys, Samuel and Jean.

"When did you learn to use a bow?" Patrick asked and Jacob told him of his early days living with the Mohawks. They had taught him how to hunt with the bow.

In the morning, Lee once more called for the British to surrender. Having seen the fires across the river, they refused. Jacob was called for and Lee permitted him to set the house on fire.

"I will have to wait until noon when it's good, hot and dry for the fire to take," Jacob explained, and Lee nodded. They kept the pressure on with the riflemen and the cannon until then but had stopped digging the approach trenches. As noon approached, all stopped to watch Jacob and the bow.

He entered the approach trench, followed by Samuel with a lit lantern and a candle. The men stood off to the side, allowing Jacob to pass by. He came to the end of the trench, able to see the house roof in the distance. He placed his pitched-tipped arrows against the dirt wall of the trench as he looked at the roof.

It was hot enough for the mirage to make waves in the air over it. Jacob nodded as he readied the bow and picked up the first arrow. Samuel placed the lantern down, opening the window to the lit candle inside. He waited until Jacob had strung the bow and was ready to draw.

"Ok, Samuel, light me," Jacob instructed. Samuel reached up with the candle, and the pitch caught and flamed on the end of the arrow. Jacob pulled the bowstring back and lifted the bow at a good angle for the shot. The arrow was nose-heavy with the burning pitch. He pulled, so the string touched his right cheek.

Twang!

Jacob released the string, the bow snapped, and the arrow flew in a fiery arch up and over the wall to land perfectly on the house's roof. Within seconds, a flame could be seen spreading from the arrow. The men cheered and the sound of orders being given could be heard from inside.

***

Captain Pearis and his men occupied the house's second floor, protected from the damn rebel riflemen and their cannon. He watched out of the window, looking at the approaching assault trench snake closer and closer to their walls. He felt confident, though, having seen the campfires in the distance, the relief column as Lieutenant McPherson pointed out. So they had to hang on for another day.

While looking at the trench, he saw the flicker of light, and then it rose into the air and arced down to the roof. *"A bloody arrow?"* Pearis thought and soon there was a shout of "Fire on the roof!" Grabbing some blankets, Pearis and some of his men exited a window that gave them access to the roof.

Sure enough, an arrow was stuck in the roof and the flames were spreading out. "Get to it, men!" he yelled, "If we don't beat it out, the house is lost!" As they beat at the flames with the blankets, they were smothering it and Pearis had a satisfied look on his face.

"Bloody stopped that one quick enough," he stated, and his men agreed. Then he looked over in time to see the muzzle of the 6-pounder facing in their direction and the linstock coming down on the rear of the gun.

"Oh damn!"

The cannon fired and swept the top of the roof with grape shot. Pearis took two of the shot through the chest, fell dead and rolled off the roof. A couple more of his men screamed and fell. The rest ran and ducked back inside the house.

***

They watched how, using a window, a few Loyalists were able to get on the roof and began to beat out the flames. As they had just about put out the fire, the cannon boomed and sprayed it with grape shot. A few of the men rolled dead from the roof. Jacob had Samuel light another arrow and Jacob let it fly once more.

The arrow caught, the roof began to burn and the gunners waited to see if anyone else would come out. Instead, a white flag appeared and the command of "cease fire" was shouted across the trenches and the hill.

Samuel smiled as he blew out the candle and the lantern, then looked at Jacob. "Now that was different," he commented. "You know they will make up more legends and stories about you and that bowshot?"

Jacob nodded, "In the end does it matter?"

Samuel shook his head, "Only at taverns and depending on who pays!" The two laughed and headed back to their camp. The men in the trenches patted Jacob and Samuel on the shoulders as they passed by.

As Jacob and Samuel made their way back up to the headquarters, Marion and Lee accepted the British surrender as the roof of the house continued to burn. Once the British and Loyalists grounded their arms, Marion ordered his men onto the roof and extinguished the fire before it spread to the house. The men quickly charged into the fort, climbed out of the windows on the second floor, and began using blankets and anything they could to snuff out the flames.

Jacob and Samuel arrived just in time to see the surrender acceptance. There had been some friction growing between Lee and Marion concerning, of all things, horses. Lee thought Marion had enough horses to equip his men and that he should give Lee any extras. Marion did not have enough horses to spare as it was.

Jacob suspected a lot of this was due to poor communications between Marion, Lee and Greene.

What bothered Jacob was when the word went around camp that General Greene was trying to take their horses to give to Lee, a good number of them went home, which reduced their number to only around two hundred. So while General Greene had apologized to Marion, the damage was already done.

There was a chasm growing between Marion's men and the Continentals. Jacob could also see how Marion chaffed at seeing the well-disciplined and equipped Continentals of Lee's Legion and his men. Jacob suspected that Marion would much rather be a conventional officer once more than a partisan leader.

In the end, with the chasm in place, Lee accepted the surrender of the British regulars, and Marion accepted the surrender of the Loyalists. The fire was extinguished, saving most of the roof and the entire house. Mrs. Motte returned, moved back into her home, and cooked dinner for Lee, Marion and the British officers as a gesture for peace.

That evening, Marion had asked Jacob to accompany him as one of his officers, mainly to help keep him in check as his emotions were still raw in dealing with Lee. The officers sat down at a long table, Patriots on one side and the British on the other. As Mrs. Motte was the host, she sat at the head of the table.

Surprisingly, her servants made a sumptuous meal and she produced some bottles of port along with Lee, who also brought some bottles. The conversation was straightforward and polite, if not a little strained. Jacob kept an eye on Marion, who was angry, but kept it concealed and polite in conversation.

As Marion did not drink, he could keep a level head. But unfortunately, due to the other officers, especially Lee's men, one of them made a comment that caused the situation to explode. During the meal, a man came in and whispered in the ear of one of Lee's officers, who exclaimed, "Bloody excellent, let the bastards swing!"

Marion stopped and looked at the officer who commented, while Jacob thought, *"Bloody hell, that can't be good."*

"Explain yourself, sir!" Marion demanded and the officer shrugged as if it meant nothing.

"Nothing really, sir," the officer replied, "We found three of these bastard Loyalists guilty and now they are swinging."

Marion dropped his fork, stood up, and exploded. "You dare to hang Loyalists without my permission? How dare you, sir! If I find that you or your men have committed a crime, I will see you all hang!"

With that, Marion bolted out of the house and Jacob did everything he could to keep up. He saw a group of men gathered around a tree, mostly Lee's men. Marion shoved his way through the crowd. They had been laughing and jeering, but now all became silent as an angry Marion stood there.

Two dead bodies were laid on the ground, and the third man was freshly hanging from the tree. Jacob could not recall when he saw Marion so angry, shaking with rage, with both hands clenched into fists. He stepped forward and pointed to the hung Loyalists, "Cut that man down now!"

He then turned and leveled an angry look at all of Lee's men standing there. Marion was seething; Jacob had never seen a more direct and angrier look ever on Marion's face.

"Let me make this blood well clear for all of you. I am in command here! Not Colonel Lee. He has been attached to my command by General Greene. If I catch anyone of you deciding to take justice into your own hand, I will kill the man responsible. Do I make myself clear?"

Lee's men looked at the ground and shifted their feet but did not respond.

"I bloody said, do you understand, or by God, I will have all of you charged under a court martial and will see you flogged! Now, do I make myself clear?"

This time the man answered with "Yes, Sir!"

Marion still scowled. "See to these men have a proper burial; the rest of you get out of my sight!"

Lee's men quickly cut the hanged man down and, with the other two men, took them over to a small cemetery near the house and began working on digging graves. Marion watched for a short moment before stomping back to his camp and avoiding Lee or any of his men. Jacob followed along until Marion reached Oscar and his camp.

Oscar could see Marion was upset and looked over Marion's shoulder toward Jacob. Nodding slightly, Jacob agreed that Marion was upset and Oscar should watch over him. When Oscar nodded, "Sir, I'll see to making some tea for you." Jacob turned and headed back to his camp. Lee must have reported the friction and General Greene arrived at Fort Motte in a couple of days.

Jacob was with Samuel, Jean, Frederick and Zacharia on top of the hill when they saw Greene ride into Fort Motte. The four watched as Marion, Lee and Mrs. Motte came out to greet the general.

"What do you think, Jacob?" Samuel asked as they watched the greeting before they all went inside.

"If I was to guess and believe me, I am guessing, Greene is here to smooth things out between Marion and Lee. He needs both commanders and as we saw with the number of our men going home to check on their families, if they don't fix the command issue, there will be no commands."

"Would that happen?" Frederick asked and Jacob nodded.

"Personalities are personalities, and how Greene, Lee and Marion conduct war are very different. One wrong comment, or what could be considered either a slight or downright insult, is enough to drive the commander away. If he goes, his men go, which is tougher for us as we are not considered Continentals. We have already seen what happens when our men get bad news; they go home."

Later in the afternoon, Jacob and the other officers were summoned to Marion's camp, where he addressed their new orders. He made no comments about the meeting between himself, Greene and Lee.

"Gentlemen, we have been directed to move against Georgetown while Colonel Lee has been directed to invest and take Fort Granby. Greene is going after Ninety-Six and when we are successful, to send reinforcements to him after we secure Georgetown. We are departing first thing in the morning; make sure your men and gear are ready to march. Any questions?"

Jacob and the other officers shook their heads. Then, finally, Marion nodded, "Alright, gentlemen, get ready, for I believe this is our time to finally take Georgetown and safely secure this area from the British."

Jacob and the others headed to their camp, and after he told the band what they would do, they automatically went to work. Samuel would lead his element to secure supplies, shot, and powder if he could. Jean checked the men's equipment for serviceability. Frederick and the other sergeants watched their men and ensured that everything was in order.

Jacob nodded in approval; the band had come a long way from the early days. Now it was all automatic; his leaders knew what they had to do, allowing Jacob more time to get his gear ready. Jacob did walk amongst the band to check on the men; their morale and to speak with them. He enjoyed the small talk, building a relationship with his men, built a trust upon.

When the sun rose the following morning, Jacob and the band were up and, in the saddle, ready to ride. As they had done numerous times, they rode over to where Marion with Oscar was waiting until the rest of the men showed up. Jacob noticed Marion looked better, no longer angry but instead driven.

He smiled when Jacob arrived to report his band was ready. "Finally, Jacob, we get to go after that long-sought prize of Georgetown! What a prize and boost to our effort that will be! Driving the British from our area and securing it once and for all!"

Jacob nodded in agreement. "Yes sir," he answered, "A long time coming."

***

"A long time coming," thought William "Bloody Bill" Cunningham as he led his Loyalist cavalry through the upcountry. While technically supporting the Crown, Cunningham's campaign of terror was first focused on those who personally harmed or insulted him. Then he decided to become the rabid bloodhounds, running down any rebels or their supporters. Supporting him, this group of Loyalists was of a like mind, all looking for more revenge than victory.

McGirtt had joined up with Cunningham's group and was riding with him. He had known Cunningham, and having learned what happened to his father when he was in Florida, rode back into South Carolina to seek justice, which he served personally. He then went after his old commander from the Third Regiment, who had thrown him in jail for refusing to march to Fort Sullivan.

McGirtt had just joined up with Cunningham's group when he paid a call on his old commander, who had retired and gone back to his farm. When they rode into his yard, Major John Caldwell was sitting on the porch of his own house without shoes or stockings. When Cunningham rode into the yard, Caldwell had a surprised look on his face as Cunningham and a few of his men jumped off their horses with their pistols drawn.

McGirtt watched as Cunningham amused himself by stamping on Caldwell's toes and kicking his shins. Cunningham laughed in glee as his men joined in, three of them keeping Caldwell's family under pistol point. Then, holding his shins and rolling on the floor in pain, Cunningham drew his pistol, cocked it and pointed at Caldwell's head.

Caldwell looked at Cunningham with fear and waited for the pistol to go off. Then, de-cocking his pistol, Cunningham bent down to speak to Caldwell. "Let's say that for this moment only, I will take mercy on you, though you didn't see it with me. I will consider this ample satisfaction for the whipping you gave me those years ago. If I were you, I would pack up your family and leave. Your kind is not wanted here."

Cunningham moved off, motioned for his men to mount up and led his Loyalists away from Caldwell's house. Now, with a vengeance in his mind, Cunningham was leading his Loyalists after another personal vendetta, Captain Samuel Moore of the Lower Ninety-Six Militia Regiment. To ensure they would meet, Cunningham sent a messenger to let Moore know he was coming for him.

"Is that wise?" McGirtt asked and Cunningham scoffed and snorted. "So, what if he comes out with all of his men? I bloody hope so. We'll make short work of them, won't we, men?"

Cunningham's men shouted in approval and McGirtt simply shrugged and rode along. He was not about to argue with Cunningham, as he was along for the ride anyways. It was just before midday when Cunningham's group crested a ridge. Below was Moore and a few men heading in their direction before them. Without breaking stride, Cunningham yelled, "There's that bloody bastard, charge!"

Their group quickly fanned out into a line, and the horses charged forward with clods of grass and dust kicking up. Cunningham drew his pistol and leveled it at the charging rebels. Just before the two groups ran into each other, both sides fired their pistols at one another. A few rebels fell, but none of Cunningham's men fell before the two lines crashed into each other, and brutal close combat began.

Spying Moore, Cunningham yelled, "Moore, I have come for your head!"

A rider turned and rode away with Cunningham in close pursuit. McGirtt stayed with the fight, assuming it must be this Moore fellow that Cunningham was chasing after. At the moment, he was drawing his saber and becoming involved in close combat with the rebels as the two groups whirled and circled one another, working on getting an advantage.

**

Captain Moore laid flat along his horse's neck, the wind whipping by as he urged his horse faster. Quickly looking over his shoulder, Cunningham was in close pursuit and closing with him. "You can't run from me, Moore!" Cunningham yelled out and Moore kept urging more speed from his horse. Both were well-mounted, excellent horse riders and knew well the ground over which they ran.

For miles, Cunningham was at a sword's length away from Moore and close enough to speak to him. "Tsk, tsk, you better get faster, or I'll have you!" Cunningham called out. "Push the rowels in, Sammy honey!" Moore started to say a silent prayer as Cunningham gave a wicked and evil laugh. He drew his saber and waved it, so the sun reflected off the blade's metal.

After a short while, Cunningham had enough of the chase and ended it like a cat playing with a hopeless mouse. As he watched Moore's horse begin to flag, Cunningham spurred his horse to come alongside Moore, rising in the stirrups, then swung his sword down in a sweeping arch.

As Moore was leaning forward, the sword struck his back and spine, slicing through and causing Moore to tumble from his horse. Cunningham pulled up on his reins, turned his horse around, and slowly walked back to where Moore was lying on the ground. Then, smiling, Cunningham dismounted and walked over to the dying Moore, saber in hand.

Looking at how Moore was lying, Cunningham suspected he had severed Moore's spine, and we could no longer use his legs. Kneeling, he looked at Moore, facing up, lying on his back. His breaths were coming shallow from the injury, terror on his face. Cunningham moved as close as he could see Moore could look at him.

"This is why they call me Bloody Bill!" Cunningham stated as he stood up and, using both hands, swung his sword up, then down in a savage blow. Moore's head rolled off his shoulders, his blood fountaining out. He left the head where it rolled, eyes still open, a look of shock frozen on his face. Then, wiping off his sword, Cunningham walked over, recovered Moore's horse, and mounted his own before returning to his men. He whistled a jaunty tune as he rode down the path.

***

Gently moving the branches out of the way, Jacob raised his telescope to look at the British picket outside of Georgetown.

After departing Fort Motte, Marion had led them to the Cantey's Plantation, where he put the call out for the militia to join him. He knew he would need more men to take Georgetown than what they had for Fort Motte.

Marion hoped that the situation with Lee's Legion, having been resolved, would get the men to return to their units. Their horses were safe, and Marion was counting on that news. As they waited for the men to arrive, Marion had tasked Jacob and his band to scout out the defenses of Georgetown.

Jacob and his section looked into the main road leading to Georgetown, while Samuel and his unit scouted the south and Jean, with his team, scouted the north side of the town. Jacob watched the picket, consisting only of three men, which was not expected. However, Jacob focused his telescope on looking more into the town instead of watching the picket. He felt that was where the actual information was.

His suspicion was later confirmed when he could focus on a wagon loaded with mostly personal baggage. Jacob lowered his telescope and slowly nodded before clicking it shut.

"What do you think, Jacob?" Zacharia asked.

"They're leaving; not sure if they are going on a campaign but I believe they are pulling out."

Frederic nodded, "How do you come to that?"

"We can see their pickets are woefully undermanned and from what I saw in the town, they are loading personal baggage into a wagon. That only happens if they were to transport their gear to a more secure location."

"Like Charles Town?" Zacharia asked and Jacob nodded. "Aye, I think Charles Town. So, they may be getting rid of their excess baggage and sending it back to Charles Town to move faster against us, or they are leaving. Will have to hear from the other scouts and see what they have seen."

They slowly and quietly pulled back, remounted their horses, and then headed back to Marion's camp at Cantey's Plantation. When Jacob rode in, he was happy to see some of the men who had gone home over the dispute with Lee's Legion had indeed returned. Jacob went over to their camping area and dismounted. After giving directions to his section on what needed to be done, and he headed over to speak with Marion.

Jean and Samuel had not returned yet; only Jacob reported to Marion what they saw. Marion was sitting in a chair liberated from the plantation, his troubled leg on a crate. Jacob also noticed his eyes were closed and he was slightly snoring. Oscar was there and smiled when Jacob arrived. Jacob took a seat on a spare crate that was there.

Without opening his eyes, Marion asked, "Well, Jacob, what did you see?" Then he opened his eyes and smiled, having guessed who had sat nearby.

Jacob chuckled, "We think the British are getting ready to move, sir."

Marion smiled, "Why do you believe that and where do you think they are going?"

"Three men on the main road only manned their pickets into the town. I also saw personal baggage being loaded into a wagon." Jacob explained. "As for where they are going, that remains to be seen. It may be that their baggage maybe being moved so they can march faster to come after us, or they are all heading to Charles Town."

Marion nodded, "It will depend on what Samuel and Jean bring back to see where we go next."

As they waited for Samuel and Jean, Marion and Jacob reminisced about the old days, back during the Middleton Regimental days when they first met. How much has changed since then, for good and for bad? Oscar brought Marion his tea and offered some for Jacob, who accepted.

A little while later, the sound of horsemen riding into camp was both Samuel and Jean returning from their scouts. Like Jacob, they took their sections to the camp before joining Jacob and Marion.

"Nice day for a ride," Samuel remarked, "Much to see, so much to see."

"What did you see?" With a smile, Marion asked, and Samuel reported, "Boats, sir, there are cargo boats in the harbor, and they are loading them, not unloading."

Marion nodded, "Do you believe, like Jacob here, that it is personal baggage?"

"Yes sir, very sure." Samuel answered, "Even could see the sick and invalids being loaded. One of the boats departed and headed south, which means only one thing."

"Charles Town!" Marion interrupted, "Then they must be heading to Charles Town!" He then turned and looked at Jean. "Can you confirm?"

Jean nodded, all serious, though. "Oui mon colonel, it was the same from the north. Only a small picket watching the north road, we saw redcoats and green coats moving around the town. We also saw baggage being loaded in wagons and brought into town."

Marion nodded and smiled. "Now is the time to strike! We can catch them off-balanced if they are packing and maybe getting ready to march."

Marion thought for a short moment before calling for an orderly. "Go get the commanders and have them report to me immediately!" The orderly nodded and then took off on the run to get the officers. Marion turned to Jacob, Jean and Samuel.

"Once again, your uncanny luck has brought us good news; thank you for the successful scout. Jacob, please remain; Samuel and Jean, you can return to your camp. Again, thank you!"

The two nodded; Samuel winked at Jacob, and then they headed back to the camp. Jacob sat and waited, sipping on his tea as they waited for the other commanders to arrive. Marion sat back in his chair, thinking as he sipped his tea. Oscar stood to the side, watching and waiting.

"What do you think, Jacob," Marion asked, "Can we take it by siege, or can we charge in? We do not have the artillery to lay a perfect siege; we could dig siege trenches to cover our approach. Then there is the bold option of simply charging in. If their numbers have been reduced to a low amount, it would be easy."

"Luck favors the bold sir," Jacob replied, "Who dares win." He thought on it for a short moment, "We can't reduce their defenses without artillery, but from what we saw, there aren't that many men to fight."

The commanders began to arrive, Colonels Richardson Postelle, McDonald, Benton and Horry, who took seats around Marion, who nodded at their arrival.

"Gentlemen, our time has arrived. Jacob here just returned from a scout of Georgetown and the time to take the town is now. The British may be withdrawing, as they observed baggage being loaded on wagons, the sick and invalids being loaded on ships and their pickets and defenses weekly manned."

The officers nodded and murmured about the news, and then Marion continued. "As we don't have artillery to reduce their defenses, our two options are digging siege trenches and approaching the defenses, to cover our men, or just throw care to the wind and charge in. What are your thoughts?"

The officers began talking amongst themselves, including Jacob, as Marion waited. Most of the discussions centered on just charging in vice a siege. None of them liked the hard work of digging and the time-consuming wait for the enemy to give up.

Therefore, the discussion focused more on a direct assault, with Jacob's scouts leading them.

When everyone finished, Marion listened to the options, nodded and made the battle plan. "Then we will assault the town, using speed and surprise to our advantage. Major Clarke here will lead the way, making use of the defenses that are small or abandoned before we attack. If they are in their defenses, we may have no choice but to start digging the siege works. We will attack in first light tomorrow; prepare your men."

The officers nodded and returned to their commands to prepare their men and equipment. "You are good leading the way, Jacob; sorry to just drop it on you like that," Marion stated, and Jacob smiled.

"Wouldn't have it any other way. We will lead the way and clear the route. I believe the British will be gone by morning."

"Is your gut telling you that?" Marion asked and Jacob nodded his head and smiled. "Yes, sir."

Nodding again, Jacob returned the cup to Oscar before returning to the band. The men were all waiting, discussing what they had seen amongst themselves.

"We are going to attack, aren't we?" Samuel asked and Jacob nodded.

"We are leading the way, so you may want to prepare your blunderbuss." Samuel and the others cheered, which pleasantly surprised Jacob. "Samuel, Frederick and Zacharia go secure any supplies we need; Jean, you check on the weapons. Make sure they are serviceable."

They all moved on to their assigned duties, whether securing the supplies, inspecting weapons, or looking at their gear. Jacob went over to check his Jaeger rifle, the amount of shot and powder he still had and how sharp his tomahawk and knife were. Once completed, he checked on his horse tied to a line near his sleeping area.

The horse whinnied when he approached, and Jacob ran his hand along its neck and patted the horse. "Well, George, it looks like another one. Are you up for it?" The horse whinnied again and even tossed his head and swished his tail. After checking his saddle, Jacob returned to the camp.

Samuel returned and brought some dried meat, biscuits, shot and powder. He brought some biscuits over to Jacob, "He was able to secure enough shot and powder for each man to have about five more rounds. How are you set?"

"I'm good; I have ten rounds of shot and powder. I have enough lead to melt and make a few more balls if need be," Jacob responded. But then, he saw Samuel with a bag in his hand, "What is that?"

Samuel smiled, "Goose shot for my blunderbuss. Going to load buck and ball for this one."

Jacob chuckled and nodded, "Makes sense to me." Samuel nodded, "Aye, to me as well."

Once everything was in order, he joined the boys, Samuel, Jean, Frederick and Zacharia, around the fire to smoke their pipes, eat their dried meat and biscuits and talk about the attack to come. They joked and boasted, reminding Jacob of the old days with the Rangers. Now it was his sons, nephews, a former enemy and new friends. The wolves sat near them, heads on their paws and golden eyes glistening in the firelight.

It was early when Jacob woke the band to back up their gear. Jacob did not know where their next camp would be, perhaps even in Georgetown. The sun was not even up yet, the darkness covering them like a cloak. Once everything was packed and secured, they mounted up and once ready, Jacob led them to where Marion was already waiting. He nodded when Jacob arrived, then waited for the rest of the commands to stage.

Once all the commanders were there with their men, Marion turned to Jacob, "Major Clarke, lead the way!"

Nodding, Jacob led his band out of the camp and onto the road that led to Georgetown. In the distance to the east, the first faint glow of sunrise was peeking. Marion waited until Jacob and his band was a decent distance to their front before leading out the rest of the command.

Jacob felt exhilaration, so close to finally achieving one of their main objectives: securing the area from the British. Everything felt right; Jacob felt buoyed with the morning, the band and what they were about to do. He could feel it in his gut.

When they arrived just outside Georgetown's defenses, the sky was pink and changing to gold. Jacob halted the band and then dismounted. Selecting Zacharia and Frederick, Jacob led them forward to see if the outer picket was manned. Moving at a crouch, still wrapped in shadow, rifles held at the ready.

Jacob could see no light, no movement, or any silhouettes that would represent guards. They moved up the picket's wooden palisade wall, Jacob listening for any sound. Not hearing any, he brought his rifle up, quickly turned around the corner to look inside and found no guards. The picket was empty.

"Well, that answers that question," Jacob whispered, then led them back to their horses. As they mounted, Samuel whispered, "Well?"

"No one, so we'll check the main defenses of the town," Jacob answered in a whisper. At a trot, they approached the outer defenses of the British line; all had their muskets and rifles held at the ready. The tension was building, not knowing they would be fired upon when they closed in on the redoubts. As Jacob likes to say, "Who dares win?"

Riding around the outer edge of one of the redoubts, rifle leveled, Jacob observed no one in the defenses. Shrugging, he turned his horse and led them into the town. They rode as far as the town's center and no British were seen. "Well, I be; I think you scared them off, Samuel!" Jacob stated as Samuel had a depressed look on his face now, not able to use his favorite blunderbuss.

Jacob led them back out of the town to meet the approaching Marion. They arrived as Marion was leading the force to the outer pickets. Marion rode up to Jacob and asked, "Well?"

"We didn't see any British in the town, nor were we fired upon," Jacob answered. In the early morning golden light, Marion smiled, waved the men forward, and charged into Georgetown. The thundering hooves of Marion's men entering Georgetown attracted the resident's attention. Marion was having the different commands search and clear sections of the town. Jacob and his band were sent to check on the British defenses.

After securing their horses at a warehouse, Jacob led the band to clear the British works and look at any British artillery pieces left behind. They found three 9-pound cannons and a carronade that had been spiked and knocked off their trunnions and carriages. Jacob looked at the spiked guns and nodded.

"They must have evacuated fast to leave this behind," Jacob commented, then looked to see a few residents approach them.

"Are you men with the Swamp Fox?" one of them asked; Jacob shrugged and nodded.

"Yes, we are. Where did the British go?"

The resident turned and pointed out to the sea. "They loaded up everyone yesterday on four boats and sailed away in the night. They sent their wagons south, I think, toward Charles Town.

There are no British soldiers here and some of their Loyalists friends left too."

Thanking the resident, Jacob went over to one of the docks and, seeing a ship in the distance, pulled out his telescope and focused on the ship. It was an armed British schooner and from what Jacob could guess, was keeping an eye on them. Then, closing his telescope, he went over to report to Marion and passed on what the resident had told him.

"Then the town is ours!" Marion exclaimed, "We did it! Find a place to billet your men as we take stock of what we have found here and destroy the British works." Jacob nodded, then headed over and looked inside the warehouse where they had tied their horses to. It was mostly empty, so he placed his men inside and set up a line for their horses.

Over the next few days, details were sent to destroy the British defenses, redoubts, and pickets. They found military supplies and uniforms in a warehouse that the British had just left behind. Marion could outfit himself in a new proper regimental uniform, though Jacob suspected the blue coat to be a British artilleryman's coat. Still, many of the men needed new clothes and helped themselves.

A messenger arrived from General Greene and Jacob was soon called to meet with Marion. Marion had occupied an abandoned Loyalist house for a headquarters, the orderly showing Jacob in. Marion sat at a table that he was using for a desk, reading messages. Greene's messenger stood off to the side, along with Colonel Horry.

"Sir, you wished to see me? Jacob asked and Marion looked up after reading a message.

"General Greene has congratulated us for securing Georgetown and requested our support as he is laying siege to Ninety-Six," Marion explained, nodding toward Greene's messenger, who nodded back. "I will lead most of the command to go and support General Greene. I am leaving Colonel Horry here in command."

Jacob nodded, "What is my task, sir?"

Marion sat back and let out a long sigh, holding up the message he had just been reading.

"This is from our old nemesis, Major Gainey. He wants to negotiate a truce between us."

Jacob had a surprised look on his face. "A truce? Does he want to negotiate a truce with us? Have we damaged them that much?" Jacob asked.

Marion shrugged and then nodded. "I believe we have. Therefore, your task is to meet with Gainey and agree to his truce. Then report back here to Colonel Horry."

Jacob shrugged and nodded his head. Marion gave him the instructions of where he had to meet with Gainey and wished him luck. "Could this be a trap?" Jacob asked, and Marion shrugged.

"Who knows, it could be legitimate or a desperate measure for trapping us; that is why I am having you meet him. I know you can meet whatever challenge you face."

Sighing, Jacob nodded, "Yes sir, we shall prevail against any challenges."

Returning to the warehouse, he called for Samuel, Jean, Frederick, Zacharia, Jehu and William Lee. "Samuel, is your blunderbuss still loaded?" Jacob asked to which Samuel nodded, with a confused looked on his face. "We are going out to meet Major Gainey, who wants to negotiate a truce with us. Jean, if this is a trap, you are remaining back here and if we are captured or killed, you are to take command."

Jean raised his eyebrows in surprise, then nodded. "You think this is a trap, no?"

Jacob nodded, "Seems fishy to me, so we must be ready for anything. We leave at midday to meet Gainey."

They nodded and then headed over to ready their gear and horses. Richard and Patrick came over as Jacob was preparing his horse with concerned looks on their faces.

"You are going to be safe out there, right?" Patrick asked. "Mama would be rather sore at us if you get hurt," Patrick paused again before looking at Jacob directly, "or killed. We should be riding with you just in case this is an ambush."

Jacob smiled and placed his hands on the boys' shoulders. "Lads, thanks for the concern, but I have your uncle Samuel and the others who will watch over me; I will be safe."

"You better be," Richard stated with a stern look on his face. Jacob chuckled and ruffled his son's hair.

"I'll have the wolves with me; we will be safe." Both boys nodded and then returned to their camp. Jacob watched them go, amazed at how much this unfortunate war had molded them into good men. He mounted his horse and rode over to meet with the rest. Once Samuel and the others arrived, Jacob led them out and headed to the meeting location.

Jacob led them to the meeting location, the old Sampit Bridge they had destroyed, so they were going to meet at the ford close by. It was a short ride to the west from Georgetown; they recalled their fight with Watson's rear guard there as they crossed the ford. As they closed in, they all focused on the task and the unknown of what would happen.

They rode down the road that led to the ford. Across the river were Major Gainey and a few of his men he sent as an escort. Jacob halted them on their side of the river and the two parties sat and stared at each other. The wolves sat next to Jacob and Samuel, staring at the men across the river.

"Are you from Marion's command?" Gainey yelled across the river. Then he recognized Jacob. "Oh, it's you, Captain Clarke. Still breathing, I see."

"Yes, still breathing. We are here to negotiate a truce, as indicated in your message," Jacob yelled back.

"It is," Gainey returned, "I agree not to attack Marion and his men for one year; I ask Marion and his men not to attack mine during the same period. Then we will see where we stand, agree?"

Jacob looked at Samuel and only shrugged. "Agreed, we have an accord. You do not attack us, and we won't attack you for one year. But, know that if you break this accord, we will bring the wrath of God upon you."

"Wouldn't have it any other way. We are in accord. See you in a year!" So Gainey turned his horse and led his men to the west; Jacob led his men back to Georgetown. Jacob reported to Horry when they arrived and told him that Gainey had agreed to the truce.

"Excellent news Jacob, bloody excellent." Horry stated, "Now I can focus on our new problem."

"Which is?" Jacob asked.

"The militia is heading home in droves," Horry complained, a frustrated look on his face. "Now that we have secured Georgetown and reduced the British defenses, they think the job is done and going home. Marion will be livid when he returns."

Jacob nodded in agreement, "Aye, while I see the militia's point of view, you are correct about Marion. He will be rather displeased with the militia."

When Marion returned from supporting General Greene, he was pleased to learn of the truce with Gainey but was rather put out when he discovered the militia went home.

"Don't these bloody bastards realize this isn't over yet!" Marion grumbled as he paced his office, "How do I keep Lord

Rawdon off balanced with what little force I have now? I have no choice but to call out the militia again, so we can keep Rawdon under pressure and press our advantage against the British.

CHAPTER 11

SHUBRICK PLANTATION

Emily Geiger was sweating from the warm July day because Loyalists were nearby. Having abandoned his siege of the fort at Ninety-Six, General Greene was marching north toward Charlotte in North Carolina to reconstitute his army. Lord Rawdon tried to pursue it, but the hot weather and rough marching conditions impacted his men, and they were forced to return to Ninety-Six.

Lord Rawdon decided to abandon the fort and took his men south. Greene wanted the pressure to be kept on Rawdon and sent out messages to the partisan leaders, including Marion and Sumter. This is where Emily came into the picture, knowing where Sumter was. Greene had given her his written orders for Sumter.

After leaving Greene's Army, Emily read the message before hiding it in her bodice. She was riding her horse toward Sumter's location when she came upon a group of loyalists foraging for food. Emily was hiding in a small patch of trees, surrounded by the Loyalists. Pulling the message from her bodice, she tore it up, then ate it so it wouldn't fall into the enemy's hands.

Once she swallowed the last piece of the message, she cantered her horse out of the trees like she was out for a typical ride. Quickly, a Loyalist yelled, "You there, stand fast in the name of the King!" Emily could hear the sounds of "clicks" as musket hammers were drawn to full cock. She stopped her horse and then turned to face the men.

It was a group of five Loyalists, their green uniforms somewhat tattered looking, with a three-day growth of hair on their faces. The leader of the group approached with his musket leveled at her. "Get off the horse, missy," he commanded, "What are you doing in these parts?"

With a stammering voice, Emily answered, "Good sir, I am traveling to take care of my sick grandmother, she has taken ill and I must see to her."

While the Loyalists lowered their muskets, they did close on her. Emily's hand shook as she held onto the reins of her horse. "How do we know you are not a spy for these damn rebels," the leader growled, eyeing her up and down. "Rebels are everywhere and you must be searched!"

Emily placed a shocked look on her face. "You, sir, dare to search me? I have heard that those who are supposed to be loyal to the King are you are no better than these bandits and thieves they say you are protecting us from. Would you be so ungentlemanly to search me, a young woman?"

"She has a point," one of the men said, "Remember what Major Maxwell said; we don't need to stir up a hornet's nest."

The leader looked at Emily and grudgingly accepted. "We'll take her to the camp and have one of the distaffs search her. Will that work?" The man who had questioned the leader then nodded. "Fine, now that is settled, follow me, young lady."

The Loyalists surrounded Emily and her horse and walked her to camp. "Miss Amanda, we need your services!" the leader called out, and one of their distaff women came over. "Please search this young lady for any contraband."

She nodded and took Emily over to a thick bush area where no one could see. "Alright young lady, start taking them off," she commanded.

"Take what off?" Emily asked and the woman looked at her and snorted. "Your clothes, I have to search you for contraband, so off with it, down to your chemise." Emily shrugged and began to take off her clothes. The woman inspected her hat and bonnet and went through her pockets after she untied them from her waist. Next, she examined her apron, bodice and sun shawl and finally patted her down when she was only in her chemise.

Emily thanked the stars she had been smart enough to eat the message, had they found the message on her, they could find her guilty as a spy and hung her. Finally, the woman was satisfied, "Put your clothes back on." She then headed back to the camp while Emily pulled her clothes back on. Once dressed, she returned to the camp, where her horse was still waiting.

The leader who had stopped her was there, "Sorry about that, but we have our orders. You are free to go." Emily nodded, mounted her horse and then calmly walked out of the camp and back to the road. Once she was well away from the Loyalist camp, she finally let out a sigh of relief and kicked her horse into a gallop.

The following morning, Emily rode into Cedar Springs and found General Sumter's camp. One of the guards escorted Emily with her horse to Sumter, sitting before his fire, eating a biscuit. When she arrived, Sumter looked up.

"Sir, I have a message for you from General Greene," Emily stated, and Sumter nodded, holding out his hand.

"Hand it over then, miss," Sumter asked, but Emily shook her head. "I can't, sir."

Sumter looked up and gave her a surprised look. "Why not, may I ask?"

Emily quickly sighed, "Because I ate it, sir."

Sumter stopped eating and looked at Emily, who started to shuffle her feet. "You ate it?"

She had a sheepish look on her face. "Because I was about to be captured and didn't want to be hung as a spy, sir."

Sumter raised his eyebrows and then began to laugh. "That's the best thing I have heard in a long time! Too bad I can't get the message."

"No sir, I read the message and can tell you what it said," Emily explained and Sumter stopped laughing. "General Greene wants you to strike Rawdon before he can join with Stewart in Dorchester."

"Is that all of it?" Sumter asked and Emily nodded, "Yes, sir, more or less."

Sumter stood up and gave Emily a big hug. "Lass, what you did was one of the bravest and smartest things I have seen in a long time. You have made us proud and helped the cause; thank you!"

Emily stood in shock but felt proud at the same time.

***

Lieutenant Colonel Stewart led his column of men down a hardly-use gaming trail, avoiding any contact with the locals. He was concerned they would report his position, and then these damn rebel partisans would strike at his command from the swamps.

His predecessor Watson, in his opinion, was a broken man. These infamous bandits, the Swamp Fox and the Wolf had worn him down to the point he was no longer a capable leader. Watson became the commander of a Provincial Light Infantry battalion, where he took command of Watson's old regiment and the Provincial Light Infantry.

He led them toward Orangeburgh, where he was to join Lord Rawdon, who had marched from the old fort at Ninety-Six. Stewart felt one of the reasons the partisans had defeated Watson was he always used well-traveled roads, which made it easy for him to be ambushed. Stewart used little-known or used roads and trails and avoided any contact with the local populace.

This paid off as they were moving along these roads; they could hear horsemen in the distance on the main roads. The oppressive heat was being kept in by the trees and brush close to the trails. The heat was starting to affect them.

When they arrived at Orangeburgh, they had not been detected and he had all of his men though footsore and worn out from the hot march. When he reported to Lord Rawdon, he asked for any supplies for his men. I am sorry to say we have no bread now," Lord Rawdon explained. "We have been on the march and our supplies have not yet found us."

Stewart also saw that Rawdon had amassed of about fifteen hundred men in different camps around the town. The next day, Colonel Cruger arrived with the former garrison of Ninety-Six, an additional thirteen hundred men. As they all camped around Orangeburgh, the lack of provisions were a significant issue. Rawdon sent out foraging parties, who were able to secure water and the wild cows they found in the woods. Still, it was barely enough to feed the army and Stewart was concerned it would affect them.

The British Army, while camped around Orangeburgh, was in a desperate situation for supplies. They could find some little beef from the wild cows; however, no salt was available to preserve the meat and as it was only July, no vegetables were ready. Unless they could get provisions soon, the army could be in trouble. Moreover, Stewart was concerned whether that they could fight if this rebel general made contact with them.

***

Jacob was hungry and had to admit it had been some time since they had anything decent to eat. Marion had been called to join the main army with Greene and Sumter's group, Washington's cavalry and Lee's Legion. They were pursuing Rawdon and Greene had amassed enough men to give Rawdon a good fight.

Greene had been concerned about whether or not Cruger or Stewart had reinforced Rawdon, but none of his cavalries had been able to locate them. Until then, they marched and the weather and lack of food started to impact the men's morale. They had been supplied a significant quantity of rice, but the only meat they would get were frogs in abundance and the few alligators they came across.

Around July 10, from what Jacob guessed, Greene ordered the army into position about four miles outside of Orangeburgh, near Turkey Hill. Washington's cavalry had confirmed Rawdon was entrenched around Orangeburgh, so Greene ordered the army to prepare for battle. The men took up battle positions and the woman and children joined the baggage train in the rear. Shot, spare flints and powder were issued, and the waiting began.

Jacob joined the officers at Greene's headquarters on the hill. First, Jacob went over to greet Sumter and catch up with his old friend. Then, when General Greene arrived, Jacob joined Marion as Greene presented his strategy.

"Gentlemen, from what Colonel Washington told me, Lord Rawdon has been reinforced by both Stewart and Cruger; somehow, we passed each other in the woods. In any case, he is reinforced and in a defensive position around Orangeburgh. I feel it would be a fruitless assault, so I plan to try to lure Rawdon out so we can meet him on our field of choosing. Until then, see to your men; any questions?"

Marion raised his hand, and Greene acknowledged him. "Sir, what about provisions? Between the heat and lack of food, the men are starting to go lame and more and more are sick with the surgeons. If I may suggest, if we don't get supplies soon, we may not be in a condition to fight."

The officers mumbled their agreements as Greene thought of it. "General Marion, you are right. As we wait to draw Rawdon out, we will send out foraging parties to see what supplies we can procure."

Jacob, the band and the army sat and waited for two days. Rawdon did not accept the challenge for a fight. Then, from the hill, Jacob looked out in the distance, Jean joining him. "What do you think, Jacob; the British will not take the challenge?"

Jacob nodded. "They are probably short supplies like we are and with the heat, they are worn out just like we are and may not be in any condition to fight. Although seeing they are coming out of the fight at Ninety-Six, they could be in rough shape." Jean nodded in agreement.

The next day, Jacob, with Marion, Sumter, Lee, Washington and Greene, rode out to better view the defenses around Orangeburgh. Greene had artillery with him if he decided to lay the town under siege. When they arrived at a vantage point, they could see that Orangeburgh would be too tough to take.

Instead of just breastworks, the British established different houses in the town as strong points, little fortifications. This would present a challenge, the cavalry would be useless, what little artillery they had ineffective and a frontal assault suicidal. Greene looked at it and then made up his mind.

"Gentlemen, we have achieved our goal of clearing the upcountry of any British foes. Taking this town with no strategic value will be a pointless loss of life. Seeing the army had just marched over three hundred miles in twenty-three days, it's time to rest."

Greene looked once more at Orangeburgh in the distance and then nodded as he was sure of his decision. He turned and looked at his commanders. "I have made my decision, and the army will break up. General Sumter, you are to pursue Lord Rawdon; General Marion, you will invest in Monck's Corner. Colonel Lee, take your Legion to Dorchester and invest in the British outpost there. I will take the rest of the army to the High Hills on the Santee to reconstitute and recruit. Thank you, gentlemen. See to your commands."

Jacob and Marion returned to their men and after packing up their camp, Marion led them away from Orangeburgh. Being tasked with investing in Monck's Corner, Marion had to find a new base of operation, as he had lost Snow Island. They established a new camp in a cleared cane break on the Santee River, in the Upper Saint Stephens Parish, near the Peyre's Plantation. Their new base was on the western edge of the Gaillard Swamp, and they soon got down to business setting up their camps.

Jacob's men took advantage of the rest period to fix equipment and mostly went fishing to get food. While some of the militia companies were rotating their men as some enlistments were ending and now required replacements, Jacob's band mostly stayed with him and Marion.

The heat of the summer grew as July arrived, sometimes stifling the air in the camp. Jacob would take his band out to scout when he was able, as they had a responsibility to keep track of the British forces and, for Marion, activities around Monck's

Corner. While Jacob did not see much action, the word was filtering down that Colonel Coates was on the move.

It was mid-July when messages arrived at Marion's camp that Coates had burned Biggin's Church. Also, Sumter had directed Marion to join him to finish off Coates. Marion arrived and joined with the rear of Sumter's column. Sumter had left his artillery baggage to catch up while he pursued Coats. Marion dispatched Colonel Horry's and Maham's cavalry to catch up with Sumter as he would protect his baggage and precious artillery from falling into the enemy's hands.

Jacob and his band with Colonel Richardson's men stayed with Marion guarding the baggage train. As they clopped along on the dusty road, listening to the jingle of the artillery being pulled, sweat rolled down their faces, Jacob frequently using a handkerchief to wipe his face. Then, about sixteen miles later, they saw the results of Sumter's fast-moving use of cavalry.

Wagons and carts were lined up along the side of the road, a small detail from Horry's dragoons guarding it. Off to another side was a group of British prisoners from the 19th Regiment based on their uniforms. As the sun was about to set, Marion directed the men to rest on their arms. The riders cared for their horses but remained saddled if they had to attack. Jacob and his band pulled their horses off to the side of the road where the forest was not as thick, tied them to the trees, and located places to sleep next to their horses.

Jacob directed them to water, feed and check their horses, then check their gear, before they started a small fire to eat their meager rations. As biscuits and rice were the staples, many men pulled out their small copper rice cookers and set them over the fire to get boiling.

Even on horseback, the hot day played havoc on the band. Riding on a heater in the cold is nice, but not in the summer.

The band lounged as best as possible, allowing their bodies to cool and rest from the long day. However, they had to face another unknown day in the morning, unsure how hot it would be or where their enemy would appear.

Jacob sat back, smoking his pipe and reflecting on the band. Thankful that while the boys have grown and been molded in the crucible of battle, they have only been lucky to receive minor injuries. The band has been extremely lucky, with only a few wounded that had to go home to heal. No one had been killed yet and Jacob had a feeling that would change soon.

Looking at his boys and nephews, Jacob hoped that if something were to happen, it would not be to them. But his uncanny gut warned him something was about to happen and he could not put his fingers on it. But Jacob also knew nothing he could do to influence it. He just had to ride out and let fate smile or frown on him.

The night passed, and the temperatures lowered enough that they could get decent sleep before once more gearing up. The wolves waited patiently as the band packed their gear and readied the horses. After mounting, Jacob joined Marion, the rest of their men and Sumter's artillery and baggage train.

The morning was already sticky and humid and the men beginning to sweat in their clothes. By midday, they had caught up with Sumter and his command, Marion riding alongside and conferring with him. From Jacob's vantage point, he could see Sumter and Marion were going back and forth on an issue and Jacob assumed they were trying to devise a plan.

Jacob admitted his old friend Sumter had changed since the Anglo-Cherokee War when he arrived in South Carolina as a shop and plantation owner. He was more agitated than he recalled, and the stories that Jacob had heard concerning Sumter's treatment of Loyalists and rumors of looting bothered him.

Sumter also told Marion that his date of rank of being promoted to a General of Militia was older than Marion's and that he outranked him. Jacob believed this chaffed Marion, as he had a different command and leadership style; therefore, these two would always clash. Jacob shook his head, having seen the same issue time and time again.

In the distance, the sound of musketry was heard that got both Sumter and Marion's attention; Sumter called up Captain Singleton, "Stay with the artillery; we are pressing ahead!" Then waving his arm forward, Sumter and his men began to trot down the road toward the sound of musketry. When the last of Sumter's men passed them, Marion waited and led them onward. Jacob rode up next to Marion, who had a perplexed look.

"Are you alright, sir?" Jacob asked and Marion shrugged his shoulders and blew a deep breath.

"Jacob, that man drives me to my wit's end," Marion grumbled, "I am about to tell him where he can stick that date of rank issue when he keeps bringing it up!"

Marion thought for a moment before looking back over at Jacob. "You knew him, right Jacob?" Marion asked and Jacob nodded. "Was he always like this, so headstrong, stubborn and self-serving?"

Jacob pursed his lips as he thought, then slowly shook his head. "No sir, to be honest, I was thinking about that, and I believe he has changed some from when I knew him last. But, then again, war can do that to a person. You know that as well as I do."

Marion nodded, then sighed once more. "We're good soldiers and we'll follow our orders, even if it doesn't make sense."

Marion, Jacob and Robinson men followed Sumter's men as he was quickly leaving the artillery, baggage and the captured British soldiers behind. The sound of battle was still in the distance but close as they rode on. Soon through the trees, a river could be seen that was following the road they were on.

When they came out into an open area, they could see a bridge crossing the river, and some of Sumter's men were arrayed in a line, firing at the other side. Riflemen were positioned to fire on the far side of the bridge and slowly but effectively picked off the British infantry, or a cavalryman would tumble from his horse.

Marion raised his hand and the column halted. Then he dismounted and headed over to observe the fight. After making sure his men were getting a drink and checking their horses, Jacob headed over to join Marion. Jacob looked across the bridge and the British started falling back to escape the deadly rifle fire.

Marion nodded in the direction of the far side of the river. "That road heads to Captain Shubrick's plantation. I fear the British will likely fall back and use it to fort up in. But, hopefully, Sumter will wait for his artillery before deciding to attack."

Jacob looked across the river and watched the rest of the British continue to fall back and head away from the fight. Thinking of the looming battle, he nodded to Marion's comments.

"We don't have enough bayonets, let alone shot and powder, to take a whole plantation under siege. So, we need Sumter's artillery."

Marion nodded in return, "Well, let's see what General Sumter decides to do once we have all of our forces here.

*⁣**

Lieutenant Colonel Coates stood on the large porch of the plantation, so he had a good view of the field and the approach from the bridge. Although he shook his head, he was not in a good position. From the amount of musket and rifle fire, he suspected the rebels outnumbered him.

Looking around as to how the plantation was arrayed, he decided upon a defensive strategy.

"Lieutenant, go get Captain Campbell, have him report to me." The lieutenant nodded and went to get Captain Campbell. As he waited, Coates scanned and took in the smaller outbuildings and the slave quarters. The kitchen and some closer outbuildings would work, but he did not have enough men to cover the slave quarters.

"Do I burn them or leave them there? The smoke will obscure our view of the rebels if I burn them. On the other hand, the rebels will use them against me if I don't burn them."

Coates turned his attention to Captain Campbell, who reported to him. "Sir, you called for me?"

"Aye, I did." Replied Coates and then pointed at the kitchen and smaller outbuildings near the plantation house.

"Pull the regiment in, form a square anchoring your right on that smaller building, then the kitchen and your left at the house here. Detach a company to take elevated positions in the windows above."

Captain Campbell looked at the area Coates indicated and nodded. "Yes, sir and the howitzer?"

Coates pointed at the center corner of their square. "Deploy the howitzer there; make sure it has a clear field of fire to support our line. Then, God willing, and our luck holds out, we'll beat these rebel scum and drive them away!"

***

Colonel Lee had joined Marion, Jacob, McCottry, Richardson and Postelle sitting in the shade, watching the bridge being repaired and waiting for Sumter to arrive with the rest of his men. Some of their infantry and cavalry held the far side in case the British decided to counterattack.

"What is taking Sumter so bloody long?" Lee commented, poking the ground savagely with a stick. "The longer we wait, the better the British will be. We don't know what they are up to."

Marion looked at Lee, "We can solve that problem without Sumter." He then turned and looked directly at Jacob. "Would you be so kind as to see what our British friends are up to?"

Jacob nodded, "Yes, sir, we'll take a look and return."

Marion nodded; Jacob stood up and headed back to where the band was sitting in the shade, their horses tied to trees. "Samuel, Jean, with me. Marion wants to know what the British are up to."

Both Samuel and Jean jumped up and gathered their gear and rifles. "About bloody time," Samuel grumbled in his typical fashion, "getting rather bored sitting here." Once they settled their gear, Jacob led them toward the bridge.

The bridge had been repaired, the men putting the finishing touches on the planks as Jacob, Samuel and Jean crossed over at the trot. Jacob led them up to the picket posted at the tree line, where the road entered a large open field.

"We're heading out to scout for the colonel. If we come running back in a hurry, we'll be yelling Ranger, Ranger, Ranger. So please don't shoot us if you mind."

The sergeant in charge of the picket smiled and nodded, "We'll try not to."

"That's all we can ask," Jacob returned with a smile before leading Samuel and Jean into the field. As soon as they broke out of the wood line, the three men crouched low and moved cautiously through tall wheat stands, moving with the breeze.

Then, using the terrain to mask them to the best of their ability, Jacob halted them when the field flattened out and they could see the plantation.

Kneeling, their heads just above the top of the grain, Jacob placed his rifle on the ground. Then, reaching into his haversack, Jacob pulled out his telescope and began scanning the plantation. He could see the British redcoats in more of a triangle of points of a square toward them. At that point, he could see the stubby barrel of a howitzer.

Continuing to scan, he could see the slave quarters and other buildings unoccupied to one side of the plantation, but when he focused on the house proper, he could see the British soldiers arrayed in a square, even could see them up in the windows. They had deployed into an effective defensive position and had made the house into a fort.

Jacob lowered his telescope and slid it closed. He slowly began to shake his head. "Does not look good, does it?" Samuel asked. Jacob shook his head.

"That's a good position," Jean commented, "Clear fields of fire, for the most part, a strong defense with their flanks covered. Anyone who charges across the field without preparation will get hit hard, no?"

Samuel looked over at Jean, "Prepared?"

"Artillery," Jacob confirmed. "We need those 6-pounders we passed way back in the rear. If Sumter is smart, he will encircle the position to keep the British from escaping or being reinforced until the artillery arrives."

"You said smart? Sumter?" Samuel returned. "If I recall, he has not done some smart things, and he recently got chased up into North Carolina by Tarleton. Let's be real, Jacob; we know Sumter does not make good decisions."

Jacob nodded, "Hopefully, today will be a first."

Motioning with his head, Jacob led them back to their lines and when they arrived where Marion and Lee were, Sumter had joined them. As they approached, he could see Marion and Lee were having another heated discussion with Sumter.

"You were saying Jacob," Samuel commented in a low voice. Jacob shook his head and headed to join them while Samuel and Jean watched him go.

"I'll be honest, Jean, I don't have a good feeling about this," Samuel said softly to Jean, who nodded in agreement.

"Oui, my friend, it does not look good for all of us." Samuel and Jean returned to the band.

"Are you out of your bloody mind?" Marion stated to Sumter, whose face was a thunderhead. Marion pointed toward the plantation. "We'll lose a good piece of our command if we attack now."

When Jacob arrived, he scanned, saw no cannons and began picking up why Marion was upset. Finally, when Marion saw that Jacob had come, he let out a sigh of relief.

"Major Clarke, please explain to *General* Sumter what you saw on your scout." Jacob could see the friction of rank between Marion and Sumter came up again as he had inflexed on the title of general. Finally, Sumter turned and looked at Jacob. "Well, out with it."

Jacob was taken aback by the gruffness of his old friend.

"Sir, from what we observed, the British are deployed in an effective defensive position using the plantation and the outer buildings to secure their flanks. They have deployed their howitzer in a way to have a clear field of fire. There is no cover on the right, except for the slave quarters in the center of the position, and they have men in the second floor's windows. Anyone crossing the open wheat field will be under heavy fire for the assault."

Jacob waited to see what reaction Sumter would have, hoping he would see and make a sensible decision. But, instead, he did the opposite.

"That is more the reason we must assault now before they can strengthen their position."

Jacob gave Sumter a surprise. "With all due respect, it would make better sense to use your artillery from range and batter them down."

Sumter stared hard at Jacob. "The artillery is delayed, caught up in mud and mire. We must go now."

Not giving up, Jacob pressed on. "Thomas, it would be more effective to encircle and hold the position, preventing any British from coming in or going out until the artillery arrives. We have enough men to do it and the riflemen can keep them occupied from a distance."

Sumter scowled at Jacob. "It's General, Major. No, we will not wait for the artillery."

Sumter faced the other commanders. "My brigade will attack in the center, Marion's Brigade on the right and Lee's Legion on the left. Our three columns will divide their fire, and we will be able to break them. See to your men. We attack in one hour."

Lee, Marion, Jacob and the other officers stood there, not believing their order. Sumter glared at all of them. "I said to see to your men, that is all!"

The officers turned and headed back to their respective commands. Marion, with McCottry and Postelle, headed back their men. Marion was visibly upset and did not like the orders. Marion looked to Jacob, "You said the right is all open, no concealment, correct?

Jacob nodded, which made Marion shake his head. "Fool, bloody thick-headed, stubborn fool! We have them; we bloody have them and can bag many of them. But our illustrious

Commanding General wants to bath himself in glory and I fear bath in our blood!" Jacob nodded in agreement; the fear his gut was warning him was coming true.

Jacob gathered his men and then looked at his boys. "You four are staying back to secure the horses. If it appears the British have won and are coming this way, take the horses and head back to our last camp to wait for any men to arrive. If, after two days, no one arrives, go home. Do you understand?"

"But papa, it's a big battle and you are forcing us to stay out of it," Richard complained, and Jacob growled back.

"You're bloody right. I am keeping you all out of it. You will obey my orders!" The boys looked shocked, and then Jacob breathed a big sigh.

"I am sorry, lads, I know you are brave, but you are not fool hearty. I feel that many of us may not make it back. However, you four must live and carry on the fight if I, Uncle Samuel, or even Jean do not make it. Understand?"

The boys shuffled their feet but nodded and looked up at Jacob.

"Know I am proud of all four of you, watching you grow into brave and strong men. I always wondered where my boys went, but time has not been fair to you, and you had to grow up much sooner. I am overjoyed and pleased to see the four men before me."

Then Jacob shocked them by hugging all four before heading to where the wolves waited next to his rifle leaning against a tree. Then, picking up his rifle, he nodded to the wolves who followed him as he met with Samuel, Jean and the rest of the brigade.

When Jacob joined, Samuel, whose own wolves were waiting, asked, "How did the boys take it that you had ordered them to stay behind?

Jacob snorted, "Not well at all, just like what we would expect from our boys. But they understand and will follow our instructions if this is bad."

Samuel nodded in appreciation, "Besides, our wives would kill us if the boys got hurt."

Jacob gave a short laugh before Marion ordered the brigade to form. Leading his band, Jacob was directed to the right side of their column, with McCottry's riflemen, Richardson's men in the center and Postelle's men on the left. Marion turned and led them to their start position.

They passed the cavalry, being held in reserve. As Marion's brigade marched by, Horry and his men doffed their helmets in salute. They moved along the road, just below a small ridge and took up their assigned position on the far right. Once they halted, Marion gave the command to prime and load. The men drew their cartridges, a choir of spitting sound as the paper was spat out before priming and then the sound of rammers being slid out to ram home the ball.

"Those with bayonets, fix bayonets!" Marion commanded; only a few who had them did. Then, looking to the left, Sumter brought his brigade up and underwent the same preparation. Jacob's heart began to beat faster in anticipation of the impending battle. Jacob gripped his rifle hard, ready for the command to charge.

Once Lee joined and was ready, the command to attack was given. Hearing the drum command, Marion pointed and led his band forward. The brigade maintained their dress until they crested the slight rise and all between them and the British line was an open field full of wheat.

"Charge!" Marion yelled and waved his arm forward, and the brigade released all of their pent-up energy and surged forward, screaming at the top of their lungs.

"Boom!" The sound of the howitzer echoed as it was fired at the mass of men charging forward. Jacob continued to trot ahead, the wolves keeping pace with him. So far, no one had fired in their direction, but Jacob knew they were waiting for them to close the distance. As they continued forward, they saw a stout fence appear before them, the end of the open field of wheat.

"Crash, boom!" The howitzer took a shot at Marion's men and struck effectively as four men fell to the ground. Instinctively, they all crouched lower, thinking that the wheat could, in some way, conceal them from the fire. The British line opened fire as they approached the fence, and the balls began to buzz around them. Men began to fall, having been hit by the musket balls. Some were yelling in pain and some were silent in death.

As they arrived at the fence line, they all dropped to the ground, some using the stout fence posts to fire from. The British balls continued to snap by, some striking the fence posts in a shower of splinters. To their left, some of Sumter's riflemen were taking up positions around the slave quarters and were firing at the British shooters in the windows on the second floor.

Jacob, resting on his elbows, aimed and fired at a British officer controlling the firing line. Then, rolling up on his side, he began to reload his rifle when his wolf Waya whined as both he and Red laid as low as they could on their bellies on the ground. The two looked accusingly at Jacob.

"What do you want me to do?" Just as he spoke to the wolves, a ball came whizzing past his ear, near enough, so Jacob felt its heat as it passed. Quickly, he rolled over and flattened himself before loading his rifle. They were stuck and Jacob knew it. He looked around as the British had them pinned down now that they were so close. Anyone who moved or exposed themselves was hit. The howitzer was dealing death and destruction across the brigades.

Once more, Jacob's mind flashed back to the bloody field before Carillon, where the British were pinned in place by the abatis and French fire. The screams of the wounded, the sound of the shot, and balls snapping all around him. Jacob had returned to the hell of that battle, just like Savannah. It kept following him.

Jacob returned to reality when another one of their men had been hit. He had been trying to move over and check on one of their wounded. The sun was beginning to set in the afternoon sky, and he knew the decisive moment was closing in. Either pushing to take the position or withdraw before losing more of their men.

From their left, Jacob could hear that the riflemen's fire was beginning to slacken as they ran out of ammunition. Looking across at the British, Jacob could see they also realized it and appeared to be forming for a bayonet charge. Knowing it would cause a hole in the middle of their line, Jacob rose and yelled, "Follow me!"

Crouching and running as fast as he could, Jacob led his men toward the slave cabins, British balls hitting the dirt in brown buffs or snapping past. Finally, Jacob recognized Taylor, leading Sumter's riflemen and slid up next to him.

"We're out of shot and powder!" Taylor yelled, and Jacob nodded. "Thought so, and it looks like our British friends know as well. Get your men out of here; we will cover you!" Taylor nodded and squeezed Jacob's shoulder in thanks before ordering his men to fall back.

As Taylor's men pulled back, Jacob's men took up their positions and began to pour fire into the British line that had been preparing to charge. The uptick in fire changed their mind, having seen Jacob's men arrive. Using the slave houses as cover, Jacob's men began to fire at the windows and the British line, keeping it hot for them both.

319

Jacob, at a crouch, his wolves moving with him, checked on his men and determined how much ammunition they had left.

"I've lost about four of my men," Samuel stated as he brought his rifle up and fired at a distant British soldier. "Have about four or five rounds left. That's all." Jacob nodded and squeezed his friend's shoulder before moving. The wolves checked on Samuel's wolves, tails doing a quick wag, before following Jacob.

Jean's men were about the same and Jacob continued until he found Marion behind one of the houses. Splinters fell from the multitude of British musket balls when Jacob slid up next to Marion.

"We've lost about a quarter of our band." Jacob yelled over the din of battle, "Down to about four rounds per man. Unless we do something soon, we won't be able to do anything, whether advance or retreat." Jacob stated with his back against the house. Marion had a dejected look on his face.

"That bloody damn fool, we should have never attacked this place!" Marion looked up at the setting sun just above the trees.

"When the sun goes down and we have the cover of night, the brigade will fall back. So, make sure your men are ready."

Relieved that someone was making sense, Jacob nodded. "We will be ready!"

Turning, Jacob continued to move in a crouch until he flopped onto the ground next to Jean. "We will fall back when it gets dark," Jacob said into Jean's ear so he could hear him. Jean nodded, then Jacob took off again in a crouch for Samuel's position next to a slave house. Just as Jacob was about to slide up next to Samuel, a howitzer shot hit. It punched through the building and exploded on the inside.

As the shell exploded, time slowed for Jacob as the bright yellow and orange light filled his view from the left, the shattering roar of the explosion drowning out everything except a new sound of ringing in his ears. Then the wall of heat washed over him from his left and what felt like a heavy hammer hit his left side.

Jacob crumbled to the ground, rolling in the wave of heat and light. He rolled over and over for a few paces from the impact of the exploding house. He could not hear Samuel yell, "No!" as he began to rise and run toward him.

Still unable to hear anything but a muffled ringing, Jacob stopped rolling and stared into the bluish-grey sky. He felt as if he was burning, yet the pain had not registered. Samuel's face suddenly appeared above Jacob, but he could not hear what he was saying.

Then Jacob did feel like someone had grabbed his shoulders and was pulling him behind the ruins of the destroyed house. The sound was coming returning from a muffled sound. First, it was a slight roar, then the typical sound of battle, except with the addition of a crackling fire. He felt like someone was pounding on him when he looked to his left to see Frederick patting out portions of his clothes that were on fire.

"Stay still, Jacob!" Frederick ordered as he continued to extinguish the small fires on his clothes. That sensation of heat went away, but a more intense feeling of heat and pain was now coming from his left leg. Jacob turned and looked down and embedded in his upper thigh, was a large wooden splinter sticking a good six inches out of his breeches.

Jacob felt someone's hands on his shoulders, "Lean back, Jacob!" Jehu stated and Jacob leaned against Jehu's legs. Propped up, he looked over and to his horror, Samuel was lying face down on the ground, with two more of his men lying with him in crumpled positions that Jacob could not recognize. The pain was rising, radiating from his burned and probably broken left ribs and his leg.

"Easy, Jacob, rest easy," Jehu said soothingly. "Know it hurts now. We'll get you out of here, don't worry." Then Jean's face appeared, looking at Jacob in concern.

"Jean, go see to Samuel. Make sure he is alive," Jacob stated, the act of talking hurting his side.

Jean nodded, turned and left. The pain continued to rise and fall like waves. Finally, the sound became muffled, his view fading to black; the last face he saw before oblivion was Marion's concerned face. Then the darkness took him and all sight and sound were gone.

CHAPTER 12

REST AND RECUPERATION

Darkness.

Floating.

Emptiness.

Jacob felt nothing but floated in a sea of darkness and no sound. He had no idea where he was, what time it was, and whether he was dead. Yet, all he knew now, he felt no pain.

Jacob then felt like he was in a dream, walking on a familiar dirt path deep in a fog-shrouded forest. He could not recognize where he was exactly, but it felt like the mountains of New York. The evergreen trees, the smell of those trees and the sound of birds. Jacob looked around; he was standing on a dirt path. Not knowing what else to do, he began walking.

He felt a cool wind on his face and strangely felt peaceful. Jacob tried to recall where he was, but this was not right. Hadn't he just been in a battle? He shook his head as he walked along the path.

The sound of woodpeckers in the distance and a lonely call of a loon indicated water was nearby as Jacob walked down the path. While it still felt familiar, Jacob could not recall where exactly he was. His footfalls made no sound as he walked along the trail; the sun shining on his face, which was comforting.

The feeling of familiarity with the woods, the dirt path, hung in his mind. Jacob felt he had stridden them before, perhaps when he was younger. He felt no pain, though he knew he should from his last memory of the explosion. Jacob caught movement from the side and quickly spun to see a young boy run through the trees, then down the path.

Jacob trotted after the boy, calling out to him to stop. The trail twisted and turned and great ferns and giant trees blocked the sun, allowing the light to only filter down. Finally, the track reached a small clearing, where Jacob spotted the young boy waiting, watching him. Jacob thought he knew him.

"Richard, is that you?"

The boy turned and ran back down the trail into the woods, Jacob in pursuit. The path continued through the forest, and it felt well-worn as it had been traveled numerous times. Jacob could see a brighter light as the way opened into a clearing. The boy was no longer there when Jacob burst from the trees into the clearing.

A man now stood, Jacob, recognizing the uniform of the militiamen he encountered outside Quebec's walls. The man had two buckets in his hands; he turned to look at Jacob. The memory returned of the militiaman carrying buckets he had surprised and nearly killed. For some reason unknown to Jacob, he released the young man.

Jacob looked closer at the man's eyes and could see the same boy's eyes he had been chasing. The realization hit Jacob like a cannon ball, as the man who must have known smiled and nodded toward Jacob.

"No, it couldn't be, Richard?"

The man smiled and nodded, turned, entered the trees and disappeared from view. Jacob took off in a sprint to catch the man but ended up running through the trees. There was no sign of the man and only the path continuing. Jacob slowed to a walk and followed it out into another clearing.

Rounding a bend, deer looked up from grazing in a field, their mouths chewing but not bounding off in fright. Instead, they watched Jacob as he walked by and returned to grazing as if it were nothing. This felt odd to Jacob, but he shrugged it off and kept walking. Then he felt a presence, looking down and seeing a great grey wolf walking alongside.

The wolf was old; his muzzle streaked with grey, golden eyes, old but all-knowing. Jacob placed his hand on the wolf and felt the fur with his fingers. Jacob could feel the wolf's great muscles as it walked next to him. Like the surroundings, it felt familiar and right. Looking closer, it seemed this wolf was Smoke, his first wolf from when he was a Ranger.

"Smoke, is that you?" Jacob asked, his voice sounding like an echo on the wind. The wolf looked up, grizzled and grey but with knowing eyes and kept walking with Jacob. Once again, Jacob shrugged and kept walking with the wolf down the trail, not knowing where he was going. Jacob felt tired; he needed to sleep. He found a soft patch of tall grass, laid down and slept. The wolf sat and watched over his sleeping form.

***

Heat.

Pain.

Sweat.

Jacob felt like he was in Hell; his body was racked with heat and pain. Jacob was stuck in the abatis at Carillon when he opened his eyes. The sharpened stake was through his left leg, pinning him in place. The flames were licking all around him, the heat and pain getting closer and closer. Gritting his teeth,

Jacob reached down to try to free his leg, but his left side was also caught up in the sharpened stakes of the abatis.

The flames licked at his feet, his side, his old Ranger uniform beginning to smoke. The sound of battle was all around him. Muskets from both sides, the cannons roaring, and the shot whistling by. The screaming and the moaning of the wounded. Many tried to free themselves, like Jacob, from the entanglements of the abatis.

The flames were steadily marching forward, undeterred by branches or men. When the fire reached the dead, the smell of charred flesh filled the air, combined with the scent of cooking flesh and meat. The screaming would then rise as the flames enveloped the wounded, who could not escape until they were silenced in death.

Jacob pulled with all his might, but he was trapped and could not remove his leg. He saw his tomahawk nearby and the thought of cutting off his leg to escape crossed his mind. The black smoke of the flames grew; Jacob thought he saw a black hooded figure amongst the smoke with a scythe in his hand. Jacob began to pull harder with all of his might.

With a crack, the branch snapped off, allowing Jacob to move, but preventing him from using his leg. Looking down, he saw the head of Captain Reynolds staring at him; fear etched on his face. Jacob looked away, focusing on moving, but the sharpened limb that broke off in his leg caught on other branches, slowing his retreat.

A peal of laughter could be heard almost in the distance. Turning to see where the laughter was coming from was the form of Sergeant Major Lovelace, looking at him from a distance and laughing. A bright crimson hole in the middle of his forehead from where Jacob's shot ended his cruel and sadistic life.

"There is no escape for you!" Lovelace yelled out mockingly. "You are going to die just like that pretty little thing I took before I died." His laughter continued, echoing amongst the screams and roar of the flames.

The flames began to rise, his uniform began to burn and the pain reached a crescendo. As hard as Jacob could crawl, he was hampered everywhere and knew he was doomed and trapped. His breaches began to burn, along with his coat and Jacob screamed until darkness took him.

***

Floating.
Ice cold.
Shivering.

It was cold; Jacob's teeth were chattering, his bones aching from the shivering. Pulling his arms around him, Jacob tried to warm himself. Looking around, he could see he was lying on the field where they had fought Jean and his men on snowshoes. The battle nearly caught them all.

Sitting up, Jacob was still shaking and shivering, the cold penetrating deep into his soul. Stumbling along a snowy path, he could see the dead, frozen blue faces of Rangers, French, Canadians and Hurons staring at him accusingly.

"Must…keep…going," Jacob stammered as his teeth clicked and clattered from his shivering. His feet made crunching sounds on the icy snow. When Jacob looked behind him, though, there were no tracks; his feet were not leaving any sign behind in the snow except for a few drops of blood that seemed to come from Jacob's left leg.

Jacob's mind was getting fuzzy; he knew it was from the effect of the cold. He willed himself to keep walking. He had left the dead behind and was walking through a thick forest, trees heavily blanketed in snow. In the distance, he saw a glow and headed toward it.

The glow turned into a bonfire, surrounded by oxen that seemed to be sitting near the fire and smelled of cooked meat. Stomach growling, Jacob slowly shuffled toward the roasted ox meat steaming platter. Dropping to his knees where the platter was, Jacob picked up a warm piece of meat and took a bite.

Warm and flavorful, to Jacob, it was the best-cooked meat he had ever had. The oxen continued to watch him, unmoving as he ate the cooked piece of meat. Next to the platter was a letter, and when he opened it, it turned out to be a thank you letter to the Marquis de Montcalm for the wonderful Christmas gift of roasted oxen. Jacob seemed to recall that moment before he toppled over and darkness took him once more. In the distance, Jacob thought he heard the sound of a wolf howling.

***

Warmth.
Soft fur.
Comfort.

Jacob opened his eyes. On one side was a grey and white fur: on the other, a black and grey one. Slowly sitting up, Jacob realized two wolves had laid next to him as he rested. One was who he thought was Smoke, then looking over at the large black furred with grey streaked wolf, Jacob asked, "Raven? Is that you?"

The black wolf joined the grey one, sat and watched Jacob with golden eyes. Then, getting to his feet, Jacob saw he was once more in the fog-shrouded forest dream world. The dirt path was still there, and he knew he had to walk it for some reason. He turned, but the wolves remained in place, sitting but with their tails wagging. They did not follow.

Smiling, Jacob waved at the two wolves before continuing his journey. He knew he had to be somewhere; he did not know how or why. The patch continued into the trees, so that is where Jacob went. As he walked along again, nothing but the sound of birds echoing through the trees and the breeze was all he could hear.

The path left the trees for a field full of wild flowers that filled the air with an herbal scent that made him feel better. Apple trees flowered and filled the air with their petals, dancing in the wind. Jacob stopped and stood, eyes closed and breathing in the herbal scent of the apple blossoms and the flowers.

Then he heard a light giggle on the wind, echoing amongst the trees. Opening his eyes, Jacob did recognize the laughter. It was Maggie, once more coming to him in his dream-like state. Looking, he saw her moving about the apple trees and Jacob pursued her. Every time he thought he found her, it was empty except for the echoing sound of her laughter.

"Jacob…"

He looked around, hearing Maggie call his name.

"Jacob…"

Looking, all Jacob could see were the flowers and the apple trees.

"Jacob…"

Finally, Jacob stopped moving and just closed his eyes. He first smelled her scent, warm and inviting. Then he felt her hands cover his eyes.

"Open your eyes…."

Jacob reached up and felt her hands and opened his eyes. Holding her hands in his, Jacob turned to gaze at Maggie.

"Well, now, look at you," she said, looking at Jacob up and down. "You turned out to be quite the man now."

Jacob blushed, not knowing what to say. He held onto her hands and looked at his feet before returning to look into Maggie's eyes. Jacob sensed she was waiting for an answer.

"Maggie, I can't stay. I have my wife and family to take care of. I am so sorry."

She smiled and reached up to caress his face. "See, was that so hard to say? You must take care of them, my love; return to your family."

She placed her hand on his heart, "I'll always be here, but you must go home and take care of your family."

"Aye, lad, you need to go," Jacob heard another voice. He looked up to see standing behind Maggie was Patrick, his first Ranger sergeant.

"You have done us all proud, lad, very proud," Patrick stated. Standing behind him were numerous figures and faces, wearing their green berets and black jockey hats, the fallen Rangers he had known. Jacob even believed he saw Konkapot, who raised his hand in greeting.

"Jacob, you need to go, lad; we'll be here."

Jacob looked at Maggie, who smiled once before lowering her hands.

"Jacob, you need to go back and finish the mission."

Looking over Patrick's shoulder, he saw the old Rangers begin to fade away.

"Jacob…"

"Jacob…"

***

"Jacob?"

The pain came crashing down on Jacob as he began to return to reality. Slowly opening his eyes, the light hurting them, Jacob became aware of his surroundings.

"Jacob! Are you awake? Jacob?"

His vision cleared and Jacob could see he was lying on a bed in a bedroom, though he did not recognize the location. He followed the voice and there sitting on another bed, was Samuel, a bandage around his head. He looked down at his left leg and splints and bandages were holding his leg in place. The pain came rushing back and Jacob knew he was still alive.

Samuel jumped up, ran to the door and yelled, "Hey, Doc, he is awake! Jacob is awake!" Then he returned and sat on the bed, looking at Jacob.

"Where are we, Samuel?" Jacob asked in a hoarse voice. His throat was raw and dry; the bed he was lying in was damp from sweat.

"Hampton's Plantation. After the fight, we had to get you somewhere you could be seen by a surgeon and fix your leg. Had we left you to the tender mercy of the regimental surgeons, you would have more and likely lost your leg."

Jacob wiggled and propped himself up, so he was in a sitting position. He pulled the blanket off to look closer at his injured leg. Stout boards, padded by linen and secured tightly, kept his leg from moving. A large, bloody bandage covered the area where the large splinter had embedded itself.

A civilian came in, a younger man carrying his surgeon's bag, grabbed a stool and sat down next to Jacob. He placed his hand on Jacob's forehead, Jacob's eyes following him.

"Good, fever is breaking," the surgeon stated and then he focused on the leg and the bandage. He nodded and then began to loosen the tight splint's binds. Once the splints were loosened enough, he began to unwrap the bloody bandage.

"Who are you?" Jacob asked, "You look familiar to me."

The surgeon chuckled, "My name is Robert Brownfield, and I was a surgeon's mate with the Second Regiment before I went off to medical school. When I learned Charles Town had fallen, I rushed back but found out everyone had been captured. Then I learned Colonel Marion was back, so here I am."

Jacob smiled and nodded, "Aye, I remember you at Savannah, or I should say after Savannah."

Robert nodded, "As I recall, you were banged up after that fight as well."

The bloody bandage was removed, and Jacob could see the extent of the wounds on his leg. It was heavily discolored and had a great gash about 7 inches long that had been stitched closed with thick black thread.

"I had to remove the splinter from the center of your femur bone, which had cracked. Luckily you have strong bones, had the bone shattered with the sliver, I would have to amputate your leg. Instead, I was able to remove the splinter and allow your cracked bone to set itself.

You have been fighting blood poisoning from the injury, running a high fever for the last few days. You were delirious, calling out names and I almost had to restrain you from preventing you from tearing open the stitches."

Jacob looked over at Samuel as Robert began making a poultice from herbs. Samuel nodded but said nothing as Robert applied the plaster to the wound, then set new bandages before tightening the splints. Jacob gritted his teeth as the pain shot up his leg, then relaxed as the pain subsided when Robert was done.

"I'll speak with Mrs. Horry to have some soup brought to you," Robert said as he stood up. "You need to get your strength up enough so we can move you. I'll tell Marion you are awake; he had been asking about you following the battle."

Robert nodded before he left the room. Jacob looked over at Samuel, sitting on the edge of his bed.

"You had me, the colonel, everyone concerned, Jacob," Samuel explained, "When you fell at the battle, we thought you had finally met your fate. But I knew you were not ready to die yet; you're too strong for that."

Jacob snorted and shook his head but then looked at Samuel. "How long was I out? How long have we been here?"

"Five days," Samuel answered, "You have been fighting this fever for five days. First, you would burn up, thrash about and then shake like you were freezing your bones. Back and forth until your fever finally broke just now."

Jacob nodded, looking thoughtfully at his leg in the splint. "Was I calling out? What names did I say?"

Samuel sat back on his bed and leaned against the wall.

"Our old friends, I think, you yelled out Richard a couple of times, wasn't that your younger brother?"

Jacob nodded. "I was in a dream or someplace, felt like back home, and I thought I saw my younger brother, so I followed him until I saw the militiaman from Quebec, then he disappeared. Then I saw my old wolf Smoke and Konkapot's Raven."

Samuel thought about it before continuing.

"Then you yelled out the fire and the flames, how you were burning up."

Jacob nodded slowly again. "I was in Hell, I think, Samuel," he explained, "I was back at Carillon but stuck in the abatis as we saw. The flames were catching up to me, and I couldn't escape them."

Samuel nodded, "Did you dream of Carillon in the Winter? You kept mentioning the snow and the oxen when you were shaking and shivering."

Jacob chuckled, "Yes, in fact, I did." He then paused and smiled, leaning back against the wall as he recalled his final moments in the dream world.

"I saw Maggie again and our friends like Patrick, even Konkapot. Our dead friends were there but said it was not my time. They were proud, Samuel; they were proud of what I and what we have done."

Samuel's eyes had misted up, just like Jacob's were, as he recalled his moment in the dream world before waking. Then a black serving girl carrying a tray and a distinguished-looking woman entered the room. Samuel settled into his place and the serving girl placed a tray before him, the woman putting the tray in front of Jacob. A large bowl of steaming chicken soup was on the tray.

"Major Clarke, may I welcome you to my home, though I wish it had been under better circumstances." The woman stated, and Jacob bowed slightly with a wince from his sitting position.

"Thank you, Mrs.?" Jacob asked.

"I am Harriott Horry, wife of Colonel Daniel Horry. I believe you know him?"

Jacob smiled, "Yes, ma'am, I do know your husband. Thank you for allowing this old soldier to heal up."

Harriott smiled and nodded, "Please do, as I fear the British may come hunting for you, and you will need the strength to escape."

She and the serving girl left and Jacob slowly ate his soup, feeling its warmth fill him and feed his body. They would remain there at the plantation for the next four days, Robert coming to check on him, change his bandages and check on Samuel's concussion. The only sign of his injuries was a tendency to talk louder than usual, as the explosion slightly had hurt his hearing.

Marion arrived on the fifth day to check on Jacob and Samuel with Jean and the boys accompanying him. Mrs. Horry escorted them to the room, and they crowded around both Jacob and Samuel.

"It's good to see you alive and well, if not for the broken leg," Marion stated," You had all of us very worried. I am glad you are still a tough old wolf." Marion turned and addressed Robert.

"Are they healthy enough to travel?"

Robert nodded. "I can remove the splint, but he must be careful and allow the bone to heal before he can fully use it again. As for Sergeant Penny, he is also good to travel."

Marion nodded. "Major Clarke, Sergeant Penny, you are both on convalescence until you are fully healed and can return to duty."

He then turned toward Jean. "Lieutenant Langy, you and the lads here will see these two men return home and remain with them on detached duty until I need the use of you."

Jean nodded and the boys smiled in excitement. Marion turned back and rested his hand on Jacob's shoulder. "Get well soon, my friend; we still need your unique skills. Besides, you saw what happened to me with my leg; go home and heal up." Smiling once more at Jacob, Marion turned and departed.

Richard and Peter came over; Richard stated, "It's good to see you are doing better, Papa; we have your rifle and gear. Waya is waiting outside with the horses." Jacob nodded his thanks, and his two sons helped him to his feet and out to his waiting horse. Mrs. Horry was waiting on the sizeable columned porch of the house.

"Thank you, ma'am, for everything. Hopefully, we didn't draw the attention of the British toward you."

Mrs. Horry waved her hand in dismissal. "We have been helping friends since the city fell; what are two more? Please do take care of yourself, Major Clarke."

With his two sons' aid, Jacob nodded, then walked down the steps to his waiting horse. Waya was sitting there, waiting with his tail wagging and tongue out in greeting. Carefully, Jacob pulled himself up onto his horse and set his left leg carefully. His upper leg still hurt due to the mending bone and torn muscle.

After Samuel mounted his horse, the band turned to leave for home, Jacob waving to Mrs. Horry. They road down the dirt road to the horse, flanked by great trees, before cutting to hunting trails they knew. Jacob wanted to avoid any chance meetings with the British or Loyalists until his leg was much better.

It was a slow and cautious journey home, ensuring they were not spotted. At night, they only built a small fire to draw less attention. Jacob and Samuel were brought up to date on what happened after the fight at Shubrick's Plantation.

"We lost about fifty men," Jean explained. "General Sumter kept fighting until the darkness prevented his men from shooting. We used it to escape."

Jacob frowned at the news, "Fifty? Did we lose Fifty men? That is about half of our brigade."

Jean nodded. "Marion was not pleased. Because of our losses, many men went home, complaining about being thrown to the wolves." Jean looked over at Waya. "Sorry, but it was true, no?" Waya just stared back, slightly wagging his tail.

Jacob shook his head in disbelief. "What happened to him, Jacob?" Samuel asked.

Jacob sighed, "You know, sometimes war can change a man; well, I think this war has changed him and not for the better."

It was a sunny morning when Jacob and the others rode home, the wolves leading the way. Jacob and his sons headed toward their house and Samuel and his sons toward theirs. Jean dismounted but was directed toward Jacob's house.

"Mrs. Clarke, there are men here," a man yelled out from the barn area; Jacob turned to see who it was. A worker stood there, leather apron on; Jacob assumed he must be working for Peter in the skinning business.

Maria came out wiping her hands until she saw it was Jacob and took off in a trot toward Jacob. Jacob's heart raced as she got closer to seeing his wife after such a long time. He felt joy for a change, seeing her beaming face.

Close behind was Peter, Maria's father, mother and her sister Otti and finally Helga, their daughter. They all started for them, except for the workers who stayed behind at the barn.

When Maria arrived, she saw Jacob was still up on his horse.

"Well now, get down from your high horse," she said, then paused, and Jacob looked for help. Instead, she placed her hands on her hips. "What happened," she asked, "Where did you get hurt? You wouldn't be here if you weren't hurt."

Jean and the boys helped Jacob down off his horse as he protected his left leg. "Now, I could have come home just to see you," Jacob stated and Maria snorted in disbelief. Then she walked up and after he was standing, threw her arms around his neck and kissed him squarely on the lips.

After she released him, she started to look at Jacob up and down, shaking her head. "You are not eating right, again." Then she paused and looked at Jacob's leg before looking back at him.

Jacob nodded, "I took a big splinter in the leg, cracked the bone."

Maria pursed her lips, looking at the leg. "How long can you stay?"

Jacob shrugged, "Marion said we are to remain here until I fully heal up, or he comes for us."

Maria nodded, "That could be a little while, my love; I guess you must stay for a bit."

Jacob smiled and nodded, "Yes, my love, I think you are right."

***

Lieutenant Stephan Jarvis led his troop of South Carolina Light Dragoons along the dirt road at the trot, their hooves kicking up dust clouds. An informer had passed on to them that they had seen the Swamp Fox himself; Francis Marion had ridden through the area and was currently staying at the Hampton Plantation. Believing they could finally box in the Fox, Lieutenant Jarvis, the closest dragoon element, had the mission to capture the Fox.

As they rode, the setting sun cast a strange light on the horsemen as they made their way down the road, filtering through the trees. The swaying Spanish Moss of the great arms of the oaks waved at the dragoons as they passed by. Finally, arriving at the road to the plantation, Jarvis led his men forward as they turned toward the house.

"When we arrive, make sure we surround the house. Then, God, we'll show Tarleton and everyone how to catch a Fox!"

**

Marion leaned back in his chair, releasing Jacob and his band to return home. Mrs. Horry offered to make dinner for him, commenting that he had not had a proper home-cooked meal. Marion agreed and knew he could not refuse the offer.

As the servants were preparing the meal, Marion had sat in a comfortable chair, and it seemed the heavy burden he had been carrying began to fall off. The ugly result of the fighting at Shubrick's Plantation, how many men they lost, and how it caused over half of the remaining men to head home. Releasing Jacob and his band also significantly reduced his force.

Marion closed his eyes and rubbed his temples as he thought about what to do. *"I have no choice. We have to go to ground, send everyone home until I can rebuild my force or morale improves."*

Marion took a deep breath, the chair's comfort seducing him, and he fell asleep. However, the stress of the recent actions, and the constant movement, prevented him from truly resting. Marion fell into a deep sleep, dreaming of a better time, hopefully when this war was over. However, he was shaken awake when Marion opened his eyes; Mrs. Horry was standing before him.

"Francis, the Loyalists are coming. You have no time! Go out the back and head toward the rice fields. We will do what we can to buy time. Now go!"

As she stood back, Marion jumped to his feet as he could hear the sound of horses coming toward the house.

"Go, Francis, go!"

Bowing quickly to Mrs. Horry, Marion spun and promptly ran out of the house. Jumping off the back porch, landing with a stumble, he maintained his footing. Then, pumping his arms and legs, Marion sprinted past the kitchen building and headed down a path leading to the rice fields. He could hear the horses coming around the kitchen; Marion's luck had held.

Crouching low, Marion moved along the path, bathed in the deepening shadows of nightfall, moving along the raised berms of the rice fields. He could hear the Loyalists yelling at the house when he came to a stream. Walking into the water, Marion sank low and waded across to the other side and once more moved into the rice fields, remaining crouched amongst the rice stalks.

***

Jarvis waved his arm to the left and then to the right, his troop dividing to ride around the house. He rode up to the large porch with Greek columns and dismounted from his horse and some other men from the troop. Mrs. Horry came out onto the porch and gave a small curtsey to Jarvis.

"How may we be of service?" Mrs. Horry asked as Jarvis climbed the steps to stand before her.

"We're looking for a traitor and a criminal, a Francis Marion; we learned he was here visiting," Jarvis replied.

"No sir, there is no Francis Marion here." Mrs. Horry replied, her eyes down cast. "We are good citizens and would not harbor any criminals."

"Is that so," Jarvis countered, "Then you wouldn't mind if we searched your house?"

She looked up at Jarvis and gave him a stern look. "Are you saying I am a liar, sir? How ungallant of you!"

Jarvis moved closer to Harriot. "If you are a good citizen and, as you have said, don't harbor any criminals, then there shouldn't be an issue, would there?"

Harriot paused before she nodded, "You are correct, sir. I am sorry for my outburst. You may search my house at your leisure."

Jarvis bowed his head slightly to Harriot, "Thank you, kind lady." He then turned and called out to the troop. "Search the house, every room!"

The troopers entered the house and fanned out; Jarvis walked through the entryway to the troopers on the backside of the house.

"Search the kitchen, the slave quarters and all of the outbuildings," Jarvis instructed, and his dragoons dismounted and fanned out. Some rode over to the slave quarters to begin their search. Jarvis walked back into the house to stand near Mrs. Horry as his men searched all the rooms. "You have a nice home, Madame," he stated and she nodded in thanks.

"Thank you, sir." She answered and thought, *Francis, I hope you made it across the stream to the fields. This indignity has to end!"*

After the house was searched, the troopers came by to report nothing was found. Jarvis had a hard look on his face, wanting intensely to be the one who bagged the Swamp Fox. "Have the men mount. Prepare to move."

He turned and bowed to Mrs. Horry. "We are sorry for disturbing you, madame," Jarvis stated with a slight bow, "Have an enjoyable evening." Jarvis turned and went over to his horse, then led the dragoons away from the house.

Mrs. Horry finally let out a sigh of relief before smiling. It had worked; Francis had gotten away and will take the fight back to the British. She was satisfied with that thought, smiled, and returned to her everyday life, such as it was.

***

Jacob lay in bed, and Maria's mother, Gerda, was applying her herbs poultice on his leg wound, just like she did some time ago when he had rested up in their home following an injury. His leg was feeling better, slowly becoming stronger. When he was not resting, he walked around the compound, exercising his leg. He was feeling better but knew it was not time yet.

His daughter, Helga, took her job seriously, as assigned by Maria, to keep an eye on him so he wouldn't reinjure his leg. She brought a meal on a tray, then sat there to watch Jacob eat his dinner, whether he wanted to or not.

She stood there with fists on her hip, just like her mother, "Mama said you are to eat all of your meal; you need to grow stronger."

Jacob looked at the seriousness of Helga's expression and replied, "Yes, ma'am."

As he ate, Helga asked him about the battle and what had happened. Jacob told her of the fighting and living in the swamps. Helga shook his head, "Now I understand why mama says you don't eat well."

As Jacob chewed on a soft, warm roll, he gave Helga a leveled look. "I heard you have been having your adventures; tell me of them."

Helga sat down; she appeared happy to tell her stories and began recalling her role in helping Maria as a spy. She said she knocked down the boy who had made fun of her, and the other kids started to leave her alone. She ended by telling of the night Maria killed the man who had attacked her.

Jacob listened intently, nodding his head. He saw how confident she was, like her brothers had to grow up earlier because of this war. "Sounds like you had your adventures," Jacob commented. "I am very proud of you for helping your mother and how you are turning into quite a lady."

Helga smiled as she stood up to take the tray and kissed Jacob on his forehead. "Flattery will get you nowhere, so behave and listen to mama. Heal up." She gave him a mischievous smile before turning and heading out of the room.

Jacob shook his head. *"That is a dangerous young woman, just like her mother."*

Two months passed and Jacob could move with a slight limp. He would chuckle to himself, seeing that Marion also walks with a limp. With Maria's cooking, Jacob's strength was returning, and he was filling back out to his standard form. Samuel was doing the same, along with Jean, who was fed and cared for by Otti.

At night, they would sit outside, smoke their pipes, drink ale and talk about their adventures. Jacob leaned back, pipe in his mouth as he listened to his boys try to out-boast Helga on who did more exciting or dangerous missions. While it did bother him that his children were now fully immersed in the war, against what he initially wished for, it turned out for the better,

Samuel leaned over, pipe in hand. "Sound familiar, eh? Like being out on the island when the new Rangers tried to out-boast the old ones." He looked at Jacob seriously. "We have done well, haven't we?" He turned and pointed with his pipe to the debating children. "They have turned out rather well, I think."

Jacob sat and smiled, nodding his head. "I do think so, Samuel, I do think so."

Peter joined them and told them what was happening in the backcountry while they fought with Marion. "The British visited Dorchester; they burned St. George's Anglican Church and a few homes. Maria's parents lived full time in the compound now, as their house was burned."

Jacob nodded as Peter continued. "Seems our old friend Bloody Bill is back up north, and the British landed near George-town and burned many of dee warehouses and homes near da water. Also, we heard Marion reformed his group and ambushed a troop of those damnable South Carolina Light Dragoons. So we are doing well and the British seem to be falling back."

Jacob rubbed his chin, taking in the information. The news sounded good, and Marion had taken the field, so he must have recruited or was able to call out the militia again following the disaster at Shubrick. The news of the British falling back was great indeed.

It had been two months following Jacob's wounding and he felt fit. He was honestly looking at his ability to move and ride to determine if he was ready to return to duty. He rode, hunted, and ensured his skills and healing were sharpened. Finally, summer was slowly slipping away as September arrived and Jacob felt ready to return to duty.

During a pleasant morning, Maria approached Jacob as he sat on their porch, Waya at his feet, watching the workers begin another batch of skins to be washed.

"Well, I sense you will be leaving soon," she stated while taking a chair next to Jacob. "You have done what I have told you to do and you seemed to have mended and finally filled out to the man I knew. That army of yours can't feed you well to stay healthy."

Jacob shrugged, "We tried eating enough frogs and fish, but it wasn't enough, I guess."

She looked at him and responded, "No, it did not." Then she became earnest. "How much longer, Jacob, how much longer will this fight go on? The news we are getting sounds like the British are heading south, and to be honest, this was a close one for you this time."

Jacob looked at Maria and could see the concern in her eyes. "I am hoping soon, and you are right; this was as close to death as I wanted to get. Besides, while I do not want to admit it in front of anyone, I am not as young as I want to be. My body reminds me and my old wounds do the same. Old wounds." Jacob looked off into the distance, recalling all the times he kept returning to the horror of Carillon.

Sighing, Jacob looked back at his wife and sighed. "I believe it won't last much longer. I believe this war has to end soon."

Later that day, a familiar face rode into the compound as fate would have it. Frederick rode up to Jacob's house as Waya came to the end of the porch, wagging his tail before giving out a loud bark. Jacob came out of the house and Frederick waved to him.

"Greetings, Jacob; I bring news," Frederick stated.

"Marion needs us, doesn't he?" he asked, and Frederick nodded.

"I knew you would figure it out before I said anything," Frederick confirmed. "General Greene is on the move now that the weather is cooling slightly. Washington has our friend Cornwallis in a bind up in Virginia and he wants us to make sure none of the British forces down here move up to support."

Samuel and Jean made their way over to greet Frederick, shaking hands. "You all look fit as a fiddle, ready to retake the field," Frederick commented. "As I told Jacob here, Marion is calling everyone back; we are to rendezvous with him at Lauren's Plantation."

Looking over Frederick's shoulder, he could see their boys jogging up. "Go get your gear together; Marion needs us back up." The boys came to a halt and quickly sprinted to their respective homes to start packing. Samuel and Jean nodded, turned and headed to pack their gear.

"Make yourself comfortable; I will be along shortly," Jacob stated as he headed into his house. Frederick occupied Jacob's chair and looked at the two wolves, looking at him expectantly. Frederick raised an eyebrow as the wolves stared at him. "Ah, I see," Frederick stated, then opened his haversack and pulled out some jerked meat.

The wolves came and took it gently from Frederick, holding it out, before dropping it to the porch in front of Frederick, holding the meat in their front paws and chewed on it. Frederick looked around the compound and nodded. *"They do have a nice place here,"* Frederick thought. *"A very nice place indeed."*

As Jacob entered the house, Maria was waiting for him. "Marion called for you, didn't he?" she asked, and Jacob nodded.

"About bloody time; you need to get back out there. Besides, you are getting underfoot and getting in the way. Would be better this way." She responded with a straight face before breaking out in her impish grin and kissing him. Then, she turned and headed to the kitchen area to pack food for the journey like always.

After an hour, they were assembled once more. The horses fattened up on grazing look refreshed and eager to go. Saddlebags had dried meat, bread and other goods that both Maria and Otti provided. Peter, Gottfried and Gerda observed Peter's hand on Helga's shoulder from the porch.

The boys mounted up, followed by Jean, Samuel and Jacob. His leg was enough to mount and settle on the horse without support. Maria came over and handed up his rifle to him, briefly holding his hand.

"I know I keep saying it, but be careful out there, and take care of one another. I want you all to come home soon."

Tipping his hat, Jacob responded with "Yes, ma'am, before bending down and kissing her. He straightened out and turned to see if everyone was ready. Samuel was finishing up with his traditional goodbyes with Otti. He looked at the porch, Peter raised his pipe in salute and both Gottfried and Gerda waved. The wolves had also fattened up. They sat with their tongues hanging out, a smile in the ways of the wolf.

Jacob looked over to Frederick and nodded, "Lead us out."

Nodding, Frederick healed his horse and began to lead the column out of their gate. The wolves ran ahead as they always do. Jacob turned and waved one last time to Maria, Helga, and the family on the porch before settling into his saddle and beginning his ride back to the war. He caught up with Frederick and he looked over and smiled.

"To be honest, Jacob, we will all be happy when you arrive, especially Marion. We think this will be a big one and could mean the war here may be over soon. The sooner, the better, I say, and with you all back, I think it will happen sooner than later. Jacob nodded in appreciation; what Frederick said made perfect sense. Maybe the war was finally coming to an end.

CHAPTER 13

EUTAW SPRINGS

Lieutenant Colonel Stewart hated the damn heat in South Carolina, having to march in the deep summer of August. As he watched his men march, he could see many were sick from the heat, and their morale was heavily affected by their losses. Having consolidated his forces following the fight against these damnable rebels under Sumter and Marion had learned that he had faced at Shubrick Plantation, nearly bled him dry. Stewart knew it had been close had the rebels brought up artillery; it could have nearly wiped him out as a fighting force.

They had captured his supply wagons and the much-needed ammunition for his infantry. He knew they needed to be resupplied. If these rebels were to attack now, he would not have much in the way of powder and shot to put up a good fight. Therefore, he ordered the men on the march to head south to a better and more defendable position where he could be resupplied by water instead of on land.

Shaking his head as he rode alongside the marching column, these rebel fighters, had odd names. Carolina Gamecock, he believed, was meant for this Sumter character, the Swamp Fox he had learned before concerned this Francis Marion. Both intercepted his supplies coming overland from Charles Town and starving his men at their pleasure.

After a few days on the march, Stewart found a suitable site for his army. He found some high ground flanked by the Congaree and the Wateree Rivers. From these rivers, he finally received some supplies; his men could rest and eat. Additionally, his sick could be cured and his fighting force could better meet these rebels and thwart their offenses.

Stewart, with an orderly, walked amongst his men as they rested and mended their clothing in the cool shade of the trees. Fresh water from the Eutaw Spring was helping those with heat sickness. Finally, the men fit for duty were dispatched to reinforce their positions at the old tabby fort in Dorchester and a new redoubt was built at Fairlawn. There, he could control the roads to prevent the freedom of movement for the rebels.

Stewart approached one of the regimental surgeons who was seeing the sick. "How are the men fairing?" Stewart asked and the surgeon took a deep breath before letting it out slowly.

"To be honest, sir, not well. Most are starting to recover from the heat now that we have fresh water and getting daily supplies from Charles Town. But, unfortunately, a small streak of Malaria is still running its course."

Stewart nodded. "Can they fight?"

The surgeon looked across the sick he was working on. Many were lying on blankets in the shade. All with distressed looks on their faces, their shirts damp from sweat. His surgeon mates were moving amongst the sick, providing scoops of grog and biscuits for them to eat.

"Sir, to be honest," the surgeon stated, "Only for a short while in this condition. The longer we wait, the better they can rest up and heal. Then you will have more men fit for duty. If we were to fight now, only about half could fight."

Stewart pursed his lips as he thought, then nodded in acceptance. "Thank you for your service to the men, doctor. I'll leave you to your duties."

The surgeon nodded, then turned and returned to the sick and injured under his care. Stewart watched him go before he turned and continued inspecting the camp.

"Lieutenant, get with the quartermaster. I want a return of serviceable muskets and abled body men who can fight. We are in bad shape, and I suspect our luck will not hold out long, and these damn rebels will find us."

***

Frederick and Jacob leading the band rode into the field next to Lauren's Plantation, where Marion's men had set up camp. In the distance, he could see the Continental Army had set up their camp.

"Well, looks like General Greene has arrived," Frederick stated and Jacob nodded in agreement. Frederick led them to where the rest of Jacob's men had set up their camp. When they saw his approach, they all jumped up, with loud voices, welcomed and celebrated his return. Jacob blushed slightly, not used to being recognized, so he dismounted.

His men came by to pat him on the back, all welcoming him back and hoped he was feeling better. Even Samuel, Jean, and the boys were welcomed. The wolves just sat on their haunches, watching.

"I better go report to the colonel," Jacob stated as he handed his reins to Samuel. "I'll take care of my gear when I get back."

Samuel nodded as Jacob headed to where Frederick pointed out where Marion was camped. When Jacob arrived, he found only Oscar there, who smiled when he saw Jacob.

"Major Clarke, so glad to see you, sir. Master Marion will be so happy to see you again. How is the leg?"

Jacob smiled in return. "My leg is fine, Oscar; thank you for asking. Where is the colonel?"

Oscar turned and pointed toward the Continental camp. "He is meeting with the general at his camp."

Thanking Oscar, Jacob headed across the field to where the larger army was encamped. As he approached, he saw roving guards and companies drilling. He could hear the "snap" of wooden flints as they practiced loading and firing. The "snaps" sounded as one. Jacob nodded in approval.

As he drew closer to the camp, he saw they had no tents, only cooking fires with mess pails and other cooking implements. *"Greene must have decided to travel light for speed."* Jacob thought.

"Halt, advance and be recognized."

Jacob stopped and saw one of the roving sentries had halted, holding his musket across his chest.

Jacob moved up to the sentry. "Major Clarke, commander of an Independent Company of Partisans serving under General Marion."

The sentry presented arms. "Enter, sir; I have been instructed that you are to make your way to the commanding general once you arrive."

Jacob nodded and entered the camp; the sentry returned to roving the perimeter. As Jacob walked, he could not help but notice the sad shape the men were in. Some were in uniform, some only in shirts and even some were just plain naked, their skin marked and discolored from the leather straps of their cartridge boxes.

The men huddled in small groups like all armies when not drilling or on sentry duty. A good number rested in the shade; others sat on the ground and spoke of the coming action. Some worked on their rations, which Jacob noticed was limited.

"A half-naked and starved army on the march to fight the British, was this, not the same issue Gates had before Camden?" So, Jacob thought as he continued to work amongst the soldiers. While the men looked raggedly and tired, it sounded like their morale was good.

In the distance, he could see the taller General Greene, his staff and the shorter Marion under the limbs of a large oak tree, providing them shade. Jacob stopped at the edge of the tree limbs. "Request permission to enter."

Marion looked out and, seeing it was Jacob, commanded, "Enter!"

Jacob had to bend low to get under the branches before standing before Generals Greene, Marion, and the assembled staff. Coming to attention, "Sir, Major Clarke is reporting to duty as ordered."

General Greene smiled, came over and shook Jacob's hand. "Good to see you up and about, Major Clarke; we need your services."

Jacob nodded, "I am here to serve, sir." Greene nodded and motioned to the map stretched out on a log with his hand. As Greene retook his place at the map, Jacob joined Marion, who also shook his hand in welcome.

"Major Clarke, I need you to locate and fix where the British are. We know they departed Orangeburgh and consolidated while pulling out of Camden and Georgetown. However, we have heard reports of the old fort at Dorchester recently seeing reinforcements and we have received word of an earthen redoubt near Fairlawn. Therefore, we think the British are heading toward Eutaw Springs. We need you to find them, fix their position and report back to us."

Jacob looked at the map; he could see where the fort at Dorchester was and compared to his house and this redoubt near Fairlawn. Looking at the direction from Orangeburgh and drawing a line toward Charles Town, it did make sense for the British to be near Eutaw Springs.

"Yes sir, I will depart with my men immediately and find them. Once we have them located, where will I be able to find you to report?"

"My line of march is along this road toward Eutaw Spring," Greene explained, using his finger to trace the road toward Eutaw Spring. "We will march slowly, as I am sure you are aware of our condition."

Jacob nodded and then Greene nodded in return before reaching out and shaking Jacob's hand.

"Good hunting Major."

Turning, Jacob saluted Marion, who only smiled and shook his hand. "See you on the field," was all he replied. Jacob smiled in return.

Jacob returned to where his band waited for him. Once more, he looked over the Continentals who were trying to rest in the hot and humid conditions of the southern summer. Seeing partially clothed men, most of their clothing in sad shape with tears and holes, yet there is still a desire in their eyes. They still followed General Greene and believed in the cause to stay with the army.

When Jacob arrived at where the band sat, in what shade they could find, even the horses hung their heads from the heat. Several men had brought buckets of water for their mounts, who drank noisily from them. When they saw Jacob arrive, they all rose to their feet expectantly.

"Well, where are we off to?" Samuel asked as the rest gathered around to hear what Jacob had to say.

"General Greene wants us to scout for the army, our British friends have stopped moving, and he wants to finish what he started. The British have encamped near Eutaw Springs; we are to pinpoint their exact location, then observe their daily activity. General Greene will bring the army up slowly; we must maintain communication with him on his line of march."

Everyone smiled, even though their hair was matted from sweat, their clothing clinging to their skin. Jacob nodded; his band's dedication always impressed and amazed him. Even after all of these years, they have been fighting together.

"Samuel, Jean, see to the men. Get what supplies you can if needed from the quartermaster; everyone checks your flints and powder. Make sure you have enough ball though we are scouting now; I believe we will go into action with Marion during the fight."

Samuel, Jean and the others automatically turned and went off on their tasks, having done it numerous times. Jacob went over to his horse, whose head was dropping, eyed him as he approached and nickered. Jacob rubbed his nose. Pulling an apple from his haversack, he held it out for his horse, who happily munched on it.

Patting the horse's neck, Jacob went through his gear, ensuring he had all that was needed. He looked down at his clothes, surprised they were still in one piece, though mostly held together by multiple patches and repairs. *"More thread than material,"* he mused.

Samuel, Jean and the boys returned from the quartermaster with supplies, including rum bottles. Jacob raised an eyebrow when he saw the bottles. Samuel just shrugged, "Strictly for our grog, nothing else. Men will need to drink with this heat; you know that as well as I do."

Jacob shrugged as Samuel smiled and headed to secure the bottles in his gear. The rest of the band packed away the supplies they had received and began to mount on their horses. Once everyone was up, Jacob motioned and led the band back out of the camp and toward the road.

The men lounging in the shade rose and waved as Jacob led his men past them, some even calling out, "good hunting" and "best of luck!" Jacob nodded back, and the band waved in return.

Jacob maintained a steady pace toward Eutaw Springs, only seven miles away. It worked nicely that it was afternoon, so with a slow pace, he will not tire out his mounts and still arrive when the sun was setting. At least the road they used was shaded, though the air was still humid, and the insects buzzed around them. Once more, the sweat tricked from under his hat down his face, his clothes clinging to his skin.

The sun was sinking when Jacob halted the men near Eutaw Creek. Then, dismounting, Jacob called Samuel, Jean and Frederick to him.

"We'll leave the horses here so they won't give us away and we'll leave a group with Frederick to watch them and get water for us from the creek. They will also be the couriers who will ride back the way we came and keep Marion and General Greene informed."

Jacob looked at Frederick, who nodded his acceptance of his task. "The rest of the band will follow the creek until we can get a good vantage point to watch the camp. Afterward, we will rotate our scouts to stay fresh and keep the information coming. We move in five minutes."

Jean, Samuel and Frederick go to get their sections; Frederick and his section gather the horses and bring them to the creek to drink. Jean and Samuel brought the rest of the band up, including the wolves. They seemed to be weathering the heat but had disgusted looks on their faces. When all was ready, Jacob led them out with his wolves moving alongside him.

The night sounds mixed with the creek's gurgle as Jacob quietly led the band toward the possible British camp. As he was taking his time to stay quiet, it was about an hour before they could see the twinkle of the campfires of the camp.

"Well, seems we found them," Jacob thought and got down to scout the camp.

Whispering instructions to Jean and Samuel, he pointed to the left and right, showing where he wanted them to go and when they would report to him in the morning.

Jean and Samuel gathered their respective sections and wolves and then moved off to their scouting positions. Moving toward a thick stand of trees and brush, Jacob could crawl in and, after moving some branches around, made a viewing hole through the bush. Jacob's section included his boys Richard and Patrick, Jehu Jones, James Lafayette and William Lee. They made places concealed in the brush where they would rest when not reporting.

Jacob crawled back and whispered, "Get some rest; we'll start when the sun comes up." His section crawled and laid upon their blankets and fell asleep. Jacob went back to look some more, his wolves keeping him company. They did rotate a watch, one man at a time being this close, while still allowing time for rest.

Jacob woke everyone for stand to as the sun began to rise. Grimacing from his discomfort, Jacob's body reminded him he was not a young Ranger anymore. His leg ached, so Jacob shook his head and watched the area around the British camp. Then, seeing no one had detected them, he had his men eat breakfast and moved up to his observation area.

Pulling his telescope, Jacob began to scan the camp now that it was easier to see. Richard crawled up and joined Jacob, having a notebook to record what was seen. He also handed Jacob a biscuit, which he nodded in thanks. Richard opened his notebook and waited to record. Then, taking a bite, Jacob held the piece of the biscuit in his mouth until it softened a little before chewing.

"I take it Samuel made the biscuits?" he asked, and Richard nodded. "How did you know?"

Jacob quietly chuckled, "I can taste fire ash in it, and he always had a small problem keeping it out of the biscuit."

Jacob could see activity in the camp and focused on his telescope. "We have an activity," he stated and Richard readied his notebook. While Jacob chewed, he took in what was developing in the camp.

The regular activity was seen in the camp. Men wake up, sit around fires, make breakfast and hold formations. It was one of these formations that stood out. It was a decent size group of mostly Loyalists based on their uniforms. What drew Jacob's attention; was that most of them were carrying shovels while only a few carried muskets.

Lowering his telescope, Jacob turned to Richard. "Looks like a foraging party heading out," he whispered, "we'll see what happens when they return." Richard recorded the information and Jacob returned to looking at the camp.

The camp surrounded a large plantation house, the line of tents located behind a large fenced-in area. There were sentries at the entrance to the fenced area and he saw one roving patrol moving between the fenced-in area and the tree line. However, from what Jacob could see, they did not enter the woods to patrol.

Jehu crawled up, along with Patrick and they rotated back to their concealed camp. Richard and Jacob moved back to where they had sent Samuel and Jean's section, waiting for their info. The sun had risen, and Samuel and Jean soon arrived with their observations. Jacob nodded to the two men, "What have you seen?"

"Seems our British friends are short on food," Samuel reported, "from my position, I can see their field kitchen, not many fires and they are not making a lot of bread."

Jacob nodded, "Makes sense; I saw a foraging party of about three hundred men armed with shovels head out this morning at first light. What did you see, Jean?"

"From our position, we counted about four, maybe five, British regiments from their uniforms and company streets. They have some artillery pieces in one corner; we also saw some mounted Loyalists head southward out of the camp."

Richard wrote all of the notes down from Samuel and Jean. It included sketches that all three had made from their positions. "I have it all, papa," he stated.

Jacob nodded, "Go to Frederick and have a courier take it to Marion and General Greene. Richard nodded and returned to where Frederick and his men held the horses. Jacob watched him go and then turned to Samuel and Jean. "Feels like it will be hot today; keep an eye on your men. Keep them watered."

Both nodded and then headed back to the observation positions. Jacob returned to his camp, laying down and closing his eyes for a short nap. William Lee woke Jacob, "Jacob, those men are back carrying shovels and they have sacks with them."

Nodding to William, Jacob crawled up to the observation area and James Lafayette handed the telescope to Jacob and then pointed. "They have just come out of the road over there."

Focusing on the telescope, Jacob took in the foraging party as they entered the camp. Sweet potatoes, from what Jacob could determine, watching the men pouring out what was in the sacks. They must have gone to local fields and dug up the potatoes for the camp. As Jacob watched, he did see men come over with buckets and secure potatoes while heading back to their camps.

"That confirms it," Jacob stated, "They are low on supplies as well. Keep an eye on them; record what you see in the notebooks. I am going back to get some rest."

Both James and William nodded, and they returned to watching the camp. Jacob went back and returned to his napping. He lightly slept for a few hours and then woke in the late afternoon. Richard was waiting, "James had ridden to the general and reported. He said they are almost here, about four miles away."

Jacob nodded and thanked Richard before going to relieve himself. Then, Jacob crawled up for his turn to watch the camp. Richard quickly crawled up, joined him, along with the wolves and lay alongside, their golden eyes watching, their noses sniffing.

"Anything new?" Jacob asked and Jehu shook his head no. Then, nodding, Jacob took his telescope and Richard took the notebook from Patrick, who headed back to the camp. They wiggled to get comfortable, the observation area now well packed down. Then, bringing his telescope up, Jacob scanned the camp and saw normal activities.

The night was uneventful; Jacob did not see anything to report and rotated when their time was up. Finally, Jacob went to his blanket and lay down. The night air was more relaxed and more comfortable than it had been. As Jacob lay there, looking at the stars through the tree limbs, he thought of the coming battle. It did not look like the British were going to move so that General Greene would have his fight. Perhaps, this battle could decide the outcome in South Carolina.

As he had been doing for many years, Jacob woke naturally before the sun rose and had everyone back up to stand. After a quick breakfast of some dried meat and one of Samuel's biscuits, he, Richard and the wolves made their way up to the observation position. Nothing happened during the night, Jacob took up his telescope and Richard readied the notebook.

Just like the morning before, the foraging party was being formed, about three hundred and fifty men. Shouldering their shovels, the foraging column marched out of the camp and down the road. Jacob scanned for anything unusual or new as the sun rose and light bathed the camp. Finally, after an hour, Jacob did see something out of the ordinary.

Two Loyalists appeared to be walking with two Continentals heading toward the camp. Jacob focused on the four and watched what they would do. First, the two Loyalists led the Continentals up to the sentries at the gate's opening. Then Jacob saw one of the sentries turn and jog toward the mansion while the rest stayed at the entrance.

"Oh, this is not good," Jacob whispered and shook his head, "Not good at all."

***

Andrew Maxwell stood there, looking at the tents, the fine clothes the British soldiers had, and the smell of sweet potatoes cooking on the fires. After enlisting in the Third North Carolina, he had been promised food and clothing and so far on this campaign, he had neither. Andrew looked down at his tattered blue and red-faced lottery coat, threadbare and patched. The thought of deserting did not bother him; he had been a lowly dockworker at Wilmington.

The other man, James Shank, stood there with no shoes or stockings, his feet covered thickly in dirt from the road. He also wore a threadbare blue and red-faced lottery coat, most of his breaches rags, his knees exposed. James sniffed at the smell of cooking food and looked over at Andrew. "Do you think they'll feed us?"

Andrew looked at the two Loyalists and the one sentry who were standing at the entrance, then back to James. "I sure hope so; it smells good, doesn't it."

The sentry returned, and Lieutenant Colonel Stewart approached the two deserters. The two men stood up the best they could in the form of attention when Stewart stood before them.

"Why should I not hang you for traitors," Stewart asked, looking at their poor uniforms, "or for being deserters?"

Andrew looked at James, then back to Colonel Stewart. "If it pleases, my lordship, we have seen the error of our ways. We want to be forgiven for our sins."

Stewart looked sternly at Andrew, "I cannot forgive your sins, not in my line of work. So, what else can you offer me?"

"We can talk about the army that is coming," James offered. Stewart looked at James quickly.

"What army?" Stewart asked.

James looked at Andrew, then back to Stewart. "General Greene's Army, we thought you knew." He turned and pointed down the road. "That way, about five miles or so. He is marching here with the whole army, even those others like General Sumter and Marion who joined them. He'll be here in a day, maybe less."

With a shocked look, Stewart looked to the sentry, "See to these men and feed them." Then, turning on his heels, Stewart headed back into the camp, moving to where Major Coffin had his headquarters. Major Coffin rose from his camp chair when Stewart entered.

"Major, take a force to reconnoiter down the road. The enemy may be marching toward us, and I need to know. Therefore, I will prepare our force here while you ride out immediately."

Major Coffin called for his bugler, "Sound Assembly!" His men rose up and quickly went to their horses to saddle them. Then, moving over to the next company, "Captain Crawford, form your company, we move quickly!"

Andrew and James were sitting near the main mansion house, savoring the fresh bread and tea they were receiving from the British, two soldiers standing close by to keep an eye on them. As they ate their bread, they watched the dragoons and infantry follow Major Coffin out of the camp. Andrew shook his head, not feeling guilty about what had just happened.

***

When Jacob saw the deserters enter the camp, his gut told them they were compromised and they needed to get back to warn General Greene that the element of surprise was slipping away. Crawling back to their camp, he ordered everyone to pack up when Jean and Samuel arrived for the morning update.

"Go back and get your men; we must ride quickly and warn Greene about the deserters."

Samuel nodded, "Thought so. We couldn't see what happened at the gate well but suspected when we saw those regimental coats enter the camp."

Jean and Samuel quickly went back to gather their men. An advantage of operating when it was warm, most of the men only unrolled their blankets to lay on, making it easier to pack up. Jean and Samuel returned within five minutes and Jacob led them at a jog to the horses. One of the sentries called out for Frederick when Jacob came jogging in and the men headed for their horses.

"Pack up. We must warn Greene," Jacob commanded; Frederick quickly turned and called his men to pack up and mount. Within five minutes, they were hopping up into the saddle. When everyone was mounted, Jacob led them back toward the line of march, hoping they would make it in time.

After riding for about twenty minutes, they saw horsemen approaching that Jacob recognized as from Sumter's group and

Armstrong from Lee's Legion. Jacob held up his hand and his men halted while, led by Colonel Henderson, he rode up and stopped before him.

"What's wrong," Anderson asked, "you wouldn't be heading back unless something is amiss."

"We saw what could be deserters enter the British camp," Jacob explained, "if they speak to the British and we can bet they will, then General Greene needs to be warned that the British are preparing for him. There will be no surprise."

Anderson nodded, "Aye, now that would be news Greene would need to know." Then the sound of hooves coming from behind Jacob could be heard. Looking over his shoulder, Jacob could see Major Coffin's lead element coming toward them.

Knowing they had no time; Jacob spun his horse while bringing his rifle up. Then, seeing Major Coffin's troop approaching, Anderson pointed and yelled, "Here they come!"

Bringing his rifle up, bracing by squeezing his legs around the horse, Jacob aimed and fired at the approaching Loyalists. Jacob's men quickly reacted, spun and fired, including Samuel's blunderbuss that thundered. Jacob's ball tore into the chest of the leading horseman, then the shot from his men, followed by both Armstrong's and Anderson's, crashed into the head of the column.

As the horses screamed, their riders falling dead, wounded, or thrown from their horses, Jacob spun his horse around and galloped away toward the approaching army, with both Armstrong and Anderson following right behind. Jacob knew they had been lucky with that chance contact, but they had to get away to reload and delay them some more.

As they galloped down the road, they could see the riders of Lee's Legion in the distance, and Jacob rode up to Colonel Lee, who was leading. He raised his hand to halt his men.

"We just ran into a Loyalist force," Jacob explained as his band rode around to reform and reload. "They may be out to locate us; we need to stop them from detecting the whole army."

Lee nodded, "Armstrong, form a line here in the open; we'll deploy in the woods and spring the trap on them!" Lee led his force to the left side into the tree line and Jacob joined Anderson's men on the opposite side. Jacob pulled his horse up to a tree and finished loading his rifle. Armstrong's men had their muskets and pistols at the ready.

Jacob looked at their position and realized it was one of the best to ambush the approaching Loyalists. Armstrong had deployed in the open field on the curve's far side. The Loyalists would not see them until it was too late. Jacob's heart raced in anticipation, excited by the looming ambush.

"Lovely, such lovely ground for an ambush," Jacob mused. He quickly looked to his left and right; all his men were ready. The wolves were coiled up like springs,

The sound of the approaching Loyalists, moving at a slower rate, having already bounced into them, but still at a quick trot. Watching in anticipation, Jacob watched the Loyalists trot by, and when they reached the far side of the curve, they saw Armstrong's line.

"Aim!" Armstrong commanded and then quickly gave "Fire!"

The line of cavalry fired, four men toppled from their horses and then Lee shouted the command of "Charge!" Lee led his men out, Jacob and Anderson leading their men out and between the two elements, quickly surrounded the Loyalists. As the horses skidded to a halt, they all lowered their muskets and pistols, the dust blowing over the shocked Loyalist infantry. Finally, they raised their muskets overhead, surrendering. The Loyalist cavalry sprinted away while the infantry was captured.

As Lee's men disarmed their prisoners, Jacob scanned the area around them when motion caught his eye. Turning, he could see the foraging party rushing toward them, Jacob believing they must have heard the firing and were coming to the Loyalist's aid. Jacob pointed toward the woods and the foraging party.

"Enemy in the woods!" Jacob yelled, pointing. As the foraging party jogged out of the woods in the open, Jacob's men, whose rifles and muskets were ready, quickly fired. Then, as the muskets, rifle and Samuel's blunderbuss boomed, the foraging party halted in place.

"Dismount!" Jacob ordered and he quickly dismounted from his horse. Then, as they had practiced and had done numerous times, every fourth man grabbed the reins of their horses and pulled them toward the rear as Jacob formed a line of battle. He and his men quickly reloaded as Anderson and Lee organized their men into a battle line, while Armstrong secured the prisoners.

"Fire by sections!" Jacob commanded; his men fired one by one as their partners covered their reload before firing. The surprised foraging party, wearing only their small clothes and no regimental coats, did wear the proper tricorns and helmets of British regulars. Jacob also saw that more were carrying muskets this time instead of shovels.

A general firefight began between the British and Jacob's men while Lee's Legion infantry, Armstrong and Anderson's cavalry reformed for another charge. As balls whizzed past Jacob and his band, they kept up a steady fire against the foraging party. Then, watching the cavalry, when Jacob saw they were ready to charge, he gave an order to "load and hold."

When everyone was ready, and Jacob could see Armstrong and Anderson were watching him, Jacob gave the command, "Make Ready! Take Aim! Fire!" Jacob's line erupted in fire and smoke, punctuated by the roar of Samuel's blunderbuss. Through the smoke, Anderson and Armstrong's cavalry charged through and crashed into the British foraging party. It was a quick and brutal fight.

What few horsemen Major Coffin had, turned and galloped away. What surviving British infantry was left ran off into the woods while around sixty men were taken prisoner. Jacob led his men forward to secure the British prisoners and strip them of their muskets. "Take their cartridges!" Jacob commanded, "Top off your boxes."

Once everyone gathered what they could, Jacob led them back to where their horses were waiting. Richard was holding their horses that day. "Got them good, didn't we, papa?" he asked; Jacob smiled and nodded.

"Aye, lad, we did. But I fear this is only the opening shot of the fight."

Richard nodded and mounted on his horse, "I'll be ready."

Jacob smiled in the affirmative, then, seeing the band was mounted, led them toward the army's main body. The army was only about a mile away, having stopped when they heard the early action with the foraging party. Jacob led the band off to the side and had them dismount while he went to look for Marion and General Greene.

As Jacob moved through the line of men resting on either side of the road, rum casks had been broken out and the men were freely drinking rum. The men were drinking, talking, and sounding happy for the moment. This did not sit well with Jacob, who would ask Marion to see what was happening. To Jacob, this was something you did not do before a battle.

Arriving when General Greene and the other commanders were standing, including Marion, Jacob reported what they observed in the camp. Greene nodded at the news, then Jacob asked, "If I may, sir, but why are the men drinking rum before action."

Greene nodded, turned and faced Jacob with his hand clasped behind his back. "I know what you are thinking, major, and you are correct. Not what professionals would allow. These men are not that professional; perhaps the rum will release the animal spirit in them that we'll need very soon."

Jacob nodded and General Greene faced the assembled officers while Jacob went to stand next to Marion.

"Gentlemen," Greene began, "we have an opportunity to break the lion's back and push the British back to Charles Town. From the information confirmed by Major Clarke, the British have stopped moving; there are no defenses to breach. We can carry the day!"

Greene looked at the assembled officers, who were nodding and waiting for him to continue. "My plan of action is simple yet effective with three lines of battle. Generals Marion and Pickens's South Carolinian brigades will be our first line, supported by Malmedy's Dragoons and two three-pound cannons in the center. I want Marion on the right, Pickens on the left."

Greene looked to see if all understood their positions before continuing. "The second line, our main line, will have Sumner's, Campbell's and William's Continentals, supported by two six-pounders and Lee's Legion, along with Henderson's troops on the flanks."

Pausing once more, Greene made sure the officers understood their location in the line of battle. "Washington's Dragoons and Kirkwood's Delawares will be in reserve following the second line."

Greene centered himself on the assembled officers who waited for his last words. "Gentlemen, we will deal with two enemies out there, the British and the South Carolina heat. Either will kill or reduce your numbers. See to your men, and we will be victorious this day!"

After some final coordination, the officers were dismissed and told to have their men ready to march in fifteen minutes. Jacob walked with Marion as they headed over to where his brigade was lined up on the road. "I need you in the line Jacob," Marion stated and Jacob nodded.

"Yes sir, where do you need me?"

"You will anchor the right, hold the place of honor as the first company as we don't have our normal companies. The rest of the group will dress off of you when we go into the fight. Be our rock we can rely on."

Jacob looked down at Marion and smiled, "Have I ever failed you?" he asked jokingly, and Marion replied jokingly, "No, but there is always a first time."

Jacob headed to his band and told them they were marching into battle with Marion and the rest of the group. "What about the horses?" Patrick asked.

"We leave them tied up with the rest of the baggage once the general releases the army at the line of departure. We are on the far right. We are anchoring Marion's brigade. See to your gear; we move in a few minutes."

The men talked excitedly with each other as they checked their rifles, muskets and shooting bags. They will finally all get a chance to fight as a brigade instead of splitting into groups of holding horses and going on raids.

Jacob looked over at his boys and thought they were marching into an actual battle for the first time, in a line instead of a small group conducting hit-and-run actions. Taking a deep breath and letting it out, Jacob knew there was not much he could do about it except prepare for the worse and hope for the best.

Looking down, he checked his rifle lock mechanism, hammer and frizzen. The sweat was rolling down his arms from under his shirt and dripping from his nose. After everyone had checked their equipment, he had them sit in the shade as they waited for the order to form.

Samuel, Jean and Frederick came over to join Jacob, sitting in the shade behind a large oak tree, his eyes closed.

"Ah, the old beloved hurry up and wait," Samuel commented as he flopped down on the ground, cradling his blunderbuss.

"Should it be any different, no?" Jean returned and Samuel chuckled.

"Aye," he replied, "I would be concerned if it was not so."

Jacob watched the men begin to move into position and slowly shook his head. A good portion of the army would be called slovenly looking; most of their clothes were in sad shape. A good number of the men had no clothing, maybe only a shirt or a loincloth. Moss was used to cushioning their cartridge box straps from rubbing their shoulders raw.

"We are taking a half-starved, half-naked army to face the British. This is madness, but what else can we do?" Jacob thought as he watched the battle lines form. The wolves were sitting in the shade, panting from the heat. Their eyes glowed, knowing they were going into action. Their ears were perked up, front paws crossed before them, watching and listening to the movement as the men marched into their positions.

***

The survivors from the foraging party were running into the camp, yelling about running into the entire rebel army just down the road. An orderly gathered Colonel Stewart, alerting him to what the foragers were saying about the rebels.

Quickly, he moved down to the camp, ordering the duty drummer to sound assembly. The long roll began and the rest of the drummers beat out the long roll from their camps.

The soldiers dropped what they were doing and quickly pulled on their redcoats, setting their haversacks, canteens, bayonets and cartridge boxes across their shoulders. Taking up their muskets and fast falling into line.

Stewart looked to the opposite side of his camp, the likely approach the rebel army would come. *"I'll send a company of skirmishers forward, locate this rebel army,"* Stewart thought as he looked at the soon-to-be battlefield. *"I have the woods to the left; the river protects my right. Such a lovely piece of ground."*

Turning, Stewart looked at the plantation house and the open fields behind it. Rubbing his chin, he looked back in the direction the rebels were coming and then back to the house. *"Must occupy the house if we have to withdraw if this rebel army is as large as they make it out to be. Can cover our retreat. Still, don't like those open fields but sometimes you can't choose all of your ground."*

Nodding, having made a decision, Stewart called for Captain Strong. When the captain arrived, Stewart ordered, "Take your company forward and scout along the Congaree Road until you make contact with this rebel army. Confirm its size, then return. We will be forming our line of battle here."

Understanding his orders, Captain Strong turned and jogged back to his company. Within minutes, a company from the 64th was trotting out of the camp. Heading down the road toward the woods. After watching them depart, Stewart called for his commanders. As he waited for the arrival, Stewart began formulating a battle plan.

When the officers arrived, Stewart began. "Gentlemen, it seems the rebels are upon us. Our morning foraging party ran into a large size of rebel infantry and cavalry only a few miles down the road from us. They state they are heading this way and probably mean to meet us in battle. Therefore, we shall give them battle here and now."

He stopped and made sure all were paying attention and he nodded to the assembled men.

"Captain Kelly, you will take the 64th and anchor or left in the woods forward of the fence line. Captain Saint Ledger, your 63rd will fall next to the 64th, and Colonel Cruger, your brigade will be in the center. Then, Captain Charles, place two six-pounders on the road to give our rebel friends a warm reception."

The officers chuckled at the comment, along with Stewart, who continued with his deployment plan. "Major Marjoribanks, you will deploy the 3rd to the right of the volunteers, followed by your combined lights and grenadiers. Keep the 84th as the reserve on the right. Major Coffin, you will be our reserve on the left. Deploy one hundred yards to the front of the camp, watch your dispersal in the woods and make sure you maintain contact across the line."

Stewart turned and looked at his officers, who were visualizing their positions in the woods before them. It was a decent defendable position; Steward felt confident he could hold against these rebels, but he was concerned as his last major fight at the Shubrick's plantation had been close.

"See to your commands, deploy!" Stewart commanded and the officers smartly saluted before returning to their commands. He remained there, looking down the Congaree Road toward the approaching enemy army. Soon the sound of tin cups and canteens banging of equipment was heard as the companies began jogging by to take their positions in the woods.

The sound of rumbling wheels and chains came from behind, along with a polite "Excuse me, sir."

Stewart turned to see the approaching six-pound cannons being pushed into positions by their crews and mattroses. It was one of the mattroses who was bowing to him that had asked him to move.

"My apology," Stewart said as he stepped out of the way to allow the gun to be moved forward. He watched as both guns were placed in positions to the front and center of his developing defensive line. The infantry was deploying in open order to have spaces between the trees while maintaining their two lines in depth.

Nodding, Stewart was pleased with how his men were deploying; now, he had to wait for the rebels to arrive.

"All I can do is wait and see," Stewart thought, *"Just have to wait and see."*

***

The order was passed along the line to stand up, form ranks and prepare to march. Jacob, positioned on the far right of the line, with Samuel behind him, looked down their rank of men and ensured all was ready.

Jacob stepped out and walked down the line, looking into the eyes and faces of his men. They looked back expectantly, almost with smiles, confident in Jacob and the battle to come. Even his son's faces, hardened from their time riding with the band, were eager.

Jacob walked up to Jean, who held the last position in their ranks and they shook hands.

"As they say, once more, dear friends, no?" Jean asked with a grin. With a nod, Jacob replied, "once more into the breach, we go." Jacob returned to his position, looking at his boys once more.

"Sons, soldiers." Jacob thought, *"No longer boys. They had been forced to grow up and they have. I hope I can get them through this day alive and well."*

"Open order!" was shouted down the line and starting with Jacob's men, the rank opened up between them, so they were spaced out about two arms lengths.

"Fix bayonets!" was ordered from their rear, mainly for the Continentals under General Greene's command. Jacob's men did not have bayonets.

Prime and load!" Command was passed along the line and the men began loading their muskets and rifles. While not parade ground perfect for their situation, Jacob was satisfied as he finished loading his rifle.

Marion approached and the men did a light cheer for him. He waved them to be quiet but did have a smile on his face in thanks.

Standing close to Jacob, "I am relying on you to be my anchor, to help hold this line together if need be."

Then Marion paused, looked down at the ground, then back at Jacob with a serious look. "If I fall, you are to take command, understood?"

As Jacob was about to argue, Marion shook his head. "Don't argue with me on this if something happened to me; you are our best hope of leading these men. I pray it does not happen, but I want to be sure. I'll have your hand on this, your oath."

Marion held out his hand, that unwavering gaze holding Jacob. Reluctantly, knowing Marion was right, Jacob shook his hand. "You have my oath, sir," Jacob answered, "Just stay healthy for the time being, sir."

Scoffing, Marion smiled and turned to head back to the center. "One never knows," he replied as he walked off.

"You know he is right," Samuel commented as he watched Marion limp off.

"Yes, I know," Jacob responded, "It doesn't mean I have to like it."

Soon, the command to "Advance to the front!" was given and the men lowered their muskets and rifles to the ready position and advanced. Marion's line began to move in front of the main army as skirmishers when they bumped into the British again.

The men advanced cautiously, scanning and listening for anything that showed the British were close by. So far, the only sound was the tall grass and bushes brushing against the men's legs as they advanced. A slight breeze and a woodpecker were knocking rapidly in the distance.

The air smelled warm, the sun trickling through the trees, providing a decent amount of shade as the line moved like a wave before the army. Jacob was impressed by how quickly the men returned to proper linear tactics, keeping their alignment with one another and not getting too far ahead or stretched out.

"Not bad for being out of practice for a while," Jacob thought as he watched the men move professionally. They were all scanning, watching the woods and trees and their scouting wolves running before them and to the flanks.

It was a short time later that Jacob began to have an uneasy feeling that something was not right. The only sound he heard was the breeze, no insects, no birds. Even the woodpecker went quiet. Jacob raised his hand in warning and all the men looked down to see the signal.

They brought their muskets and rifles up in a more "On guard" position, quickly cocking the hammer back to fire. What alarmed Jacob, he did not see the wolves. As they continued to advance, the men instinctively crouched lower and began to zigzag to be near trees to get behind.

Then, all four wolves lay in the grass before them, ears up and a low growl coming from their throats. Jacob quickly moved up to the waiting wolves and saw what had their attention.

Redcoats were advancing toward them, in open order as well. They were roughly fifty yards away and Jacob's men had them by the flank. They had not seen them yet, but they would soon know the line was before them.

Jacob turned and was able to get the attention of Samuel and his men. He pointed his finger like a gun to their left front and they saw the advancing British line. Jacob quickly motioned his hands to the left and the right for the men to find cover behind trees. Nodding, his men rapidly fanned out and took up firing positions behind trees.

Patting the wolves, Jacob brought his rifle up to his shoulder and aimed at an officer. But, as fate would have it, the British were walking into an "L" shape firing line. "*I hope those others see them soon,*" Jacob thought.

His question was quickly answered when the British line halted, as they must have seen the rest of Marion's men. Then, for the quickest moments, both sides just stared at one another before Marion gave the order to "Fire!"

As Marion's center fired, Jacob had his section fire, catching the British in the middle of the "L." Being hit from two sides caused confusion in the British line.

The Battle of Eutaw Springs had begun.

The line erupted into flame and smoke, the balls crashing into both trees and soldiers in the British line. While at close range, with the British advancing in open order, it was not as effective as a volley in ranks.

As Marion's men began to reload, it was the British who, in turn, made ready to fire. Seeing the British bring their muskets up to the present, Jacob yelled, "Cover!" His men dove behind trees or flattened themselves on the ground, though he could see none of the British was engaging him. However, Jacob did see some of the other companies do the same. Jacob's men automatically loaded.

"Give, Fire!"

The British line returned a volley that flew in and amongst Marion's men. Jacob did see a few fall but most of the balls missed as they were in open order. The British began to reload; Jacob had his men resumed their firing positions.

"Independent fire, fire at will!" Jacob commanded. Now the men fired in pairs, keeping a steady flow of shots going into the flank of the British line. Finally, Jacob raised his rifle, aimed at another officer across from him, and pulled the trigger. The officer fell straight down, which now drew the attention of the rest of the British line.

Seeing Jacob had them by the flank, the British commander bent his line back so a portion of it faced Jacob to stop being raked by his effective fire. Jacob's men remained behind cover and kept up their fire. Jacob could see the British were wavering, and soon they began to withdraw. It started orderly, but as soon as Marion kept pouring fire into them, they broke and began to run back toward their line.

"Get after them, boys!" Marion yelled and the entire line surged forward at the trot to keep pressure on the British. Jacob made sure he tied back into Marion's line and, as they came up on the backs of the British, or what few turned to face them, poured fire into them. Again, resistance was minimal, the British focusing on getting away.

Jacob nodded, caught up in the moment as they drove the British through the woods, now and then the snap and whiz of a musket ball flying by. Then as they came over a slight rise in the woods, a long line of British stood facing them in open order and the surviving skirmishers ran through them.

Marion commanded them to halt, and the line reformed, facing the British across from them in the trees. Their muskets were at the ready as Marion gave the order, "Prepare for a brigade volley; make ready!"

Up and down the line, muskets and rifles came up to the ready positions. Hundreds of clicks as the hammers were cocked back. The men stared down the British across from them, standing still as they watched the British muskets drop to point at them. Jacob and the rest of the brigade braced for the incoming fire.

"Give, fire!"

The British line exploded with fire and smoke as the volley crashed and balls flew toward their line. While Jacob cringed for a second, he realized that most British balls went high, flying mainly between the men and hitting the trees above them. Bark, branches and leaves fell on top of the men as the British balls tore into the trees. Now, it was their turn.

"Aim!" Marion raised his sword, looked left and then looked right to ensure the brigade was ready. Then with a downward sweep of his sword, "Fire!"

The entire brigade fired a near-simultaneous volley; the grey smoke and orange flames pointed toward the British line. The difference was noticeable as a good number of British soldiers spun and fell, either dead or wounded, from the effective volley.

"Prime and load!"

Jacob watched his men automatically go through the loading procedures, all of their eyes staring at the British line. With no fear in these eyes, Jacob noticed strong determination. Looking behind their line were the four wolves, laying low to the ground, but they also had an expectant look, ready to charge. Looking across the space, the British were ramming their cartridges down, and Jacob knew this would be a stand-up fight.

***

Colonel Stewart was pacing, his hands behind his back as he looked toward the woods. They had heard something that sounded like musket fire in the distance; he assumed that his skirmishers had made contact with the approaching rebel army. Then there was some silence, and no one had exited the woods. His line was stretched across inside the woods, yet no action.

Turning to look to his right, he saw it was well anchored, almost impenetrable and unassailable by the rebels. A steep and thickly grown riverbank stretched down to Eutaw Creek. Then a short distance from the bank was scrub blackjack oaks. Cavalry could not get through it to turn his flanks.

Positioned behind it was three hundred light infantry under the command of Major Majoribanks that would assail any rebel infantry who would be foolish enough to attempt to take the flank. But, if fate was fickle, not too far away, hidden in the hedges was Major Coffin's surviving cavalry and infantry being held in reserve.

"Sir, men are coming from the woods," an orderly shouted. Colonel Stewart turned and looked to see where the lieutenant was pointing. In small numbers, British light infantry, more and likely from the skirmishers he had sent out, were heading toward the camp. Then, just as he started asking the question, a loud crash of musketry came from his left.

"It seems our guests have arrived," Stewart told an orderly standing near him. "Have the artillery prepare to fire on the rebels when they come down the road if you please."

The orderly nodded, then moved down to where the Royal Artillery gunners were staring toward the musketry. There were the two loud crashes of musketry, a full battalion or better volleys, and then there was a familiar sound of a roar, then a pause, then another roar of an orderly procession of volleys.

Smoke from the musketry began to filter out of the woods, the battle having been joined. As the skirmishers filtered through the fence line, they began to reform their ranks and Stewart noticed there was far less assembling than what was sent out. He turned to watch the fight before him. Either the rebels will break or his line. Only time will tell.

***

Jacob watched as his men kept up a steady rate of fire, as the command to fire by companies had been given. First, they would fire and then as they loaded, Richardson's men, next to Jacob, took up the next round of volleys. After Richardson's men fired, the next in line, Benton, would prepare to fire.

Seeing motion behind them, Jacob took a step out to look and saw the blue coats of the Continentals marching up. General Greene had arrived and was pushing his first line into action. Marion had his men move more to their right, overlapping the British line to allow the Continentals to take a position next to them.

As soon as the Continentals took their place, they opened with a battalion volley, followed by company volleys. They would fire a few more times and, equipped with bayonets, decided to charge forward against the British across from them. Seeing the Continentals preparing to charge with their bayonets, Marion had his men cover and support.

"Pick your targets," Jacob ordered. "Aim for the officers and sergeants!" His band, armed with rifles, took good aim, looking for shiny gorgets, gold, silver or red epaulets. Jacob looked over his rifle, having spotted a British captain and took aim. Then, taking a deep breath, let it out slowly and pulled his trigger. The officer fell to the ground.

"Nothing personal," Jacob said to the dead man across the woods, "just business." Jacob's riflemen were having a telling effect on removing the regiment's leadership across from them. While corporals and lieutenants were taking charge, they were being carved into a smaller formation.

The Continentals charged forward and smashed into their opposing side. Jacob and his men continued their slow, methodic fire into the other regiment so they would not become involved in the bayonet fight.

"Boom…boom…boom!"

With the sound of artillery, British cannons had become involved, and as Jacob suspected, the Continentals began to fall back as they had been hit in the flank by artillery shots. *"Must have been grapeshot,"* Jacob thought, *"That would have broken up the attack. Must be three-pounders."*

A runner came down to Jacob, "Sir, orders from General Marion, you are to move to the left, as General Greene is going to try and take this flank with his Continentals."

Understanding his order, Jacob turned to his men. "Load and come to shoulder; prepare to move!"

Once everyone was ready, Jacob moved down the line to where Jean stood and gave the command, "Double files left!" Both ranks turned and faced to the left; with a curt nod, Jacob gave the order, "March!" and led them around Richardson's line, who was doing the same. Richardson was standing at the left of his line and as Jacob's men passed, fell in beside them. The wolves kept pace with Jacob and the band.

As Marion's men peeled away, Greene brought more of his Continental brigade up to take their position. Two 3-pound cannons were being pulled into place to support the Continentals as they engaged the British. Jacob could see Marion waiting for them and brought his men to where Marion pointed. They were now on the far left of their line, and when Jacob arrived where Marion wanted him, he commanded, "Halt!"

His men faced back to the right and Jacob made his way back down to his position. As he passed his men, he checked on them and asked how they were doing.

"We're ready to go, Jacob," Frederick shouted, "Let's take the fight to them!"

The men chorused their approval, wanting to get at the British. "Don't worry, lads; soon enough, we'll bring them to grips. Be patient, lads, be patient!" The wolves looked up in excitement, yearning for action. The men liked having the wolves along; they were good luck charms.

Jacob returned to his position in the line, watching as the rest of Marion's brigade marched past and snaked into their position in the line. Once the brigade was reformed, Marion walked along the line, speaking to the officers. When he arrived at where Jacob stood, he found Jacob leaning on his rifle, watching.

Jacob turned and nodded to Marion, who stated, "Your men look agitated, ready for action." Marion looked over and scratched Waya's ears. "You four look ready too."

"Aye, sir," Samuel responded, caressing his blunderbuss, "we're ready to get up, close and personal with our British friends."

Marion chuckled and shook his head.

"Orders, sir?" Jacob asked. Marion looked along the line. "As before, though now you are my anchor for the left. Greene and his Continentals are on the far right, Sumter and the others in the center. If they try to flank us, it will be here. Stay vigilant."

Jacob nodded, "We'll hold, sir, don't worry."

Marion smiled, "Aye, that is true. I do not have to worry about you. It's these others I have to worry about." Marion headed to talk with Sumter and Pickens in the center of the line. Jacob turned back to his men.

"Check your pieces, wipe down your pans, frizzens and check your flints. Then, sergeants check for cartridges and evenly distribute them."

They could hear the musketry pick up from their right as the Continentals opened fire on the British. Jacob walked back along his line, then back to Samuel. "How are we set for cartridges?

"About half a box, or a little less," Samuel replied, "we redistributed the best we could."

Jacob nodded, "Be ready to take from wounded and dead."

The fire was intensifying from the right but was growing louder toward them. The four wolves turned; their ears perked to the left. Then a call came down the line, "The British are advancing; it's an all-out attack!"

Jacob looked out; sure enough, a line of redcoats was advancing through the trees toward them. "Well, this is different," Jacob commented as he retook his position in the line. "Make ready!"

You could hear the shuffle of the feet and the clank of canteens and cups on the British gear as they marched with their muskets shouldered. Jacob was waiting for them to stop or get closer to have their fire becoming more effective. The British were continuing to advance, and Jacob shrugged. "If that's the way they want it."

"Take aim!"

In unison, the muskets and rifles came down, the men braced and looking over their barrels. The muskets and rifles were steady, the men all breathing on the controlled breaths of veterans. Then, when the British advanced to within forty yards, Jacob commanded, "fire!"

With a roar, the balls swept into the British line, several of the soldiers tumbling to the ground.

"Prime and Load!"

As his men loaded, Jacob watched the British line prepare to fire. He observed that the uniform had more of a buff or beige facing to it, not recalling the unit designation. Their muskets came down, but he saw they were aiming more up than at them. Jacob shook his head but braced for the volley.

The British line fired its volley, but Jacob noticed the balls, for the most part, were still flying a good four to five feet above them. Moreover, while the trees were taking a beating, none of his men, especially his boys. He also saw the wind had slightly shifted and the smoke from their muskets was blowing into their eyes.

When his men were ready, Jacob fired another volley. He could see several men fall, and their smoke blew into the faces of the British. *"Their smoke and ours blind them; they can't see."* So Jacob thought, and then he smiled. While strange, it seemed they were in the safest place on the battlefield.

The two lines blasted away at one another, the British line and Marion's men. However, like two great warships firing broadsides after broadsides, there were more British causalities than Marion's men. Jacob nodded in satisfaction when his men began to yell, "Down to one cartridge." They were running out of ammunition.

Jacob had his line fire their last volley, then stood their ground. Jacob went to tell Marion, but it seemed they were all in the same situation. All were out of ammunition and not enough men had bayonets to charge. Therefore, they had no choice but to withdraw to fill their cartridge boxes.

A messenger was sent to General Greene about their situation, and the messenger returned with instructions for pulling out to fill up their cartridge boxes. Marion had the brigade immediately pull out of line and a brigade of North Carolina Continentals quickly replaced them. The smoke from the firing helped to cover their withdrawal.

***

Colonel Stewart was highly agitated, watching and listening to the battle unfolding before him. After the initial contact with the rebels, Stewart and his staff moved forward and entered the woods where his line was supposed to be. Instead, he found that the entire line had gone forward in attack and was not defending.

"What in the bloody hell is going on?" Stewart roared as he saw that his orders were not being followed. "Who bloody ordered this attack?"

The closest officer Stewart could find was Lieutenant Colonel Cruger of Delancy's Provincial Battalion.

"What is happening here?" Stewart demanded and Cruger could only shrug his shoulders.

"Good question, sir," Cruger replied, pointing down to their left. "It started down there, then the whole line just went forward and are now fighting toe-to-toe with those damned rebels. They are giving us a hell of a fight."

Stewart scoffed and moved forward to the line of battle, with the two 6-pound cannons of the Royal Artillery in the center. When Stewart arrived at the guns, he saw the gunners were only firing one gun, the other crew watching.

"What is the matter with this gun?" Stewart asked, "Why are you not firing?"

"Sir, the trunnion cracked. We cannot fire," the gunner explained and Stewart nodded. He moved over to where the 63rd and 64th regiments were pouring fire into the rebels. Through the thick grey, sulfurous smoke, Stewart saw blue-coated so-called Continentals. He saw more of his men lying on the ground or limping from the woods than the rebels.

Stewart stayed behind the line of the left, watching the battle. Then it seemed that favor finally looked fondly upon him, and the rebels appeared to be breaking. Having been caught up in the action, Stewart drew his sword. He rushed to the front of both regiments and commanded, "Charge!"

With their bayonets lowered, the 63rd and 64th Regiments surged forward and forced the Continentals, who had been firing so efficiently and stubbornly, to fold up and began to fall back at a run. Then, caught up in the yelling along with his men and sword raised, Stewart charged forward through the grey smoke and into fresh sunlight.

Eyes opening wide, Stewart saw the following line of rebels advancing toward him, their muskets and bayonets lowered. They stopped just as Stewart gave the command to "Halt!" As he turned, the Continentals brought their muskets up and, as the rest of the two British regiments broke out of the smoke, added to it by firing a vicious volley.

Stewart could hear the balls whistling around him and the slap of wet flesh as they struck soldiers. Then, finally, the British advance came to a halt and the Continentals continued to fire volley after volley into the now-disorganized British regiments. Then the regiments began to dissolve and started back toward their original lines.

The Continentals closely pursued, not wanting the British to reform. Soon across the entire line, the British regiments were in retreat as the rebel forces charged forward. Finally, the wave of blue swarmed over the two British 6-pounders, capturing them. However, they kept coming, and Stewart continued racing ahead to the stone plantation house.

The soldiers inside the brick house took up positions with their muskets, aiming out of the windows, intending to use it as a fort. Instead, Stewart began to rally his men and slow the flood of retreating British troops. He began to quickly organize a defensive line, hoping to stem the rebels' advance, though now he was in the open.

Using a handkerchief, holding his sword under his armpit, Stewart wiped the sweat from his face as he looked out across his camp. His camp was the only obstacle between the advancing rebels and what was left of his force. He had to hold to either drive the rebels away or make them pay.

Nodding after he put his handkerchief away, *I'll make them bleed for every foot of ground.*

***

Jacob and his men were loading cartridges into their boxes and bags. The order for the all-out advance came down the line. Looking up from where he was packing his shooting bag, Jacob saw the entire line of Greene's Army advance out of the woods. Watching his men, he stood up and followed the advancing line toward the British once everyone was reloaded.

Jacob's men, having reloaded, were following him, their weapons being carried at trail arms. Once they exited the woods, they trotted across the open field and could see the line of Continentals breaking up and moving around the British camp, all except the militia.

For the most part, the militia, who had been in the center, charged into the British camp. Then seeing all the clothing and supplies, stopped and began to loot. Jacob looked with disdain at the situation, the Continentals were advancing, but a gap was growing in the center as the militia broke off to loot.

"What in the bloody Hell is this?" Jacob growled, looking at the militia completely losing control and started to go after all the clothing and supplies. While he understood, seeing several naked men happily start picking through shirts and trousers, there was still a fight, which was still in the balance.

Shaking his head, Jacob motioned his men forward. "With me, lads, there will be time to look for trinkets after the fight!"

Jacob's band continued their trot forward, moving into the space vacated by the looting militia. His was a small group where the entire brigade had been before. Still shaking his head, Jacob tied his men with some Continentals from Virginia and Lee's Legion.

Looking off in the distance, Jacob saw a threat of Loyalist cavalry coming up to the flank of the British line. Moving quickly, Jacob took his men and formed an "L" with Lee's Infantry to protect the flank if the Loyalist cavalry attempted to turn their flank.

"Prime and load!" Jacob commanded, and the men went through the loading procedures, keeping their eyes on the Loyalist cavalry. Jacob scanned the field and could see the brick house in the distance. Massive fighting was happening around it; British soldiers were up in the windows, while Continentals and British soldiers were fighting hand-to-hand before it. Leaning his rifle on his shoulder, Jacob pulled out his telescope and focused on the fighting around the house.

"What do you see?" Samuel asked, leaning forward.

"Strange things, my friends, very strange. The British must have secured the house door and are not letting their own in. British soldiers were pounding on the door but not being let in."

Jacob lowered his telescope, "Very close fighting around the house." They all stared at the fighting, very heavy on their left, as it appeared General Greene was throwing their entire left side of the army at the house

Muskets cracked, cannons boomed and the cries of the men in action echoed across the field. Men were falling on both sides. They were piling up around the base of the house and in the space to the camp.

"Horses on the move!" Richard yelled out, pointing across the field at the Loyalist cavalry. They had drawn their swords, resting against their right shoulders as the horses began to trot out.

Jacob retook his position and then turned to Samuel. "I believe it is time for your blunderbuss."

Samuel took a step out, an evil grin on his face as he took a knee and cocked back the hammer of his weapon.

Turning back to his men, Jacob gave the command, "Take care to defend against cavalry; make ready!" The wolves sank to the ground, watching.

Looking to their left, the Legion Infantry was doing the same, *"Would be nice to have the Legion's cavalry; I wonder where they are?"* Jacob thought. Quickly shaking his head, he focused on the approaching cavalry. Timing would be everything. Fire too early they will crash into them when unloaded. Fire too late and they won't have enough time to fire as the horses would close the distance rapidly.

The horses began to spread out and form into a line to charge. Then the trot started to get faster, the riders rising up and down rapidly with the gait of the house. Jacob watched intently, *"Wait until they commit."*

The horsemen turned and were down-angled at the point of the "V" between the Legion's infantry and Jacob's men. The horses were about a hundred yards away and Jacob watched as their commander turned his head to give the order. *"Now."*

"Take aim!"

All their muskets and rifles came down in a snap, the men stepping back slightly with their right feet and subconsciously digging their heels in. They looked over their barrels at the approaching riders. The wolves tensed in anticipation, low on the ground.

From the horses, Jacob could faintly hear their command of "Charge!"

Waiting just for that right moment, he gave the command of "Fire!"

The muskets and rifles went off in a large sheet of flame, fingers of death reaching toward the approaching dragoons. From their flank, Samuel's blunderbuss roared like a small cannon. The men came to the ready position, muskets and rifles coming up to the ready position. From what Jacob could estimate, the volley went off when the dragoons were only twenty yards away.

The results were high pitch screaming of the horses falling and kicking, having been torn through by the balls. The riders tumbled from their saddles, either shot dead, wounded, or thrown from their falling horses. Then, between Jacob's men and the Legion's, what dragoons survived turned and rode away.

Seeing the wounded were on their hands and knees, Jacob ordered, "Go get them, boys!" They rushed forward, taking the weapons off the fallen dragoons. The wolves pounded ahead and surrounded the wounded, who held their hands up as the wolves growled. Jacob's men helped the wounded who could walk to their feet and Jacob nodded for them to be taken to the rear.

"Richard, Patrick, make sure those prisoners get turned into the provost," Jacob instructed.

The boys nodded; their rifles lowered at the backs of the prisoners. Jacob motioned to the wolves with the thumb over his shoulder and the four trotted off with the boys, trotting around the prisoners, growling. The small group moved around the camp and back toward their rear lines.

Major Rudolf, the commander of Lee's Infantry, came over to Jacob, "That was bloody well timed, I do say." Jacob nodded in response.

"Seeing those horsemen are no longer a threat, how about we get into this fight? What do you say?" Rudolf asked.

"Sounds like a good idea," Jacob responded, and Major Rudolf smiled. He trotted over to his infantry, who had finished loading their muskets. Jacob turned to his men, who were waiting expectantly, even the wolves following behind.

Jacob followed the Legion forward as they angled toward the fighting but not getting too far in front of the right side of the Continental line. The action was still heavily involving their left side. They were not making a dent in the British position in the brick house.

It was turning into a slaughterhouse; anyone who would break from any cover would be shot down by the British. Greene even rolled up the two captured 6-pounder cannons to blast holes into the house. While Jacob applauded their bravery, they were well within point-blank range. As a result, the artilleryman was shot down and the cannons became useless.

"We're pulling out!" was shouted down the line. As Jacob's men were on the furthest of the right flank, they could see that the British had charged the left side's flank and were pushing the Continentals back. Soon the Continentals had fallen back far enough that the two 6-pounders were sitting alone.

The British came out and began to push and drag the cannons back into the fenced area near the house. Shaking his head, Jacob had his men cover while moving backward. As they moved closer to the camp, Jacob and Rudolf supported one another, bounding back to the woods. The British did not pursue them.

General Greene was at the edge of the woods, directing the men and reforming his line. Men were moving back into small groups or companies, except for the militia, piled high with looted items. Several shirts and trousers in their arms, a stack of hats, looking more like gypsies than soldiers.

Once in the woods, many men just dropped their equipment and regimental coats. Instead, they made for the ponds to cool off from the heat and quench their thirst. Jacob, having found

Richard and Patrick and the prisoner detail, moved the band to a shady area where they all slumped to the ground.

As they usually do, the boys gathered up their canteens and headed to the pond to get water. Leaning against a tree, Jacob closed his eyes briefly and realized how tired he felt.

"We almost had them, didn't we?" Jacob heard, opening his eyes and seeing it was Marion sitting next to him. Oscar was off to the side, holding onto Marion's horse. Seeing the sweat on Marion's face, Jacob handed him his handkerchief.

"Yes sir, we had them," Jacob replied, "until the militia found the camp. That is where we lost them and the momentum. Couldn't get them started, and the British forted up."

Handing his handkerchief back, Marion nodded. "Very much so; while I understand the wants of the men, we could have finished this fight here and now. But, instead, this bloody war will keep going on."

Jacob nodded, "Just like back at Shubrick's place; we could have finished it then had Sumter waited for the artillery to arrive."

Jacob stared at the ground as Marion closed his eyes. *"Sumter. It was Sumter at Shubrick, and his men were part of the mob of looters that could have finished this fight. What had happened to him to change him so?"* Jacob thought.

"Master Marion, sir?" Oscar asked; Marion had fallen asleep. He opened his eyes, looked around really quick and nodded.

"Yes, Oscar, let's get the brigade reformed. I can sleep later." Marion stood up with a groan and then looked at Jacob. "Take care of your men and yourself, Jacob."

Jacob nodded in reply, "Yes, I will do my best. You as well, sir, take care of yourself."

CHAPTER 14

RETURN OF BLOODY BILL

Colonel Stewart surveyed his shattered command around the brick house. Surprised by the vicious fighting by these rebels, the number of survivors and casualties coming in told a brutal story.

He lost about half of his force in nearly three hours of fighting. When he heard the return of the numbers from the 64th Regiment of Foot, twelve were dead, two officers and fifty men wounded, and another two officers and fifty-four men missing. Slowly shaking his head, Stewart knew he was no longer combat effective. He would have to retreat to Monk's Corner if not to Charles Town.

Stewart called the remaining officers to him and ordered the withdrawal. "Sir, what of the dead and wounded? Should we not see to them?" an officer asked.

Stewart, thinking for a moment, shook his head. "Dire times require dire needs. Leave some surgeon's mates with the wounded under a flag of truce; the rebels can see to their needs better than we can. Leave the dead as they lay."

"Sir?" a captain asked and Stewart gave him a hard stare. "I said leave them. In addition, burn all stores and muskets we cannot carry. I don't want them to fall into rebel hands."

The officers nodded and went about getting their commands ready to march. A rear guard of light infantry set fire to the supplies in the quartermaster area.

Stewart looked over to where about seventy wounded men were being cared for, a white sheet used as a flag of truce tied to a pole. Then, shaking his head, Stewart headed to his horse and began to lead his column away from Eutaw Springs.

While it started as an orderly withdrawal, muskets that had been loaded had been thrown into the fire or set on fire began to go off. Then, thinking the rebels were attacking again, a general panic took over the withdrawal that turned into a rout.

The waggoners cut their horses from the wagons and rode off. The distaff and camp followers ran screaming through the ranks, completely disorganizing the column. Only when the sound of the muskets stopped was order restored. Stewart only shook his head, embarrassed at how this victory, in his mind, was turning out.

***

In the morning, Greene swept the abandoned British camp. The regimental surgeons went to assist the British wounded and the men were able to find over a thousand muskets that they could use again. But fortunately, not all the supplies had been burned, so Greene had the quartermaster take stock.

Jacob and his band helped to sweep the battlefield and what was remaining of the British camp that the other militia groups had not looted. His boys and Samuel's mostly weathered the fight well, with minor scrapes from splinters. They had been lucky that the British were firing high. As they searched, the wolves moved along the dead, noses to the ground.

Some of Marion's other units had not fared so well; a good number had lost about half of their men and even more, were wounded. When a messenger arrived, Jacob and his men helped move the wounded British soldiers who had been left behind.

"Sir, General Greene is asking you and your band to report to his headquarters."

Jacob nodded to the messenger, who turned and rode off. Then, he turned and gathered his men and they headed over to their camp and horses.

"What do you think he wants?" Jean asked as he and Samuel joined Jacob as they walked across the field.

"If I was a betting man, I say we are going to chase the British, keep an eye on them for the Generals so they can plan the next move," Samuel replied. He looked up to see both Jacob and Jean were looking at him.

"What?" he asked.

Jacob smiled and shook his head. "Well, look who has a head for tactics."

"Ah yes," Jean replied, "Seems learning has occurred, no?"

"Harrumph," commented Samuel, "my friends!"

Jacob's band broke camp mounted their horses, then rode down the road the way the army had marched. Greene was at Burdall's Plantation, where the army was reforming to continue the attack.

Leading his men in a column of twos, Jacob located where Marion was camped and found a space amongst trees for shade. Dismounting, Jacob wiped the sweat from his face, dealing with the end of Augusts hot temperatures. *"When will this summer end?"* Jacob thought as he tied his horse to a branch. Finally, the wolves settled down under some shady bushes.

It was not long until a runner arrived for Jacob, "Well, time to see what the generals want," Jacob stated to Jean and Samuel, then headed off to Marion's camp. As Jacob approached, he saw

Lieutenant Colonel Lee coming as well. He raised his hand in greetings.

"Glad to see you survived this little skirmish," Lee stated with a grin, and Jacob returned the grin.

"Aye, luckily, the British proved to be poor marksmen, so here we are."

Due to the heat, Marion worked under a fly instead of a tent. He preferred the shade and openness for the slight breeze. Marion, with a few officers and Oscar, looked at a map when Jacob and Colonel Lee arrived.

Looking up, Marion nodded. "Right, let's get down to business; time is of the essence. General Greene does not want the British to march away unmolested. So we must keep a sword or bayonet at his back until they stop to face us or retreat to Charles Town."

Marion looked at Jacob. "Due to our losses at this recent fight, you have the largest detachment of mounted infantry."

He then turned to Colonel Lee, "General Greene has attached you to our command for this."

Marion then looked at both men, "You are to leave immediately and pursue the British. If possible, pin them down and prevent them from reaching Fairlawn. See to your men; we ride within the hour."

Understanding their orders, Jacob and Colonel Lee gathered their men and prepared to ride with Marion after the British. When he arrived at their site, Jean and Samuel were waiting. Jacob pointed to Samuel, "We are going after the British. Have the men see to their horses; we ride immediately."

The band scrambled to their horses, checking their equipment, girths and weapons. Once complete, everyone mounted up, and when Jacob saw all were ready, he led them in a column of twos and went to where Marion was waiting.

Jacob looked at the tired and waned face Marion had, and Jacob looked at Oscar, who mouthed "Heat."

Marion looked up and, when he saw Jacob, gave a weak smile. "Tell me again of these cold scouts you used to go on up north? I could use some snow right about now."

Jacob chuckled, "Aye, sir, I believe you are correct. I could use some nice cold, fresh mountain air than this heavy air."

Marion gave a weak smile, the weight of the heat wearing on him along with time in the field. Then, as the rest of his men arrived, Marion forced himself to sit erect and put on his serious face, not wanting Lee's men to see him tired.

"Let's get after those Brits on the road with me!" Marion kicked his horse and trotted out with both Jacob's men and Colonel Lee's men trotting behind. The horses' hooves kicked up the dry dust as they rode in pursuit of the British. The wolves took their places along the front and flanks.

Sweat was beading down Jacob's face as the heat of the day swirled around him, though there was a slight cooling effect from the ride. Riding through the woods at least kept them in the shade; Jacob suspected it was much warmer out in the sun. *"Definitely a hotter year this year."*

The column came out of the woods and into an open plain that had been a plantation field. In the distance, horses and wagons could be seen resting in the shade. Motioning, Marion pointed Jacob to lead his band to the left, Colonel Lee was going to the right and Marion right up the middle as he yelled, "Charge!"

Following the direction Marion pointed, Jacob saw a British rear-guard resting in the shade. He could see men trying to mount their horses, running toward the wagons and infantry forming into a line to face Lee's cavalry. Jacob kicked his horse and raced forward, his band right behind, with a loud yell coming from their mouths.

As they did not carry sabers like real cavalry, he would move them close enough to engage with their muskets and rifles. They quickly closed the distance, Jacob pulling the hammer back on his rifle to full cock, before pulling on the reins and forcing his horse into a sliding stop. A dust cloud rolled into the eyes of the British, fully blinding them.

"Ka-Boom!"

Samuel's blunderbuss roared, along with a few muskets just as the dust cloud cleared enough for the Loyalist cavalrymen to be seen. The shock was enough, along with seeing Jacob and the rest of the band with lowered muskets and rifles pointing down at them from their horses, enough for the Loyalists to surrender. But, of course, having four wolves snarling and growling helped as well.

A crackle of musketry could be heard and Jacob looked over to see who appeared to be a Highlander firing into Lee's Cavalry as they did the same tactic as Jacob did. However, Jacob could see only one horse drop to the ground from Lee's Cavalry as his men, sabers drawn, encircled the British Highlanders who had their muskets held above their heads in surrender.

Jacob dismounted and his men moved about to secure the Loyalists while a few of his band held their horses. These Loyalists were from Major Coffin, with only about ten being secured as prisoners. Jacob walked over to Marion, who was watching the scene. The wagons were secured, and the British infantry was herded.

"71st Highlanders," Marion stated, looking at the prisoners, "Seven wagons of baggage and stores we can use. But, of course, their captured muskets shot and powder."

Jacob nodded, "Do we pursue the rest of the retreating British?"

Marion looked at the number of wagons and prisoners and shook his head. "This is a good enough message to send; we captured their rear guard with no casualties. We are successful; let's take all of this back with us."

The prisoners were loaded into the wagons. They were kept in the middle of the column between Jacob's band, with his wolves and Lee's Cavalry. Marion led them back to their camp location, arriving at night where General Greene watched and nodded in approval at the success of Marion's capture.

Marion came over to Jacob, "Go through the baggage, make sure your men replace anything they need, fill up your cartridge boxes, replace your muskets if they are in bad shape. I want you to be fully capable before I turn the rest of this over to the quartermaster. You and your men deserve it."

Jacob looked at a smiling Marion, but he could see in Marion's eyes that he was exhausted. The campaign was having a telling effect, even with Oscar taking care of him. Marion had been on campaign much longer than Sumter, who had gone up into North Carolina to rest and refit. Marion and primarily Jacob's band had been in the field except for the few short times he had been allowed to head home.

Jacob sat next to a small fire that Samuel and Patrick were working on, and he ached more now than in his early days. A groan escaped his lips and Samuel gave him a chuckle.

"Feeling your age?" Samuel asked teasingly and then as he settled back, his bones creaked and popped. Then, everyone started to giggle and laugh, and Samuel only raised an eyebrow.

"What? I never said I was a young man. Although, I admit I am feeling my age, so respect your elders!"

That just made the group laugh even harder. Then, as everyone was exhausted, they laughed harder, some even rolling on the ground, holding their stomachs. Even Samuel eventually joined in as well.

***

William Cunningham was now a Loyalist Major and had been given his own command to do with as he wished. Initially, he had ridden with General Robert Cunningham when his column departed Charles Town in a punitive expedition to chase down rebels. However, after running into the rebel General Sumter near Orangeburg, Cunningham was released.

"I know you have a bone to pick with these rebels up north," General Cunningham stated as he and Bloody Bill walked around their camp. "I will set off against this Sumter fellow and see what I can do."

He stopped and looked at Bloody Bill with a level look. "Major, you have complete autonomy over your command. Take the fight to these rebels, I have seen you in action and I know of your reputation. Impress me."

The two stopped walking and Bloody Bill looked back at the general with a slight grin coming to his face. The general looked back again with a level look.

"Impress, sir?" Bloody Bill stated, "You haven't seen anything yet. I will make them all pay one way or the other. They will all pay!"

Bloody Bill headed to where his men were camping, sitting around a fire and passing a bottle of rum around. They all stopped talking and looked up at Bloody Bill when he reached for the bottle. One of his men gave it to him and he took a long swallow.

"Boys, the general has cut us loose; we are heading north to put all bastards to the sword and flame. Then, after that, we are on our own; we can do as we wish. No British officer is going to tell us what we are to do. They want us to ride north and bring the pain."

His men began to nod and welcome the news. Bloody Bill took another swig before wiping his mouth on his sleeve and passing the bottle back.

"We ride first thing in the morning," he instructed and then he looked at two specific men. "John, Gabriel, head to the Danuwoa's village; he should be in the low country. I think he and his warriors would like to seek some vengeance right now."

The two men nodded their understanding, rose and headed for their horses. The rest of the men began to joke. Some bragged about their upcoming raids against the rebels in the north. Finally, bloody Bill wandered over to his sleeping area, sat down and leaned against a tree. He began to list who he would go after and how he would savior his revenge.

The following day, Bloody Bill departed and headed north, eventually linking up with the Cherokee Danuwoa and his small warband of warriors. Bloody Bill raised his hand and the column stopped. He then rode forward and greeted the Cherokees.

Danuwoa nodded to Bill when he rode up, "I hear you are on the warpath?" he asked Bill, who smiled and nodded.

"Are your scalping knives and tomahawks sharpened?" Bill asked back, and in turn, Danuwoa smiled and nodded. "Always."

"Let's ride the warpath together, take many scalps and put many rebel homes to the torch!"

They arrived in the upcountry at the beginning of October and found out where the rebels were. An informant told them that a group of rebels was at Pratt's Mill on the Little River and Bloody Bill led his raiders past the Town of Abbeville and along the river until they found the mill.

Hiding in the woods, Bill was waiting for the sun to go down to strike. The Cherokee were applying their war paint and some of his men did likewise. When the sun had set, Bill waited until he felt the rebels would be the most off guard before he had his men mount and then led them in a charge against the mill.

While he did catch them by surprise, all the rebels could escape, but not their horses, and one officer was wounded. Not satisfied that they all got away, Bill turned the horses they captured over to the Cherokee and then spoke to their wounded prisoner.

"I am going to leave you here," Bill growled at the wounded officer, Captain Norwood. "Tell them Bloody Bill is coming and the devil is coming with me. Tell your rebel friends there is nowhere they can hide where I cannot find them. You tell them I am back!"

Bloody Bill stomped off, leaving the prisoner behind. He mounted his horse and led his raiders to look for more rebels. A few days later, thanks to an observant Loyalist, he was given a location of another group of rebels camped near Hartley's Creek.

Bloody Bill had his men dismount and quietly approach the camp in the dark. Moving slowly, they could see the fires flicker and hear some voices in the distance. Finally, Bloody Bill moved them all to just within the circle of light from the fires, when he rose and led the raiders in a blood-curdling yell as they charged into the camp.

The rebels had no chance, most being caught in their sleep. It was a slaughter, the Cherokee falling on the sleeping rebels, their knives and tomahawks flashing in the firelight. Bloody Bill himself strode into the camp like a vengeful demon, hacking and slashing with his sword. By the time it was done, twenty-eight laid dead, hacked to pieces.

The Cherokees raised their voices in a war cry, holding their bloody scalps up in the air. Then they stripped the dead, taking all the muskets, gear, food and supplies they could. Bloody Bill walked amongst the dead, some of the Cherokee chopping and dismembering the dead, nodding to himself.

"This will send a message if there ever was one." Bloody Bill commented, nodding his head as he watched the camp activity.

With the taste of blood, Cunningham started to go through his list and began attacking rebel homes. He relied on hit-and-run tactics to keep the rebels off balance, never staying in place too long. He took as much food and other supplies as possible during his raids to keep his men, and the Cherokee fed.

Bloody Bill began to rove between Orangeburg and Rowe's Plantation, looking for reported rebels who were raiding Loyalists. When he found a lead, he would take his raiders and attack the rebel home, showing no mercy or care before burning it all down. As he was in the area, Bloody Bill decided to find his old rebel commander John Caldwell from his Third South Carolina days.

The raiders rode into the front of the house and Caldwell came out after Bloody Bill called for him. "Come out, you bloody bastard!" Bill yelled, "Come out and face that which you created! Time to pay the piper!"

John Caldwell came out of his house and saw the many men sitting behind Bloody Bill, who was in the middle, his saber out and cradled in his arm. Caldwell had a musket in his hand, ready to shoot.

"You brought it on yourself, you traitor," Caldwell shot back. "We took you in the regiment, served together and showed the world we will stand for liberty. Then you turned your back on us and now you are no better than a monster!"

"Monster, you say!" Bill yelled back, his anger starting to grow. "You denied my promotion that I earned and deserve. Deserved, you bastard! Then you violated my enlistment agreement to defend my home when you wanted to take us all to Charles Town."

"Charles Town is your home, like all of South Carolina! You turned your back on us; we all know you and your family's Loyalist leanings. You are the only bastard here!"

With a sneer on his face, Bloody Bill pulled his dragoon pistol and shot Caldwell in the chest. As he dropped to the ground, his wife just came out of the house and fainted at the site of Caldwell's death.

Cunningham looked at where Caldwell fell, where his wife lay on the ground and sighed. He felt mixed emotions; Caldwell had not been that bad of an officer and had treated him fairly. On the other hand, who knows if Caldwell had not forced him to march to Charles Town? Perhaps he would still be with the rebel cause. *"Doesn't mean anything now; what is in the past will stay there."*

One of his men came up, torch already lit. "Sir?"

Cunningham nodded, "Burn it."

His bloodlust not sated, Bloody Bill led his raiders across the Saluda River and followed the Cherokee Path to Anderson's Mill. There they found the mill abandoned, as it had been a militia outpost. Bloody Bill ordered it burned before heading on with his Bloody Scout.

Continuing, Bill learned of the Patriots garrisoning at Hayes Station and made the best speed to get there before the rebels withdrew. Bloody Bill picked up the pace and charged down to encircle the station. Bill could see the rebels running inside as they rode up and the doors shut tight. Bill had his men surround the entire station.

Bloody Bill rode up toward the front of the station. "Listen to me. We will let you go if you surrender now and do not fire upon us. If not, all of you will die. Your choice!"

Bill sat on his horse and watched, not hearing anything from the rebels, so he sent a few of his men forward. Just as they approached the door, a shot rang out and one of the men approaching the door dropped to the ground dead.

"Kill them all, no prisoners!" Bloody Bill yelled and all his men opened fire on the building. Moving off to the side, Bloody Bill watched as their balls struck the walls. Then, not having any artillery, he began to think about how he could force the surrender.

Danuwoa came over to consult with Bill. He pointed at the roof of the building. Danuwoa pulled his ramrod from his musket. "We tie rags to theses, shoot at the roof and catch it on fire. Drive them out."

Bloody Bill nodded and Danuwoa returned the nod and went to get a few of his warriors. They wrapped pitched dipped rags on their ramrods, loaded powder in their muskets, then placed the thicker end of the rod down first, the rag sticking out.

The Cherokee warriors moved to a good position and lit the rags. Then, raising the muskets to their shoulders, fired their muskets and the ramrods flew with the flaming rags arching through the air and thudding into the roof. After a short while, the wooden shingles began to blaze.

Smiling, Danuwoa walked up to Bloody Bill. Holding his now useless musket, "Need new musket."

The roof quickly grew into a full fire with choking smoke from its openings. Then, finally, the door flew open, and the rebels came out, their muskets raised over their heads.

"There you go," Bloody Bill said with a smile, "new muskets. Go help yourselves."

Bloody Bill's men quickly took them all prisoner. Cunningham walked over and faced the rebel prisoners, his face a thunderhead. "I gave you a choice and you threw it in my face! Against my better judgment, I tried to show mercy and now I have no mercy to give. Hang them!"

His men tied the prisoners' hands tight, threw ropes over the cross beams of the fodder shack, and began to hang the prisoners. Bloody Bill stared emotionless as each prisoner swung back slightly in the breeze.

As one of the men was about to be hung, a young boy ran up yelling, "Brother Daniel, what am I to tell mother?" Spinning on the boy, Bloody Bill drew his saber and slashed the boy, nearly cutting his head off. Then, as fate would have it, their rope broke when the last two men were strung up, and they fell to the ground.

Stalking over, Bloody Bill began hacking and slashing, his saber rising and falling. Blood was flying as he raised his sword and when the blade arched down. Bloody Bill continued to hack away until he stood there heaving breath, tired from the exertion. Both men were nearly indistinguishable from the multiple wounds.

Exhausted, Bloody Bill knelt on the ground while his men went about to check on the rebels; any found wounded were killed. The Cherokees moved among the dead, taking scalps. After catching his breath, once all was over, Bloody Bill remounted his horse and led his raiders to Odell's Mill. Believing his message was sent, Cunningham decided it was time to head back to Charles Town.

Bloody Bill was satisfied; for the most part, those who wronged him had been killed or chased off. He also was a realist and knew that soon the shock would wear off, the rebels in great numbers would be in pursuit and he would be at a disadvantage. Once his raiders were ready, Cunningham led his men back toward Charles Town

***

While Jacob's band had not suffered any losses from the fight at Eutaw Springs due to the British shooting high, some other companies were not so lucky. Combined with the numerous wounded, Marion was so short on men that the brigade could not conduct any operations.

General Greene needed Marion in the field, so he attached Colonels Isaac Shelby and John Sevier's Over-the-Mountain

Men and Major Maham's horses were replaced. They were encamped on the north side of the Santee River, near John Cantey's plantation.

Jacob had learned that Maham had led his men and some of Sevier's riflemen against a British redoubt near Wappetaw and the British abandoned the redoubt without firing a single shot. He shook his head as he walked to where the band was camped. *"They ran without firing a shot and were in a redoubt. Perhaps this is the beginning of the end."*

When Jacob arrived, Samuel, Jean and the others were excited and joyful as he walked into the camp.

"Have you heard?" Samuel asked as he placed his hands on Jacob's shoulder, "They beat him, they beat him!"

Jacob was confused and Jean took over.

"We just received a message that General Washington, with the help of the French, defeated our good old friend General Cornwallis near Yorktown, Virginia. However, he was forced to surrender and I also heard that he couldn't surrender his sword; another had to do it in his place."

It was great news, and Jacob nodded. "So they beat General Cornwallis at his own game."

"Oui, my friend," Jean replied, "At least the dead of Camden can rest in peace, no?"

The news spread quickly through the camp, and Marion organized a ball at the Cantey house and invited all local ladies to entertain his officers. One of those invited was Jacob, concerned, as he had not bathed in a good while and his uniform was not in great shape.

Samuel led Jacob to the river, where Jean was tending a fire, a bucket of water from the river and a stool. Jacob stripped out of his clothes and sat on the stool. Jean handed a bar of scented soap to Samuel, who had a cloth and began to scrape the grime off Jacob.

The wolves followed and laid down to watch Jacob, their tongues out in the method of wolves laughing. Jacob gave them all a reproachful look and the wolves promptly ignored him, watching the show.

Samuel and Jean looked at Jacob with a critical eye, "Maria is going to be angry at you," Samuel commented, "You are all skin and bones again and scars, of course." Jacob shrugged and sat there as Samuel scrubbed.

"You are getting grey hair as well," Jean commented as Samuel poured some water over Jacob's head and Jacob gave Jean a hard look. "Just adding to the conversation Mon ami." Jean gathered up Jacob's clothes and he walked off with them, chuckling. "Going to find a laundress."

Jacob sat as Samuel scrubbed and with a cool breeze from the day, the temperatures were lower than they had been. Grudgingly, Jacob admitted to himself it did feel good, scraping the layer of grime off.

Samuel brought him a blanket, and Jacob sat before the fire to dry off, smoking his pipe. Samuel was pulling Jacob's hair back into a queue and tying it off. Then, hearing movement, Jacob looked to see Jean returning with a set of new clothes, including a dark blue civilian coat, a new linen shirt and a matching blue waistcoat and breaches.

Where did you get those?" Jacob asked. "The quartermaster doesn't have regular clothes.

"No, he doesn't," Samuel replied with a smile. "Mrs. Cantey does. Or rather did. When she heard the mystical Wolf was coming, she handed me these clothes for you."

They started to help dress Jacob, who gave them both a dirty look. "I have been dressing for a good while, you know." Samuel shushed Jacob. But, looking down, the wolves were still watching him with what looked like smiles.

"You are representing us, so you don't need to look like a pig farmer," Samuel stated as he helped straighten out his breaches. Jacob looked over at Jean, "Where is the rest of my clothes?"

"Your small clothes are being burned; your frock and trousers and being cleaned and your leggings will be repaired," Jean explained as he handed Jacob the waistcoat. Next, Samuel went to get Jacob's old boots and brought them over.

As Jacob stared at him, Samuel shot back, "You are not going to this ball wearing your moccasins!"

"But they are more comfortable than the boots," Jacob shot back. Both Samuel and Jean gave him a hard look.

"Not when you are in civilian clothes do you wear moccasins," Samuel replied while Jean shook his head. Jacob sighed and accepted his fate while Samuel and Jean finished dressing him.

Jacob stood and both Samuel and Jean nodded in approval. "He cleans up nicely, doesn't he?" Samuel asked Jean, who replied, "Oui, we shall make a gentleman out of him, no?"

Jacob looked at them and muttered, "My friends."

They then handed him his black Second South Carolina helmet with a new black feather covering the top. "They didn't have any new hats, though," Samuel explained, and Jacob smiled as he accepted his helmet. He pulled his coat down, wiggled his shoulders so it fell into place, and sighed again.

"Alright, I guess I am off to the ball," Jacob stated, and both Samuel and Jean clapped lightly, making Jacob shake his head as he stalked off in the direction of the house. The two watched Jacob move off before joining the band at the campsite.

They could hear his men hoot and applaud as Jacob went by, even some whistles. Samuel and Jean just smiled as they made their way back to the camp, where a bottle of rum and a bottle of port were waiting.

The house was two stories and well-constructed, the windows open with light pouring out and the sound of music playing. Taking one more deep breath and settling his coat on his shoulders, Jacob mounted the front porch stairs and entered the front hall, where a servant was waiting.

The servant held his hand out for Jacob's helmet and asked, "Your name, sir?"

The servant handed the helmet to another servant with a good number of hats before leading Jacob into the main hall.

Clearing his throat, the servant announced, "Ladies and gentlemen, Major Jacob Clarke." The guests turned to watch Jacob enter; he noticed many women present, along with the officers he recognized from Marion's command and a few others who were not.

As eyes followed him, he could see numerous fans in the women's hands, a few speaking to each other behind them. Jacob could hear the whispers, "That's the Wolf and even the Old Grey Wolf."

Not familiar with the protocols of a ball, Jacob quickly moved off to the side, where a servant with a tray of glasses of wine stood. Jacob accepted and thanked the servant, who moved off to service the crowd.

Small groups of people were around the ballroom. Major Maham was holding court with three young ladies listening to his animated tales. Colonels Richardson and Sevier were in deep conversation. Officers dressed in the uniform of Lee's Legion were engaged in conversations with the young ladies, the tinkle of their laughter mixing with the music.

Jacob sipped his wine as he watched, trying to blend in with the wall and unobserved. Finally, Peter Horry moved up and stood next to Jacob, giving him a smile and nod. "Not a ball person, I see?" he asked, and Jacob shook his head with a slight smile.

"No sir, not really. Not my cup of tea, so to say." Horry nodded in agreement.

"What are your plans once all of this is over?" he asked, and Jacob thought for a moment before answering.

"Just go home, be with my family, watch my children hopefully grow in peace. I've had my fill of fighting."

"Would you think about going into politics, representing your area like myself and Marion have? I think you would be a great representative."

Jacob looked at Horry, "Why would you say that?"

Horry smiled again, "Because you have no fear and no one can intimidate you. You are honorable and truthful to a fault sometimes. You take care of your people." Then he turned and pointed to the ball, "Except attending the events like this, where the true politics occur."

Chuckling, Jacob shook his head.

"Well, think about it," Horry advised.

"We have to finish this fight before I can consider anything."

Horry nodded, a serious look replacing his smile. "Aye, that is true." He looked at Jacob. "Bloody Bill is back; we just received reports he is massacring Patriots up north. We may have to do something about it."

Jacob nodded, "We are ready if you need us."

Horry smiled and patted Jacob on the shoulder, "Aye, that is true; we can always count on you and your band."

As Jacob took a sip from his glass, two young ladies approached Jacob and cornered him. Jacob looked up at their approach. *"Oh no, I don't want to deal with this."* Jacob thought.

"Major Clarke, are you Major Clarke?" one of the young ladies asked as she gave him a curtsy, allowing him an amble look at her cleavage pressed up by her stays. She had dark hair and brown eyes that Jacob could see when she rose to stand before him.

Her friend, a blonde girl with blue eyes, curtsied, displaying her ample cleavage before rising. "My name is Harriet Acland," she said in a light tone, then pointed to the girl's dark hair. "This is my friend, Grace Elliot."

Jacob gave a slight bow to both young ladies as they introduced themselves.

"Are all of these stories we have heard about your bravery true, Major Clarke?" Harriet asked, followed by Grace. "Is this legend about a Cherokee gauntlet that you walked through unscathed then spat on the ground of their chief?"

"Not this story again," Jacob thought before answering. "I am not sure what you mean by bravery, miss. I am doing my part like everyone else. As for the gauntlet, it's not exactly like that. But, trust me, I was scathed."

The two young ladies gave a light laugh as they pulled out their hand fans to laugh behind them, but showing their eyes. *"Wolf's eyes,"* Jacob thought, *"they are on the hunt and I am not going to be their prey."*

The two young ladies kept asking Jacob questions and he politely answered them. Then Grace asked if Jacob was married and he replied he was, in fact, married,

"Is she here?" Grace boldly asked, looking over his fan while batting her eyelashes.

Before Jacob could respond, he heard, "Master Clarke, Master Marion would like a word with you, sir. If you would accompany me, please?"

It was Oscar, and Jacob nodded. "Excuse me, ladies, but I must go see General Marion. Please excuse me."

"Hurry back," Grace called after him, "We'll be waiting."

Jacob walked with Oscar with a slight smile, leading him to where Marion was waiting. "I could see you needed rescuing, Jacob," Marion stated and Jacob nodded.

"Yes sir," he replied, "Not my type of battlefield."

Marion nodded. "I will dispatch your band, Sevier's riflemen and Maham's cavalry to take another British outpost, Fort Fairlawn. General Greene wants all these small outposts taken and the British pushed into the city. I hope that with Cornwallis out of the picture, we will get all of those northern troops to head down here and we can finish our fight. Go see to your men."

As Jacob left, he could see the two young ladies looking at him, speaking behind their fans. He shook his head and returned to the entrance, where he took back his helmet and the servant wished him a good evening.

When he returned to his camp, his new small clothes, frock and leggings were waiting. The entire band was sitting around the fire with mugs in their hands, waiting expectantly. Even the wolves looked up; their ears perked.

"Please, Major Clarke, a bedtime story," started Samuel and the rest of the band joined in with "Please?"

As Jacob changed into his regular clothes, he told of the ball and what he saw. But, of course, the men wanted more details about the two girls, Grace and Harriet. Jean smiled as he collected the civilian clothes to take them back. The band mostly asked questions about how they were dressed.

Once Jacob was back in his regular but cleaned clothes, he told the band about their next task of riding out with Maham and Sevier to attack Fort Fairlawn. Then, nodding their acceptance, they returned to relaxing, for they knew they would be on campaign soon to retake Charles Town piece by piece.

Fort Fairlawn and British Hospital

CHAPTER 15

MARCH ON CHARLES TOWN

Captain Murdock MacLaine looked at the position he had been ordered to secure with his company from the 84th Regiment of Foot. Known as the Fairlawn Plantation, a strong brick house that had been built for both comfort and defense. The original British force had already had an abatis in place. The defensive position had been designed to protect a vital boat landing on the Cooper River.

MacLaine began to shake his head as he took into account his other tasks. Not only was he responsible for the garrisoning of this plantation, but the safety of a field hospital about a mile away and man a blockhouse overlooking Biggin's Bridge two miles away. Although one hundred and fifty Hessian soldiers had initially garrisoned it, their commander told him, "You don't need to worry about the hospital, but the bridge must be held at all costs."

"How in the bloody Hell am I going to accomplish all this with only fifty men when the Hessians had three times as many. It's bloody impossible!"

Heading to his office in the plantation, MacLaine penned a message to Charles Town, asking for clarification on his orders, as it did not make sense to him. The letter was sent to his commander, Major Brereton of the 64th. While waiting for a response, he got down to business to figure out how to divide his force to protect these key areas.

A few days later, on November 9th, MacLaine received his instructions. *"You are to occupy the current post and the Colleton's House hospital. Leave the blockhouse in its present situation."* Tossing the message on the table next to his chair, MacLaine rubbed his chin as he thought about the message.

"Well, that is as clear as mud; I still have no idea how to defend this place with fifty men. The Hessians said you do not worry about the Colleton's House hospital, yet he was now ordered to protect it. What do they want me to do?"

The Hessian commander had told him that the main army was between him and Charles Town, so the hospital was safe. Taking a piece of parchment, MacLaine wrote a warning to the doctors at the hospital to be on guard against the rebels and ready to evacuate at a moment's notice. He sent a messenger to the hospital as he walked the defenses. He thought of the one hundred and thirty sick and wounded soldiers at the hospital and wondered how he could evacuate them quickly.

"Right, let's get down to business!" MacLaine stated to no one and called for his second in command. He pointed out where he needed the defenses improved. "We're next, you know," he said to his lieutenant, "This rebel General Greene is coming this way and we are between him and the city. We must be ready."

Using local slave labor, MacLaine started improving their defenses and fortifications while sending out scouting parties. Finally, a group of South Carolina Loyalists arrived from Camden that he sent to cover the blockhouse and bridge. He knew he was racing against time.

This was confirmed the following morning when a group of his scouts came riding into the camp. "They're coming; they're coming! A large group of rebel horsemen is heading this way!"

The duty drummer played the long roll and the British took up their positions within the fortification around the house. MacLaine sent warning messages to all outposts and the hospital they were about to be engaged. Later that afternoon, a rebel deserter surrendered to the British, said he had been part of Maham's men and a large group of mounted riflemen was coming.

MacLaine quickly sent a rider to Stewart, asking for reinforcements. He then sent another message to the hospital, directing all sick and wounded who could move to evacuate and head to Charles Town. Unfortunately, all of the slave labor was also sent to Charles Town. He knew he could not defend the hospital, so he ordered it abandoned; the only men remaining were the medical staff and the wounded who could not move.

MacLaine's reinforcements from Stewart arrived and twenty militia horsemen he sent to the blockhouse to help protect the bridge. He waited for the rebels to arrive, confident they could hold out from their strong brick house and fortifications.

**

The column of horses moved along the dirt path, the cool November air refreshing after so many months of hot, sticky air. Jacob relished the ride; now it seemed the war had turned back to their favor; the British were now the hunted, and they were the hunters.

Their task was to secure the British outpost at the Fairlawn Plantation and they would have to rely on their accurate rifles to do the job, as they had no artillery for a siege. Jacob's band rode alongside Maham's horse and Shelby's riflemen, all with very determined looks on their faces.

As their lead scouts rode up, Maham halted the column, indicating they found a British forward post. Maham ordered them to lead them, "Our first catch of the day!" The scouts led them along a side trail and when they came out, it was an open field, and on the opposite side was a redoubt.

"Jacob's band on the left, Shelby's men on the right, Maham's form line and draw sabers!"

Jacob led his men to the left side of their line and they rested their rifles across their saddles. Shelby did the same on the right with his riflemen. The sun reflected off the saber blades of Maham's men. The wolves moved along the side, itching for action.

Jacob and Maham pulled out their telescopes to see who they were dealing with and could see it was a cavalry outpost. Jacob lowered his telescope, "It's a cavalry outpost; I don't see any cannon or infantry," Jacob yelled out so his band could hear. They nodded and smiled in anticipation. Samuel, Jean and Frederick joined Jacob.

"What do you think, Jacob?" Frederick asked and Jacob shrugged as he looked over at Maham. "I think we may see a duel between cavalry, as I believe our young commander is full of piss and vinegar and may do something rash."

As Jacob stated, Maham led his men forward at the walk while yelling, "Riflemen, cover us!"

Shrugging, Jacob ordered his men to dismount, his musket men holding the horses while the riflemen took up shooting positions. Looking to his right, Jacob could see Shelby's men doing the same.

As the cavalry was making their way across the field, Jacob's men began taking bets and calling shots, though he could not see much from where he stood. Standing, he leaned his rifle against his chest as he opened his telescope again to see what was transpiring. The wolves sat down with disappointed looks on their faces.

Maham had stopped his men and he could see a green uniformed man speaking over the logs. While he could not hear what was being said, he could see hand gestures back and forth toward the field.

"I don't think he is going to get his duel," Jacob replied as he lowered his telescope. Soon after, Maham returned to their line and commanded, "Mount up, follow me."

Jacob's band remounted their horses and joined Shelby as they rode behind Maham's cavalry. Maham continued to lead them toward Fairlawn Plantation. As they rode toward the outpost, the British cavalry at the post they had just left rode right and shadowed them.

It was in the early morning of the 17th of November 1780 when they arrived at the plantation. Maham haled them at the edge of the wood line. "Officers to the center!" was ordered and Jacob made his way down to the middle of their line. "Have fun!" Samuel called out as he left. The wolves sat on their haunches.

When Shelby arrived, the three commanders looked at their objective. Jacob looked at it with a critical eye, using his telescope and shaking his head.

"Your thoughts Major Clarke?" Maham asked.

Still shaking his head, Jacob answered, "We are not taking that without artillery; the position and the brick house are too strong. It is like it was back there at Eutaw Springs. We can send a message to the general to bring up artillery, but that will take time."

Shelby nodded, "Aye, as Major Clarke stated, that's formidable. My riflemen won't be able to do much."

Looking at the position across from them, Maham nodded in agreement, "True, this is true. But the British are there and we must have them! So there has to be a way to get them!"

The scouts came riding back and reported to Maham. "Sir, we found an undefended outpost just a mile from here." After being dismissed, the scout nodded and waited to see what Maham wanted to do.

Nodding, he addressed the officers, "Well then, I believe prudence will say we shall attack the undefended position before trying a fortified position. Scout, lead us!"

The scout turned and led Maham, and the rest of the column followed. The scout arrived just outside the field hospital at the Colleton house. Raising his telescope, Maham smiled and nodded before bringing his telescope down.

"There are no sentries, no fortifications; it is completely undefended. Shelby, you will ride with me; Major Clarke, you will support." Once the instructions were issued, the column split into their assigned positions. As Maham rode across the field, Jacob watched as he placed Shelby's riflemen to cover their flank from the British redoubt.

Samuel, Jean and Frederick joined Jacob as they watched the raid come together. Maham rode up to the hospital and from their position, they could see the medical staff, along with the sick and wounded who could walk, were being herded toward Jacob. Then the prisoners who could not move were carried out and placed on the ground. A short time later, the black fingers of smoke and flame reached upwards as the hospital was set afire.

A messenger came for Jacob to bring his band up. When they arrived, Maham was sitting with a smile on his face. "Major Clarke, please secure all the muskets and equipment you can, plus escort these walking wounded back to the camp. I have already paroled the medical staff, these others who can't walk."

Jacob nodded, "As instructed, I shall do." Maham nodded as Jacob turned and led his band over to where the prisoners were waiting. Jacob sent a few of his men to guard the eighty walking wounded prisoners and then went to inspect the captured muskets and equipment.

"Three hundred, Jacob," Frederick came up with a smile, "We have secured three hundred stands of new Brown Besses, cartridge boxes mostly full and bayonets. We can use these when we get back to the camp."

Smiling in return, Jacob watched as the band gathered all of the stands of muskets and secured them to extra horses they had found. They didn't have enough for the prisoners, so that they would walk with the band surrounding them. When all was ready, Jacob turned and led the column of his men escorting the prisoners. The snap and crackle of the fully engulfed Colleton House wished them farewell.

**

Lowering his telescope, MacLaine watched the hospital go up in flames. Then, he looked at his small garrison of men, who watched the building blaze even with it a mile away. Then, shaking his head, he could see the line of dragoons lead the captured British wounded away and into the woods.

MacLaine shook his head and closed his telescope as his lieutenant arrived next to him. "Your orders, sir?" he asked.

"Have the men stand down; there will be no action today, lieutenant. Post normal sentries."

The lieutenant nodded and walked off to see that the men stood down from the walls. *"They are going to crucify me,"* MacLaine thought, *"Even though they outnumbered me four to one, and any counterattack would have been foolhardy against those riflemen, I am sure to be blamed for this. What a way to fight a bloody war!"*

**

"I hope the rest of the war is like this," Samuel commented as they walked their horses, escorting the prisoners. "Better than ducking with all of that lead flying around. I could even get into enjoying it." As if they could hear, the wolves looked up at Samuel with disgust, as though they were missing the action.

The band gave Samuel a hard time about his suggestion, hooting and scoffing at the proposal for the rest of the war. Jacob shook his head at the jabs between Samuel and the rest of the band, though he did agree it would be a much better way to end this fight if they didn't have to go into action again.

When they arrived at the camp, the prisoners were moved off to be consolidated with the others from Eutaw Springs. Scouts were sent out to keep an eye on the Loyalists and to look for any British scouts in their area.

Word arrived that the British were evacuating Wilmington up in North Carolina, which Marion thought, like the Yorktown victory, more men would be released to come south and help finish off the British.

At the end of November, malaria arrived in the camp and it struck hard at the already tired men and the wounded. While Jacob had already fought through his bout of malaria, it did strike Richard and both of Samuel's boys caught it. They spent their time in the sick area of the camp, keeping isolated from the rest of the men until they recovered.

Orders arrived and Marion marched his men, including the walking wounded and those still fighting malaria. These men were wrapped in blankets on their horses, with a rider next to them so they would not fall off from the shivering.

The column marched southwest until they came to Round-O Plantation on the Edisto River. There the different columns consolidated, and a large field hospital was established. With around seven hundred sick and wounded, it was all it could take for the regimental surgeons to keep up between malaria running its course and the wounded from Eutaw Springs.

Jacob and Samuel went to the field hospital to check on the condition of their boys. One of the regimental surgeons from Greene's Army met them, still not wanting them to get too close.

"How are the lads doing?" Jacob asked the surgeon, a man named Linctus. Nodding, he replied, "Those are some tough lads you have there, the malaria is about to run its course and after a few more days, they can return to duty."

Jacob nodded, thanked the surgeon and headed back toward their camp. Halfway there, a messenger came for Jacob and told him General Greene wanted to see him. Samuel raised his eyebrows, "I'll get the band ready!" he yelled after Jacob, who walked away, shaking his head.

Arriving at Greene's command area, a small marquee with the outer sides down to let in the fall air. Along with Greene were his officers and Marion. Looking up from a map, he smiled when he saw Jacob arrive and properly salute, even though his clothes were a little ragged.

"Sir, I hear you need me?" Jacob stated as he stood before General Greene.

Greene waved for him to stand easy. "Yes, Major Clarke, we need your knowledge of Dorchester, especially of the fort there."

Jacob nodded. "Not much of a fort; the walls are made from local tabby, so it's as strong as stone. Rectangle in style, small bastions on the corner, the main feature being the powder magazine near the center. Of course, it will depend on if the British maintained the fort and it hasn't fallen apart."

"Does it mount cannon?" one of Greene's officers asked and Jacob shook his head.

"We have never seen it mount cannon, other than some swivel guns on the corner, one pounder," Jacob answered and he could hear the men mumbling to one another in the background.

"General Marion has informed me you have extensive knowledge of Dorchester and the area, correct?" Greene asked and Jacob nodded.

"Yes sir, trained Middleton's Regiment there, garrisoned it a few times during the early days of the war and my home is south of there in Goose Creek. My wife's family used to live there."

Greene nodded, "The British have occupied it and we will drive them out. I want you and your men to lead Colonel Hampton's men in an assault to take the fort. From what we have gathered, maybe three hundred men, mostly Loyalist militia."

Jacob nodded, "Yes, sir, we would be honored to lead Colonel Hampton and his men. When do we leave?"

"In the morning, so see to your men, get anything you need from the quartermaster," Greene instructed, "With a little more effort, we will have pushed them all back into the city and plug the bottle on them!"

As the officers cheered, Jacob turned and left, with Marion walking with him. "How are the lads doing?" he asked.

"Surgeon says they are through the tough part, a little while longer before they will be released back to duty."

Marion nodded, "That's good to know; they are strong lads, those three." He gave Jacob a sly look, then a wink, "Look who they are related to."

Jacob shrugged, "I would say their mothers more than me, but thank you all the same."

When they arrived at the camp, Samuel, Jean and Frederick prepared them for their task.

Marion looked at Samuel, "Is it always like that, Jacob knows when a task is coming?"

"Yes sir," Jacob replied, "Goes back to our Rangers days; it's natural to believe every time Major Rogers called for me, we were off on some scout or raid. Still the same today."

Marion nodded, "Makes sense then." He turned and shook Jacob's hand, "Good luck out there and don't be a hero. You have survived this long; we are so close to finishing this thing, so you don't do something rash and get killed."

Then Marion turned and headed for his camp, "Besides, your wife would kill me."

Jacob gathered the band, about twenty of them available for duty. "We're leading Colonel Hampton's men on an attack against our old home of Fort Dorchester. We will be more guides; let Hampton attack the fort. Everyone check your muskets and gear; let the sergeant major know if you need anything."

Once all was ready, they settled in for the night, sitting close to a small fire as the air was getting much cooler at night. Some men wrapped their blankets over their shoulders as they sat, talked, and smoked their pipes. The glow of the pipes looked like fireflies across the camps.

Jacob had them up with the sun, getting some warm food, tea or coffee into them. Once they were more or less alive, he had them prepare their gear and horses. The morning was chilly; Jacob considered pulling out his blanket coat but decided against it. It would warm up later.

Seeing the Legion heading their way, Jacob ordered his band to mount and form into a line of twos behind him. As Colonel Hampton rode up, Jacob nodded to him, and Hampton nodded back.

"Good morning," Hampton cheerfully greeted, "A great morning for a ride. Are your men ready?" He raised an eyebrow seeing the wolves waiting.

"Yes sir, we are ready to lead you out," Jacob responded.

"Well, sir, Rangers lead the way then," Hampton instructed, motioning with his hand forward. Jacob nodded, turned his horse and led the band forward with Hampton and his men following. Riding on familiar roads, Jacob tried to lead the column along routes that kept them hidden from the view of the locals.

***

As the column of horses rode by, Mary Firth, still dressed as a man, watched from her concealed location. She had been lucky riding her horse back toward King's Tree when she heard the horses approaching. She pulled her horse into the trees and watched the column ride by.

As the end of the column went down the road, Mary took another trail and kicked her horse into a gallop. As there were no other British positions in the area, they must be heading to the only remaining British outpost in the area, Dorchester.

Having given up the life of crime riding with the bandits, she became a scout and spy for the Crown. It paid well for the information she found, and this piece should be well worth it. As a small-framed woman, it was not hard for her horse to keep a fast pace, getting ahead of the rebel column. However, the trail she used was a more direct route and she quickly got ahead of the rebels.

Riding through the town of Dorchester, Mary stopped with a skid in front of the guards at the entrance to the fort. Luckily, they recognized her simply as "the scout" and let her in. She went straight to the commander of the fort, Major Crawford.

"Sir, you are about to have a lot of company soon," she said. "I just saw a huge column of rebels heading this way."

Major Crawford nodded to Mary and went out to the fort's interior. "Get me, Lieutenant Walker!" he commanded. Then, turning, he looked to Mary, "Can you take our cavalry and lead them, in your best opinion, the route they are taking to get here? I want to see how enormous they are."

Mary nodded she could and went over and remounted her horse. Lieutenant Walker came jogging up to the commander, then went to fetch his cavalry troop. These men were South Carolina Royalists and came trotting out to meet Mary. The rest of the garrison was assembling, and the long roll was played on the drums.

"Lead on!" Walker stated and Mary turned to lead the troop of dragoons to the northeast out of the town, then onto Dorchester Road. As Mary led them forward, Walker asked, "How many were there?"

"A lot, sir, she answered, "a lot."

**

Jacob and his band led the column through familiar trails and roads, a feeling of home flowing through him. Even the wolves had a spring to their trot, recognizing the scent. Still, he had a job to do and refocused on keeping vigilant and aware as they moved closer to Dorchester.

They were rounding a bend on the road, heading toward Dorchester, when they saw the approaching Loyalists. They were less than a hundred yards away and Jacob had little time to react.

"Loyalists to the front!" Jacob yelled as he pulled his horse to the right and led his band away to clear a path for Hampton and the Legion. Then, wheeling his horse around to face the now-reacting Loyalist, Jacob raised his rifle and set himself to fire.

As his rifle barked, so did a few of the band who could get their rifles up to fire. Hampton and his dragoons charged forward and were met by the charging Loyalist Dragoons. Sabers flashed and the two bodies of dragoons crashed into one another into a maelstrom of combat.

As the dragoons fought one another, spinning and turning, Jacob had his men dismount and reload their rifles. Samuel stood with his blunderbuss, waiting in anticipation. Jacob watched, keeping his rifle at the ready. The dragoons were caught up in close combat and there were no clear shots to be had.

The dragoons would wheel away and then charge back in to slash with their sabers. Now and then, a sound of a pistol being fired was heard. Then Jacob saw a target of opportunity ride away from the fight, a Loyalist in civilian clothes, who appeared to be aiming a musket at Hampton. Jacob brought up his rifle in a smooth motion and fired. The Loyalist tumbled from his horse.

From their vantage point, Jacob saw that these were no simple Loyalist militia cavalry; instead, they appeared to be well-armed and trained dragoons proficient in saber and pistol. Hampton would pull back for a short moment, reassemble and then charge back again to the crash of combat.

While the Loyalists fought well, Hampton seemed to do a better job of it and the Loyalists retreated from the field with Hampton in pursuit. Jacob led his men across the open area to where the bodies of the injured and dead lay. The field was strewn with numerous green uniformed Loyalists and a few of Hampton's wounded or dead men.

Jacob directed his band to help assist with Hampton's wounded and dead while he and the rest of the band searched and collected the wounded Loyalists. In all, they found ten dead Loyalist dragoons and twenty wounded who were taken prisoners, the wolves helping to herd. The prisoners were stripped of their weapons; the dead were also searched.

Jacob went over to the body of the civilian-clothed Loyalist he had shot. The body was lying face down; Jacob knelt and rolled the body over. As the body rolled, the hat fell off, and long hair spilled out. It was a girl's dead eyes staring up that shocked Jacob.

While she had been wearing men's clothing, the ball tore through her side and blew out a large hole in her chest. Her shirt was dark with blood and her cold, lifeless eyes stared into infinity. Jacob shook his head and closed her eyes. Then, he motioned to members of the band who were collecting up the enemy dead and they carried her dead body to join the rest.

Colonel Hampton rode back, a pleased look on his face. "Damn buggers got away," he commented as he looked around.

"What is the butcher's bill?" Hampton asked.

"From our count, they lost ten dead, and we captured their twenty wounded. Your men fared better, only three dead and eight wounded," Jacob answered.

Hampton nodded, "Can your men take care of the wounded and prisoners while you lead us the rest of the way?"

"Yes sir," Jacob replied, "give me a moment and we'll be ready to ride."

Hampton nodded in reply and Jacob ran to find Jean. He was with his section of the band watching the prisoners. He smiled when Jacob approached.

"I take it I am the lucky one, no?" Jean asked, "Do I take them back or sit on them until the army arrives?"

"I would say sit on them here; General Greene is heading this way. Would be easier to keep an eye on them."

Jean nodded, "You go and lead them to Dorchester?"

Jacob nodded, and Jean nodded in return. "Hopefully, no one we know is fighting for the British; we hate to hear we lost a neighbor because of it."

The wolves waited, and Jacob pointed to Jean, and once more, they did their part in securing the prisoners, who gave the four large animals fearful looks. Jean only smiled in his wolfish way.

Jacob nodded and then jogged to where Samuel was holding his horse, his blunderbuss resting on his hip. After pulling himself up, Jacob saw his section was ready, then looked over to see if Hampton was ready.

General Greene rode up and conferred with Colonel Hampton as they were about to leave. Jacob rode over and joined the conversation.

"Seemed you had a little excitement here," Greene asked with a half-smile, "and from the looks of it, they took the worse of it."

Hampton smiled, "Yes, sir, they did put up a stiff fight, but we prevailed in time."

Greene nodded, looked skyward and then looked to Hampton and Jacob. "I'll see to the care of your men and the prisoners; you go take care of that fort."

Jacob and Hampton nodded to the General. Then, turning and with Jacob leading once more, the column continued down the road. Finally, they crossed the bridge that the Loyalists had retreated across. Jacob recognized the area and knew they would be at Dorchester soon.

As they turned onto the road that entered the northern part of Dorchester, Jacob could smell the smoke of a fire. Then, when the town came into view, they could see a large column of smoke rising from the southern end, where the fort stood.

The horses clopped down the road between the buildings of Dorchester. Some of the people who Jacob recognized waved and smiled at their passing. Jacob saw no Loyalists or British regulars as they closed on the fort. Jacob and his section and Hampton dismounted and entered the fort.

The tabby walls stood, but what was burning was supplies. Jacob and his men quickly cleared the fort and found it completely abandoned. However, they found two small iron cannons, some gear not being burned. Also strewn about were some personal items, as if they had evacuated quickly.

"Looks like our little action at the bridge scared them enough to abandon the fort," Hampton stated as he walked up to Jacob, who nodded in agreement. "We have them on the run."

Jacob and the band returned to Marion's camp on the Cooper River after dropping off the prisoners. General Greene had provided food and supplies to Marion and the men settled into their new home. They had been tasked to watch the British right flank and ensure they did not move.

Jacob would lead his band of scouts north of Charles Town and would occasionally stop by his home at Goose Creek. Maria, Otti and Peter would say a quick hello, bringing some refreshments. Both mothers would check on their boys, though they were men. The band spoke freely, becoming just a larger extension of Jacob's family.

Jacob walked with Peter while the family mingled with the band. "Any news?" Jacob asked, and Peter nodded.

"Ya, we have news of our old friend Bloody Bill," Peter responded, puffing on his pipe. "He is back to his old tricks but claiming he does it for the Crown. Killing a good number of people, like he used to do."

Jacob nodded, deep in thought. "We had heard earlier he was back. Where did he come out of?"

"Cherokee lands," Peter answered, "Our Catawba friends who had been watching the Cherokee saw him and his group of bloody bandits leave their lands and come south. Heard now he is around Orangeburg and has a few Cherokee riding with him."

Jacob shook his head. While the main Cherokee are staying out, they support the Loyalists who take refuge in their lands. "We may have to do something about him, as we seem to have driven the British into the city."

***

Bloody Bill was not happy. Having led his men from the Cherokee Lands, recuperating and getting some much-needed rest, he has been doggedly pursued by this General Pickens and his force of rebels.

Since his expedition started a month before, Cunningham was able to gather Hezekiah Williams and some more refugees from Charles Town. His group had one focus, revenge and retribution against the rebels for the loss of their lands, homes and way of life.

Bloody Bill found most of those who wronged him or supported the rebel cause and ended their lives. As he sat on his horse, watching his men cross the Edisto River. He smiled as he learned how they called his campaign the Bloody Scout.

They had ridden to Mount Willing and put it to the sword and flame, plundering all of the settlers' possessions. Then he and his men rode into Union County, chasing down rebels and burning more homes. His reign of terror was making an impact.

Cunningham scoffed, shook his head and then returned to watching his men cross. His reign of terror also had him the most wanted man in South Carolina and all of these rebel commanders wanted his head.

"Well, come and get it, you bloody fools; I'll cut you all down to size!" he thought as an evil grin played across his lips. *"I welcome it!"*

***

Jacob and the band, wolves trotted alongside, were heading up toward Bulls Swamp on the Edisto River. Marion had instructed him to join General Pickens and his men as they chased Bloody Bill and his Loyalists. He had learned that Pickens had been chasing Bloody Bill and had him on the run.

In time, they found Pickens camp. After reporting to the sentry, Jacob and the wolves led the Band into the camp. Then, dismounting, Jacob left the band to Jean and Samuel while he reported to General Pickens.

Pickens sat on a stump when Jacob approached, talking with his officers. Then, turning, Pickens stood and approached Jacob. A tall thin, almost stern-looking man with a beak of a nose, Jacob bowed in salute.

"Sir, General Marion's compliments; I am Major Jacob Clarke and here to offer my service to you and your command."

Pickens bowed in return, "Yes, I have heard of you, Major Clarke; what services can you offer my command?"

"I am well acquainted with Bloody Bill," Jacob replied, "myself and most of my men have been tangling with him and his cutthroats since the Regulator War.

Pickens nodded, then gave Jacob a half-smile, "I hear you have a nickname?" he asked.

"Yes sir," Jacob answered, "Spirit of Okwaho."

Pickens nodded, "Which means?"

"Spirit of the wolf." Jacob returned.

"That's the one. This war gives us all nicknames, your General Marion as the Swamp Fox, Sumter the Carolina Game Cock."

Jacob smiled and nodded, "And you, sir?"

"The Cherokee of all people named me Skyagunsta or Wizard Owl," Pickens continued. "During the last one with the Cherokee, we received no nicknames. Anyways, let us see about your old friend Bloody Bill. We have a location of one of his camps."

Pickens formed his command early the following morning before the sun rose. Jacob and his men were mounted, the wolves sitting off to the side, waiting as they did. When the column was ready, Pickens led them out, Jacob's band following behind Pickens's men.

Pickens had a guide leading them through the forest along a game trail. The sun was slowly rising, the forest going from a black to a grayish cast. There were clouds and the air was crisp; it felt like the rain would fall later that day. Jacob inadvertently shivered, then returned to focusing on the task.

In the distance, a soft glow of fires could be seen, and the guide halted the column. Pickens motioned for everyone to dismount, and Jacob and his band followed suit. Making his way up to the front quietly, Jacob met with Pickens to get the battle plan. Pickens, the guide, and three of his officers were already gathered.

"Ah, Major Clarke. Seems we have them, and they are all in their camp. I want your men to move to the opposite side of their camp. My men will attack from here and drive them toward you. The rest I will leave in your capable hands."

Jacob nodded, "How much time do I have to get in position?"

"Twenty minutes," Pickens answered in a whisper, looking at the soft glow of the Loyalist camp. "Will that be enough?"

"Yes sir, it will," Jacob answered, "I'll see to my men."

Jacob moved back to the band; they tied their horses to branches so that he could take all of them on the attack. He pulled everyone close and told them they were the anvil for the Loyalists to be hammered against. Everyone nodded their understanding.

Smiling in the dark, "Right, lads, off we go."

Jacob turned and led his men at a slow trot, the wolves following closely. Watching the location of the fires, Jacob kept them at a safe distance so they would not hear them. Once they were at the opposite side of the camp, Jacob halted the band. Turning to their right, the band formed a line, and with rifles and muskets at the ready, they advanced slowly to the edge of the woods.

Walking at a crouch, rifle at the ready, Jacob scanned the camp for any sign of sentries. The wolves crept, noses to the air and ears perked up. The wolves froze, Jacob held his fist up, and the band stopped. Motioning his hand down, the band all sank to their knees. Looking at Waya, Jacob passed his rifle to Samuel and drew his knife.

Jacob and Waya moved slowly and softly forward to detect what the wolves had spotted. It was answered soon when they found a Loyalist squatting in the bushes near a tree, his trousers down. Jacob placed his hand on the back of Waya and the wolf sank to the ground. Jacob waited for the men to finish his business. Then, as he walked around the tree, buttoning up his front flap, Jacob leaped up, covered the man's mouth with his left hand and drove his fighting knife into the back of the Loyalist.

When the body stopped moving, Jacob lowered it to the ground. Then paused to see if they had been heard. When he looked at Waya, he had a disgusted look. "What, it wouldn't be fair if I killed him with his trousers down," Jacob whispered at the wolf, who ignored him. Then, shaking his head, "*I am arguing with a wolf; I have been out way too long.*"

Jacob returned to the line, took his rifle from Samuel and motioned the men forward. They arrived at the forest's edge, and Jacob motioned for the men to spread out and find cover behind trees. Then, looking left and right, he saw the band was ready; they had to wait for Pickens to start the game.

The camp was small, from what Jacob could see. Four fires were burning; about twenty men were lying in their blankets near the fires. He still couldn't see any sentries and wondered if the one man he caught in the bushes had been the sentry. There were horses tied on a picket line off to the side.

It wasn't long when the far side erupted in yells as Pickens' men charged into the camp. As the Loyalists tried to rise from the sleeping rolls, muskets and rifles barked. A few Loyalists had turned and were running right at Jacob's line. But, as they closed, Jacob commanded, "Wait for it!"

The Loyalists who were running mainly looked over their shoulders at the pursuing Pickens' men, not at their front.

Jacob gave the command of "Fire!" The wolves charged forward and the four crashed into a Loyalist who somehow survived the musket and rifle fire. The wolves brought the man down and Waya finished the job with a loud "crunch" as his jaws closed on the Loyalist's throat. None of the Loyalists survived, there were no prisoners.

Jacob advanced the band forward, surveying the site. All twenty bodies of the dead Loyalists were strewn around the camp. Pickens' men searched the dead and secured items of interest and the Loyalists' horses. Pickens stood in the middle camp, nodding in satisfaction in bringing justice to the Loyalists.

"Thank you, Major Clarke; we were able to crack them between my men and yours. But unfortunately, this is just one of Bill's camps; we have learned he has broken up his command. Once we have secured the site, we'll head after the others."

Word must have gotten out to Bloody Bill's men, who seemed to have fled in every direction when Pickens with Jacob searched for their camps. Local farmers told them they saw the Loyalists all ride out as if the devil was chasing them. Pickens nodded and smiled, "Aye, you may be right."

***

Bloody Bill was riding his horse hard down Dorchester Road toward Charles Town. He had learned the rebel general Pickens and his men had wiped out one of his companies, and then the rest of his men took to flight. Now he was on his own and justice was coming after him. The horse was wavering, flagging from the long ride.

Turning onto the road that led straight to Charles Town, Bill could see the outer defenses of Charles Town in a short time. Never letting up, Bill kept the horse galloping until he felt safe behind the walls and fortifications of Charles Town. The city grew in size as he approached.

With the last bit of energy, the horse rode into the protective walls of the Great Horn Works of Charles Town. Bill Cunningham stopped and dismounted to report to the sentry, his horse's legs wobbling. As he approached the sergeant of the guard, his horse collapsed and died.

For the first time, Bill showed concern when he went over to his horse. Kneeling, Bill placed his head and hands on his horse and wept. "Oh, Ringtail, I am so sorry. I did not intend to kill you; I know I was pushing you hard. Those damn rebels would have arrested me and turned you into a plow horse." Tears actually made tracks down Bill's dusty face.

CHAPTER 16

THIS IS THE END

Jacob and his band were getting supplies at Round-O plantation, where General Greene still had his headquarters. It was a cold January of 1782, and Jacob felt it in his bones. It had rained for several days, turning the roads into a sea of mud. He had been waiting for the roads to dry before returning to Marion's camp.

While at Round-O, Jacob and the band saw a welcoming sight as reinforcements arrived from up north. Three Continental Regiments from Maryland, Delaware and Pennsylvania, along with 400 head of beef cattle. With the surrender of Cornwallis, as Greene had expected, General Washington was sending reinforcements so they could finish their business in the south.

As they gathered supplies, Jacob felt odd that the City of Charles Town would be encircled and again under siege. General Greene's plan had been very effective, as the only British strongholds left were Wilmington in North Carolina, Charles Town and Savannah in Georgia. Jacob led the band and the wolves out when the carts were loaded.

They received strange looks from the new Continentals that had just arrived from Virginia. They eyed the rugged look of Jacob's men, the rough condition of their clothes, and four large wolves in winter fur trotting by. Finally, they nodded and whispered that Jacob and his men must have been one of these legendary partisan companies they had heard about up north.

Jacob led the band and the carts toward Wambaw Creek near the Santee River. As one of the telltale signs of the war was closing, he was concerned about the friction between Maham, Horry, and Marion. Unfortunately, they had no one to fight, so they ended up fighting one another.

Maham believed he was under an independent command and only answerable to General Greene. Maham would not take any orders from Horry and even barely took orders from Marion, who was not a Continental officer, only a militia general.

When Jacob arrived at the camp, he sent the carts to the quartermaster. Then, he sent the band to their campsite and went to find Horry. But, instead of Horry, Jacob found Colonel McDonald and reported in.

"Sir, we have returned with supplies from General Greene," Jacob reported, and McDonald nodded.

"Any news?" he asked.

"Yes sir, we have received roughly two thousand more Continentals that have marched from up north and they brought some 400 head of beef cattle with them," Jacob answered. "What is our situation here?"

"A mess," McDonald answered, "a bloody mess."

Jacob looked concerned and nodded.

"As we know, General Marion was elected to the South Carolina General Assembly and left orders that Colonel Horry would be in command of the brigade. Of course, Maham still won't follow Horry, but that isn't important as it seems Maham was elected and is also at the assembly."

"Where is Colonel Horry then?" Jacob asked.

"He went to visit his plantation, so now I am in command of what is left of our brigade. If our luck turns bad, now would be the time for the British to attack. We are all over the place, confused."

Jacob agreed, "I will see to my men; we will be ready to ride at a moment's notice." McDonald nodded his head in thanks.

The prediction came true a few nights later when scouts rode into camp around dinnertime. McDonald and some of the officers were eating when the scouts rode up. Major Benison said to McDonald, "Sir, a large British Army is heading this way!"

All of the officers looked up and started to laugh. "You must be joking," one of the officers stated, looking up from his bowel, "there isn't enough British around to form a force, let alone a raiding party!"

"I saw them, sir, there are at least several hundred of them, a mix of infantry and cavalry, and they are heading this way." Again, the officers laughed and scoffed at the report, not believing it. Major Benison, frustrated, stormed off and saw Jacob's band off to the side.

"Major Clarke, I need some help," Benison called out. Jacob, Jean and the others looked over as Benison approached. "Where is General Marion? We have a situation he needs to be aware of."

"He is at the assembly; what is happening?" Jacob asked.

"There is a large force of British heading this way, several hundred soldiers I personally saw, and those officers over there don't believe me. Can you ride with me and see for yourself? I know they will listen to you."

Hearing his voice's urgency, Jacob commanded his band to mount up. His men scrambled and mounted their horses, the wolves jumping to their feet and tails wagging. Benison ran over to his horse and his men joined up with Jacob. McDonald came over, "Major Clarke, where are you going?"

Jacob looked down at Colonel McDonald. "Sir, the Major here just reported on an approaching enemy force. I am going to ride out and determine the strength of this force. However, I recommend you prepare the men here just in case."

Jacob kicked his horse and the band followed Major Benison out of the camp and toward the approaching British. As they began to close on the location of Durant's Plantation, they could already hear the sound of musketry. Jacob and Benison rode around a bend and into the open field with a bridge in the distance. There, they could see the militia under Colonel Benton being engaged by the British.

From his position, Jacob could see they were facing a large British and Loyalist force, not a raiding party. As they began to deploy into a line of battle, Jacob could see the militia and cavalry under Colonel Benton falling back. Colonel Benton himself appeared wounded.

"Cover fire. Give them time to fall back!" Jacob ordered and the band dismounted, quickly brought their rifles up and opened fire. Benton's men were riding back across the bridge, with the Loyalists in close pursuit firing pistols at them. Amid this fight, there was a loud cracking noise as the bridge collapsed from all of the weight.

"Band, with me!" Jacob yelled as he began to run forward to provide what cover or help, he could for the men who just fell into the water. Balls began to whiz and snap past as Jacob and his band. They were under fire from the British and Loyalists on the opposite bank. Jacob took a kneeling position, raised his rifle and fired at a Loyalist across the way, toppling him from his horse.

The British fired at the men in the water as they tried to swim. A few sank beneath the water and drowned. Jacob shook his head at the unnecessary loss but continued to load his rifle, as the British were not stopping. They now had the taste of blood in their mouths, and they were giving no quarter.

"Band, fall back to the horses!" Jacob commanded, seeing they were outnumbered almost seven to one. A small group of Loyalists seemed to have been across the bridge before it collapsed, charged from their left. Jacob stopped when he heard the men approach and fired a snapped shot. A rider tumbled from his saddle.

The wolves sprinted as Jacob dropped to a knee to make himself a smaller target. However, the wolves snapped at the horses' legs, causing them to rear up. More of the band turned and faced the Loyalists, getting their shots off before they turned and rode away. Jacob resumed running, with the wolves catching up quickly.

Remounting, Jacob looked across to the far bank and saw a large number of British and Loyalists quickly moving along the bank and toward their camp. *"Damn, McDonald better listen now!"* Jacob thought as he kicked his horse into a gallop.

The band rode to the camp and at least McDonald did follow his advice and had the brigade ready to move. "Is it true, Major Clarke?" McDonald asked. "Is there a large force coming?"

Jacob nodded, "There are several hundred infantry, cavalry and even a cannon with them. We have no choice but to evacuate."

The brigade evacuated and moved to a new campsite at the Tydiman Plantation, between the Echaw and Wambaw Rivers. Word reached back to the brigade that the British were running rabid around the countryside, attacking at will. Jacob shook his head, though he had to admit he wasn't surprised.

With all of the string victories they were enjoying, they were lacking. The fact that Marion and Maham were elected to the State Assembly and left the camp, only to have Peter Horry leave to go home, showed that their focus had shifted from the war.

"Perhaps this is just a way fate warns us; it's not over until it's over. We still have enemies out there and we can't rest until the race is won," Jacob thought as he cleaned his rifle and shook his head again.

Frederick walked up and knelt. "Did you hear they got old Charles Pinckney?"

Jacob stopped cleaning his rifle and looked up to Frederick, "What did you say, they got Pinckney?"

With a sour look, Frederick sat down next to Jacob. "Aye, the same bastards that gave us such a pasting the other day over on the bridge, well they have been riding around and causing all sorts of Hell while we get our act together."

Frederick picked up a stick and poked the ground. "Aye, he had been visiting his home, like Horry and the others and the Loyalist cavalry caught him."

Jacob nodded; he knew Pinckney from his early days in the First Regiment. He was both surprised and glad that the Loyalists did not kill him.

Jacob went over to speak with Marion, who had come racing back from Jacksonboro from the State Assembly. While Peter Horry did return, Maham rode onto his plantation and left Captain Smith in charge of his cavalry.

As normal as it can get, there was Oscar with Marion, who must have been handed a cup of tea as Marion was sipping on it. When Marion heard Jacob's approach, he turned and looked up. "Ah, Jacob, what can I do for you?"

"You have heard about what happened with Pinckney, correct?" Jacob stated and Marion nodded.

"Aye, terrible that, but at least he wasn't murdered." Marion stopped and looked at Jacob in earnest. "You didn't come to see me over the news I already have; what is it? We have known each other for far too long to hang on formalities. What is on your mind, Jacob?"

"Sir, we just got struck by a sizable British and Loyalist force, with yourself, Colonel Horry and Major Maham away. When the news arrived, the British were closing and McDonald and the other officers failed to take the scout seriously. We nearly got caught flat-footed but still suffered just the same."

Marion was listening and knew that, in a simple but easy way, Jacob was chastising Marion for a tactical blunder. "What would you recommend, Jacob?" Marion asked.

"We must return to the old ways, keep moving to keep the British and the Loyalists off-balance. Make it harder for them to find us, then strike fast when we can on a field of our choosing. We may be coming to an end, but we are not there yet."

Marion nodded; even Oscar agreed. "As usual, you are correct, Jacob. However, perhaps a part of me wants this damn war to end and may not be focusing on what is happening around me."

***

Colonel Thompson was pleased with the current outcome. The near destruction of who he believed was the Swamp Fox himself, free reign to bring justice to those disloyal families across the countryside. Everything was coming up roses.

"Sir, this Swamp Fox may not have been there at the bridge," Captain Saunders of the Queen's Rangers stated, "We have learned that this Francis Marion, the so-called Swamp Fox, had been elected to this State Assembly and was away from his men."

Colonel Thompson turned and frowned at Captain Saunders. "You wouldn't be a little jealous and would be saying this out of spite, would you now, Captain Saunders? If I recall, this Swamp Fox has thrashed you and your Queen's Rangers a few times and even took your base of operations, Georgetown, no?"

There was some light chuckle around the assembled officers but Captain Saunders kept his composure. Then, finally, Colonel Thompson became serious, scratched his chin and then looked back at Saunders.

"That does make sense, though," Thompson commented. "What would you suggest if you were in my position?"

"A trap," Saunders answered. "Have a small detachment of our men lead some of the captured cattle in plain view, make it look like another foraging party. We know eyes and ears are working for him out here. Then, as we draw Marion and his rebels away from their camp, the mounted troops will circle around while a supporting detachment remains with the cattle. Then, as Marion fights the cattle, we strike his camp again."

Saunders finished, noticing the officers were not snickering anymore and were listening closely. Even Colonel Thompson was thinking hard about it.

"Your plan is sound; I like it. But, gentlemen, let's go bag that old Swamp Fox once and for all!"

In the morning, Thompson led all the mounted men out of their camp and began a circular route back toward the Wambaw area while Major Doyle of the Volunteers of Ireland was leading the false foraging party.

***

Jacob followed Marion and Captain Smith from Maham's dragoons as Marion was taking Jacob's advice and went out to locate any of the British or Loyalist forces still in the area before moving their camp again. Some of the men had returned to the base to pack up what they had for supplies.

It was a clear but cool February morning. The mist from the horses' noses mixed with the riders' breath. Even the wolves who padded along, their fur were thick to protect them from the cold, though it looked like it did not affect them. Jacob scanned the woods to either side of their column; Marion and Smith's horses were in front of his band. He could see movement in the woods before them only a short time later. Then, quickly pulling his telescope, he saw it was the Loyalist cavalry again.

"Damn, Loyalist riders to the front!" Jacob yelled out as Marion, who must have also seen their approach, had ordered Smith to charge the Loyalists before they could form a line of battle. Jacob motioned for the band to come on line, Samuel to his right and Jean to his left. Samuel cocked the hammer on his blunderbuss.

They watched Smith lead his cavalry in a charge and suddenly, he veered away to the right.

"What in the two blazes is he doing?" Samuel asked. Jacob shook his head in disgust and sighed heavily.

"They are running, Samuel," Jacob replied, "The bastards are turning tail."

Before Marion could order him, Jacob kicked his horse, and the band followed him as they raced after the retreating Smith as the Loyalists were charging after his now exposed rear. The fight was chaotic as horses ran in different directions and Jacob could hear splashing as men were jumping into the Santee.

The Loyalists and the British began to fire on Smith's dragoons in the water, as Jacob and his band rode up and took them under fire. The Loyalists and British spun around and began to return fire; Samuel's blunderbuss roared in defiance. Jacob jumped from his horse and stood next to a tree while Richard grabbed his reins.

Sighting at a Loyalist dragoon, Jacob fired and saw the man fall from his saddle. Then, as Jacob turned behind the tree to load, two balls whizzed by and smacked into the tree, spraying him in small splinters. Jacob quickly dropped to a knee as he finished priming his rifle, then bent around the tree to fire.

With the rifles barking once more and a British rider falling this time, Jacob could see that the enemy was starting to pull off from the shooting of Smith's men in the river. He watched them ride away before calling the band together and remounted. Leaving the field, they rode to where they found Marion trying to rally what few men were left. It was only a small group assembled that Marion led them back to their old camp.

It was a sorry site that Jacob found, as once more, the British and Loyalists had killed another twenty men and roughly another twelve were missing and presumed captured. Horry's and Maham's Dragoons had been decimated and they lost a good number of arms and some supplies. Marion was angry but did not yell though Jacob could see how red Marion's face was.

Oscar came over to Jacob. "Master Marion is rather upset at those horsemen," he stated, pointing toward Captain Smith, who had survived. "The English stole Marion's tent. I am not sure what he is angrier at; we lost the fight, or they took his tent."

"Oscar, to be honest, I think he is angrier at losing his tent than the arms or the loss," Jacob responded. "Though I don't think Captain Smith there has a career in cavalry much longer."

Marion moved their camp and what survivors they had across the Santee River. As Jacob thought, Captain Smith resigned. As for their dragoons, due to the losses, both dragoons were combined into one and placed under Maham. This, of course, angered Horry but Marion would appease his old friend by making him the commander of Georgetown. Colonel John Laurens, Jacob had not seen him since Charles Town, had been sent by General Greene to support Marion's brigade.

In early March, the British were still foraging around the countryside near Charles Town, and Jacob was sent to see if he could locate one of these parties and chase them off. He was sent by Marion to scout along the Ashley River, as there were many large plantations in the area. As with all siege warfare, he knew, you had to keep the enemy hungry and prevent his freedom of action and movement.

It was a warm day, the horses plodded along but the men did keep a watchful eye out. But, Jacob believed it was becoming difficult for his men to pay attention in some cases, as their minds thought the war was ending. Some, like Samuel, still thirst for action, while most thought of going home. This, Jacob knew, was a dangerous time.

As they were following the dirt road near the Ashley River, just below the Middleton's Plantation, through the Spanish moss and trees, Jacob spotted a small foraging party. They had gathered a few milk cows and a cart holding rice from a family arguing with a British soldier.

When the soldier slapped down the farmer, Jacob kicked his horse and led the band forward through the trees toward the foraging party. When they rode out into the clearing, they could see four soldiers; when they saw Jacob and his band, three started to run away. Jacob, Jean, and Frederick stopped their horses, brought their rifles up and fired nearly simultaneously. The three runners fell to the ground. The fourth raised his hands in surrender.

Jacob came over as the farmer picked himself up off the ground, wiping the dirt off. Two of the band covered the prisoner; Samuel led his group to secure the dead British soldiers. "Are you alright?" Jacob asked the farmer, who was in shock but nodded.

"Take your animals and rice and go home. We will see to these men," Jacob instructed. The dead British were tied over a horse. The prisoner had his hands bound and then placed in front of Samuel, who jammed a pistol in his ribs.

"Don't get any ideas," he warned in a whisper, jabbing the barrel into the prisoner, "understand?" The prisoner nodded quickly. Samuel could see this was a young recruit who was already shaking and would cause no problems.

Once the dead were secured, Jacob led them back to their camp, where the prisoner was transferred, and the dead taken to a burial area. Jacob reported on what they had found along the Ashley near Middleton's. Marion accepted the report, "Not much movement out there, eh Jacob?" Marion asked.

"No sir," Jacob replied with a nod, "I think we finally have them bottled up in Charles Town. It seems the boot is back on our foot this time."

Marion smiled and nodded in agreement. "Aye, Jacob, I believe you are right."

As General Greene's Army continued to surround the city of Charles Town, it was a ragged-looking army. As with their militia and partisan brigade before Eutaw Springs, now the Continentals were wearing rags, low on food and morale was being affected. There were even grumblings about mutinies within the ranks. A small portion of the army was deserting and going to the British.

Jacob kept a firm hand on his band, just as Marion kept a strong hand on the brigade. They knew they had to be patient and wait out the British. However, it bothered Jacob, learning that not only were there deserters but some had even plotted to have General Greene captured and turned over to the British. This infuriated Jacob, who kept vigilant eyes and ears open when dealing with the Southern Army.

As the Spring progressed, some good news arrived on how General "Mad" Anthony Wayne from up north was now going after Savannah. Like Greene, Wayne was driving in all of the British outposts. While not strong enough to take the city, he kept the pressure on the British, trying to entice them to desert. But, unfortunately, Jacob learned that the British had called on the Cherokee and they attacked one of Wayne's camps at the end of May; but proved to be a Cherokee failure, losing over twenty warriors.

While Jacob admitted he, too, was beginning to think of home, his wife and finally seeing his children grow up in peace, he also knew the war was not over, and the fighting could start again at any moment. Furthermore, not all of the Loyalists ran and hid in Charles Town; one of those was Major Micaiah Gainey. Jacob had learned that Gainey was commanding all of the Loyalists in the area of the Pee Dee River.

Gainey had been quiet for the past year. Had been captured and agreed to a truce near Georgetown, but that truce was about to expire. Jacob was concerned because he was a troublemaker for Marion, having threatened to see Marion captured or killed personally. His fear was confirmed when reports came into the camp of Loyalists gathering around the Pee Dee region.

Their eyes and ears network were reporting that someone calling themselves a "Scotsman from Charles Town" had been going around and telling people the British had a much larger force than the rebels and the Loyalists and Highlanders should rise and join. While they did eventually find this person and hang them, the Loyalists were still gathering. This would place an enemy force behind Greene.

Marion received a message from Governor Rutledge and called his commanders, including Jacob, to him. When everyone arrived, Marion began. "Gentlemen, peace will have to wait a little while longer. The governor has learned our old nemesis Gainey is back and there is a gathering of Highlanders and Loyalists. Both Governor Rutledge and the Governor of North Carolina want this threat removed. Therefore, we will ride out and see to this problem. Gather what supplies you can and have your men ready to ride in the morning."

Jacob and the band were ready, and the wolves sat with their tails wagging, looking forward to some action. Once the entire brigade was formed that had horses, Marion, with Oscar at his side, led them out. Jacob was amazed by everything Oscar did for Marion, following him into action unarmed, that he was never wounded or even received a scratch.

"What a lucky man," Jacob thought, *"Marion is lucky to have a friend like that."*

As they approached the Pee Dee region, a messenger came galloping up to Marion and gave a report. Quickly a call of "Officers to the front!" was passed. Jacob trotted up along with the other commanders and sat on their horses around Marion.

"Seems one of the other columns have found Gainey and are not big enough to tackle him but can keep him in place." Then Marion looked up and smiled, "We have him!"

Returning to the band, Jacob told Samuel, Jean, and Frederick the news, and soon they were at the trot following Marion as the messenger led them to where Gainey was pinned down. They only rode for about thirty minutes when they came upon rifle and musket fire. Marion waved one column to the left and Jacob's band to the right. The column that had Gainey pinned remained in the middle; now Marion created a "U" around Gainey.

Jacob dismounted, handing his reins to the designated holder, Patrick, for this round. "Good hunting," Patrick said with a wink; Jacob smiled and nodded. The band formed a line with Jacob in the center and they advanced through the trees until they could see Gainey's men near the Ashley River.

"We have time; pick your targets!" Jacob yelled and then brought his rifle up and, with a slow and methodic pace, aimed and fired at a distant Loyalist. The ball hit him square in the chest, and he fell into the river with a splash. Several barks of rifles came from the band, all having a telling effect.

Soon, all Loyalists remained hidden, not presenting themselves as targets. The band decided to have fun and kept the Loyalist pinned by firing close enough to have wood chips and splinters hit them. Soon enough, a white flag appeared on a ramrod.

"We want to talk; stop shooting!" the Loyalist yelled. Jacob called out, "Cease fire, load and cover in case this is another one of their typical tricks." The band reloaded and then watched the open area to see what would happen next.

As they watched, they saw Marion, with Oscar and a few selected men, approach the Loyalists who held the white flag. While they could see a conversation, they were just far enough away not to hear what words were exchanged. Whatever was said, the Loyalist nodded, turned and walked away. Marion did the same.

Word was sent down the line to reform and once everyone was remounted, he joined with Marion. The column rode out and Marion led them to Burch's Mill, where he had the brigade dismount. Jacob joined the other officers with Marion as the men dispersed to set up a perimeter around the mill. When Jacob approached, he could hear arguing.

"There is no way Gainey will respect or follow you," Captain Birch commented, followed by, "Gainey is nothing but a thieving, murdering bastard who deserves nothing but the end of a rope!" Jacob had to agree with the sentiment; a good number of the officers wanted nothing more than to see Gainey pay for his traitorous joining the British and vowing to capture Marion.

Marion nodded and listened to his officers, but Jacob saw how Marion had set his face; he had made a decision. "Gentlemen, if I may," Marion started, not raising his voice but keeping a strong, steady tone. "If we are to be united once all of this fighting is done, we will have to forgive our enemy, no matter how hard it will be."

The men grumbled but knew Marion was correct. Gainey's party arrived about midday and he went to speak with Marion while the officers, on the other hand, stood and stared daggers at one another.

"Forgiving our enemy may be harder than what Marion thought," Jacob thought, seeing how the sides were facing one another. But unfortunately, the situation worsened as Marion and Gainey were negotiating; a fight eventually broke out between the Loyalist officers and Marion. Jacob tried to stay out of it, but then men began to hoot and holler, and it was turning into a spectacle.

At that point, Jacob saw it was escalating and needed to be stopped. Squaring his shoulders, Jacob drew his tomahawk. Jacob strode into the fight and knocked both officers to the ground with the backside of the axe, opposite one another. Both men fell back, shaking their heads and looked up at Jacob, whose face was a dark thunderhead.

"Enough!" Jacob roared, his eyes flashing as lightning, "The next one I find fighting, I will knock all of their teeth out so they can't talk."

Jacob stood there, staring at everyone, his tomahawk held tightly in his right hand. "Am I understood?" He stared at Marion's men, and they nodded, then he stared at the Loyalists.

"You can't order us around," the Loyalist man stated from the ground. As he began to stand up, Jacob knocked his legs out from under him, once more knocking him to the ground. Finally, Jacob knelt on the man's chest, pinning him to the ground.

"Try me," Jacob whispered. At that moment, all four wolves walked up behind Jacob and stared down at the Loyalist, low growls coming from their throats. The Loyalists began to whisper about "the wolf, he is the wolf," and they began to nod. Jacob stood up, the wolves moving up and taking position next to him, staring at the Loyalists.

Later that afternoon, Marion and Gainey came out, and Gainey led his Loyalists away. Jacob and the other officers approached Marion to get the outcome of the meeting.

"Gentlemen, Gainey is through," Marion answered. "His men will lay down their arms in Bowling Green; they will try to return all plundered property and attempt to become good, peaceable citizens who submit to the law and sign an allegiance to South Carolina."

The officers nodded and then Jacob asked, "What about Gainey himself?"

"Gainey told me he had to relinquish his commission to Colonel Balfour, who had given him his commission in the first place. Once he resigns, he is to return and perhaps even join us," Marion answered.

"Gainey join us?" Jacob replied with a concerned look, "Sir, that man can't be trusted. He changes his allegiance based on who is winning. Who is to say he won't try to stab you in the back?"

Marion shrugged, "We have to give him a chance to change his ways. The treaty does not protect Bloody Bill and Samuel Andrews. They will be shown no mercy."

***

With a few of his men, Fanning rode in the center of the column of the First Continental Dragoons, led by Colonel Baylor. He had given Baylor a false story that they were members of Marion's command scouting the area near Charles Town. After they rode through the rebel lines with Baylor, Fanning left the dragoons as if they were continuing with their scout.

Now that he was through the lines, Fanning and his small party rode to Charles Town and took stock of the situation. The city was full of refugees escaping the wrathful rebels as they pushed all Crown and Loyalists south. Accepting the situation, Fanning decided to speak with this Marion about bringing his wife Sarah down from North Carolina.

Under a flag of truce, Fanning and a few of his men approached where Marion was operating. Jacob and his band rode out to confront Fanning as he was following a road along the river. Jacob spread his men out into a line, stopping Fanning from approaching further.

"State your business!" Jacob ordered as his men rested their rifles and muskets on their pommels, Samuel staring at the Loyalist with his blunderbuss.

"I need to speak to Marion concerning a family matter," Fanning replied.

"Whose family?" Jacob returned and Fanning answered with, "Mine. I want to bring my wife from North Carolina to join the refugees in Charles Town."

Jacob nodded and then turned to Jean. "Go get Marion; we'll keep an eye on our Loyalist friends here."

Jean nodded, then, with his small section, rode back to get Marion while Jacob and the rest of the band watched the Loyalists. Fanning looked at Jacob, who returned the look.

"You have a name?" Fanning asked, trying to make small talk. Then he looked down and saw the four wolves sitting on their haunches next to him. "You are the wolf, aren't you?"

Jacob shrugged, "I have been called many things and Spirit of the Wolf was my Mohawk name. And you?"

"Fanning, Colonel David Fanning."

Jacob nodded, "I have heard of you but up in North Carolina."

The two groups remained watching each other, a tense situation between two partisan officers and groups. No love was lost between the two, but Jacob wanted to ensure no blood was spilled, especially when there was a flag of truce. The Loyalists would use it against them.

When Marion arrived, Jacob blew out a quiet sigh of relief. Jean rejoined the band as Marion rode up to face Fanning, who bowed at the waist on his horse.

"What can I do for you? Marion asked and then looked to Jacob, who provided, "Colonel Fanning, sir."

Marion nodded, then looked at Fanning, "What can I do for you, Colonel Fanning?"

"General Marion, I humbly ask permission and safe passage for my wife from North Carolina to Charles Town to join the refugees there."

Marion did not see any issue, but his officers did. "This is like Gainey; we can't have Fanning in Charles Town. He is a murderer and a brigand just as bad as Gainey. You don't want any relations of his to be safe behind the walls of Charles Town. Then he'll be riding around and fighting us, which we don't need as we have just about cleared out any Loyalists."

Marion listened to the officers while he understood; he did not see the young wife of Fanning to be of any threat. However, to be fair to his men, when Fanning and his wife returned, Marion only allowed the wife and Fanning to pass, but none of their baggage or slaves. This infuriated Fanning, who demanded why Marion would not let any of his property through.

"You asked for safe passage for your wife, which I did," Marion retorted, "You did not ask about your ill-gotten booty. They are now confiscated, be satisfied. We do not arrest you for what you did here in South Carolina. However, I recall your crimes, be happy with your wife and move on."

Marion stared hard at Fanning, who starred back, before turning away and leading his wife to Charles Town. As Marion turned and saw Jacob was watching, he winked and then trotted off.

"Why that wily old fox," Jacob commented, and Jean answered, "He knew all along. He was playing this Fanning, no?"

Jacob nodded, "He sure did, Jean, he sure did."

A few days later, Jacob learned that General Greene had sent a warning that Fanning was determined to see Marion, dead or alive, so to be careful. Although Jacob snorted, *"I would like to see him try."*

Jacob and his band continued to ride patrols around Charles Town and stopped by his place at Goose Creek when able. In addition, the band will go out with a troop of horses from Horry's Dragoons from time to time to stay busy. During the summer, Jacob and his band rode a few scouts with Captain Caper's troop. Jacob, like Caper, seemed very energetic and one of those people who found goodness in everything. Jacob doubted he ever had a bad day in his life and his men always seemed to be in a good mood.

They were riding down in southeastern Berkley County when they came upon Loyalist dragoons, the Independent Troop of Black Dragoons, led by free black men. Three farmers with their hands behind their backs were sitting on the ground before them. As the Loyalist dragoons turned to face them, Jacob yelled, "Caper, take the dragoons; we'll get the prisoners!"

With a yell, Capers led his dragoons in a charge as they drew their pistols and fired at the Loyalists. The Loyalists quickly turned their horses and began riding away as Capers galloped after them and Jacob's men rode up to where the prisoners were. As a few of his men kept a watch out for the Loyalists in case they tried to circle back, Jacob and the others released the prisoners.

The three were local farmers, who nodded and said their thanks. "Those bastards called us disloyal, and rebels and we were to be drug off to be tried. While I appreciate being saved, I know that I am on no one's side but my family's."

Jacob nodded, "I understand; glad we could stop them from carting you off. I know you wouldn't get a fair trial."

The released farmers nodded their heads. "Aye, you be right," another farmer stated, rubbing his wrists from where he had been cuffed. "I want to thank you and I am sure my wife and children would want to thank you."

Jacob waved it off. "Not necessary; go home to your families. That is thanks enough."

The men moved off and Jacob remounted his horse, followed by the band. Capers returned with still a pleasant look on his face. "That was invigorating! Too bad those rascals got away."

Jacob nodded but saw at least two of Caper's dragoons were wounded. "Do your men need help?"

Caper looked over his shoulder at his wounded and shook his head. "Just some minor flesh wounds. I asked the lads if they needed help and they told me when we got back to camp, the surgeon would see to their injuries."

Shrugging, Jacob nodded in deferment and followed Capers as he led their column back to the camp, where his two men went to see the surgeon. The band headed to their camp and went through their ritual of seeing to their horses, then their gear, followed by themselves.

As Jacob was leaning back against his saddle, smoking his pipe, Samuel sat next to him with his pipe, followed by Jean, Frederick and the boys. The wolves were already curled up, but their eyes were watching over their tails.

Samuel sat with a groan, then commented, "I don't recall during the last war, we were this less active and sitting around."

Jacob nodded; they had stayed busy right up to the very end of the French and Indian War. Even when Rogers began to send some of the Ranger Companies home, he and Samuel had been sent to South Carolina and became immersed in the Cherokee War. He was correct; this is the longest time they have been inactive.

"Perhaps there are no more British or Loyalists to fight," Jacob responded around his pipe, "Even the Cherokee have finally been stopped."

"Then, is it over?" Richard asked, "Is the war finally over? We won?" There was excitement in his voice, and he could see it in the eyes of his sons and nephews. Even Frederick and Jean chuckled but said nothing.

"No, lads, I don't think so," Jacob answered. "That's up to those government ministers and gentlemen to talk and negotiate. We are simple fighting men, waiting for the next orders."

Jacob had to admit he had the same thoughts. Each passing day was less contact with British or Loyalist units out foraging, scouting or raiding. No word on Bloody Bill or any of the other brigands and cutthroats. Perhaps peace was coming; they could not see it yet through the fog of war. Then, finally, they received a message that the British and Loyalists had evacuated Savannah, and it was back in their control.

Some of the fog could be attributed to the summer humidity as, once again, the deep summer arrived with August. As with the previous summers, it was hot and sticky; Jacob volunteered the band to go out on as many scouts or foraging parties as possible. Most of the time, they went fishing along the river, sitting in the cool shade, yet he always ensured he had guards watching. It did feel like the war was over, but no one told them.

A few days later, Jacob and his band had escorted Marion, who paid a visit to Horry in Georgetown. Marion inspected the rebuilt defenses and saw many of the town residents had returned and it seemed life was returning to a sense of normalcy. Then, meeting his approval and spending some time with Peter, Marion returned to his base at the former Loyalists house of John Colleton on the south side of the Wadboo River.

When they trotted into the front of the house, a messenger came and went straight to Marion.

"Sir, Loyalists have crossed the Cooper, including a troop of black cavalry and South Carolina Royalists. They appear to be heading for Biggin's Bridge and Strawberry Ferry."

Marion nodded at the news and began looking around. Then he asked the messenger, "Who is in camp right now?"

The messenger replied, "Well sir, there is yourself, Major Clarke there," he said, pointed at Jacob, then with reluctance, "Some of the Williamsburg District men under Witherspoon, and Gainey with his men."

Jacob had heard Gainey had done what he had promised so far and after giving up his Loyalist commission had joined Marion's brigade. It had been one of Jacob's self-appointed duties to keep an eye on Gainey in case he tried to get Marion.

"Go get Witherspoon and Gainey; bring them here," Marion instructed. Jacob trotted up and joined Marion.

"Do you trust Gainey?" Jacob asked and Marion sighed. "I know the men's feelings, Jacob," Marion answered quietly. "I want to try and forgive and reform our split country. But there, sometimes you and the men are correct."

Marion gave Jacob a very level stare. "Sometimes you cannot forget or forgive, which is my burden."

Captain Witherspoon and the newly appointed Major Gainey arrived at Marion's summons. "Gentlemen, it seems the fight goes on. Loyalists are across the Cooper and heading for Biggins and Strawberry Ferry. We will ride to Fair Lawn Plantation and give a warm welcome."

They nodded and went to gather their men. When they were out of earshot, Marion turned back to Jacob.

"I have grave concerns Jacob, about the composition of the brigade."

Jacob could see the concern in Marion's eyes. "Sir?"

"We don't have many veterans left. Your band is all I have that I can rely on. Most of these men are newly made Whigs, having seen they were on the losing side and switched to us. We are so desperate for men that it was allowed by the governor. But, as you have always advised me, can they be trusted?"

Jacob nodded; he understood where Marion was coming from. They were getting ready to go into action with a brigade of mostly former Loyalists, a former Loyalist officer and a Second South Carolina traitor.

"Jacob, I want you and your band to be with the infantry when I emplace them. I know you will keep them straight." Again, Jacob nodded in understanding.

When Witherspoon and Gainey arrived, Marion led them out and headed toward the Fair Lawn Plantation. The ride was only about thirty minutes when the plantation, a large brick house with an avenue of cedars, led up to it. Marion halted the element at the entrance of the plantation.

"Captain Witherspoon, lead your section north and watch the road, lay an ambush to draw the Loyalists to us here. The rest of the brigade will be waiting in ambush for their warm welcome," Marion instructed, and Captain Witherspoon led his section off. Then Marion began deploying the rest of the men around the plantation. He placed Jacob in the cedars with some of the men; Gainey and the others were spread out amongst the slave cabins.

Jacob and his men had dismounted, three ready to fire while one held the reins of their horses. Jacob made sure the "new

Whigs" were between his veterans, checking his left and right. He placed Samuel with his blunderbuss on their left to cover the road, while Jean took the right while he remained in the center.

Now for the waiting and as long as he had been doing this, the waiting was always the worse. It was a hot day, the cicadas chirping, a slight breeze blowing the sweet cedar scent of the trees. While Jacob's shirt had a few holes in it, the sweat still caused it to cling to him. Using an old piece of shirt, he wiped his face.

"Ka-pow; ka-pow!"

In the distance, the sound of musketry was heard. Jacob's heart began to thump, excitement rising as he knew the battle was about to be joined. "Steady lads, steady," Jacob instructed, holding his hand out. "Wait until I give the order to fire." Jacob brought his rifle up to the ready position, cocking his rifle. The rest of the band did likewise.

The sound of galloping was soon heard and Captain Witherspoon, with his men, came racing by and galloped through the ambush line, drawing the Loyalists behind them. However, Witherspoon did not follow his men but turned and brought his carbine up.

Soon, the sound of the Loyalist cavalry was heard, and then, coming up the avenue, were the Black Dragoons that Jacob had seen before and some other Loyalist dragoons. Witherspoon calmly brought his carbine up and aimed at the charging Loyalists. Nodding, Jacob gave the command, "Make Ready! Take Aim!"

A lone Loyalist dragoon, saber raised and with a fierce yell, charged at Witherspoon, who calmly brought his carbine up and fired. Having loaded it with buckshot, the enemy dragoon was blasted out of his saddle. Witherspoon turned his horse and dashed into the trees.

Jacob waited until the rest of the enraged dragoons closed to within thirty yards before giving the command to fire. The new Whigs shouted and fired, when his band aimed and fired in a thunderous crash of musketry. Numerous Loyalists tumbled from their saddles, the survivors pulling up their reins and retreating a short distance.

"Sir, the ammunition horse!"

Jacob turned to see their wagon of extra ammunition was being quickly pulled away by a horse that was not used to the sound of battle. Marion dispatched five men to go chase down the fleeing horse and wagon, while Jacob returned to reloading and watching their line for the next move by the Loyalists.

"Pick your shot carefully; don't waste them, "Jacob ordered, knowing they would have to be careful without the extra ammunition. The Loyalists, like a predator, kept circling and looking for a way in for the kill. They would get hit from multiple sides every time they tried, either the cedars or the slave quarters. The fight continued for an hour before the word arrived; they were just about out of cartridges.

Marion had a strong position, but without the cartridges, it will become useless. The five men he had sent to go after the fleeing wagon returned empty-handed after explaining they had run into the black dragoons who took the wagon. Now the Loyalists had more ammunition than Marion did.

Letting out a frustrated sigh, Marion gave the order. "Pass the word, fall back by section's and to cover one another. Then, head to the Santee, where we will regroup."

Marion, Oscar and his section turned and rode off. Jacob and his band remained concealed as they had more balls than the regular men. Jacob looked down at the other infantry, "Go head back to the Santee; we'll stay here and keep them off you."

The men nodded while Jacob's band carefully, slowly and methodically loaded, aimed, and fired. The accurate fire the band was providing was keeping the Loyalists back; the number of dead and wounded Loyalists with their horses were strewn across the plantation. Once Jacob saw Gainey and his men pull off, he ordered the band to mount up and depart. After determining none, he watched to see if there was any pursuit and rode on to the Santee.

The men settled back at the camp, repaired their equipment and cared for their horses. Oscar came over as Jacob mended his poor, torn shirt, which surprised him. Jacob was finishing tying off a knot in his sewing.

"Master Clarke, Master Marion needs to speak with you, sir," Oscar asked. When Jacob looked up, he could see the concern in Oscar's eyes, which meant something was amiss with Marion. Nodding, Jacob stood and followed Oscar.

"What is on your mind, Oscar?" Jacob asked as they headed over to where Marion camped.

"I think he is done with fighting, sir," Oscar said in a whisper, "I think he has had enough."

Jacob could understand Oscar's concern and when they arrived, Marion sat in a chair under a large tree in the shade. When he saw Oscar had brought Jacob, he shook his head.

"Going to go get some tea, eh?" Marion reproached and Oscar shook his head.

"I am off to see to your tea now, Master Marion; I thought it might be best you speak with Master Clarke here, sir. It may help you feel better."

Oscar gave a slight bow before turning and heading to the house kitchen to prepare Marion's tea. Seeing another chair that happened to be there, Jacob sat down and looked at his old friend.

"How are you, sir?" Jacob asked. Marion rubbed his face with both hands, leaving it red for a quick moment.

"Tired Jacob, very tired and very old," was his answer. Then he scoffed and looked back at Jacob.

"Odd that I would say that to a man like you, who has been fighting since you were sixteen?"

Jacob snickered and smiled but shook his head. "Longer, sir; I was younger when I saw action with the Mohawks. That was how I earned my name Spirit of the Wolf. But I, too, am exhausted and feel very old."

Marion nodded and the two laughed before becoming serious again.

"We were asked to go out after more foraging parties coming out of Charles Town to keep the British and their Loyalists contained."

Jacob nodded, waiting to see what Marion would say next as he could see he was having a difficult time before he looked Jacob in the eye.

"I told them we could not do it." Jacob gave Marion a questioning look but also began to see Marion's point of view from their discussion just before the action at near the Fair Lawn Plantation. Oscar arrived with Marion's tea, who accepted it and sipped.

"Jacob, we are done. We are not the old Second Regiment; we are not even the brigade we began with after Charles Town fell. My ranks are filled with veterans and civilians who have shed enough blood already. Even a few who have seen more than enough since 1775."

Marion paused to take another sip of his tea and Jacob waited to see what he would say next. Jacob knew this must be difficult, as he knew Marion had always been a regular officer, even when he was leading the militia. A professional officer at all times and this must weigh heavily upon his tired shoulders.

"I did tell General Greene that if ordered to attack the enemy, then I would follow that order to the best of my ability and the brigade. However, with my consent, I told General Greene that no other life would be lost. Therefore, though we know that the British are preparing to evacuate Savannah, so far from being molested by me, I shall rather protect them and speed them on their way."

Now Jacob understood why Oscar was concerned; Marion had enough of the bloodshed and only wanted the war to end. However, he was a realist and knew the British would not fight anymore; it was time to be patient and wait for them to leave our shores. The war had, in fact, ended.

"Do we have orders, sir?" Jacob asked. "Is the militia to be sent home?"

Marion nodded his head, "While General Greene has not directed me to disband completely, I am using my authority to release the militia under my command. I will leave it up to the commanders, as I know Maham is a Continental officer and will remain. Horry Dragoons are also on the Continental rolls."

Jacob nodded and stood up, "Then, with your permission, sir, I would like to speak to my men about whether we go home or see it to the end."

Marion nodded and raised his teacup to Jacob in salute.

Jacob was deep in thought when he arrived at his camp. Jean, Samuel and the boys with the wolves were still there. "Band, gather on me!" Jacob called out and waited for the men to join them in a circle.

Once all were present, Jacob looked at the faces of his band, twenty hardened faces even for his sons and nephews. They had seen so much, lost friends and earned their release to go home.

"Men, Marion just informed me he is going to use his power as a general of the militia to release the militia companies and go home. Only Maham and Horry's are still considered on the Continental rolls and will continue to serve."

"What are you getting at Jacob?" Frederick asked.

Letting out a sigh before looking at his men. "I have never been prouder to have led and known men like you. If anyone deserves to go home, it is you. Nevertheless, in my mind, we are not done yet and I hate to leave things unfinished. I may stay behind and work with Marion."

The men began to speak amongst themselves before Richard spoke up. "Papa, I mean Major Clarke, sir, are you not, along with Uncle Samuel and Jean, still Continental officers?"

Jacob chuckled, thinking he knew where this was leading. "Yes, Richard, I am still a Continental officer as I did not surrender or relinquish my commission. Neither did Jean, while Samuel did not of his free will surrender."

Catching on, Frederick spoke up next. "So, what you are saying, we have a basic company of mounted infantry under the command of a Continental captain, a Continental lieutenant, and a sergeant major. Well, does not that then make us an independent Continental command? Did you not say you were in command of the Colonel's Company?"

Jacob could feel a catch in his throat for the first time in his life, seeing where this line of questioning was going. He nodded that he was.

"Well then," Frederick stated, "Then I volunteer to join the Colonel's Company of Independent Continentals!"

Shaking his head, careful not to show the emotion he was trying to control, Jacob, nodded as the band stepped up to volunteer.

"I will let Marion know," Jacob stated as he returned to Marion's camp. There was excitement in the camp, which surprised Jacob, who had thought they would go home. However, when he arrived at Marion's camp, he sat in his chair, sipping his tea, while Oscar sat in the other chair.

"I take it you have some words for me?" Marion asked with a twinkle in his eyes, "Your men want to stay, correct?"

Jacob smiled and stood at attention before Marion. "Sir, Major Jacob Clarke of the South Carolina Militia would like to relinquish his commission."

Marion nodded, "Why is that may I ask?"

"Sir, as a Continental officer who never surrendered or relinquished his commission, Captain Jacob Clarke of the Colonel's Company, Second Regiment of the South Carolina Continentals, must humbly ask permission to depart your command and return to the senior ranking Continental officer, General Greene."

Marion raised his eyebrow, still lightly chuckling as he sipped his tea before continuing. "Well then, Captain Clarke, where will you recruit your officers and men to fill your company?"

Playing the game, Jacob continued. "Sir, my company is formed. I have Lieutenant Jean Langy and Sergeant-Major Samuel Penny, Sergeant Frederick Nasonne and seventeen fresh volunteers I just recruited from a former militia group that was disbanded."

Marion nodded, placed his teacup down, stood and approached Jacob. "I would have been concerned and shocked had you not done this. I have known you long enough that you always keep fighting until the fighting is done. But what about your family?"

"My wife would be disappointed in me if I didn't keep fighting," Jacob answered. Marion agreed and then shook Jacob's hand.

"It's been an honor and a pleasure to know you, Jacob," Marion said. "Hopefully, you won't see any action and can truly be assured the war is over."

The following morning, Jacob, with the wolves trotting alongside, led the band out of Marion's camp for the last time and headed up to where General Greene had his headquarters. When the sentries stopped Jacob, he reported he was Captain Clarke of the Colonel's Independent Company and was here to report to General Greene.

Trotting up to where the command marquee for General Green was placed, Jacob had the band dismount close by and then Samuel went with a few men to the quartermaster to see what they could get. Outside of the marquee was an orderly and two sentries. Jacob approached and stood before the orderly.

When he looked up, he gave a start, as Jacob did not look like an appropriately dressed soldier or officer. While he still wore his scuffed and well-worn black leather helmet with its crescent, his clothes were threadbare and torn. "Ah, yes, may I help you?"

"Captain Clarke to report to General Greene," Jacob stated. The orderly gave him a rough look based on his outward appearance.

"Jacob, Jacob Clarke, is that you?" a voice boomed from inside the marquee. General Greene came outside, the sentries stood to attention and even the orderly stood up. Greene came over and shook Jacob's hand.

"So, the old Grey Wolf has come to call, eh? Greene stated, "Has Marion changed his mind?"

Jacob shook his head. "No sir, I am here as a Continental officer to report to the army commander. I have a new Continental independent company ready to serve, formerly the Colonel's Company from the Second Regiment."

Greene looked over Jacob's shoulder and saw the band in their rough clothing and mounts.

"Well then, I welcome your independent command. Your company will work for me. You will be my independent company that I will use to gather information and help finish off the war. I will see you and your men fully clothed and equipped. Without you and Marion and the rest of the partisans, I would not have been so successful. I owe you and your men that."

Jacob led the band to an open area and set up their camp and the men settled in. General Greene sent the quartermaster a few new clothes and uniform cartloads. While not the deep blue and red of their South Carolina uniforms, they were known as "lottery coats" of different colors of blue and red facings. New small clothes were issued and the band's old clothes were simply burned.

As they had access to armorers, Samuel had the band take their muskets and rifles over to have them looked at and repaired. Some were in such bad shape they were taken and the men received brand-new Charleville muskets. The band stood around, admiring themselves in their new uniforms, a sense of pride evident on their faces.

"Major Clarke, your uniform is ready?" a quartermaster stated. Jacob turned and looked at the man holding a new coat for him with a major's epaulet on it.

"I am Captain Clarke; you are mistaken," Jacob replied, and the quartermaster shook his head.

"Ah, no, sir. According to General Greene's specific instructions, you are a major and should be uniformed." The soldier stood there and handed Jacob the uniform, a new sash and a gorget. He even had a new tricorn, but Jacob shook his head.

"Thanks, but no," Jacob explained, "My good old helmet will still work for me." The quartermaster shrugged and then returned to his duties. Once Jacob had settled on his new uniform, he went to see General Greene. When he approached the marquee, the orderly looked up. "The general is expecting you," he stated.

Tucking his helmet in the crook of his arm, Jacob entered the command marquee, where General Greene was waiting. "I was wondering when you would show up," Greene stated. "I know you were a captain on the Continental rolls, but you were a major under Marion and I like him, believe you should continue as a major."

Greene walked over to a field desk, picked up a document, and handed it to Jacob. "Your commission as a major in the Continental Army and appointment to my personal escort."

Jacob accepted his appointment. "What are your orders, sir?"

"We are having some problems with British foraging parties near Edisto Island. While we control the interior, the British use longboats and are raiding from the ocean and rivers. The local militia will not turn out to stop them. I am attaching you to Colonel Lacey's command and see to this problem."

Nodding his head, "Yes sir, we will see to it immediately." Greene nodded and then Jacob left the marquee and went to find Colonel Lacy to inform him he was attached to his expedition to Edisto Island.

"Oh, most excellent," Colonel Lacey beamed when he found out Jacob and the band were attached. "I have heard so much of you and your band of fighters. Some say some of the best in South Carolina and the best marksmen that can ride a horse!"

The band prepared their equipment and on the following day, Jacob, with his band, joined with Colonel Lacey and headed down to Edisto Island. Colonel Lacey was mounted while his men marched and Jacob rode next to him while the band served as an advance guard and flank guard.

"I heard the damn militia won't turn out as they think the war is over and there is no need to get killed if we are simply waiting for the British to leave like Savannah," Lacey commented.

"Yes sir, I have heard the same from other groups," Jacob replied, recalling the same sentiment from Marion.

Lacey leaned over his saddle closer to Jacob, "Some say it's over politics too. Their Colonel Harden had not been promoted to general and they refused to serve under General Barnwell. Bah, politics and we are so close to finishing this war."

When they arrived at Edisto Island, he placed Jacob and his band in a supporting position on the high ground lined with bushes.

"I will take my men and look for any raiding parties; if we find them, we'll lead them back here, and you, with your excellent marksmen, are to take care of them."

Sounding like a decent plan, Jacob nodded and started to deploy the band into a line, with their horses tied to branches a few yards behind them. They settled into the waiting, Jacob watching his men. The weather was cooling, as August had moved into September. As they were near the river, a cool breeze moved the bushes.

Only an hour later, the word was passed down the line as to the sighting of smoke columns. Jacob went to the far right of the line and, using his telescope, looked at the smoke in the distance. Two plumes of smoke were rising over the trees.

"Well now, it seems Colonel Lacey bagged himself some boats," Jacob commented, then returned to the center of the line. "Be ready; expect Colonel Lacey and his men leading the British to us."

The band brought their rifles and muskets up to the ready position, watching the approach to their hidden line.

"There they are!" Samuel called out and Jacob looked to see where he was pointing. There was Colonel Lacey and his men running as fast as they could toward Jacob's ambush position. Jacob returned to the center and commanded, "Make ready!" All the hammers were pulled back, with clicks being heard along the line.

A few minutes later, the British landing party appeared in pursuit of Colonel Lacey and his men; a few British were firing on the run. Jacob waited until the distance closed with the landing party.

"Take aim!" Jacob commanded and the band brought their rifles and muskets up to their shoulders, aiming at the approaching British. Then, waiting a few more seconds to make the shots count and for Colonel Lacey with his men clearing out of the way, Jacob gave the command, "Fire!"

The ambush line erupted in a torrent of fire and smoke. A few of the landing party spun and collapsed on the area in front of the bushes. Not knowing what had happened, in shock, the landing party froze in place. Then, seeing an opportunity, Jacob commanded, "Load!"

The landing party started to shoot in different directions, their balls flying by harmlessly. Finally, they pulled themselves into a small circle only thirty yards away. Shaking his head, Jacob was about to give them a lesson in battlefield tactics. He looked over at Samuel, who must have read Jacob's thoughts and had traded out his rifle for his small cannon of a blunderbuss.

Seeing the men were loaded once more, Jacob commanded, "Make ready!" The band brought their weapons up and cocked their hammers back.

"Take aim!"

The rifles, muskets and Samuel blunderbuss all were leveled and aimed at the mass of the British landing party before them.

"Fire!"

With a more thunderous roar with the blunderbuss mixed with rifles and muskets, more of the landing party were shot to pieces and fell to the ground. That was all it took, and the British turned and fled away from Jacob and his men. Waving his hand forward, Jacob led the band out of their ambush line, searched the dead and secured any wounded prisoners. There were very few wounded prisoners, just broken bodies whose blood mixed with the island soil.

"Marvelous, bloody marvelous! It worked, and that will teach them to stay inside the city and not forage. That sent a clear message!" Colonel Lacey was happy with the result, and Jacob nodded in agreement. Colonel Lacey remained behind to care for the wounded prisoners while Jacob led his band back to the army.

News arrived in camp that Andrew Pickens and Elijah Clarke moved against the remaining Cherokee in Georgia. The Cherokee had been conducting small raids, plundering farms and killing farmers. They led an expedition of over five hundred men into the Cherokee lands and would eventually get them to sign a treaty.

Then word that their old nemesis Bloody Bill Cunningham had somehow left Chares Town and made his way through their lines where Pickens had been before he had departed for the campaign in Georgia. Finding a few Loyalists to ride with him, Bloody Bill moved back into the upcountry, unaware that Pickens had left a force behind for such an emergency.

Captain Butler and his men had been left behind to watch that area when he learned that Bloody Bill had arrived. He had a personal reason for hunting Bloody Bill, as Bloody Bill had killed his father. Butler had been able to find their camp and quickly moved his thirty men in to surround it. Butler wanted to capture Bloody Bill alive so he would pay for his crimes, so he advanced on the camp just as the sun rose.

Butler was able to quickly move into the camp, as it seemed the Loyalists mistook Butler for Bloody Bill. His men charged into the camp and the Loyalists ran in every direction of the compass, with Butler's men in pursuit. Bloody Bill jumped on his horse and Butler took off with his to chase Bloody Bill down. It was a tight race between two excellent riders, Bloody Bill shooting over his shoulder with his pistols at Butler. He then tried to draw his sword, but a branch took Bloody Bill's sword. Butler urged his horse to catch the Bloody Bill, but he rode into the Saluda River and swam away.

Butler stood at the riverbank, watching Bloody Bill swim away as he was only armed with a sword and could not shoot at Bill. He heard Bill laughing, "Better luck next time, you bloody bastard; you can't catch me!"

Butler rallied his men and quickly continued the pursuit of Bloody Bill's men; at least they could bring them to justice if they could not catch Bill. That must have been enough, as Jacob never heard anything about Bloody Bill. He must have escaped or returned to Charles Town, but Bloody Bill never hurt anyone again.

A report from Colonel Mahan indicated they took over eighty prisoners near Monck's Corner, as he stated, "In the very sight of the British themselves." Then Jacob heard that a Continental expedition led by Colonel Kosciuszko attacked British positions on James Island south of the city.

At the end of November, Jacob was called to General Greene's marquee. After Jacob reported to the general, Greene held up a report.

"Jacob, we just received a report that the Royal Newspaper reports that Marion and his men caught a spy and then executed him by cutting off his head. Then they placed it on a stake near Greenland Swamp. This doesn't sound like Marion. Can you confirm this, Jacob?"

Jacob shook his head. "Sir, Marion is too much a professional to stoop to such a low act as murder and beheadings. While another group may have done it, the British may be desperate to smear Marion's good name. As you also know, sir, Marion has not taken the field, waiting for the evacuation to occur."

Greene nodded. "That was my thoughts as well. It did not sound like Francis, and you are correct. The British are getting desperate. I have seen other reports of misinformation and straight lies written about our men to discredit us. It is a sign of their desperation. The war is closing, and they lost."

Crumbling the report, Greene nodded to Jacob. "Thank you for your confirmation; you may return to your duties."

***

Lavinia Trout sat behind the bar, smoking her pipe. There were no patrons in the tavern; word must have spread quickly that she used poison on some of her patrons to sell their goods and steal their coins. Unfortunately, her last brew was not mixed correctly, and the traveling merchant survived and escaped.

She turned to the right, the pipe smoke circling her head as she looked where Mary Frith used to sit, dressed as a man and sharpening her knives. If Mary had been there, she would have taken care of the merchant and not been in this hot water. She sighed deeply, knowing Mary had been killed riding with the Loyalists as she wanted more excitement.

Then the sound of what she had been waiting for, the sound of hooves as horses stopped and the thump of men dismounting. The tavern door swung open and four armed men dressed in uniforms of white with sabers at their sides and pistols in their hands.

"You know why we are here?" the leader asked, and Lavinia nodded. He looked sternly at her, "Are you going to resist or come peacefully?" Lavinia snorted and looked at the cocked pistols in their hands.

"Oh, of course, I will come peacefully; I can't bloody well fight you," she grumbled as she stood up and walked around the bar. "Let's get this over with."

***

December 14th, 1782. It was over; the war was finally over. Having crossed the river at Ashley Ferry, Jacob with his band had ridden with Colonel Lee's Cavalry as the advance guard into the city after the morning cannon was fired. General Wayne led the column, along with three hundred infantry and even two 6-pound cannons. They could see a small detachment of German Jaegers guarding the open gate as they approached the outer defenses. When they came closer, the Jaegers turned and went into the city.

As they rode up to the front of the gate, Jacob looked at the Hornworks in the defensive line. He had helped build it along with the men of the Second Regiment. They followed the old road through the fortification gate and entered Charles Town. They passed through the Hornwork, now empty of any British soldiers. Memories flooded into Jacob's mind.

General Wayne led them slowly, keeping a respectful two hundred yards from the British rear guard. Then, finally, they walked down Boundary Street toward Gadsden Wharf, where the last British evacuated.

They rode through the streets with the advance guard moving through the city. The British had promised not to destroy anything if they were allowed to leave in peace. Jacob and his band were instructed to keep the peace, to keep the local citizens from venting their vengeance on the departing British.

The town was eerily quiet, though some people peered out from their windows as they walked down the street. Colonel

Lee leaned over to Jacob, "We learned that General Leslie had ordered the civilian inhabitants of Charleston to remain in their houses so as not to interfere with the British withdrawal and to prevent noncombatants from getting injured in the event of a fight."

A sea of sails appeared when they came into view of the rivers and the port. Jacob could not recall when he saw so many ships of different types; up to around three hundred was Jacob's guess. They were full of the remnants of the British Army, the Loyalists and their families, all leaving the city for places unknown. He also saw a few man-o-wars facing the shore; their guns run out.

"I am guessing our British friends have trust issues as well," Jacob commented and Lee nodded in agreement. General Wayne led the column down King to Broad Street, turned east and halted in front of the South Carolina State House at the corner of Meeting Street. General Wayne sent out small detachments from this post to inspect the town and assess the situation.

Jacob and his band were sent to the old barracks that had been their home in the Second Regiment. The large wooden structure was there, standing empty and silent, but it was more like seeing his old home on Rogers Island. *"Hello old friend,"* Jacob thought. Then Jacob was dispatched back to the gate to meet General Greene.

Jacob had his men lined up on opposite sides of the road as General Greene and his party of distinguished men approached. Jacob could not help himself when he saw General Moultrie riding behind Greene. When General Greene rode through with the new Governor Matthews who was escorted by a small troop from Lee's Dragoons, Jacob saluted and Greene returned the salute.

"If you wouldn't mind, please escort General Moultrie," Greene called out with a smile and continued his entrance into the city. When Moultrie with General Gist approached, not only was Jacob and his men smiling but so was Moultrie. After the band took up their escort positions, Jacob rode up next to Moultrie, who now wore the rank of a Major General.

"Sir, it does my heart good to see you are alive," Jacob stated, "After we evacuated Marion and Governor Rutledge from the city, we lost word on what happened to you. We feared the worse, based on what Samuel told us when he was out on the prison hulks."

"Yes, that was so true," Moultrie answered. "After the city's fall, the British made me the senior commander of all the prisoners they held here. It took all of my patience when advocating for the men against the harsh treatment by Balfour. Then would you believe the audacity those bastards had in trying to recruit me to join them! Ha!"

Jacob nodded in agreement as Moultrie continued.

"You made a name for yourself or a unique name like I learned of the Gamecock for Sumter and the Swamp Fox for Marion, the Wolf who struck in the night. The British feared you and your men." Then Moultrie looked to either side and raised his voice.

"You hear that, you wonderful pack of wolves and terrors of the night? The British feared you and Marion!" Moultrie looked down and saw the four large wolves showing grayer around their muzzles. "Even you, there were many stories of you four."

As they accompanied Moultrie, the city had changed from quiet to full of excited people. Jacob could see the expressions on the faces of his men; some had tears in their eyes along with the joy shown on their faces.

People stood on the sides of the street, from the balconies, crying out, "God bless you, gentlemen! You are welcome home, gentlemen!" Even Jacob felt a catch in his throat and tears forming in his eyes. The shock of the reality, the war was over. Moultrie looked over, "What a homecoming, eh?" he asked, and Jacob nodded.

"It is my first one sir," Jacob commented, "I have always gone from one war to another."

When the city people saw Jacob and the four wolves walking with Moultrie, they called out, "The Wolf, the Wolf! See, there goes the Wolf with General Moultrie, huzzah!"

Jacob and Moultrie quietly rode for a short time, the crowd cheering and yelling as they marched by. Then, finally, Moultrie gave a short chuckle. "Jacob, you and the rest of the men who served aught never to be forgotten by the Carolinians; it ought to be a day of festivity with them, as it was the real day of their deliverance and independence. But, like Marion and Greene, we are here today because of your dedication to duty. Victory at last!"

EPILOGUE

"*Clack…clack,*" The sound of the cane clicking on the paved walk was nearly drowned out by the sound of excited voices shouting about victory over the British and how they will prevail. Jacob shook his head and hobbled along using his cane to help him walk.

It was December 14th, 1812, and what had been celebrated as "Victory Day," as Moultrie spoke about so long ago, seemed to be fading away. Perhaps that was because so few veterans were left to remember or be remembered, or Charleston's collective attention became focused on the new war with Britain, which some began to call our "Second American Revolution."

Again, Jacob scoffed, seeing how they changed the City from Charles Town to Charleston. But time kept marching and new changes occurred.

"What's on your mind, dear?" Maria asked as he walked arm and arm with Jacob.

"Oh, just thinking about how much has changed," Jacob replied. *"And how much it has not,"* he thought. They slowly walked along the path. Their daughter Helga with her husband Stephen walked with them.

"Do I have to do this?" Jacob grumbled and his daughter playfully punched him in the shoulder.

"Yes, papa, Uncle Samuel had done it, even Uncle Jean. You are owed this, and they need to know what you did."

"Humph," Jacob replied, but knew she was right. He was not getting any younger, now 68 years old, and he felt every year in his bones. He walked with a slight bend to his back, no longer the stout fighter he had been, his wound in his leg now requiring him to walk with a cane.

When the war ended officially, Jacob did return to his compound and back to his life as a hunter. Some of the free black men, like Jehu, came to work in the tannery or hunting. The band was a family and they did come to visit from time to time.

The boys did grow up, got married and started their families. Helga had married and they lived in the compound with Jacob. Same with Samuel and Otti; while an old couple, their children grew up and made lives for themselves. While his wolves died from old age, they continued their practice of having wolves as pets, though cats were now included to keep the rodents under control.

Even in 1812, there were not a lot of them left. Time caught up with the older ones, the younger ones got older.

Marion had passed away already and Moultrie followed in 1802. However, they did honor him, renaming old Fort Sullivan to Moultrie. Sumter was still around, having retired from serving in the United States Senate. Jacob was surprised he had outlived them, but Maria kept reminding him he "was too stubborn, and she won't allow him to die yet."

As they walked along the walkway, Jacob saw an old coffee house, which brought back memories. Then they overheard conversations about "beating the British this time," Jacob shook his head and chuckled.

"What is it, love?" Maria asked.

Shaking his head, Jacob answered, "Just like before, they keep thinking we can beat the British. We wore them down, that is all.

Back in the Revolution, they still had a larger army than us up north. We just wore their resolve down and made them give up here in the south."

Maria smiled and patted his arm as they walked. Finally, they turned, walked up to the probate office and opened the door to the sound of a small bell hanging on the wall to announce the door had opened. Jacob and his family entered, and the clerk stood from his desk.

"Oh, Colonel Clarke, it is my honor to meet such an esteemed veteran. I will let Mr. Dawson know you have arrived." The clerk left and went into the office. Jacob stood there and waited, listening to the soft sound of the clock on the wall.

"Hmph, colonel," Jacob thought, *"I am glad I did not accept that commission as general of militia; colonel is enough for me."*

"Why not sit down, Jacob?" Maria asked and Jacob shrugged and tapped with his cane. "I might not be able to get back up." He smiled, and the family chuckled with him. Then, the door opened, and the clerk came out.

"Mr. Dawson is ready for you, sir."

Jacob walked into the office and took the chair that Mr. Dawson presented to him, and the family took chairs around the room. Mr. Dawson, the probate, sat down and picked up his quill. Before him was a pension application that Maria and the others had forced Jacob to come and complete.

"Welcome, sir, welcome! I am sure you hear this all the time, Mr. Clarke," Mr. Dawson said, "I recall and love all the stories of you and your wolves from the war. So inspiring"

Then he paused and followed with, "Oh, where are my manners? Shall I address you as Mr. Clarke, or would you prefer Colonel Clarke?"

Jacob waved his hand, "I am not serving anymore; Mr. Clarke or simply Jacob will be fine."

Mr. Dawson nodded, dipped his pen and then looked up at Jacob. "Jacob, I need you to recall as much as you can from the beginning, when and where you served, who you served with, what battles you saw."

Jacob sat for a moment, silence in the room as he began to think back. Then, reaching up, he took off his battered and scuffed old leather helmet, a crescent still fixed in the center. His eyes took on a faraway look, the faces of his lost friends passing through his memory. He could see them all in the distance, smiling.

"Jacob?"

Jacob cleared his throat and placed his old helmet on the desk.

"When and where it began. It was 1755 at Fort Lyman, or you may have known it as Fort Edward with Rogers Rangers...."

This concludes the series of Jacob Clarke, Ranger, Continental Officer, and Partisan

Review Requested:

We'd like to know if you enjoyed the book.
Please consider leaving a review on the platform
from which you purchased the book.

Ingram Content Group UK Ltd.
Milton Keynes UK
UKHW011945140623
423431UK00001B/50